D0035586

OY JUL 2014
FA JUL 2015

"One more dance. Please?"

Friedrick lifted his hands into dance position, but Livy hesitated. Their other two dances had been lively and fun, not intimate like the waltz. The teasing challenge in his blue eyes was unmistakable, though he lowered his arms to his sides.

Livy took a quick breath and tilted her chin upward. "I like to waltz."

"Good." His confident tone produced a strange thrill in her stomach. She stepped into his arms, and they joined the other couples spinning about the room.

Friedrick held her in a way that made her feel completely safe and cherished. She felt a heightened awareness of him in every sense. His firm touch on her back, the masculine scent of his shaving soap, the pleasure of his laughter in her ears. Not for the first time, she contemplated what it would be like if he kissed her, if they were to dance like this all night.

Afraid he'd read the longing on her face, Livy kept her chin lowered, her eyes trained on his shoulder. She shouldn't be thinking such things about Friedrick. She'd only ended things with Robert right before coming to Hilden, and then there was the whole dilemma of Friedrick being German-American. They couldn't be more than friends, no matter how much she secretly wished for something different . . .

Hope at
Dawn

Stacy Henrie

FOREVER

NEW YORK   BOSTON

This book is a work of fiction. Names, characters, places, and incidents are the product of the author's imagination or are used fictitiously. Any resemblance to actual events, locales, or persons, living or dead, is coincidental.

Copyright © 2014 by Stacy Henrie

Excerpt from *Hope Rising* copyright © 2014 by Stacy Henrie
All rights reserved. In accordance with the U.S. Copyright Act of 1976, the scanning, uploading, and electronic sharing of any part of this book without the permission of the publisher constitute unlawful piracy and theft of the author's intellectual property. If you would like to use material from the book (other than for review purposes), prior written permission must be obtained by contacting the publisher at permissions@hbgusa.com. Thank you for your support of the author's rights.

Forever
Hachette Book Group
237 Park Avenue
New York, NY 10017

www.HachetteBookGroup.com

Printed in the United States of America

First Edition: June 2014
10 9 8 7 6 5 4 3 2 1

OPM

Forever is an imprint of Grand Central Publishing.
The Forever name and logo are trademarks of Hachette Book Group, Inc.

The Hachette Speakers Bureau provides a wide range of authors for speaking events. To find out more, go to www.hachettespeakersbureau.com or call (866) 376-6591.

The publisher is not responsible for websites (or their content) that are not owned by the publisher.

ATTENTION CORPORATIONS AND ORGANIZATIONS:

Most Hachette Book Group books are available at quantity discounts with bulk purchase for educational, business, or sales promotional use. For information, please call or write:

Special Markets Department, Hachette Book Group
237 Park Avenue, New York, NY 10017
Telephone: 1-800-222-6747 Fax: 1-800-477-5925

For my grandma

Thank you for reading my early, less-than-stellar attempts at writing and thinking they were brilliant anyway. If books could be delivered to Heaven, I'd send you this one with all my love.

Acknowledgments

While writing is a very solitary act, this book wouldn't be possible without the loving support of my family. Thanks to my kids for your excitement over what *Mom* is doing. And a lifetime of thanks to my husband for holding my hand, so often literally, through all the ups and downs of being an author. You are my real-life hero!

Much thanks to my agent, Jessica Alvarez, and my editor, Lauren Plude, for seeing the potential in not only this story but the series in general.

Thanks to Ali Cross, Elana Johnson, and Sara Olds for being much more than critique partners. Thanks, too, to Amber Perry—it's amazing how just a few years of knowing each other can feel like a lifetime of friendship.

A final thank-you to family, friends, and readers who have cheered me on. I hope this story touches your heart as much as it has mine.

Author's Note

While this story, its characters, and the town of Hilden are all works of fiction, many true events inspired those experienced by Livy and Friedrick. The governor of Iowa did, in fact, proclaim the use of foreign languages in public to be against the law in 1918. This law was unique in that it forbade the use of *any* foreign language, not just German. The proclamation was issued in May, but for the sake of the story, I had the language law come into effect at the beginning of February.

There were four liberty loan drives during the course of America's involvement in the Great War, in which all citizens were encouraged to buy bonds in order to help pay for the cost of the war. A fifth "victory" drive occurred after the war ended. The third drive, which figures into this story, actually began in April. Again, for the time frame of the story, I moved the drive to March.

The Spanish influenza epidemic of 1918–1919 is well known for its deadly sweep across the globe. Of lesser note is how the epidemic hit in three waves. The first and second waves occurred in the spring and late summer/early fall of 1918, and the third during the beginning months of 1919. Because the influenza epidemic played a pivotal role in the Great War and the year 1918 in particular, I wanted to capture the essence of this experience. While I have Friedrick contracting the illness during the first wave, when the number of deaths was comparatively small, his symptoms and the high potential for death in young adults his age are both true to life.

Although the Eighteenth Amendment to the Constitution, which prohibited the making, selling, and transporting of alcohol, didn't come into effect until 1920, Iowa had its own statewide prohibition law by 1916.

Before researching for this book, I knew very little of what so many German-Americans faced during World War I. The few incidents of persecution I've shared in this story—coercion to buy liberty bonds, arrest, prison sentencing, homes and buildings painted yellow, and tar and feathering—actually did occur. The widespread use of propaganda during the war was likely one of the biggest contributors to inspiring fear and mistrust of German-Americans, who were often viewed as potential enemies to the United States. This suspicion typically resulted in ordinary citizens meting out justice against other citizens, in sometimes violent ways, as shown here in Livy and Friedrick's story.

Having now studied much about World War I, I have a great respect for not only those men and women who served in the Great War, but those who, like Friedrick and Livy, fought prejudice and injustice on the American home front. Most German-Americans chose not to resist, for the sake of their lives and their families. But whether they stood in silence or stood vocally, most remained ever loyal to the country they had come to call home.

Chapter One

Of all the birthdays Livy could recall, this one would certainly go down as the most memorable—but for all the wrong reasons. *Ironic*, she thought, smoothing the skirt of her blue silk taffeta dress for surely the hundredth time. *I always thought turning twenty would be special.*

She fanned herself with her hat, wishing she'd selected a chair near the back of the dance hall, where the door had been thrown open to let in the cool night air. The catchy strains of a one-step filled the crowded room as couples danced in front of her.

Livy glanced at the hall's entrance, then to the clock on the wall. Where could Robert be? He'd told her he needed some work done on his automobile, so he would meet her at the dance hall at seven o'clock. But with Robert's army training, Livy knew he meant six fifty-nine. That had been an hour ago.

The song ended and the couples stopped moving to applaud the band. Livy let her gaze wander over the unfamiliar faces. A tall young man with blond hair and broad shoulders caught and held her attention. Not only because of his handsome face and blue eyes, but also because of his lack of a uniform. Most of the men here tonight were older and married or baby-faced youngsters almost out of high school. The few who looked to be in their mid-twenties like the blond young man were dressed as soldiers, likely having returned home wounded, like Robert.

With his cane, Robert didn't enjoy dancing as he once had, but he'd promised to take Livy for her birthday. The few times they'd come to the dance hall, mostly just swaying to the music, Livy couldn't help seeing the adoring looks the other girls gave Robert—or the jealousy-tinged ones they threw at her when Robert refused to dance with anyone else. The appreciative glances and wistful sighs were the same wherever they went together.

But tonight she sat alone, with her polished dance shoes and her carefully curled hair. Without Robert. Livy simmered with frustration. She'd looked forward to a lovely evening all week. What would make him so late? A sudden thought turned her insides to ice and she dropped her hat into her lap. The inside of her cheek found its way between her teeth.

"Please let him be sober, God, please," she whispered, the next song drowning out her quiet pleas. "I'll forgive him any other excuse, if he's sober."

Robert had vowed, just three weeks before, that he was done imbibing—much to Livy's relief. She couldn't entirely blame him for turning to the bottle. There was so much he wanted to forget about his time overseas. Things he'd whispered to her, during moments of insobriety, which made her cringe in horror.

Robert's stories had only increased her anxiety for her two older brothers, fighting in France. What were they experiencing there? Would they be driven to drink because of it?

Livy mentally shook her head at the thought. She couldn't imagine Joel or Tom ever becoming drunk. They wouldn't be alone in that resolve either. There were other men in their hometown who hadn't succumbed to drinking—some had even lost arms or legs or their eyesight. So why were they able to stay away from alcohol and Robert couldn't? Not even Iowa's statewide prohibition or Livy's increased compassion toward him had stopped Robert from finding the bootleggers when he wanted.

For a moment, Livy imagined she could smell the fermented scent of Robert's raw alcohol. She hated that smell and the way it clung to his breath and clothes. She gagged at the memory and sucked in a breath of the stale, warm air inside the dance hall to clear her nose.

She'd learned to read his drunken mood, too. If he was lumbering around the barn, muttering things to himself, he was angry. Angry at the Germans, at God, at her sometimes. She didn't like the barbed comments he tossed her way, but those were preferable to the intense sadness he experienced more often.

If he was lying back in the hay, bottle in hand, he was consumed with sorrow. No matter what she said or how long she sat holding his hand, she couldn't talk him through the guilt and regret of his memories. And that cut worse than the smell. Still, she'd always try to coax him into a better mood, then return home exhausted, doing her best to dodge her parents' questions about her evening.

Robert had promised to give it up, though, and Livy

clung to that promise. Especially as her birthday approached. The past three weeks he'd been solicitous and sober, as he had when he'd first come home. At least until tonight.

When another fifteen minutes had crawled by, Livy forced herself to accept the likelihood that Robert—for whatever painful reason—had chosen to spend her birthday with a bottle cradled in his arms instead of her. Hot tears of anger sprang up behind her eyes, and no amount of blinking could keep several of them from leaking onto her face.

"Are you all right?"

Livy whipped her chin up and found herself peering into eyes more brilliantly blue than she'd suspected from her seat across the room. Their clear depths exuded friendly concern in a way that made her feel immediately safe, though she didn't know this young man. Up close, his Sunday shirt and pressed trousers, though worn, accentuated his strong-looking physique.

She blinked, trying to remember what he'd asked her. Something about her being all right? "Yes. Thank you. I'm fine."

She swept away the salty drops from her cheeks. Of course her first real cry in ten years would be witnessed by a stranger, and yet his self-assured, compassionate manner made her suspect he didn't find her silly.

"You look like you could use a dance." He crouched down in front of her and held out his hand. "How about it?"

Livy darted a quick look at the entrance again. "I'm... um... waiting for my boyfriend."

"Ah." He let his hand drop to his side. "Seems to be a bit late."

She blushed. Who else had noticed her sitting here for over an hour? "I'm sorry," she offered lamely.

"No, it's all right." He stood and started to walk away.

Who was she kidding? Robert wasn't coming. If he happened to, he'd likely be drunk and unable to dance anyway.

"Wait." Livy shot to her feet. She could have at least one dance on her birthday. Why should she spend the whole evening hurt and angry over Robert's absence?

The young man slowly turned back around.

She attempted a genuine smile. "I'd love a dance."

His face lit up as he smiled in return and held out his hand a second time. Setting her hat on her chair, Livy placed her hand inside his larger one and allowed him to escort her onto the dance floor. The band began to play a fox-trot—one of Livy's favorite dances. She and Joel had become fairly adept at the steps before he'd left for the war.

It felt strange, at first, to be in another man's arms, but the feeling soon left her. The way he held her hand in a confident but gentle grip, his hand warm on her back, helped Livy relax. He led her around the floor, their feet walking or spinning in time with the music. He was as skillful at the fox-trot as her brother, and Livy relished the chance to do more than just sway to the music.

"Are you from around here?" he asked her after a minute or two of dancing.

"About an hour away. And you?"

He shook his head. "I live outside of Hilden. In the county north of here."

Livy vaguely recalled hearing the town name. "You drove all the way down here, just to go dancing?"

"We don't have a public dance hall in Hilden. So we have to come here, or head farther north, or drive all the way to Sioux City. Do you come to this one often?"

"I used to, before I went to college in Cedar Falls."

With slight pressure to her back, he expertly led her through a spin before he picked up their conversation again. "What did you study in college?"

"Teaching."

"Are you a teacher now?"

Livy frowned, doing her best to tamp down the seeds of resentment the question unearthed. She loved her family and wanted to lift the burden her brothers' absence had created, but she missed college and the chance to pursue her own dreams.

"I was only able to attend for a year before I was needed here." Her words drew a look of sympathy from him.

"I know what that's like," he murmured. Before she could ask what he meant, he poised another question. "Do you still want to be a teacher?"

"Very much. I'm hoping someday I'll have the chance."

The understanding in his blue eyes changed to enthusiasm. "That might be sooner than you think. The teacher at one of the township schools outside of Hilden was recently..." He shot a glance at the floor, his jaw tightening. Livy wondered at the change in his mood. Then he guided her through another spin and his expression relaxed. "Suffice it to say, she's gone now and I don't think they've found a replacement. It's a little far away, but you might want to inquire about it."

A possible teaching job? A flurry of anticipation set

Livy's pulse moving faster at the prospect. She tried to squelch it with the reminder she wasn't likely to be hired with only one year of college completed and no teaching certificate, but she couldn't destroy the hope completely. How wonderful to be on her own again, and not learning how to teach this time, but actually being the teacher.

Livy met his open gaze and found her thoughts moving from his idea to the man himself. She didn't even know his name, and yet she felt comfortable enough in his presence to share some of her regret at having her dream of teaching cut short. She hadn't even voiced those feelings to Robert yet.

"Thank you," she said, hoping he sensed how much she meant it. "I may look into it."

"I hope you will." He smiled in a way that made her stomach twist with unexpected pleasure.

She searched her mind for a more neutral topic, one that wouldn't mean spilling more of her secrets to this stranger. "Do you live with family, up there in Hilden?"

He nodded. "I've got my father, stepmother, and two half siblings. What about you?"

"I've got more than two siblings." Livy laughed. "I'm the third of seven. Five boys and two girls."

She studied the firm shoulder beneath her hand. He appeared quite fit and healthy, so why wasn't he a soldier? "Can I ask you something?"

"Sure."

"How come you're not fighting overseas?"

Livy wished the question back at once when a shadow passed over his face, erasing the easy camaraderie between them. Before he could answer, the song ended. He released her hand at once, though he didn't join her or the other couples in clapping.

She gnawed at her cheek, embarrassed at her apparent mistake. He'd been so kind to notice her distress earlier and suggest the teacher position in his town, and she'd repaid him by bringing up something he clearly did not wish to discuss.

"I'm sorry. It's none of my business," she said, rushing her words in an effort to keep him from disappearing into the crowd before she could finish. "I didn't mean to pry."

He watched her, his expression guarded. What could she say to erase the awkwardness her inquiry had caused? They'd been having such a lovely time talking and dancing.

"I appreciate the dance. You see it's my birthday and I adore the fox-trot. So you've saved my evening, Mr...." She waited for him to fill the pause with his name.

The corners of his mouth worked up into a smile. "How about you call me 'the birthday rescuer'?"

Livy chuckled. She wasn't sure why he refused to give his name, but she wouldn't press it—not after her blunder moments ago. His kindness had completely changed her botched evening. "Thank you for the dance, birthday rescuer. And for telling me about the teacher position."

"You're welcome. Do I get to know the name of the birthday girl?"

Two can play this game, Livy thought with a smirk. "How about 'the girl I danced with once'?"

His deep laughter pleased her. "How about we dance again?" He gestured to the floor, where the couples were pairing off for the next song. "Then you could be 'the girl I danced with twice.'"

"No. I'd better go."

"Without your beau?" He raised an eyebrow.

"I did get my birthday dance."

A dark-haired girl approached them. She threw a haughty look at Livy and possessively pulled the young man toward the dance floor. Did the two of them know each other?

"Good night. Happy Birthday," he called over his shoulder.

Livy waved good-bye. The frustration she'd felt earlier threatened to overwhelm her now that their pleasant encounter had ended, but she refused to shed any more tears tonight. With head held high, she wove her way back to her chair to collect her hat and coat. If the drugstore hadn't closed up shop yet, she could telephone a neighbor to run over and ask her father or her younger brother Allen to come collect her.

Outside the dance hall, she inhaled the crisp air to clear away any lingering moisture from her eyes. She descended the steps and started past the wagons and automobiles parked in front of the building.

"Livy!"

She spun around and saw her father standing beside the family wagon.

"I was just about to come inside and look for you." Josiah Campbell placed his worn hat on top of his brown hair. A few gray strands had sprouted near his temples since Livy's brothers had left to fight, but he still didn't look his true age of fifty-one.

"How'd you know I needed a ride?" Livy asked as she walked toward him. Had something happened to one of the family? Or perhaps Robert was hurt or ill—and not drunk after all. "Is everything all right?"

"Everything's fine." Josiah gave her shoulder a reassuring squeeze that soothed her concern. "Mrs. Drake came over an hour ago to say Robert wasn't feeling well. She was sorry to hear Allen had already driven you here. I came to drive the birthday girl home." He smiled, but Livy struggled to return the gesture.

Her suspicions tonight about Robert had been correct, after all. Mrs. Drake always used the excuse "he isn't feeling well" when she and Livy both knew the truth—he was passed out from drinking.

"Up you go, sugar," Josiah said as he helped her onto the wagon seat. Livy sat numbly as he unhitched the horses and climbed up next to her. He guided the horses away from the dance hall and onto the street. "Pretty night, huh?"

Livy glanced up at the stars scattered across the black sky. "I suppose." She began gnawing at her cheek again, wishing she had the courage to tell her parents about Robert, but she kept her lips clamped together. Robert's continued trouble with alcohol embarrassed her. Why couldn't he lean on her instead?

"Something on your mind?"

"Just thinking I feel old." *And tired.* She linked her arm through his as he laughed softly. "Thanks for coming to get me."

"Sure thing, sugar. I'm sorry Robert wasn't able to make it. Did you have a nice time anyway?"

"Yes," Livy answered and she meant it. She thought of her "birthday rescuer" and a real smile lifted her lips. Once she'd stopped waiting around for Robert and actually danced, she'd felt much better.

Maybe that's what I need to do from now on. She

was tired of waiting—waiting for her life to start again now that she'd left college, waiting for her brothers' safe return, waiting for Robert to give up alcohol, waiting for a proposal.

Robert had mentioned marriage for the first time about a month ago—the same day he'd received word a buddy from his squad had been killed. Livy doubted he could remember much of their conversation, even when his hangover had ended. If she did marry him, how many more nights would she find him that way? How many times would she have to drag his unconscious body into the house and nurse him back to awareness?

The possibility brought a prickle of cold fear creeping over her. She didn't think she could live that way. She wanted a marriage like her parents had—one full of love and warmth.

A feeling of being trapped grabbed hold of her, squeezing at her throat and lungs. Was there nothing she could do to change her life, her circumstances? The conversation she'd had with the kind young man about the teacher position repeated itself through her mind. This could be her chance to pursue her dream and give her and Robert some needed space, too. It might be a long shot, but surely one worth taking. Even considering the idea resurrected Livy's earlier hope and excitement. The sensation of claustrophobia faded in the wake of her enthusiasm.

"Daddy, what would you say if I were to get a job?" No matter how badly she wanted this, she wouldn't do it without his and her mother's blessing.

"What sort of job?"

"A teaching one. I heard about an opening at one of the

township schools, north of here, near Hilden. I'm hoping they'll take a teacher with only one year of college behind her."

"Is that so?" He glanced at her, and though she couldn't see his expression from the shadow of his hat, she sensed he was studying her face. "Would that make you happy, sugar? I know leaving school wasn't what you planned to do."

"It's more than that." She fiddled with one of the buttons on her coat, anxious to have him understand but not sure how much to share. "Things have been a little strained with Robert, and I think some distance would be good, for both of us."

"So there's more to it than him missing out on your birthday tonight?"

"Yes." Livy feared he'd ask more questions, ones she didn't want to answer. Tonight needed to be about hope and the possibility of new beginnings, not uncertainty and past frustrations.

His answer nearly made her fall off the wagon seat. "Then I think you ought to give the teaching job a try."

"Really?" she squealed. She twisted on the seat to face him straight on. "Are you sure? What about needing me here, to help around the farm?"

"You've done a great job of that already, Livy." Josiah pushed up the brim of his hat and smiled at her. "We would've been hard-pressed to run the farm this last year, without Joel and Tom around, if you hadn't come home. But your younger brothers are growing and learning more responsibility now. I think we'll be just fine."

"You could use some of the money I earn to hire one of Allen's friends to help out, if I do get the job."

His head dipped in a thoughtful nod. "That's an idea."

"I can apply then?" She already knew the answer, but she couldn't quite believe the gift he'd just presented her. Not something material, like the new mirror and powder compact he and her mother had given her earlier that day, but something infinitely more important—a promise of better days ahead.

Josiah shifted the reins to his left hand and put his arm around her shoulders. "If that's what you want to do—need to do—sugar, then you do it. The kids up there would be lucky to have you as a teacher. We'll be all right here. Don't you worry."

"Thank you, Daddy!" Livy kissed his cheek. His confidence and approval were worth more to her than a night full of fox-trots. "Could you drive a little faster?"

He chuckled at her impatience. "Anxious to get a slice of your birthday cake?"

"Nope." Though the thought of her mother's chocolate cake did make her mouth water. "I've got to write a letter to the school superintendent in Hilden."

"Well, in that case, I suppose we'd better hurry."

Livy laughed and gripped the wagon seat as he urged the horses to pick up their pace. With any luck, this birthday would mark the beginning of a new chapter in her life.

* * *

Friedrick stepped silently through the front door and eased it shut. The smell of the family's bread, sausage, and cheese supper still hung in the air. Murmurs of conversation and the clatter of dishes came from the kitchen, where his stepmother and half siblings were cleaning up.

He quietly removed his dirty boots, a grin on his face. He was going to win their little game tonight.

He crept down the hall toward the parlor. A glance over his shoulder assured him he was near victory, until he brought his weight down on the squeaky floorboard. The loud *creak* that erupted brought squeals of protest from the next room.

"It's Friedrick," Harlan shouted. "Hurry!"

In his stocking feet, Friedrick skidded into the parlor, the sound of footfalls close behind him. He dove for the sofa, but not before Harlan's small frame slid past him. The two ended up in a laughing heap among the cushions.

"Boys, boys," Elsa Wagner scolded in German from the doorway, her hands on her hips.

Friedrick had been nine when his father had remarried, but in no time at all, Elsa had quietly and easily filled the absence his own mother's death had left in his life. She and Friedrick's father spoke little English, and never in their own home, though they'd made certain their American-born children had learned the language.

"The sofa is for sitting, not wrestling." She shook her finger at them.

"I won, I won," Harlan said, ignoring his mother and bouncing up and down on the sofa.

"Not so fast." Friedrick sat up and pulled the boy into a sitting position beside him. "Greta isn't here yet."

Harlan's brows scrunched in irritation at his little sister. "Aw, Greta," he hollered. "You made us lose."

Greta came into the room, a miniature version of blond, blue-eyed Elsa, down to the hands resting on her waist. "I had to finish drying the plates, Harlan." She sauntered to the sofa and snuggled in beside Friedrick.

"In that case," Friedrick said, playfully tugging one of Greta's long braids, "we should give one point for thoroughness to Greta and one point to me for being done with evening chores first."

"What about me?" Harlan protested.

Friedrick tousled his hair. "You get a point for speed."

"Then we all won tonight," Greta said, beaming.

"Good, good." Elsa picked up her sewing basket and went to sit in her rocker by the fire. "Now get the Bible, Harlan. The English one."

"I'll go get Papa." Friedrick stood as Harlan hopped up and retrieved the Bible from a corner table.

Elsa shook her head, the lines around her eyes appearing deeper in the light from the fire. "He said he is too tired this evening."

Friedrick frowned as he accepted the Bible his brother handed him and sat down again. He missed having their father join them in their nightly ritual of reading. Perhaps once the warmer weather arrived, Heinrich Wagner's health would improve some.

Opening the book, Friedrick removed the frayed piece of silk from the third chapter of Proverbs and began reading out loud.

Trust in the Lord with all thine heart; and lean not
onto thine own understanding.
In all thy ways acknowledge him, and he shall direct
thy paths.

Harlan shifted restlessly next to him. "What does that mean?"

"Well." Friedrick searched for the right words to help

his nine-year-old brother understand. "It means doing what God wants us to do, even though it might not make sense to us at the time. God's saying if we trust Him enough to guide us, things will work out much better in the end."

"Like you not having to fight in the war, Friedrick." Greta smiled up at him. "We prayed you wouldn't have to and then you got that de...de-fer..."

"Deferment," he finished.

"That's it."

His sister's grateful tone did nothing to ease the regret and unanswered questions any reference to the war dredged up inside him. If it was God's will Friedrick stay home and run the farm, then why did he still feel so guilt-ridden every time he saw a war poster or passed a wounded soldier in town? Did God really have a purpose for keeping him here, or did He simply have little use for a twenty-six-year-old farmer in rural Iowa?

His own doubts didn't make answering others' questions about why he wasn't fighting in the war any easier either. He typically didn't evade the question, though, at least not until last night.

When the pretty girl with the large green eyes had asked him at the dance hall why he wasn't fighting overseas, he'd decided not to answer. She struck him as sweet but spirited, too, and he hadn't wanted to ruin their short time together by revealing he had a farm deferment because his German father was dying.

Thankfully she dropped the subject and hadn't pressed him for his name either. Inwardly he smiled at the memory of how she'd beaten him at his own game by not revealing her name either.

"Children," Elsa said, glancing up from her mending. "Let Friedrick read, please." The creak of the rocker punctuated her words.

Friedrick settled back against the sofa and continued reading to the family. They'd nearly reached the end of the chapter when a loud knock at the front door interrupted him.

"Who's that?" Harlan scrambled to a standing position on the sofa and peered out the curtains.

Friedrick glanced at the carved cuckoo clock hanging above the mantel. *Must be a neighbor with an emergency*, he thought as he stood, *to come over after eight o'clock*.

"Harlan, get down." Elsa continued to sew.

"Uh…Mama." Harlan's frightened voice stopped Friedrick on his way out of the parlor. He crossed to the window, and Elsa did the same.

Through the slit in the handmade curtains, Friedrick saw at least a dozen men gathered in the yard, torches in hand. The lights stood out brightly against the heavy dark clouds above them. Friedrick recognized most of them as folks he'd seen around Hilden, but several were strangers. A few of them held rifles at their sides, but it was the man with the coil of rope that made cold fear run down Friedrick's spine.

"Stay here. Out of sight," he said to the children. They nodded quickly, their faces pinched and pale. "You, too, Mother."

"Merciful God." She collapsed into her rocker. Harlan and Greta scurried to her and she put an arm around each of them. "What do you think they want?"

"I'll find out." Friedrick exhaled slowly, offering a silent prayer for God to be with him, and walked to the door. He slipped his boots back on and tucked in his shirt before reaching for the handle.

Another weighty knock sounded. Cold air rushed in around him as Friedrick opened the door. If this took longer than a few minutes, he was going to wish he'd grabbed his coat. He pulled the door shut behind him.

"Good evening," he called out with forced politeness to those on the porch, grateful he didn't have an accent. With America fighting Germany, it was better to appear as un-German as possible these days.

The harsh smell of smoke from the closest torch stung Friedrick's nose and momentarily made his eyes water. He blinked back the moisture. "What can I do for you, *gentlemen*?"

"We need to see Heinrich Wagner," a stranger near the door demanded. Murmurs of approval swept through the group.

"My father is ill. But you may address any questions to me. I'm in charge of this farm now."

"Are you?" the man holding the noose said as he stepped forward. "Well, then we've got some business to conduct with you, son."

"That's right, Joe. You tell 'im," another man hollered. Friedrick recognized him as a store owner from town.

Friedrick straightened to his full height of six feet, two inches and crossed his arms over his chest. He relished the fact that he stood at least half a foot taller than Joe. "What seems to be the trouble?"

Joe looked him up and down and smiled, but his expression looked warped in the torchlight. It reminded Friedrick of a wolf, like those in the Grimm Brothers' fairy tale book he liked to read aloud to Harlan and Greta.

"No real trouble. Just out doing our patriotic duty as Hilden's vigilance committee." Joe strolled up the porch steps as though he belonged there. He twisted the rope into a tighter coil in his hands. A distant crack of thunder added emphasis to the sinister gesture. "You see, the schoolteacher, Miss Lehmann... Do you know Miss Lehmann, son?"

Friedrick sensed a trap. Miss Lehmann had been Harlan and Greta's schoolteacher before she'd been fired. She also attended the same church as the Wagners, which meant Friedrick would have to answer with care. "I'm familiar with who Miss Lehmann is."

"Did you hear she's been speakin' German in our school?" Joe added. "And that's against the law."

The reminder had Friedrick fisting his hands. The governor had recently issued a statewide proclamation prohibiting the use of any foreign language in public. No more speaking German in the schools or on the telephone or in public places.

"She's also been prayin' for the Kaiser's safety in front of the children." Joe sent a stream of tobacco-laced saliva toward the porch. Friedrick didn't flinch or back away as the dark liquid sprayed his boots.

He eyed the noose again and prayed Miss Lehmann hadn't come to any harm before she'd left Hilden. However foolish she'd been to openly oppose the proclamation, she didn't deserve any ill treatment.

"Did you hear we fired her?" the store owner shouted. His words were accompanied by cheers.

"We were aware the school was closed," Friedrick said with dismissal, "but thank you, gentlemen, for the reminder." He remained where he stood, though, certain their reason for being there wasn't to share the old news about getting rid of the schoolteacher.

Joe released an ugly chuckle. "We're not quite finished, son. Since Miss Lehmann is likely a German spy, we're visiting all our good German neighbors tonight and seeing where their loyalties lie."

Anger ignited inside Friedrick at the man's veiled accusation. He and his half siblings had been born on American soil, same as these men. His father and Elsa, while German-born, were still as loyal to this country as anyone he knew.

He fought to keep his voice calm and even as he said, "We're American citizens, same as you folks, and we honor the laws of this country."

"Then how come you ain't fightin' over there with our boys?" a man at Joe's elbow demanded.

Joe glanced at his friend and gave a thoughtful nod. "That's a good question. What do you say to that, son?"

Friedrick's growing resentment was making it hard to stand still and breathe normally. Why should he have to answer to the likes of them? "I have a farm deferment. My father is dying, so I run the place now."

"Looks like your neighbor George Wyatt told us the truth about you," Joe said.

Hearing the name of his neighbor caused a spark of shock to run through Friedrick. He looked past Joe to see George standing near the fence, hat in hand. His face remained expressionless, but his eyes reflected his sorrow. He and Friedrick had helped each other with their harvest the last few years. Though George's presence in the mob bothered Friedrick, he appreciated the man's defense.

"You might not be able to fight, son, but you can surely buy liberty bonds."

"I bought a fifty-dollar bond last fall. Paid for it in full that day." Friedrick stuck out his chin in pride. No one could accuse his family of slacking in their effort to fund the war.

"Times like these call for another demonstration of loyalty." Joe brought his face so close to Friedrick's he could smell the chewing tobacco resting inside Joe's cheek. "So what's it gonna be? You going to be the proud owner of a hundred-dollar bond, as part of our great country's third loan drive?"

The outrageous sum hit Friedrick like a punch to the gut. His family didn't have extra money to throw at bonds. His father's costly medicine and frequent doctor visits had drained them of nearly all their savings.

"And if we decline, respectfully?" Friedrick said with intended sarcasm.

Joe examined the rope in his hand. "I'll put it to you real simple. You buy a bond tonight, or you can try this rope on for size. You choose, son."

Had things deteriorated so quickly for the German-Americans in Hilden that Friedrick must buy more bonds or risk his life? Rage burned hot through his veins at the injustice. He was being treated as an enemy, when he was as loyal and American as these men watching and waiting for his response. Would they have been any less insistent of his family if he'd been fighting overseas?

He pushed such a question from his mind—it was futile. He hadn't been allowed to fight, at least not on the battlefields of France, but that didn't mean the war had passed his family by. Friedrick was beginning to see there were battles here, too. Not between trained soldiers, but between townspeople and neighbors. While he couldn't protect his country, he would protect his family. Even if it meant buying a bond with their remaining savings to satisfy these men and keep them from coming back.

Friedrick schooled his voice once again to hide his fury, though he took great pleasure from being able to look down his nose at Joe. "I'll get the money," he ground out between clenched teeth.

Joe nodded approval. "Good boy."

He went back inside, though he left the door partway open to keep the men from thinking he wasn't returning. Elsa and his siblings stood at the parlor entrance. Their expressions reflected concern but also innocence—they hadn't overheard the awful conversation.

"Everything's going to be all right." His reassurance erased some of the tension radiating from the three of them. Friedrick went to the kitchen and pulled an old Mason jar from the back of one of the cupboards. His family followed him.

"What are you doing, Friedrick?" Elsa asked. "What do those men want?"

"We need to buy a liberty bond." He removed all but one bill—and their $50 bond—from the jar.

"But you already bought a bond." Her eyes narrowed in on the money in his hand. "How much?"

Friedrick put the jar back and shut the cupboard. "A hundred dollars," he replied in a flat voice.

Elsa gasped, her hand rising to her throat. "But that leaves us only five dollars. What about your father's medicine? We cannot—"

"Mother." Friedrick waited for her to look at him. He

was only too aware of how Harlan and Greta watched the two of them with wide eyes. "We will figure this out. I told you everything will be fine. You must trust me." He didn't want her coming outside in protest or upsetting his siblings any more than they had been at the sight of the mob. "Please."

She studied his face for a long moment, then she lowered her head and nodded.

"Stay inside. I'll be right back."

He placed a comforting hand on her shoulder as he walked past them into the hallway. A noise from his father's bedroom made him turn.

"Friedrick?" Heinrich swayed in the doorway. Friedrick hurried to support him. "I heard a noise outside."

"It's all right, Papa. Go back to bed."

"What are you doing with that money?"

Before Friedrick could answer, the front door squeaked open and Joe's loud voice boomed through the hall. "Hurry it up, son. We've got other people to visit." *More like people to terrorize.* Friedrick strangled the bills in his hand.

"Who is that?" Heinrich asked him, his tone weary and concerned.

"I'll explain later. Right now you need to let Mother help you back into bed."

Elsa took Friedrick's place at his father's side, her face set in a determined expression. "Come, Heinrich. We must help you lie back down. Friedrick will take care of everything."

He was keenly aware of all four of them watching him, looking to him for guidance. His responsibility, as man of the house, had never felt so daunting.

"Harlan," Friedrick directed in a low voice as he moved down the hall, "you and Greta go wash up and put on your pajamas." He wanted them far away from the men in the yard.

For once, the boy didn't object. "Let's go, Greta."

When the two of them had disappeared up the stairs, Friedrick strode to the open door. He slapped their money into the man's open palm. "There's your hundred dollars."

Joe pocketed the cash. "Now all's left is to fill out your application." He withdrew a paper and pencil from his coat and handed them to Friedrick.

Friedrick turned to use the doorjamb as a desk. Every cell in his body screamed at him to rip the application in half and take back his family's money, but another glance at the noose silenced the urge. He filled in the required information, but he had the pencil pressed so hard to the paper, it tore in one place. Not caring, he thrust the application and pencil at Joe.

The man grinned as he took them in his free hand. "We'll see this and your money get to the bank. You can pick up your bond there." He swung the rope over his shoulder. "I knew a smart, patriotic young man like you wouldn't be needin' the likes of this. Have a nice night now." He whirled around and marched down the porch steps. The rest of the mob trailed him across the yard and out the picket fence.

Friedrick watched them from the doorway, making certain every last one of them left before he shut and bolted the door. His hands shook slightly as he removed his boots for a second time. Instead of carrying them to the kitchen, he dropped them in a heap beside the front door. Elsa would surely forgive him if he left them there tonight.

"Oh, Friedrick." Greta appeared in her long, white nightgown and threw her arms around his waist. "I'm so glad you weren't hurt."

Friedrick gave her a tight hug in return. "Me, too."

Harlan joined them in the hall. Though the danger had passed, their faces were still pinched with worry. Friedrick didn't want them to go to sleep and think of nothing but seeing their mother upset and their family threatened. "Why don't you two go wait in your beds? I'll come up and read you a story."

Harlan lifted his chin. "Really?"

Friedrick nodded.

The two raced back up the stairs. Friedrick went into the parlor and grabbed the first storybook he found from the bookcase. Before heading upstairs, he decided to look in on his father. He paused outside the door when he heard Elsa talking.

"It will be fine, Heinrich. You'll see." The bright tone to her words sounded forced to Friedrick, but his father was likely too sick to notice. "Remember how trouble always comes before the dawn, before the sun returns. Friedrick will make things right. You'll see."

Friedrick turned away, not wishing to disturb them. There was nothing more to be said at the moment. He started up the stairs but halted halfway up as the weight of what he'd had to do tonight descended with full force upon him.

With his free hand, he gripped the banister tightly, one foot resting on the step above him. They'd skirted the danger this time, but what about the next? He didn't think for a second the conflict was over. And now he had the added burden of stretching their last five dollars.

He could buy seed for spring planting on credit, but if the crops didn't produce well... There was the option of selling both bonds for cash, to recoup their money, but he feared Joe and the mob finding out. How disloyal would he and his family appear then?

The weight of providing for and protecting his family pressed down on him, threatening to crush his spirit. He'd given away their money—money meant to help his father—but was that really protecting the ones he loved? Or hurting them? If he'd refused to buy the bond, he might have ended up half-dead, or worse. What would Elsa and his siblings have done then? Whether he fought against the injustice or submitted to it, his family lost something either way.

Friedrick pushed away from the banister and resumed climbing the stairs. Harlan and Greta were waiting for him. But the opposing viewpoints and compromises still squeezed at him, making it hard to swallow. Almost as if he had Joe's rope around his neck after all.

Chapter Two

Friedrick shepherded his mother and siblings into the white clapboard church and up the aisle to their usual pew on the left, three rows from the front. The murmur of German voices pitched and roiled, louder than normal. An undercurrent of tension pulsed through the room.

"What is going on?" Elsa asked him.

Friedrick shook his head. He hadn't seen the congregation this agitated since the United States had entered the war overseas.

Elsa twisted in her seat and voiced her question to her friend seated behind them. "What is all the talk about, Hannah?"

Hannah leaned forward, her buxom frame pressing against the pew, her heavy perfume overwhelming Friedrick's nose. "Pastor Schwarz has an announcement. And not a good one, if the rumors be true. Something about the new language law."

Friedrick faced the pulpit again. Concern tightened his

jaw. What would the pastor say? Friedrick had expected more trouble after his dealings with Joe and the vigilance committee two weeks earlier, but not this soon.

The moment Pastor Schwarz took his place behind the pulpit, the noise in the church plummeted into silence. In the sudden quiet, Friedrick could hear the squeak of a boot against the hardwood floor and the soft snore of a baby several rows behind them.

The pastor cleared his throat. The lines around his eyes appeared deeper and his shoulders slumped forward. Today his body showed every one of his sixty years.

"*Geehrte mitglieder und freunde*," he began before stopping. He coughed. When he opened his mouth again, he repeated what he'd said, only in English this time. "Dear members and friends."

Even to Friedrick's ears, the words sounded as garish as a fire gong. The songs, sermons, and prayers had always been conducted in German. Friedrick exchanged a glance with Elsa. Her eyes were large with shock.

"It is with heavy heart," the pastor continued, "I announce that our humble services will no longer be given in German. As you well know, our governor has decreed no foreign languages may be spoken in public, which includes church meetings."

Startled cries of outrage swept through the congregation. Pastor Schwarz raised his hand and the chatter faded to fierce whispers.

"I have been informed that those of you who do not wish to worship in English or who do not understand the language must hold services in your own homes." He took a long, visible breath and squared his bony shoulders. "Now we will begin today by singing…"

Friedrick hardly heard the rest of the service. His family had always worshiped in German. Like most of the American-born children of the congregation, Friedrick felt deep pride for his German heritage. Joining with others each Sunday who spoke his parents' native language allowed him to honor a culture as much a part of him as his American one and helped him feel connected to those relatives who hadn't immigrated.

It wasn't enough his people were being robbed of their savings. Now they were being forced to give up their very identity—all in the name of being loyal citizens. The injustice galled him and he couldn't sit still.

He rested one leg on top of the other, his knee moving in a steady tense beat. How many of these families would choose not to attend anymore? Like the Wagners, most of them had been coming here for decades. Friedrick hated to think of their close knit congregation dividing.

Would things ever return to the way they'd been? Or had life for him, his family, and his people been changed forever? Friedrick dropped his foot to the floor and rested his arms on his knees, his forehead nearly touching the pew in front of him. He couldn't sit by, but he couldn't openly protest either.

By the time the last song had been sung, in halting English, and the benediction given, Friedrick had made up his mind to speak with Pastor Schwarz. There had to be something he and his family could do to help.

"I'll be a minute," he told Elsa. "I need to talk to the pastor." Elsa nodded before speaking with Hannah—in whispered German. Friedrick would have to remind her it was no longer safe to do so, even in church.

Hat in hand, Friedrick headed toward the back of the

building, where a line of people had already formed near the pastor. Clearly he wasn't the only one wishing to speak with the man.

He nodded at the couple waiting in front of him. He and the husband exchanged predictions about the weather and spring planting until someone latched on to Friedrick's coat sleeve. He glanced down, knowing it was eighteen-year-old Maria Schmitt, before he saw those violet eyes and dark, fluttering lashes.

"Hello, Friedrick." Her mouth curved in a coy smile, in spite of the devastating blow they'd all received today.

"Morning, Maria."

"Are we going dancing this weekend?"

He searched his mind for yet another excuse—he hadn't taken her to a dance hall since the mob had shown up. Still, it might do him good to get away for a while. Dancing would give him something else to think about besides how his family was going to survive on so little.

"All right." His acceptance was laced with more resignation than joy, but Maria didn't seem to notice. "I'll pick you up at six on Friday."

"Good. I was beginning to think you were avoiding me." She hooked her arm through his. "Will your family keep coming to church, even with the sermons in English?"

"I don't know if Elsa will want to, but I think we should."

"I hope you will," she said softly as though imparting a secret. "The church's spring social would be such a bore without you." She gave an indignant shake of her head, making the dark curls around her face sway. "Did you hear that my mother—with my help, of course—is planning the whole thing?"

She prattled on about the details of the upcoming event—the baseball game, the dance, the music. Friedrick didn't have the heart to stop her. Let her find a bit of happiness where she could.

He liked Maria well enough. She was the only girl in the congregation near his own age who wasn't married or had a beau overseas. Maria clearly hoped to be among the former, based on the not-so-subtle hints from her and her mother. Friedrick couldn't imagine marrying anytime soon, though. He had nothing to offer a wife but a crowded house, a dying father-in-law, and no extra money.

The couple ahead of him bade the pastor farewell. Friedrick gently pried his arm from Maria's grip and stepped forward with purpose. "I must talk to Pastor Schwarz now. I'll see you Friday, Maria."

"Friedrick," the pastor said, gripping his hand. "What do you make of the announcement?"

"I think we'll lose many good people."

Pastor Schwarz lowered his hand to his side, his eyes taking in the still crowded room. "I fear you are right."

"Can I help in some way?"

The pastor clapped his hand on Friedrick's shoulder. "People look to you, Friedrick. If you continue to bring your family, I think others will follow."

"I will," he said without hesitation.

Elsa would take some convincing. More than any of them, she loved singing and praying in German. She'd told him more than once that doing so helped her feel close to her aunt and grandmother still living in Germany.

"Did you hear if the vigilance committee visited anyone else?" he asked the pastor.

Pastor Schwarz nodded. "At least twenty other families. They all bought bonds." His face reflected his compassion. "Like you, they have little left over."

"Is that what we must do, Pastor? Stand by and let them…" Friedrick lowered his voice. "Let them rob us of our savings and our language, just to prove we are loyal Americans?"

Pastor Schwarz looked past him toward the nearest window, but the man's wistful gaze suggested he wasn't seeing the houses across the street or the bare trees. "I miss the forests the most," he said, his voice soft, reflective. "I can still remember the great trees near our home in Germany. My mother's family still lives there." He glanced at Friedrick, anguish in his gray eyes. "My boy Johann may be fighting his own relatives at the front lines."

Mention of the war caused familiar guilt to nibble at Friedrick. If he were a solider in France, would he be fighting his German relations like Johann? Would his family be any safer in his absence?

The pastor coughed, and a sad smile lifted the corners of his mouth. "You ask an excellent question, Friedrick. Fight or stand down? The Bible teaches us to love our enemies, to do good to those who hate us."

Friedrick ran his hand along the brim of his hat. He hadn't planted a fist in Joe's face; that was something good. He'd also given the mob their money—money for his father's medicine, money to help pull them through the winter if the crops failed.

"And yet…" Pastor Schwarz paused until Friedrick lifted his head. "And yet we are also told there are different times and seasons. There is a time to keep silent, but there is also a time to speak. Only you and the Lord will know when it is time to stand down, to be silent, Friedrick and when it is time to act."

The church member behind him cleared his throat in impatience, ending their discussion. "Thank you, Pastor." The man's words had given him much to think on. "We'll be here next week."

Friedrick set his hat on his head and walked outside. Harlan and Greta were playing with some of the other children. He called to them, and they headed to the wagon as Elsa broke free from a circle of women talking beneath one of the trees. After helping Elsa onto the seat, Friedrick unhitched the horses and climbed up beside her.

"Can you believe that?" she muttered in German as they set off for home. She seemed to have forgotten the children in the back of the wagon. "Forcing us to speak English in our own church? What will they do next? My family and I came to this great country when I was twenty years old because we wanted more freedom, more opportunity. Now they want to snatch it away."

"I think we ought to keep coming," Friedrick suggested.

Elsa made a noise of disgust. "Why? We can worship—in German—at home."

He decided to try a different approach. "What are the other families doing?"

"Ach. Most of them will come back. There are even one or two who have changed their names to be more American. Mrs. Schwarz says she and the pastor will go by Black now. I guess that is what their son Johann chose to do before he left to fight."

So the pastor believed this was a season for keeping silent. The thought depressed Friedrick. His father and mother had both come to this country as teenagers, and he and his siblings had never even been to Germany. Why should the sins of the fathers, so to speak, be visited upon his American family?

"I still think we ought to keep coming. You'd miss your friends if we didn't, and as a people, we need to stick together."

Elsa crossed her arms in anger, but Friedrick sensed her resolve weakening, especially at the mention of her friends. She'd always looked forward to Sundays when she could visit with other German women.

He could think of other reasons for returning as well— ones Elsa wouldn't like but needed to hear. "There's something else we need to consider. If our loyalty to this country is in question, we don't want to do anything to call attention to ourselves. Staying home and worshiping alone in German might do that." He threw a look over his shoulder at Harlan and Greta before continuing in a lower voice, "We can't afford to buy more liberty bonds, Mother."

To his surprise, Elsa covered her face with her hands. Her shoulders shook as she began to weep. Friedrick shifted the reins into one hand so he could put his arm around her.

"He's almost out of medicine, Friedrick. How will we get more?" Her voice rose in pitch with the question. "Oh, I wish we'd never joined this war with Germany."

"What's the matter, Mama?" Greta had noiselessly moved up behind the wagon seat.

Elsa shook her head without answering.

"Is she upset about not having the sermons in German no more?" Harlan asked.

Friedrick nodded—better to have the boy think it was that, instead of fear over the future. He squeezed his mother's shoulder and took the reins in both hands again.

"I like it in English better," Harlan added. "I don't have to concentrate so hard."

"When you pay attention," Greta retorted.

"Whatdaya mean? I listened good today. Besides, I wasn't the one—"

"All right. That's enough," Friedrick said in a firm tone. Elsa straightened on the seat and swiped at her wet cheeks, but she stared silently into the distance.

A despondent feeling settled over the wagon as suffocating as a blanket on a hot summer day. Friedrick struggled to think of a funny song or story to amuse his siblings, but nothing came to mind. The drive back to the farm took them past the children's schoolhouse. Friedrick's gaze flicked to the building and away. He didn't need another visual reminder of what they'd lost in the last few weeks.

As he urged the horses to pick up their pace, something inside him whispered to slow down, to look again. Puzzled, Friedrick turned to stare directly at the school. A large number of shingles were missing from the roof, cracks riddled the brick exterior, and the outhouse leaned to one side. The building had been neglected for some time. He recalled Harlan mentioning a young man from a neighboring farm who was supposed to come several days a week to do upkeep.

"Whatever happened to that boy…Francis…who used to clean up the school?"

"Don't know," Harlan said. "I think he might've left to go fight last year."

"So nobody's been keeping up with repairs?"

Harlan shrugged. "Haven't seen anybody there but Miss Lehmann."

Elsa twisted on the seat to study Friedrick. "What do you have in mind?"

"Just an idea," he said in a noncommittal tone. It likely wouldn't work out, but he couldn't completely snuff the tiny flame of hope growing inside him. "I'll see what comes of it tomorrow when I go into town."

* * *

Livy clasped her hands in her lap to hide their slight trembling from the man seated at the desk in front of her. In the stillness of the superintendent's office, the tick of the clock on the wall and the rustle of the secretary's magazine pages in the next room sounded loud.

Mr. Foster set down his pen and removed a small set of keys from one of his desk drawers. "Now that we have all the information we need and you know where to find the school, here are the keys for the building and the teacherage. It's not much more than a glorified cabin, but it is all yours, Miss Campbell."

"So I have the job?"

He laughed. "Didn't I say as much in my telegram?"

Livy blushed as she took the keys he handed over. Her stomach had been in knots nearly the whole three-hour wagon ride to Hilden. She feared Mr. Foster would change his mind about hiring her, despite her letters of recommendation and his desperate need for a teacher. She still couldn't believe he'd willingly overlooked the fact she had only one year of college completed. And now she had a job—away from the farm and Robert.

"I hired a young man this morning to take care of the school maintenance, so don't be surprised if he comes around this week."

Livy climbed to her feet, the keys clasped tightly in her palm. "Thank you, Mr. Foster."

"You're most welcome." He stood and came around his desk. "I'm glad to have the position filled. I didn't have much in the way of replacements—not any non-German ones, at least. You can open the school as soon as you feel ready. But the sooner, the better."

She followed him out of his office. "Certainly."

"You may pick up your first month's wages at the end of April." He shook Livy's free hand.

Livy pumped his hand several more times in gratitude. "Thank you—again."

"Good day, Miss Campbell. Let me know if there's anything you need."

She gave him a genuine smile and even spared a wave for the secretary, though the woman didn't look up from her *Ladies' Home Journal*. As she rushed down the stairs, Livy's smile grew into a grin. If she ran into the handsome young man whom she'd danced with on her birthday, she might have to kiss him for mentioning the job in the first place. He'd popped into her thoughts more than once the last few weeks.

Would she see him in town? she wondered, exiting the building. Her gaze swept the street as though he might suddenly appear. Livy ruefully shook her head. She had no idea where he lived.

"Did you get everything you needed, sugar?" Her father pushed away from the side of the wagon, where he'd been waiting for her.

She dangled the keys and did a little skip. "I've got the keys to the school and my house, and directions on how to get us there."

"You want to head over there now?" Josiah asked as he helped her onto the wagon seat.

"I ought to purchase some food items first. Mother's hamper will only last me so long."

He climbed up beside her. "To the grocer's then."

His patience and acceptance of her plans resurrected the guilt she'd been battling the past few weeks about leaving home again. "Are you angry, Daddy?"

"For wanting to go to the grocer?"

"No." She couldn't help a giggle. "About me abandoning the farm."

He scratched at his stubbled chin. "I suppose I don't look at it that way, Livy. You saw an opportunity and seized it—something we've always taught you kids to do. Your mother and I only hope it'll bring you happiness."

She didn't have the heart to tell him she was already happy—more so than she'd been in a year. "Allen and the boys didn't seem too thrilled when you told them about their extra responsibilities."

"They'll manage. You, Joel, and Tom were doing that and more when you were younger."

The reference to Joel and Tom eased her guilt—almost—and reminded her of the other reason she'd applied for the job. The empty chairs at the supper table at home were a constant reminder her brothers were gone and in harm's way. Hopefully being a teacher here would keep her from worrying so much about their safety.

She sat up straighter and pocketed her keys. "I still wish you'd accept my offer to hire one of Allen's friends to help out." If she stretched her meals a little, she could send home a few dollars to pay for hired help. The gesture would certainly ease her conscience.

Josiah guided the horses into the street. "I didn't say I wouldn't accept. Why don't we wait and see how your first month goes? Sixty-five dollars a month is a good amount, but you'll still have to pay for food and things."

"All right. You win—for now." She smiled and slipped her arm beneath his as they headed toward the grocer's.

Though the morning had dawned cold, the sun now warmed her cheeks and almost made her want to shed her hat and new jacket. With less than two weeks to get ready, Livy's mother had expertly made over some of her old dresses for Livy's use. The brown wool suit Livy wore today consisted of a long jacket with matching skirt and a belt. With the superintendent's approval and her stylish outfit, she felt every bit like a real teacher.

Her gaze hopped from one store sign to the next as she looked for a grocer, until a storefront painted haphazardly in bright yellow snagged her attention.

"That's not a very good paint job. Allen or the boys could have done better. No wonder there are no wagons waiting out front."

Her father frowned instead of laughing as she'd expected. "I doubt it was the store owner who painted it."

Livy cocked her head. "Why would he let someone do that? It looks awful."

"He's likely from Germany, sugar. His store was

painted that way so everyone would know it was owned by a German."

His words made Livy swallow hard, even as her eyes sought out the building again. Mr. Foster had told her the reasons the last teacher had been let go—how she'd been accused of being a German spy and violating the language law. Livy knew she had nothing to fear on that front. She didn't know a single German here or back home, so she couldn't be accused of being a German sympathizer.

What she wasn't so confident about was her students and their families. The township school would likely be full of German children, from German parents. She might be teaching the distant relatives of those fighting against her brothers or those who'd wounded—and changed—Robert.

The reality that her new situation wasn't completely carefree and rosy brought a sick feeling to her stomach. Her earlier excitement faded in its wake.

"You're going to do fine, Livy." Her father's hand closed over hers. The confidence behind his words erased some of her nervousness. "There's something you need to remember, though—"

The honk of an automobile horn made the horses dance toward the sidewalk, and Josiah turned his focus to soothing them. "Horses just aren't used to those contraptions yet," he grumbled when the team settled down. "You know, your mother wants one of them Ford touring cars."

"But she isn't the only one, is she?"

He shrugged, but his green eyes sparkled.

"There's a grocer's," she said, pointing.

As he helped her to the curb, she realized he hadn't finished sharing his advice. *Oh well*, Livy thought, her mind already darting ahead to what things she needed to purchase for her very own kitchen. He'd probably meant to tell her not to forget who her brothers were fighting overseas. And she wouldn't.

* * *

Once her food staples had been stowed in the back of the wagon, along with her things from home, Livy and her father set off for the schoolhouse. Less than an hour later, much to Livy's relief and anticipation, the teacher's cabin and the school appeared in the distance.

The cabin sat off the road, south of the school. An outhouse had been tucked in the copse of trees behind it. Red curtains hung in the south-facing window, and the spot of color in the brownish landscape brought a smile to Livy's face. Another hundred yards or so up the main road stood the one-room brick schoolhouse. Three large windows were visible along its side.

"What you do think?" Josiah stopped the wagon beside the cabin.

"It's perfect," Livy said.

He tipped his chin in the direction of the school. "Looks a little run-down. I didn't bring any tools with me, but we could ask at one of the farms close by."

Livy shook her head as she hopped down from the wagon seat. "Mr. Foster said he hired a young man earlier today to handle maintenance and repairs."

Josiah joined her at the back of the wagon and hefted one of the sacks of flour as Livy grabbed her suitcase. In her eagerness, she nearly dropped her keys as she fumbled to open the cabin's sturdy-looking door. If her father noticed the display of nerves, he didn't comment.

Livy stepped inside the single rectangular room and felt as if she'd gone back in time, some forty years. Beneath the north window, which faced the school, sat an iron bedstead. A bureau with a mirror and a washbasin stood against the far wall next to the large pantry cupboard. The cookstove and table with its two chairs completed the kitchen area, and a fireplace flanked the wall beside the door. A good layer of dust lay over everything and the place smelled unlived in, but Livy would set it to rights in no time.

"Good thing Mama taught us how to cook on the old stove before you bought the new oven," she said to her father. He chuckled as he set the bag of flour on the floor beside the cupboard and returned to the wagon.

Livy sat on the bed and gave it a good bounce. The padding wasn't thick, but it seemed firm. *At least it isn't a tick mattress. That would be a little too archaic.*

The cabin might be small and primitive when compared to her family's spacious, five-bedroom farmhouse with its bathroom and electricity, but this place was all hers. With the kerosene lamps from the farm's attic and the large supply of quilts her mother had insisted she bring, Livy felt certain she could turn this place into a proper home.

"There's a pump out back," Josiah announced when he came back inside. "I'll get you some water." He found a bucket near the stove and took it outside with him.

Livy placed her suitcase next to the bed and went to help unload the wagon. When everything had been carried inside, including a full bucket of water, she surveyed the boxes littering the wood floor. "Now which one has my dishes, so we can eat lunch? I'm starving."

Josiah peered into one. "These must be your teaching supplies. Do you want me to take them up to the school?"

"No. I'll go over there when I'm finished organizing things here."

She located some rags she'd brought and used one to wipe off the table and chairs while her father unpacked the contents of the hamper. To the clean table, Livy added the dishes her mother had given her. The sight of all those nice plates and cups brought a sharp sense of sorrow. She hadn't expected to need them until she married and had a family of her own, but it hadn't worked out that way.

Livy swallowed her sadness and forced a bright voice to say, "Time to eat."

Her father sat down and Livy joined him at the table. How strange it felt to share a meal with only one other person. She was used to scrambling for a big helping and talking loudly to be heard. The quiet felt wrong to her ears and the amount of food unusually large.

"Think you'll like it here, on your own?" Josiah asked, as if reading her thoughts.

"Very much," she said with assurance, despite some of her misgivings.

"Don't miss us too much now," he teased, coaxing a smile from her.

"I'll miss you all very much."

He studied his food as he asked, "What about Robert Drake?"

"What about him?" Livy feigned interest in her own plate.

"Will you miss him, too?"

Memories of her disastrous conversation with Robert two days earlier filled Livy's mind. He hadn't been drunk, but he had been angry at her for accepting the job and in a different county, too. His reaction had only fueled Livy's desire to leave—and to stay away as long as possible.

"I'll miss spending time with him," she finally said. At least the times when Robert had been sweet and she'd enjoyed being together.

Her father gratefully let the subject drop. They talked instead of home and their neighbor Mae Norton, who'd moved to Hilden a few years earlier, after her husband died, to live with her daughter.

"If you need anything, I'm sure Mrs. Norton would be willing to help," Josiah reminded her as he stacked their dirty dishes.

Willing to help, yes, Livy mused, but also ready to blab to everyone else what she needed. Mrs. Norton was well known for her gift of gossip.

With lunch finished, Livy's father stood and pushed in his chair. "I'd better start back, so I can help Allen with the evening chores."

Livy trailed him outside. Something like homesickness rose into her throat for the first time all day. "Thank you, Daddy. For everything."

He put his arms around her and hugged her tight. "Seems like yesterday you were runnin' around after your older brothers, in braids and bare feet." Releasing her, he gave her nose a playful tweak. "Now look at you. All grown up and going to be a teacher."

The lump in her throat grew larger, preventing any words.

"Make sure you write."

She nodded.

"I'll try to see if I can't get your mother up here for a visit, at least before school lets out in a few months."

Livy forced a smile and gave him another quick hug. "Maybe I can come home for a visit, too."

"Let me know and I'll drive up to get you."

He turned away, but not before Livy caught the glimmer of tears in his eyes. She felt a similar sting in her own as he unhitched the horses and climbed onto the wagon seat.

"Bye, sugar." His voice cracked as he said the familiar nickname. Livy fought to keep her tears in check. She must appear brave and strong. This wasn't any different than when she'd gone off to college. She hadn't cried then, and she wouldn't do so now.

"Bye, Daddy." She kept her chin up.

He smiled at her feigned courage. "You take care now."

"I will." She lifted her hand in a wave, which he returned.

As he clucked to the horses, Livy went back inside, but she stood in the door frame and watched until her father and the wagon were specks in the distance. Some of the pleasantness of her little home seemed to go with him.

When she finally shut the door, she drew herself up and surveyed the cluttered room. "No one to share the dresser with or make noise when I'm sketching. This is going to be perfect."

Rolling up her sleeves, Livy changed into an old work dress and threw herself into the task of cleaning her small house. She heated water on the stove and used it to scrub every inch of the floor and furniture. Sweat formed on her hairline, and her clothes were soon damp and dirty.

When the single room shone with cleanliness, she turned her attention to unpacking. The more of her things she put away or set out, the more she felt at home. The work also drove away any lingering nostalgia she felt for the farm.

At last, only one box remained—the one with her school supplies. "Now is as good a time as any to take it over," she murmured to herself.

She covered her disheveled hair with her traveling hat and her work clothes with a coat, in case she should happen upon any of her neighbors or students. Taking the box in hand, she left the cabin and headed toward the school.

The sky in the west burned with brilliant pink and orange streaks. Livy shivered as the cold air penetrated her coat. Thankfully she didn't have far to walk. In front of her, the school stood tall and stark, its windows black.

Livy slowed her steps as she approached, suddenly reluctant to go inside. What would she find? Splashes of yellow paint, books in a foreign language, a German flag displayed prominently? Or perhaps things would be in complete disarray, in protest of the last teacher being fired.

An archway loomed over her, revealing a door on one side of the wide entry. Livy gulped. Perhaps she ought to wait until morning. She glanced back at her little cabin, but it looked as shadowed as the school from this distance.

"You're being silly," she told herself firmly.

She set down her box to retrieve the keys from her pocket. In the dark of the archway, she had to stick her face close to the lock to see where to fit the key. She twisted it and the door opened with a ominous *creak*.

Gnawing her cheek, Livy lifted her box and entered the building. Deep shadows pressed in on her as she walked past what appeared to be a coat closet. A loud *thud* made her heart leap into her throat. She rushed forward to escape, only to stumble over something on the floor. Her cry of fear echoed against the walls, but nothing jumped out at her.

When her pulse had slowed, she reached down to pick up the object off the floor. It was one of her books, which had fallen from the box and nearly tripped her. Livy let out a nervous laugh as she walked into the schoolroom.

In the dim light from the windows, she spied four neat rows of desks. A blackboard covered most of the far wall, except where a map of the world had been hung beside the American flag. The patriotic symbol brought Livy a measure of relief. She wouldn't have to take down any German flags or pictures of the Kaiser.

Livy set her hat and box on the teacher's desk at the front of the room and went to stand before the map. She placed her finger on Iowa and traced a line across the ocean to France. Joel and Tom weren't allowed to tell the family where they were stationed or fighting, but they were somewhere in that country.

She calculated the difference in time between Iowa and France. Joel and Tom might still be sleeping or perhaps they were awake and getting an early start on the day. What would they say about her job? Livy knew they'd be proud of her for becoming a teacher, but she wasn't sure how they'd feel about her possibly teaching German students.

An intense longing to see them welled up inside her. Her older brothers had always been her greatest friends, despite Tom being three years older and Joel five years. They were a close-knit trio and always had been. Every day she lived with the fear one or both of them might not come back.

Livy lowered her hand and frowned at the map. It would be another reminder of her brothers' absence, but one she could control. She yanked out the nails holding the map to the wall. After carefully rolling the large paper, she placed it against the small bookcase on one side of the room.

"Better," she whispered as she surveyed the now empty spot on the wall.

She shed her coat and unpacked more clean rags to dust the desks and windowsills. Though she suspected they could benefit from a good scrubbing as well, she was too tired to do a more thorough cleaning tonight.

After dusting, Livy unloaded her supplies. Some of her enthusiasm—and energy—returned as she placed the pencils, paper, and books inside or on top of the teacher's desk.

My desk now, she thought with a smile.

When everything was in order, she slipped outside and locked the door. The sky had changed to twilight blue. Livy drew her coat tighter around her shoulders and stepped quicker, anxious to be out of the cold. She found a dwindling pile of wood along the cabin's back wall and put as many logs in her now empty box as she could carry. She'd have to see about borrowing an axe to split more or she'd freeze at night.

Inside she lit one of her lamps and stoked the dying fire in the stove. She kept her coat on as she warmed the leftovers from lunch, until enough heat penetrated the room to stop her shivering. She sat down at the table to eat and eyed the empty chair across from her. If eating with only her father for company had felt odd, sitting alone felt twice as foreign. Even in college, she'd taken meals with her aunt, whom she'd lived with, or she'd invited friends to dine with them.

The stillness pressed down on her, magnifying the scrape of her fork against the plate and the distant bark of a dog outside. The food itself tasted less appealing without someone to share it with.

What is everyone at home doing now? she wondered.

A sudden pang of loneliness tightened her throat and made eating difficult. The family was probably gathered around the dinner table, talking and laughing and jostling for more of Mother's biscuits. Livy imagined Joel and Tom were there, too—every seat filled but hers—though she knew that was impossible.

She forcibly replaced such thoughts with ones about her job. Since she'd just arrived today, none of the children would know school could resume. She would need to make visits to the neighboring farms tomorrow and let them know she was the new teacher.

As her gaze swept the room, she told herself she was doing the right thing. She would find happiness here, a place where she belonged. She had to. Going back home, especially with Robert there, was not a choice anymore.

Desperate to wash off the dust and grime from cleaning, Livy grabbed the lamp and the empty bucket by the door. Full dark covered the land now, and even with the lamp in her hand, she wished Allen or even her littlest brothers were around.

She walked inside a tiny pool of light to the pump

and set the lamp down. The sudden hoot of an owl made her gasp. She forced a laugh at her jumpiness—something she hadn't experienced at home or at college—as she primed the pump and filled her bucket.

With the dishes rinsed and her face and arms scrubbed clean, Livy dressed for bed. Exhaustion tugged at her mind and body, but she found satisfaction in the feeling. Today she'd worked hard at setting things in order, and very soon she'd be hard at work teaching her students.

She released a yawn and knelt beside the newly made bed for her nightly prayers. Her lips moved in silence as she thanked God for her job and her new home and petitioned Heaven's blessings on her time here. Next she prayed for each member of her family and for Joel and Tom's continued safety. She nearly ended her prayer there, but instead, she found herself praying for Robert's return to sobriety. Even if it meant he married one of the ogle-eyed girls at church, Livy wanted him to find true happiness.

The thought of someone else as "Robert's girl" inspired a prick of jealousy within her, but memories of their unhappy times together surfaced to drive it away. If Robert did remain sober, she still wasn't entirely convinced they were the match she'd envisioned before he'd left for the war. She might miss his kisses and his handsome, dark looks, but deep down, she believed she'd made the right decision in leaving.

Livy slipped beneath her covers and shut her eyes, willing sleep to come. The air felt too still and yet noisy, too, with all the wrong sounds. She missed Mary's soft snoring and the younger boys' whispered ghost stories in the next room. Remembering some of those toe-curling tales, she burrowed deeper into her blankets and squeezed her eyes shut. *I'm a grown woman; I'll be just fine.*

* * *

The sounds of a team and wagon lumbering by penetrated her drowsiness. Livy jerked her eyes open, feeling wide awake again. She told herself it was likely someone driving past on the main road, until she heard a strange bump close to the cabin. Heavy footfalls neared her door and the handle rattled. Cold fear clutched Livy's heart. She'd been so tired earlier she'd forgotten to lock the door.

Her heartbeat pounded in her ears, nearly drowning out the soft *screech* of the handle as it twisted. Someone was coming inside. The hair on the back of her neck stood on end.

The door inched opened. Livy's pulse raced so fast it almost hurt. She searched the room for something to protect herself. Her gaze latched on to the fire poker. With one eye on the door, Livy sprang from her bed and grabbed up the fire poker. She grasped it tightly in both hands and prepared to face her intruder.

Armed with some way to protect herself, her fear changed to anger. *I have a right to be here*, she told herself. She'd done nothing wrong by accepting this job. But as the door swung fully open and a tall figure appeared on the threshold, she couldn't help thinking her decision may have been a mistake after all.

* * *

Friedrick entered the cabin, his arms full of wood. He'd meant to leave it outside, but he figured the new teacher might appreciate not having to carry so many logs inside when she arrived.

He turned toward the fireplace and nearly collided with a white figure brandishing something long and dark in its hand. The sinister-looking item swung through the air toward his shoulder.

"Easy there," Friedrick cried in surprise. He raised a log to block the blow, but it didn't come.

Instead a feminine voice demanded, "Who are you? What you do want?"

"I just want to put your wood by the fireplace," he countered. He hadn't expected the new teacher to be here already. "Look, I'm not here to hurt you. I was told to bring you more wood. The door was unlocked, so I figured you weren't here yet."

"Well, I am." He could see she still held her weapon aloft.

"Tell you what." Friedrick took a backward step toward the fireplace. "I'm going to set your wood down over here, while you put down whatever it is you've got there."

A tense moment of silence followed his suggestion. "It's the fire poker," she finally said, a note of sheepishness in her voice. He watched her slowly lower it to the floor.

Once he felt certain she wasn't going to bash him over the head, he knelt beside the firebox. "I'll be done in a moment."

"I can light a lamp, so you can see."

The room lit with a soft glow as he stacked the wood

neatly in the box. When he'd finished, Friedrick stood and turned around. He was prepared to see a spinster woman with eyeglasses, similar to Miss Lehmann, standing there. Instead he found himself peering into the vibrant, green eyes of the girl from the dance hall.

"You're the new teacher?" he asked at the same moment she declared, "I know you." They shared a laugh.

She glanced down at her nightgown and blushed. He'd barged in on her sleeping. Embarrassed, Friedrick spotted a coat near the door and reached for it. "Here you go." He handed it to her.

She gave him a grateful smile as she pulled it on. The coat and nightgown hid her small waist and curves, but he still thought she looked every bit as lovely as she had the night they'd danced. Especially with her dark blond hair falling over her shoulders and framing her pretty face.

Friedrick realized he was staring. He cleared his throat and focused his gaze on a knot in the pantry cupboard, right above her bare head. "I'm glad to see you got the job."

"You must be the new maintenance man Mr. Foster told me about."

"Yes." A job that suddenly held more appeal to him than just earning money, especially if he got to see her more often. "Sorry about coming in unannounced. Mr. Foster wasn't sure when you'd arrive and I wanted to be sure you had wood."

"Thank you." She lowered her gaze and fingered the hem of her sleeve. Friedrick recognized it as a gesture of shyness.

Funny, she hadn't struck him as timid the other night. Could that mean she might like him? Might have thought about him since their last meeting? His chest swelled a bit at the possibility.

"I best get going." He angled toward the door, but stopped when she spoke again.

"My name's Olivia Campbell, by the way," she said in a rush. "But most people call me Livy."

Friedrick dusted his wood-flecked palms against his pants and stuck out his hand. "Pleased to meet you again, Livy Campbell." His hand swallowed hers as it had when they were dancing. He liked the soft feel of her fingers in his grip. "I'll be working on the school roof this week, but let me know if I can help you with anything else."

"And your name?" She smiled, her face reflecting her eagerness to know.

He released her hand and glanced at the open door. If only he could give her a more American-sounding name, one that wouldn't crush his chance to get to know her better. But he couldn't lie. "I'm Friedrick Wagner."

"Wagner?" she repeated, a note of surprise in her voice. "Are you from here?" She quickly shook her head. "From America, I mean."

"My parents are from Germany, if that's what you're wondering." He didn't bother to hide the annoyance that colored his words. This was the very reason he'd chosen not to tell her his name before. He'd repeated this very scene so many times while dancing the last year, he'd lost count. "I was born in the United States, though, same as you."

Her cheeks turned pink at his comment, but that didn't prevent her from opening her mouth again. "How many of the children at the school are...of German descent?"

Irritation leapt inside him, despite knowing the question wasn't entirely unfounded. "Every farm in our township but one has ancestral ties to Germany. Does that bother you?"

"No." She kept her chin tilted up as she said it, and yet a flicker of wariness in her green eyes belied her response. "I only hope the children will know I don't plan to continue..." She visibly swallowed. "I will be dispensing with some of the practices of the last teacher."

The resentment he'd harbored over all his family had suffered the past few weeks roiled inside him, despite knowing Livy Campbell wasn't to blame. He was powerless to stop his next words from pouring out with the tide of frustration. "Worried you might have a whole room of little Kaiser-praising loyalists? The last teacher was accused of spying, too. But that won't be a problem for you, will it, Miss Campbell? You'll beat out any lingering love for the fatherland, won't you?"

Her eyes widened at his accusation, then narrowed with barely controlled anger. "You certainly have some nerve," she fired back. Her brow furrowed and she gripped her coat tightly against her. "You don't know anything about me or what I can handle or what sort of discipline I plan to administer, so don't mock me with your sarcasm. If you want to be a German patriot, that's your choice, but don't assume you know what I think or feel."

Her answering fury, and the memory of Joe and his mob, cooled Friedrick's bitterness by a few degrees. He couldn't afford to court trouble—not when he'd just been given this job. He realized his hands had balled into fists. Relaxing them, he softened his tone. "I assure you, I am not a German patriot. My loyalty is, and will always be, to this nation and her allies."

Livy arched her eyebrows. "Then how come you're not in Europe fighting for America?"

Friedrick folded his arms and took a determined stance. There was no need to hide the answer from her tonight, now that she knew he was German-American. "I have a farm deferment," he said simply without apology.

"I see." She gazed coolly at him. "That's certainly preferred to risking your own life or limbs for the cause." The cynicism behind her barbed words reminded him that she very well could have family fighting overseas.

"My father's dying, Miss Campbell." He locked his eyes with hers. She fell back a step. Whether from his scrutiny or his answer, he didn't know. "If I had gone overseas to fight, my stepmother and half siblings would've had to run the farm alone while caring for him, too."

"I—I'm sorry. I just presumed you didn't want to—"

"Participate?" he finished with a bitter laugh. "Believe me, it would be much easier than staying behind." He scrubbed his hand over his face. "Especially when I have to answer to judging busybodies like yourself," he muttered.

He didn't say it quietly enough, though. The muscles in her delicate jaw clenched. "I think it's time you left, Mr. Wagner. And don't bother with the wood anymore. I'm perfectly capable of chopping it myself. I wouldn't want you to have to help a judging busybody."

If he hadn't been so mad, he might have been inclined to laugh at her stubbornness. He had no doubt she could fend for herself. Her aim with the fire poker might have been a bit off, but she could hold her own in a verbal battle.

"Suits me fine," he grumbled as he stomped out the door. He didn't bother to shut it. Let *Miss Capability* do it herself.

He marched to the wagon, regret nibbling at his conscience. If word got back to Foster that Friedrick had made an enemy of the new teacher, he'd surely be fired. He didn't have to like her, but he could be civil.

He drew on every ounce of willpower to turn around. She hadn't completely closed the door. "There's something you need to know." Friedrick prided himself on sounding calm.

Livy glared at him, but she didn't slam the door shut.

"If you light the school stove in the morning, the children who live close by will see the smoke and know class is back in session. Word will spread to the others."

Without waiting for a reply, he climbed onto the wagon seat and slapped the reins. He couldn't get away from here fast enough. He'd foolishly believed Livy was different, at least until she'd found out who he really was.

Friedrick turned the horses toward home, not sparing a glance at the cabin. His eyes narrowed on the stars above him. There were other things as constant as the heavens—people's prejudice, for one. He was kidding himself if he thought things would change anytime soon for him and his family. As long as the war lasted, they would be viewed as a target, a threat. That wasn't going to change, and the sooner he accepted it, the better.

Chapter Three

The alarm clock's insistent ring jerked Livy awake the next morning. She rubbed her tired eyes and climbed, unseeing, from her bed. As she started across the floor, her big toe connected with a hard knot in the floorboards. Pain shot up her foot. Groaning, she flopped back onto the mattress and rubbed the injured limb. What a fitting omen after her less-than-restful night.

She hadn't been able to quell her fury over Friedrick Wagner's arrogance, but once she had calmed down, confusion replaced her anger. Where was the kind young man she'd danced with on her birthday? She'd gotten a glimpse of him before their argument and afterward when he'd offered the helpful information about the stove. But his ill opinions, and the accusation of her being a "judging busybody," still stung her memory.

And to think I entertained the idea of kissing him for telling me about the teaching job.

With an indignant shake of her head, Livy limped to

the bureau and carefully selected a striped blouse and a green, high-waisted skirt for her first day of school. If anyone came...

Friedrick had likely woken the neighbors last night and repeated all of Livy's comments. The thought made her already unsettled stomach lurch with fresh nerves. She needed this day and the next and the rest of the school year to go well, or she'd have to return home. There she'd be forced to once again face the absence of her brothers and Robert's insobriety.

"No." She slammed the drawer shut to emphasize her determination. She wouldn't let Friedrick's remarks or actions tear her down. She would go over to the school, light the stove, and prepare for the day, as if all the students were coming.

Once she was dressed, Livy eyed her humble kitchen. Despite her resolve to be strong, she wasn't sure she could eat anything. She settled on grabbing an apple from yesterday's lunch hamper. If her stomach felt better later on, she would eat it. She bundled into her coat and hat and pocketed her keys. The short walk to the schoolhouse was still a cold one.

Livy shivered as she unlocked the door and stepped into the frigid room. Beside the stove, she found a neat pile of kindling and wood that hadn't been there yesterday. There was only one explanation—Friedrick Wagner.

She easily dismissed the nice surprise with the reminder he'd likely brought wood to the school first before barging into her cabin last night. Which meant she didn't owe him any more gratitude. This thought, however misguided, eased her guilty conscience.

What was it about this man that made her speak without thinking? she wondered as she worked at starting a fire. She'd seen and experienced plenty of heartache and frustration with Robert, and yet she'd never lost her temper with him. *Perhaps I should have.* There was something almost liberating about sharing what she truly felt, instead of hiding it.

She forced her mind off the insufferable Mr. Wagner and soon had a strong fire going. When the room began to thaw, Livy removed her coat and hung it in the tiny cloakroom. She straightened the already straight desks and managed to down a few bites of her apple.

After peeking out one of the windows at the road, she checked the clock on the wall. Forty minutes past eight. School was supposed to start in twenty minutes. Had any of the children seen the smoke from the schoolhouse chimney? Would anyone come?

Her stomach wound tighter and tighter as she paced the room, from the blackboard to the stove and back. Finally she dropped into her chair and pulled out one of her sketchbooks. She closed her eyes as the end of the pencil found its way between her teeth. What should she draw?

Unbidden, Friedrick's handsome face materialized in her mind. She'd visualized it plenty since the night of her birthday, but today, his image was sharper with recent memory. Like the way his blue eyes had lit up with appreciation as he studied her in her nightgown last night. Or the way his tall, strong frame seemed to fill the cabin.

She recalled how his undisguised joy at seeing her again, at least at first, had made her stomach quiver with strange delight. She hadn't felt that dancing. But her memory argued otherwise. There *had* been a moment, after he'd smiled at her on her birthday, when she felt that same tremble of excitement. She couldn't recall Robert inspiring such emotion in her, even when he kissed her, though she found his kisses pleasant enough.

Livy opened her eyes and scowled at the blank sheet of paper. She didn't want to sketch a picture of Friedrick. Or think about him or dwell on what feelings he might have stirred inside her. Right now the only emotion she felt toward the man was contempt.

She decided on a quick sketch of her family's farm, but she hadn't managed more than a few strokes of the pencil when the school door clattered open. Jumping up, Livy smiled with relief as an older boy and a young girl quietly put away their things and slid into their desks.

"Good morning," she said cheerfully. They nodded back without speaking. She wouldn't let their reticence unnerve her—she had students.

A steady trickle of children filtered into the school, some looking as young as five, some nearly as old as her brother Allen. All of them remained silent, shooting Livy wary glances, as they sat down. One or two of the younger girls sent shy smiles in her direction, to which Livy responded with a little wave. Apparently she had a ways to go before winning the rest of the students' trust.

When the door ceased banging open, Livy counted the number of children seated before her. There were fifteen students altogether—more than she thought would see the chimney smoke. Had someone, possibly Friedrick, let those farther away from the school know she had arrived? If so, the man was proving to be a wealth of contradictions.

She waited until exactly nine o'clock, then she

straightened her shoulders and greeted the students with a genuine smile. "Good morning, class. I'm Miss Campbell, and I'm excite—"

A tiny girl with tight, reddish-brown braids raised her arm.

Livy clasped her hands together, hoping to appear patient despite the interruption. "Do you have a question?"

The braids bounced as the girl gave a vigorous nod.

"And your name is?"

"Yvonne. Yvonne Fischer."

"Hello, Yvonne. What is your question?"

"Is Miss Lehmann coming back?"

A chorus of murmurs filled the room before Livy could ask, "Who is Miss Lehmann?"

"Our teacher," a tall boy in the back said, his chin tipped at a defiant angle.

Livy squeezed her fingers tightly and tried to maintain the calm demeanor she'd been instructed by her college professors to display. "I am your teacher now. At least until the end of the school year."

"But what happened to Miss Lehmann?" an older girl asked. "One week she was here, then the next there was a notice on the door saying the school was closed."

Livy opened her mouth to tell them the truth—their teacher had been fired—but as she stared into their innocent faces, she knew she couldn't do it. No wonder they watched her with suspicion. Their former teacher had disappeared on them and no one had bothered to explain. If their parents hadn't felt the need to tell them Miss Lehmann had been accused of being a spy and had broken the language law, then Livy wouldn't either.

"I don't know where Miss Lehmann went," she answered honestly. "But I'm sure she would be here if she could. In the meantime, I will be your teacher and I'm looking forward to getting to know—"

The crash of the door and the rush of footsteps interrupted her introduction for a second time. A boy and girl, still in their coats, hurried into the room and slid into their respective desks.

"Sorry we're late, Teacher," the boy said as he placed his lunch at his feet. The smile on his face looked anything but repentant. "Our farm's the farthest out. Plus we had to help Friedrick with his chores 'cause he got an extra job."

Friedrick? These had to be the half siblings he'd mentioned. "We've only just started. What are your names?"

"Harlan Wagner, ma'am. And that's my sister, Greta." He pointed a thumb at the cherubic-looking girl across the aisle.

Friedrick had sent his siblings to school—to *her* school—despite his sour opinion of her. Livy glanced down at her joined hands in confusion. The man was certainly a study in paradoxes. She pushed the thought aside to greet the newcomers.

"We're glad you made it," she said.

The older girl raised her hand.

"You are?" Livy inquired.

"My name's Anna. And Miss Lehmann didn't tolerate tardiness." Livy read the unspoken challenge in Anna's gaze—this was a test. If Livy pardoned Harlan and Greta, she might appear weak to the rest of the class. But she also didn't want to punish them for what seemed to be a plausible reason for being late.

"Thank you for bringing that to my attention, Anna."

Livy turned from her to Harlan. "Are you and Greta typically late, Harlan?"

The boy shook his head. "Not really. It takes us longer to walk here. But now we're helping Friedrick in the morning, too."

Livy bit down hard on the inside of her cheek. She had to maintain an orderly classroom and prove her mettle as a teacher, but she didn't want to fault Harlan and Greta for helping their brother either. With no previous teaching experience to fall back on, she would have to use what she'd learned watching her parents raise seven children. As she considered what they might do in a similar situation, an idea popped into her mind.

"I'd like to put this to the class," she announced. "How can we promote punctuality and still do what we can to assist Harlan and Greta with their new responsibilities?"

Several of the children eyed each other with uncertainty. Finally, the tall boy who'd spoken earlier raised his hand. "What if they got up earlier?"

Livy nodded in acknowledgment of the suggestion, then looked at Harlan. "Could you and your sister wake up ten minutes earlier?"

"I think so."

"Any other suggestions?" She let her gaze sweep the room.

"Miss Lehmann always used the wooden paddle," a short boy with round cheeks said, his brow creased with distaste.

Livy fought a similar expression from seeping onto her own face. The sting on her backside and the humiliation of being paddled for making what the teacher deemed "smart remarks" in school felt as fresh as yesterday. She'd had to repeat the experience twice more during her school years, and she'd vowed never to use such discipline on any child—her own or someone else's. Here was another way she would differ from Miss Lehmann.

"Have you had the paddle before, Greta?" she asked in a soft voice.

The little girl blushed. "Once."

Spinning on her heel, Livy went to her desk and searched through the drawers until she found the detestable paddle. She removed it and dropped the paddle into the nearby wastebasket with a satisfying *thud*.

"There will be no paddle in this classroom anymore." A few of the children clapped. Livy bit back a smile. Even Anna looked relieved. "Do we have any other suggestions for dealing with tardiness?"

"What about a grace period?" a girl with dark brown curls suggested

Yvonne scrunched her face. "What's that?"

"It means you're allowed a few extra minutes after school starts to be in your seat," Livy explained, "before a consequence comes into effect."

"I like that one," Anna said. "If you aren't here by five minutes after nine, then..." She pursed her lips in thought. "Then you have to clean erasers."

This time Livy allowed her smile to break through. The discussion was a small victory, but one nonetheless. "I think that's a wonderful solution, Anna. The grace period will go into effect tomorrow. In addition, Harlan, can you and your sister promise to wake up ten minutes earlier and come in quietly?"

"Yes, ma'am," they said in unison.

"That's settled then." Livy picked up her sketchbook

and pencil and turned to a blank page. "Now that I've met Anna, Yvonne, Harlan, and Greta, it's time to learn the rest of your names. Then we'll get to work."

* * *

Livy sat in the shade of the school building, bent over her drawing. The happy sounds of the children running and playing, their lunches duly devoured, filled her ears. The morning had gone well, though she didn't mind the chance to rest for a few minutes and sketch.

"Whatcha drawin'?"

Livy lifted her head as Harlan plopped down beside her. She turned the book so he could see her picture.

His face scrunched in concentration as he studied her work. "Looks like a farm."

She smiled. "That's what it's supposed to be."

"Is that where you live?"

"Where my family lives." Livy twisted the book back toward herself. The drawing was nearly complete—just a few more chickens near the barn and the lilac bushes by the porch.

Harlan leaned back against the bricks. "Do you got any kids?"

"No," Livy said with a chuckle. "I'm not married."

"Do you got any brothers or sisters?"

She set her pencil down. "I have one sister and five brothers."

Harlan's eyes grew wide. "They all live in that house?"

"No. Two of my brothers are fighting in the war right now."

"Wish I was old enough to fight." Harlan puffed out

his small chest in a way that might have made Livy laugh if they weren't talking about something so grown-up and awful.

"How old are you, Harlan?"

"Nine."

"And which side would you fight on?"

Harlan threw her a perplexed look. "For America, Miss Campbell. I know we're fightin' Germany and all, and that's where my mama and papa came from, but we aren't Kaiser lovers at our house."

Ashamed at her own question, Livy tempered it with a smile. "I think you'd make a brave soldier, Harlan, though I'm sure your mother and father are very glad you aren't old enough to go fight."

"Yeah, I guess so." He leaned over her drawing again. "Say, can I draw something?"

"All right." Livy found a blank page and handed the sketchbook and pencil to him. She watched in amusement as he stared hard at the paper.

"What are you doing, Harlan?" a boy named Oliver asked him.

"Drawing. What do you think?"

Oliver looked at Livy. "Can I draw, too?"

Several other students had drifted over to their little group. Murmurs of interest followed Oliver's question. Livy looked the children over and smiled. "Tell you what, Oliver. Why don't you and Joseph gather up the paper and pencils in the top drawer of my desk? Anna, will you get some books off the bookcase? We can use those as desks. Then anyone who would like to draw is welcome to."

Anna and the two boys rushed off while Livy directed

the children to sit down on the grass. By the time the trio
returned with the supplies, all the students had collected
around Livy and Harlan.

Livy passed a paper to each one. "I only have two sets
of drawing pencils, so we'll have to share." She placed
the pencils in the middle of the seated group.

"What should we draw?" Yvonne asked.

Livy's gaze wandered across the school yard to her
tiny cabin. "I want each of you to draw something you
dream of, something you wish for."

Noise rippled through the group as the children talked
excitedly to one another about what they wanted to draw.
Once the pencils had been divided up and the students
bent over their work, the school yard became as quiet as
a church. Only the scratching of pencil against paper and
the occasional whisper disrupted the stillness.

Livy had traded a paper with Harlan for her sketchbook, but it sat neglected in her lap. Instead of working on
her own drawing, she found herself caught up in watching her students enjoy something she loved.

How many hours had she spent sketching outside or
in her room at home? Pouring her hopes and dreams and
feelings into her drawings? She might be inexperienced
when it came to teaching, but she could share, with confidence, her appreciation for art.

When most of the students had completed their
projects, Livy stole back inside to check the clock. To her
surprise, the school day was over. She had the children
carry the supplies and drawings into the classroom. A few
hurried to finish their work at their desks, but most of the
children gathered up their things to leave.

Livy bade them good-bye, by name as best she could.

Soon only Harlan and Greta remained. Both of them were still hard at work on their pictures.

"Don't you two have a long walk ahead of you?"

Harlan shook his head, his eyes still on his paper. "Naw. Friedrick said he'd meet us here in the wagon 'cause he wants to work on the school roof."

Panic tripped up her spine. Friedrick was coming here? She wasn't ready to see him again. The day had gone so well—she didn't need it ruined by another encounter with the unbearable man. She couldn't very well leave, though, not with two students still here. She'd have to stay and face him. And pray for the power to be more civil and polite, as her mother and father had taught her to be. After all, she didn't want any of her students' parents refusing to let their children come to school if she offended one of their own.

She busied herself with looking through the children's drawings. Some of their renditions were impressive; others made her smile. The task wasn't so engrossing, though, that she missed the sound of the door opening or the thud of boots against the floor.

Friedrick entered the room and removed his cap. His gaze momentarily locked with Livy's, his expression guarded. Her tongue felt suddenly thick and dry in her mouth. What could she possibly say to erase the awkwardness radiating between them?

She settled for an amicable, "Afternoon, Mr. Wagner."

He nodded at her. "Afternoon."

There, she'd been courteous. She lowered her head and feigned renewed interest in her students' work. With any luck, he'd hurry right back outside and start in on his task.

"Friedrick," she heard Greta say with childlike enthusiasm. "Look at my picture."

"Is that Papa?" he asked.

"Yes, and see, he's all well."

"Look at mine," Harlan said. "It's the gun I want. Someday I'm gonna be a brave solider for America. That's what Miss Campbell said."

Heat infused Livy's face. If only she could slip under her desk, unnoticed. Of all the things the boy could have said, he had to pick the one that made her look every bit the self-righteous busybody his brother already suspected her to be.

Perhaps if she could explain. Livy forced her gaze upward, but the fury in those piercing blue eyes rendered her momentarily speechless.

*   *   *

Friedrick glared at Livy, his jaw clenched, his breath coming hard with anger. This was what he had feared the most after their argument last night. She was already pushing her version of American loyalty onto her unsuspecting students. Next thing he knew, Harlan and Greta would be crying "traitor" at him for his farm deferment.

With Harlan's picture in hand, Friedrick took two steps toward Livy's desk. "Miss Campbell said you'd make a great solider, huh?" He directed the question to his brother, but he kept his eyes trained on Livy's blushing face. The extra color in her cheeks made her look that much prettier—a fact he did his best to ignore.

"Look, Mr. Wagner." She stood, her hands splayed on the top of the desk. "It isn't what it sounds—"

He didn't let her finish. "Fortunately, you're too young to fight now, Harlan," he threw over his shoulder. "But there are other things you can do for the war effort besides fighting. Isn't that right, Miss Campbell?"

To her credit, she didn't sit down or back away as he advanced another step. Instead she lifted her chin in challenge. "I don't know what you're talking about."

"Of course you do. Inspiring the children to know their duty at such a young age? Plucking out their evil roots? Keeping an eye out for possible spies?" He crossed the remaining distance to her desk. "I'd say you're the picture of patriotism, Miss Campbell. Without the gun, of course," he added in a rueful tone as he placed Harlan's paper in front of her. He didn't like going toe to toe with a woman, but this one got his ire up like no one else.

She folded her arms and glowered up at him. "I'm afraid you're mistaken, Mr. Wagner." She spoke his name with all the frostiness of ice in January. "Harlan merely expressed a desire to fight for his country. I told him someday he would make a brave solider, but fortunately for your family, such a day won't be anytime soon. That is all I said on the matter."

Friedrick could see from her fierce expression and the way she refused to break eye contact that she wasn't lying. Standing so close to her, with the bright light of afternoon coming through the windows, he noticed her eyes weren't solely green in color. There were flecks of gold and blue there, too, which he hadn't noticed when they were busy dancing. As he continued his study of her face, her eyes widened and her lips parted slightly. What would they taste like if he were to kiss them?

"Friedrick?" Greta's concerned voice broke the

charged moment. He'd nearly forgotten she and Harlan were still there—listening to every word.

Friedrick ground his teeth together. He'd made a fool of himself twice over. First by jumping to defend his siblings when there'd been no need, and second by arguing with their teacher in front of them.

He swallowed hard, hating the way his pride tasted going back down. But when he was wrong, he would admit it. "I'm sorry, Miss Campbell. My mistake."

"I should say so," she muttered, but he heard her plainly as he slammed his cap on his head and turned around. "Are you ready to hand your picture in, Greta?"

Greta nodded, throwing a glance between her teacher and Friedrick.

"Go on," Friedrick urged, giving her a smile. "Then you two can play outside while I work on the roof."

Greta skipped forward to hand in her picture, while Friedrick sought solace outside from the suffocating tension indoors. He'd meant to come in, collect the children, and start on his job—not lose his temper. Or give Livy another excuse to run straight to the superintendent and relay all the things Friedrick had felt inclined to voice.

Most of what he'd said could be misconstrued as pro-German, something Mr. Foster had warned Friedrick against. If the superintendent caught even a whiff of German patriotism, he'd promised to have Friedrick fired faster than Miss Lehmann had been.

None of those things had been foremost in his mind, though, when he'd walked into the school. Deep down, he'd been hoping to find fault with Miss Campbell. If he could prove she was as bad as the other self-righteous

Americans he'd encountered lately, his changed opinion of her would be justified.

Then the children had showed him their artwork—a subject Miss Lehmann had never taught the class—and he'd been forced to consider he'd misjudged Livy Campbell last night. That is, until he'd heard Harlan's comment. Now he didn't know what to make of the new teacher.

Friedrick grabbed his ladder from the back of the wagon and propped it against the side of the schoolhouse. After collecting his tools, nails, and shingles, he maneuvered up the ladder and onto the roof.

He was well into his project by the time he heard Harlan and Greta exit the school. "Be careful, Friedrick," his sister called up to him. The way her forehead furrowed with consternation reminded him of Elsa. If only the possibility of him falling off the roof could be her only source of worry.

With a nail gripped between his teeth and his hands full, he couldn't answer, so he waved his hammer. Greta accepted the gesture as proof he was fine and raced after Harlan. The boy was headed to the copse of trees behind the teacher's cabin. Probably looking for something to chase or throw.

Friedrick returned to his task. His thoughts soon moved from the chores waiting for him at home to his most recent argument with Livy. While he did derive a certain satisfaction in finally speaking his mind, he would have to be more careful about what he said. He couldn't afford to lose this job—his family needed it too badly.

At that moment, Livy exited the school. She didn't

even spare a glance in his direction, but Friedrick sensed the irritation still emanating from her.

He watched as she bade his siblings good-bye and walked toward her cabin, her shoulders bent slightly forward. Unlike the nightgown she'd worn last night, her green skirt accentuated her trim waist and the swing of her hips as she moved. Friedrick forced his gaze back to the ugly roof.

He threw himself into his work, knowing it would purge the memory of Livy's gold-flecked eyes and red lips from his mind. The sun baked his neck and back and his knees ached from kneeling, but he wanted to finish.

"You done yet, Friedrick?" Harlan hollered.

"Almost," he called back.

He hammered in the last few shingles and climbed down the ladder. After setting his things inside the wagon, he eyed the teacher's cabin. Was there something he could do to smooth things over with Livy, keep her from tattling to Mr. Foster? He studied the length and breadth of the small house. Some of the shingles were missing from its roof, too.

"Harlan, can you and Greta wait another twenty minutes? There's something I need to do for Miss Campbell."

Harlan shrugged. "Come on, Greta, let's go look for arrowheads in Old Man Zimmermann's field." Friedrick smiled at the memory of doing the same thing as a boy.

Armed with another stack of shingles, he strode to the cabin and rapped a knuckle against the door. He braced himself for an abrasive reaction to his presence.

Sure enough, the friendliness on her face hardened into a frown when she opened the door and saw him standing there. "Is there more you wish to accuse me of, Mr. Wagner?"

He pushed out a long breath, reminding himself to remain calm, no matter what. "No, Miss Campbell. I'd like to apologize again for earlier."

"Oh." From the way her brow creased, she hadn't expected his apology. "What do you want then?"

"I want to fix your shingles."

"Why?"

His silent reminder to be patient was fast losing its hold on him. "Because there's at least a dozen missing," he answered, "and if you don't have good shingles—"

A hint of a smile pulled at the corners of her mouth, surprising him, but she tamped it down. "I understand the importance of shingles. My question is why do *you* want to fix my roof?"

Couldn't he just fix her shingles and be done with it? Did she intend for him to grovel? "It's my attempt to make up for my...behavior...last night." He paused, then added, "And this afternoon."

"Well, you can't do it alone."

"Miss Campbell," he said through clenched teeth, "I single-handedly reshingled half the school roof. I think I can manage yours without difficulty."

Instead of challenging him further, she fiddled with the door handle, without meeting his eye. "I only meant that I'd like to help. To make up for my behavior as well."

Friedrick cocked an eyebrow. Where had the angry, verbal slinger gone? With her softened expression, she reminded him much more of the woman he'd danced with. "You afraid of heights?"

"No."

"You might want to change," he said, motioning to her skirt. He swallowed a chuckle when she blushed. He liked eliciting the infusion of color to her cheeks. "If you don't own any overalls, you might not want—"

"I have a pair of trousers, thank you very much. Now if you'll excuse me." She slammed the door before he could reply.

Friedrick shook his head with amusement. He'd admired her spunk from the moment they'd met at the dance hall, but he hadn't expected her to use it against him. Her pluck was as much a virtue as a vice.

While he waited for her, he went to collect his ladder and tools. His thoughts turned from Livy to the nearly empty jar in the kitchen cupboard. Surely enduring her displeasure a little longer was a small price to pay to help his family. At least he hoped so.

* * *

Dressed in old work trousers and a sweater, Livy climbed the ladder propped beside the cabin door. She ascended over the lip of the roof to find Friedrick setting up his supplies. He glanced her way, his brows arched in amusement at her manly attire. But his blue eyes shone with a different emotion, and Livy realized with a mixture of confusion and delight that he appreciated the sight of her in pants. Friedrick looked away first, and the moment between them dissipated, though Livy was left feeling a bit breathless, despite her earlier irritation toward him.

"Why don't you hand me the shingles and nails when I need them?" he said, motioning with his hammer to a rusted can and a stack of shingles.

"All right." Livy crawled slowly over the rough roof. The sun seeped through her sweater, warming her. A slight breeze ruffled wisps of her hair across her face. The thrill of being high off the ground made her smile and reminded her of hours spent in the hayloft as a girl, sometimes with Joel or Tom, other times alone with her sketchbook.

"Shingle."

Livy passed him the shingle. His brow furrowed in concentration as he positioned it just so. The focused look added to the handsome planes of his face and jaw, though Livy preferred his smile.

Embarrassed by her thoughts, she busied herself with grabbing a nail and extending it toward him.

He cocked his head as he took the nail from her. "You've done this before?"

"I liked helping my father fix things around the farm. I was the official nail handler." She fingered the stack of shingles she'd placed in her lap. "My older brothers always looked as if they were having more fun working with him than I did in the kitchen with my mother."

Friedrick hammered the shingle into place, then accepted the next one she passed him. "Are you one of those girls who can shoe a horse but can't bake a pie?"

Livy frowned at his bent head. "I'm quite capable of doing both." His mouth quirked upward with hidden laughter—he was teasing her. This playful side to him reminded her of Tom. Her brother had always been able to coax her from a defensive mood.

"The horse shoeing was a relatively recent lesson," she admitted with a chuckle. "After I came home from college."

"That's right, you weren't able to finish." He held out his hand. "Shingle."

Livy handed him another shingle, impressed he remembered such a detail from their conversation during the fox-trot.

He took the nail she offered him next and hammered the shingle into place. "Do you miss it? College, I mean?"

She brushed some hair from her face. "I miss some things." Her classes, her friends, the excitement of living in her aunt's opulent house, but all she'd really wanted was to be on her own, doing something she loved. "I like where I am now."

"Teaching German-American children?"

Her eyes met his, but she couldn't read his expression. Was he baiting her again? "I'm grateful for this job...and to you...for mentioning it."

"Fair enough."

Relieved they'd skirted another battle, Livy helped him finish mending the roof. When they were done, Friedrick gathered up his hammer and the remaining shingles and moved toward the ladder, but Livy lingered behind, enjoying the view. From up here she could see the top of the schoolhouse, the neighboring farms stretching outward from the road and the branches of the nearby trees swaying in the breeze. The world lay in peace around her—no painful memories, no reminders of war.

"'She sat like patience on a monument,'" Friedrick said. "'Smiling at grief.'"

Livy turned around. He stood perched on the highest rungs of the ladder. "Is that a poem?"

"It's Shakespeare. *Twelfth Night.* Would you hand me the tin of nails?"

"You've read it?" she asked, her surprise seeping into her voice. She scooted to the ladder and passed him the nails.

"I've read most of Shakespeare's plays—albeit in German." He threw her a probing look and climbed to the ground. "We aren't all the uncultured brutes they portray us to be in the war posters."

Warmth flooded Livy's cheeks as she maneuvered over the roof's edge and down the ladder. She hopped off the last rung. "I didn't mean—"

"You don't have to explain." Friedrick faced the school, his expression pained. "I would have liked to go to college—to read more books, learn new things." Livy found herself staring at his large hands, curled into relaxed fists around his tools. She could imagine them holding a book in their gentle grip as he'd held her hand while they'd danced. "My father's illness takes any extra money, though." Resignation settled onto his face.

Livy had a sudden desire to reach out and touch his arm, soothe the sadness radiating from him. How often had she complained, if only to herself, about having completed only a year of college, and yet it was evident how much one year would have meant to Friedrick.

"I'd better get Harlan and Greta home. Good day, Miss Campbell."

"Thank you," she called out as he walked away.

She entered the cabin and shut the door behind her. Why did the success of her first day feel less rewarding now that she was alone?

Happy squeals disrupted the silence in the cabin. Stealing to the window that faced the schoolhouse, Livy peeked out the curtains. Friedrick had his eyes closed and was lumbering around the school yard, attempting to capture Harlan and Greta. As Livy watched, the two children ran almost within his grasp, then darted away again before he could catch them.

The sight brought a physical ache to her chest, and she dropped the curtain on the cheerful scene. How many times had she felt like this, as if she were watching life from behind a window?

While the other girls her age had married or gone off to college, Livy had waited behind, hoping for her turn at traveling or love. When she was on her own at last and enjoying school, she'd had to leave. When she had finally secured Robert's attentions, she'd realized the hollowness of their relationship. Where did she belong? She folded her arms against the crushing weight of the question. She certainly didn't belong at home anymore, not at the age of twenty and with her older brothers gone. Not with Robert. Not at college. Would she find the sense of belonging she craved here in Hilden, with her students?

At the sound of wagon wheels, she glanced out the window once more. The Wagners were headed home. She watched them until she could no longer see the wagon. When she turned away, she felt as empty as the road stretching away from the cabin. She was alone again.

Not inclined to wallow, Livy busied herself with preparing supper. The task kept her thoughts occupied, though a few errant ones pulled her back to the conversation on the roof with Friedrick.

Which side of him truly represented the man? Was Friedrick the type of person who was quick to judge and condemn? Livy frowned at the possibility, until the memories of him quoting Shakespeare and playing with his siblings entered her mind. Did those actions better embody who he was as a man? Someone intelligent and playful, but also strong and protective of those he loved? She had to admit she'd seen more of those qualities in him than the negative ones.

Regardless, her mind argued as she sat at the table and began to eat. *He is German.*

The plain fact caused her appetite to fade. She pushed her dinner around her plate with her fork as she tried to recall what she'd heard or read about Germans. She'd seen the war posters, had felt the sense of pride they inspired in her at her brothers' service and the fear and anger they stirred at what the enemy might do. But she'd never given any thought to those Germans living here, in America.

Did Friedrick secretly harbor German sympathies? Livy worried the inside of her cheek at the thought.

She still knew so little about him, and yet she wouldn't call him unpatriotic, despite his not being able to fight. What about herself, though? Would she be considered disloyal to her country if she continued to associate with him? After all, she told herself, Joel and Tom were likely facing off against Friedrick's distant relatives. What would she do if one of them were to hurt her family?

Livy shivered, despite her sweater. She set down her fork, not sure if she could eat any more. The unanswered questions soured her stomach and left her feeling queasy and unsure. She'd been taught all her life to love her enemies, to see others as God saw them. Did that apply to Friedrick?

Loving her students came easily, German though they may be. It was different with someone closer to her own age. Would her parents approve of her acquaintance with Friedrick? Would they have let her come had they known the idea for the job had come from a German-American? That she'd be seeing more of him, with him doing maintenance at the school?

"Perhaps I'm being silly," she scolded herself out loud. She picked up her fork, determined not to waste the food in front of her.

It wasn't as if she planned to be anything more than a casual friend to Friedrick. She certainly wouldn't do anything that might worry her parents or her brothers.

Determination restored her appetite. Having only picked at her food all day, she ate hardily. The quiet of the evening magnified the shift of her weight in the hardbacked chair and the sigh from her lips, making them sound unnaturally loud. The breeze had picked up outside, and now it whooshed with plaintive notes through the cracks in the cabin. Livy shivered again and added more wood to the stove.

Too soon the kitchen area had been set to rights and she found herself staring at the four walls once more. "Maybe I ought to get a cat," she murmured.

At home the family would be heading into the parlor for homework or reading the newspaper. An intense longing to be there cut through her, but she steeled herself against it. She'd wanted to be on her own for so long. It was only the second night; surely living by herself would get easier. To help assuage the temporary homesickness, she penned a letter to her parents, telling them about her first day teaching, then readied herself for bed.

She stayed longer on her knees tonight, offering a sincere prayer of thanks for her new position. Despite the arguments with Friedrick, she still believed his mention of the job on her birthday had been providential. Surely this was where she needed—wanted—to be.

Livy slipped beneath the covers and shut her eyes, but sleep was slow in coming for the second night in a row. Her feet ached from standing most of the day and her throat felt scratchy from talking, but she couldn't relax her exhausted mind.

With an exasperated sigh, she threw back the blankets and padded on bare feet to the crate she was using as a makeshift bookcase. She pulled out one of the two volumes of Shakespeare she owned. She'd only read *Romeo and Juliet*, but if Friedrick had read most of the other plays, then it was high time Livy did, too.

Chapter Four

With the roof repaired, Friedrick decided to spend an afternoon splitting wood behind the schoolhouse. Though spring had begun unfolding its greenery along the branches and hollows of the local farms, the mornings and evenings still held winter's bite. Before he started fixing the cracks in the mortar, he wanted to ensure both the schoolhouse and Livy's cabin had adequate fuel for the stoves.

Friedrick wiped the sweat from his brow with his shirtsleeve and threw a quick glance at the school yard. Greta wandered nearby, her eyes focused on the ground. She was probably hoping to find some early spring wildflowers. He hadn't seen Harlan yet. Had the boy gotten himself into trouble with Livy? If so, it clearly ran in the family.

He and Livy hadn't spoken much in the past few days. Friedrick had kept to himself, to avoid saying something he might regret. It still rankled him she'd been surprised by his knowledge of Shakespeare. He was grateful her acceptance of the teaching position meant he also had a job, but he wished the superintendent had found a docile, older—and less attractive—replacement for Miss Lehmann.

Tossing more split wood onto his growing pile, he frowned in the direction of the school. Why hadn't Harlan come out yet? Could Livy be coming down hard on the boy, based solely on her annoyance with Friedrick? The possibility tightened his jaw. She could berate him all she wanted, but he wouldn't tolerate her doing the same to his brother.

Friedrick swept up an armful of wood and marched into the school, prepared to go toe to toe with Livy—again—if Harlan proved blameless. He entered the room and froze. Harlan sat at his desk, while Livy stood at the blackboard, writing sums.

At the sound of his footsteps, Harlan turned around and grinned. "Hi-ya, Friedrick."

"What's going on?" He hoped the words sounded less threatening to Livy than they did to him.

The guarded expression in her green eyes when she spun around proved he'd thought wrong. "Harlan didn't finish his arithmetic. He said he didn't understand it, so I was reviewing the lesson for him."

Self-reproach at his unfounded conclusions kept him from responding. Instead Friedrick busied himself with filling the wood box. He heard Livy ask Harlan a summation question, which the boy answered correctly.

"Very good," she announced. "You are free to go."

"Whoopee," Harlan cried, racing for the door.

Friedrick followed after him. Outside, Harlan scrambled up one of the trees bordering the school. Greta sat at its base, entertaining herself with what looked like a leaf or flower chain. Friedrick returned to the woodpile and stuck another log on the chopping block. Hefting his axe, he drove the blade into the wood's center. Why did he keep thinking the worst of Livy's motives and actions? She wasn't out to hurt his family, despite her reticence toward him since learning of his German ancestry. She obviously cared about her students and their progress. Which meant just one thing—he'd been too quick to judge her at their second meeting.

Friedrick tossed the split wood to the ground with a grunt. He didn't like the idea of rethinking the box he'd placed Livy inside. The action reminded him too much of the judgments those in town had made about him and the other German-Americans. Was he being as intolerant as they had been? He wasn't sure he wanted an answer.

Soon the pile of split wood had doubled in size. Friedrick surveyed his handiwork and decided there was enough wood to last Livy and the students awhile. He gathered a second load for the school and retraced his steps inside. Livy sat at her desk, a pen pressed between her teeth. Friedrick took a moment to admire the way her lips pursed around the object before he spoke. "You still working?"

She blinked and pulled the pen from her mouth. "No. Just writing a letter."

He set the wood inside the box. "To your beau?" he threw over his shoulder.

"No," she repeated, her tone curt. Was she no longer with the boyfriend she'd been waiting for on her birthday? A ripple of triumph ran through Friedrick at the idea, though he couldn't see the point. Livy didn't see him as anything more than the man she'd danced with once or the German-American who cared for the school.

"I'm writing my good friend Nora. She's promised to my brother Tom. He and my other brother Joel are fighting the..." Her quick intake of breath sounded unusually loud in the schoolroom. Friedrick knew exactly what word she'd been about to say. "They're both in France," she finished.

Friedrick stood to face her. "May I speak plainly?"

"That shouldn't be a problem." Livy clapped her hand over her mouth, her cheeks turning pink. "I'm sorry. I don't know why—"

"You can't seem to keep a civil tongue? Why the first thing you think comes right out of your mouth?"

She laughed softly. "Yes."

He walked slowly to her desk, remembering the last time he'd done this and how angry he'd been. No frustration filled him now, only a desire to improve things. And an irrational need to be closer to this beautiful woman seated at the front of the room.

"I need this job, and from the few things you've said, it sounds like you want to keep yours, too." He placed a hand on the top of the desk and bent slightly toward her. "So what do you say to throwing out the white flag? Calling a truce?"

She lifted an eyebrow in question.

"I'm asking if you'd be willing to get along, for the sake of our jobs."

Livy glanced down at her letter, her long fingers drumming the desk. Would she refuse his offer for peace? Had he jumped to the wrong conclusion one too many times to salvage things now?

"All right," she said, lifting her head. "I agree to the terms of your peace treaty."

"Shall we shake on it?" he half teased, though the idea of holding her hand again wasn't an unpleasant one.

"Of course." She stood and walked around the desk. Her head came only to his chin, as it had when they'd danced. She stuck out her hand and he clasped it in his own. Similar to the last time they'd shaken hands, her touch felt decidedly feminine but also firm. Much like the woman herself, Friedrick mused. Soft but full of pluck, kind but capable of standing her ground.

Friedrick released her hand and smiled, relieved to have struck a truce. Livy offered him a smile in return, though it looked a bit more reluctant than the one he'd seen on her face at the dance hall. Still, her large, green eyes shone with warmth and sincerity. As he stared into them, he suddenly couldn't remember why he'd been irritated at her in the first place. If he could keep himself from making unfounded assumptions, a cease-fire with Livy would surely prove to be as satisfying as sparring with her had been.

* * *

Livy kept a hand on her best hat as the wind pushed her down the sidewalk toward the church up ahead. *Of all the Sabbaths to be running late, it would be Easter Sunday.* If she hadn't fallen asleep in the large bathing pot she'd dragged in from outside, she would have been able to pick which of Hilden's two churches to attend. As it was, she had to settle for the closest.

She raced up the steps of the white building and slipped inside the double doors. Organ music greeted her ears, but no singing. They hadn't started yet. She paused to smooth her blue silk dress. The heady scent of flowers, from the arrangements on either side of the chapel entrance, filled her nose. The smell reminded her at once of Easter the year before. She'd come home from college to visit and Robert had showed up to services handsomely dressed in his Sunday suit. He'd been encouraging her brothers to enlist soon, as he planned to, before he spotted Livy eavesdropping.

"Will you miss me when I go fight, Livy?" he'd asked, speaking to her directly, as if she wasn't just the kid sister of his two best friends anymore.

She gulped. "Yes, of course."

He smiled, a charming smile that made her feel a bit light-headed, and leaned close to whisper, "I'll miss you, too."

Fresh loneliness washed over Livy at the memory. She'd been so happy then and so naïve. She'd returned to school with starry-eyed visions of her and Robert marrying after the war. Little did she know how the fight across the ocean would affect him or her hopes and plans for the future.

Sudden quiet tore the recollection from Livy's mind, and she jerked her head up to find the pastor already standing at the pulpit. She hurried into the chapel and sat on the back pew. A girl, seated farther down the row, glanced in Livy's direction. Livy recognized her—it was Yvonne. She waved to Livy, and Livy smiled back. If she couldn't be home with her family today, then she liked the idea of seeing some of her students.

After the pastor greeted the congregation, the notes of the opening hymn filled the crowded room. Livy picked up the hymnal and opened it. The words weren't in English. She shut the book and gazed at the people seated across the aisle and in front of her. She spotted several more of her pupils, including Harlan and Greta—and Friedrick—sitting near the front of the room.

Her heart beat faster in alarm. She'd inadvertently chosen to attend the German church her first Sunday in Hilden. She glanced at the doors behind her. Would a hasty exit be noticed? Probably.

Grateful at least to be in the back, Livy slid down on the bench. Maybe no one would notice her presence. She attempted to sing without the aid of words, but she wasn't the only one struggling to sing the song correctly. Most of the congregation stumbled through the verses as though they hadn't sung them in English before. The poor organist kept slowing her accompaniment, in a vain attempt to help.

When the song, thankfully, ended, Livy folded her arms and bowed her head for the prayer. Surely God wouldn't care where she chose to worship today, and yet she couldn't shake the nervousness in her stomach. Had she made a grave mistake? She tapped the toe of her shoe with impatience as the pastor began petitioning the Lord on behalf of people she didn't know. It was going to be a long meeting.

Someone down the aisle made a shushing sound. Livy peeked to see the source of the scolding. Yvonne's mother was frowning at her. When she caught Livy staring, the woman nodded at Livy's bouncing leg.

Mortification roiled through her as Livy quickly shut her eyes and ceased her impatient tapping. At that moment, a name from the prayer leapt out at her.

"Please bless Marta Lehmann," the pastor said in a loud, clear voice. "Bless her, Lord, to be safe. Watch over her as she endures her time in prison. Help her to feel of our love and of Thy love."

Prison? A cold prickle ran up Livy's backbone. Mr. Foster had failed to tell her Miss Lehmann had been sent to prison.

At the sound of sniffling, Livy stole a glance down the row. Yvonne wiped her nose with her sleeve as tears dripped down her small face. *Poor girl*, Livy thought. Several of the women nearby were wiping at their eyes as well. What a shock to her students—and apparently many of their parents—to learn the last teacher had gone to prison. Would they blame Livy?

She suddenly couldn't seem to fill her lungs with enough air. She felt as if everyone in the room was aware of her intruding presence—the one who'd taken Miss Lehmann's place. If only she could disappear beneath the pew and not have to see the congregation at the end of the prayer. For a moment, she reconsidered her plan to leave, but if the pastor ended his prayer before she reached the outer doors, she'd draw even more attention to herself.

She sat frozen in indecision too long. The pastor said "Amen" before she could move and Livy forced her eyelids open. She darted a quick look at Yvonne's family, but none of them paid her any mind. Maybe she would get through this unscathed. She could still slip out during the closing hymn.

After a silent prayer for strength, Livy did her best

to concentrate on the pastor's Easter sermon about hope and redemption. Her thoughts soon wandered, though, to home. The family would be in church, too, only six of them this year. Afterward her mother would serve a delicious ham. Once everyone had eaten their fill, the family would congregate in the parlor to read from the Bible. Homesickness filled her throat at the mental picture and she had to cough to release it. Unfortunately the sound produced another humiliating glare from Yvonne's mother.

Was being on her own really what she wanted? So far she didn't fit in here as she'd hoped. *Give it time*, her mother would probably say. *You've only been there a week.* But Livy couldn't help thinking she'd already been the recipient of more misjudgment this week than she'd experienced in her whole life. How much more would she have to endure?

When she'd applied for the teaching job, all she could think about was getting away from home, away from Robert. She hadn't considered trading one set of problems for another.

The tightness in her throat increased, alerting Livy that tears were near. She bit down hard on the inside of her cheek to stop the rise of moisture. She wouldn't cry over this situation. While things might not be what she'd imagined, she would save her tears for true sorrow and heartache, as she'd felt as a ten-year-old girl. No use wasting her tears on something like homesickness or prejudiced neighbors.

Tilting her head up, she let out a soft sigh and refocused her attention on the pastor.

"At this time of great turmoil and strife in the world,"

the pastor said, his face earnest, "we must be willing to endure what God intends. Only then will we become stronger. Only then will we become His tools. Only then will we be worthy to be counted as followers of His Son. That is my hope this glorious Easter morning."

This time the man's words filled Livy's mind, fortifying her resolve to make the best of her new life. Surely God would help her, as He had in guiding her to this job in the first place.

She sang the closing hymn with gusto—and at a slightly faster tempo than those around her—which garnered her several peculiar looks. She did her best to ignore them. After the closing prayer had been offered, she slipped out of the pew and stood behind it. This way she could greet any of her students who filed past.

She waved good-bye to Yvonne as the girl and her family exited the bench.

"That's my new teacher," Yvonne announced with obvious pride. Her mother sized Livy up, then offered a curt nod. It wasn't exactly friendly, but Livy preferred that to the woman's earlier glares.

She greeted Anna, Oliver, Joseph, and the other children she recognized. Most of them smiled shyly at her as their parents quietly studied her. Did she meet with their approval?

"Miss Campbell," Harlan called out before someone shushed him. The boy ran down the aisle toward her. "I didn't know you'd be at our church. Good thing they changed everything to English last week."

So she'd been right about the songs. Livy was aware of the governor's language law, but she hadn't seen how it would affect her or anyone she knew.

"It was a nice service," she said with conviction.

"Can you believe what the pastor said about Miss Lehmann?" Harlan's face shone with horrified awe. "Going to prison and all?"

Livy cringed. How should she respond? She was saved from having to give Harlan an answer, though, when Greta came and stood beside her brother.

"Happy Easter, Miss Campbell."

"Nice to see you again, Greta."

She looked up to see Friedrick moving toward them. He looked every bit as handsome in his Sunday suit as he did in his work clothes. A woman about forty years of age—his stepmother, mostly likely—walked beside him, while a pretty, young lady clutched Friedrick's arm and stared coyly up at him. An unexplainable slice of jealousy cut through Livy as she recognized the girl as the one Friedrick had danced with the night of her birthday. Was he her beau?

Livy watched him, trying to read at a distance how he felt about the girl at his side. Before she could reach any conclusions, Friedrick lifted his head and looked directly down the aisle at her. Something sparked in his blue eyes, but Livy wasn't sure if it was friendliness or amusement. Despite their truce, would he tease her for coming to the German church today? Or call her a hypocrite? She wasn't sure she wanted to stay and find out.

"Why don't I walk out with you?" she announced to Greta, taking the girl by the hand.

Livy led her from the chapel and out the main doors. The wind had settled down, leaving a nice breeze and plenty of sunshine. A crowd had gathered around the pastor at the bottom of the stairs. Livy held Greta's hand tightly as she struggled to maneuver a path through all the people.

Several women, standing in a tight bunch, blocked her way as she and Greta came down the steps. Livy paid them little heed as she started to squeeze past, but one of the ladies began talking in a loud whisper that caught Livy's attention.

"Did you see the new teacher in the back?" the woman said, her accent thick. "I do not understand why she chose to come here. She is not even German."

One of her companions leaned toward the others. "I hear she is after Friedrick Wagner." Her friends gasped at this remark. "With nearly all the young men off to fight, I suppose, the American girls want to take ours."

The color drained from Livy's face. Had anyone else overheard their nasty gossip? Someone jostled her shoulder from behind and she looked up to see Friedrick standing above her. He frowned, his gaze jumping from hers to the group of women and back.

"Miss Campbell," Greta said, her voice loud with frustration. "Someone stepped on my shoe."

At hearing Livy's name, the women fell silent. All three turned to gape at her in shock, their faces red.

"Come on, Greta." Livy gently tugged the girl forward and guided her past the speechless group. "Good day, ladies," she managed to say in a cool but polite tone. "Happy Easter."

That set them to whispering again, but Livy hurried across the lawn, chin up, to escape from hearing. Had Friedrick overheard them? He'd been too close not to. Did he believe them? She wasn't here to marry him or any other young man right now. For once, she wished she'd stayed in bed on Sunday. The morning had been nothing but disastrous.

Out of the corner of her eye, she caught sight of Friedrick moving swiftly toward her and Greta. She couldn't face him, not with those gossipmongers' words still ringing in her ears.

"I'd best be off," she told Greta, forcing a smile.

"Do you have a wagon?"

Livy shook her head. "No, but I have two feet. I'll see you and Harlan tomorrow."

Greta nodded and raced to join some girls near one of the trees. Livy walked with quick steps toward the sidewalk. Someone called her name, but she didn't slow down. The sooner she reached her cabin, the sooner the morning would be over.

* * *

Friedrick followed after Livy. He wasn't worried about catching up to her—her strides were no match for his long ones. Though she could move fast when she wanted. He didn't blame her for practically running from the church. Not after the unkind remarks of those older women.

He hadn't expected to see her today, in their German church of all places. But it didn't mean he wasn't happy to look up and find her there, watching him. She had on the same blue dress she'd worn when they danced. He liked the way the color heightened the blue in her eyes and the fit accentuated her slim curves.

She might be pretty, but she wasn't made of fluff. Her reaction to the women's wagging tongues had been nothing short of regal. Friedrick had swallowed a chuckle after she'd confidently bid the gossipers a "Happy Easter."

Though she appeared to be fine, he needed to assure himself this was true. He knew what it cost to remain calm in the face of discriminating remarks, and he hated to think those women might have hurt Livy. She'd done nothing to merit their malicious gossip.

"Miss Campbell?" he called out.

She didn't slow down, though Friedrick could see by the way she flinched that she'd heard him. He moved faster and managed to catch up to her before she crossed the next street. Reaching out, he snagged her arm to stop her. She whirled to face him, her gaze spitting sparks.

"Let me go." She tugged against his hand. "It isn't true what they said back there…"

Friedrick kept a gentle grip on her arm. "I know."

"Y You do?" She stopped resisting him and stood still. The faint scent of vanilla wafted off her skin and hair. She licked her lips, probably nervous about what he meant to say next. But nothing came to mind, except how inviting that mouth of hers looked. This woman sure did crazy things to him—inspiring anger in him one moment for her narrow-minded opinions and making him want to kiss her in the next.

With great effort, he reminded himself that kissing Livy in the middle of Hilden would not go over well—for her or for him. He lowered his hand from her arm and took a deliberate step to the side. To his delight, something akin to disappointment flashed in her eyes.

"It might help to know," he said, "that one of those women you overheard is Mrs. Schmitt. She's Maria's mother."

Livy shook her head in confusion. "Who's Maria?"

"She and I typically go to a dance hall on the weekends."

A look of understanding crossed her face. "She was walking beside you in the church just now."

He nodded.

"Does that mean…" Livy crossed her arms. "Are you her beau then?"

"No. But Maria and her mother still hold out hope our mutual enjoyment of dancing will turn into something much more permanent."

"Ah." A hint of a smile played about her lips. "So I'm competition."

"Afraid so."

Friedrick managed to say it in a teasing tone. No need for Livy to know the truth of her statement. The more time he spent around her, the more he knew he couldn't see himself bringing Maria to the farm as his wife. While she had many qualities to recommend her to a young man, there were some things she didn't possess. Things he was only now beginning to realize were important to him.

"Thank you—for explaining." She took a step backward. "I'd better go."

Friedrick didn't want the conversation to end yet. "Would you like a ride home?"

"I'm fine to walk. It's a lovely day."

"Then I'll join you."

"Really?" Was she happy or disappointed? Friedrick couldn't tell. She cut a glance in the direction of the church. "I don't want to cause any trouble."

"It's just walking." When she still didn't look convinced, Friedrick started past her.

"What are you doing?"

"Walking. This is the direction I live." He stopped and turned around, feigning sudden surprise. "Come to think of it, that's the direction you live, too. I guess it makes sense for us both to head this way."

She tried to keep a straight face, but at last, she laughed. Friedrick loved the sound of it. Her laugher was full and joyful and made him want to make her laugh again and again. "You win."

"Good. I'll be right back."

"Where are you going?" she asked with a chuckle. "I thought we were walking home."

"We are. I just need to tell Elsa to drive the wagon."

Friedrick strode back to the churchyard to find his family. Harlan darted past, and Friedrick stopped him. "I'm going to walk Miss Campbell home. Will you tell Mother to drive the wagon?"

"Can I come?" Harlan asked.

Friedrick wanted to refuse. He was looking forward to some time alone with Livy, now that they were on civil terms with each other again. But having Harlan with them might keep anyone from cooking up more gossip. "All right. Go tell Mother what we're doing. She and Greta can pick us up at the school."

He waited as Harlan bolted toward Elsa, who was talking near the church steps. A few moments later, the boy ran back.

"She said okay."

Harlan took off down the street. By the time Friedrick reached Livy, Harlan was already bending her ear about his collection of arrowheads. He and Livy would be lucky to get a word in until the boy finished.

Resigned to wait, Friedrick walked beside them, Harlan between him and Livy. She glanced at him, over Harlan's head, and smiled. It was a real smile, like the one he'd seen when they were dancing. One that almost made him wish he'd left Harlan behind.

Once they'd moved past the town buildings, Harlan abruptly stopped talking and sprinted ahead. "I'm gonna find me a good rock," he called over his shoulder.

Friedrick chuckled. "He can talk a streak when he wants to."

"Reminds me of my two youngest brothers, George and Charlie. George is a year older than Harlan." Her wistful tone betrayed her homesickness. Friedrick couldn't imagine being away from his family and living all alone. As nice as it might sound at times, his place was caring for them.

"You miss your family?"

She shot him a sheepish glance. "More so than I thought. Even more than when I was at college."

"What about that beau of yours?" Friedrick regretted the question when Livy stiffened and stared at the ground.

"I'd rather not talk about him."

He searched for something else to say to bring back the camaraderie between them. "How does it feel to be a real teacher now, Miss Campbell? With your own school and students?"

She threw him an appreciative look—she was grateful he hadn't pressed the subject of her beau. "It's wonderful. However..." Her lips lifted in a rueful smile. "I don't think anyone over fourteen should call me Miss Campbell. It makes me feel quite old."

Friedrick laughed. "You'd rather I call you Livy?"

"Yes." The nickname fit her perfectly, more so than Olivia.

"Then please, call me Friedrick."

"Friedrick," she repeated softly. He liked the American way she said it. "What do you usually do on Easter?"

"We'll have roast lamb and a honey cake with custard." He murmured his approval, which made her laugh. "Instead of eating it in the kitchen, though, we'll eat in my father's room. So he can be a part of it."

Livy kicked at a pebble with the toe of her high-heeled shoe. "What sort of illness does he have?"

"The doctor doesn't know." Friedrick gazed at the bare fields beside them. "He's steadily grown weaker over the last few years and he gets sick easily. Winter is the worst time for him."

"I'm sorry." She lifted her hand as if she might touch his arm, but instead she swept some hair from her eyes.

"We make do."

"What happened to your mother?"

"She died when I was six."

"That must have been very hard." Her tone conveyed her genuine compassion.

Friedrick bent and picked up a rock. "I remember a little about her. She had long hair, more white than blond. And she liked to laugh." He rubbed the rock between his fingers. "Elsa married my father three years later, so she is as much a mother to me as my real one. She's the one who raised me."

They walked on in silence for a few minutes, but it wasn't uncomfortable. Livy broke the quiet first. "I know a little of what it's like to lose someone you care about at a young age. Not a family member, but a dear friend."

Friedrick checked to see that Harlan was still in sight as he waited for Livy to continue.

"My best friend, Blanche, contracted scarlet fever when we were ten. The doctor was confident she would pull through." Livy folded her arms as if cold, though the sun still shone. "She died a week later. Because they were worried about the fever spreading, I didn't get to say good-bye."

An urge to pull her into his arms and soothe her sadness nearly overwhelmed him. But would she let him? Friedrick wasn't sure. Instead he gripped the rock tightly in his palm. "I'm sorry to hear that, Livy."

She lifted her slender shoulders in a shrug. "I think that's why I miss my older brothers so much. They've always been around. After Blanche died, they were my playmates and confidantes." She coughed and gave him a crooked smile. "Enough about that. Tell me more about your family. Did you resent Harlan and Greta coming along, after so many years alone with your father and Elsa?"

"Harlan maybe," Friedrick said with a laugh. He welcomed the change in conversation, if only for Livy's sake. He didn't like the helpless feeling in the pit of his stomach at seeing her sad and withdrawn. "Never Greta, though. She could charm anyone with those big, blue eyes and sweet temper."

The despondency that had etched Livy's features a moment ago faded as she nodded in agreement. "She is sweet, although I believe Harlan has his charms, too."

Friedrick stopped walking long to enough to throw the rock in his hand. To his satisfaction, it nearly reached Harlan, who'd beaten them to Livy's cabin.

"Do you play baseball?"

"Sometimes. Harlan and I like to toss a ball around. I think he'd like to play on a team when he goes to the high school. Did any of your brothers play?"

Livy shook her head. "Only around the farm. They enjoyed football more, but we'd play impromptu baseball games when we were younger."

"We?"

"I played, too," she said, her tone smug.

Friedrick reached down and selected a rock similar in size and weight to the one he'd picked up. "Let's see your throwing arm."

Livy held out her hand. "All right." Her green eyes flashed with determination, bringing a grin to Friedrick's face as he dropped the rock into her open palm.

She cocked her arm, squinted her eyes to slits, and let the rock go. While it didn't travel as far as Friedrick's had, her rock landed within five feet or so of his.

"Nicely done." The petite woman strolling next to him continued to surprise him. "Do you want to be on our team for the church's spring social game?"

Her triumphant smile drooped. "I'm...um...not sure I'll be attending there again. I wanted to check out the other church in Hilden."

Her words, though not entirely unexpected, had the same jarring affect as a slap. Friedrick had let himself believe he and Livy were like any other man and woman, getting to know each other. But they weren't. He was German-American; she was not. Before the war, such a fact might not have mattered—now it meant a chasm lay between them.

They came to a stop beside her cabin. Friedrick heard

the sound of wagon wheels and looked up to see Elsa and Greta coming down the road.

"Thanks for walking with me." Her words sounded sincere, but Friedrick recognized in the way she held her shoulders and stood apart from him that her guard had returned. He wished he hadn't brought up the spring social at all—things had been going swimmingly until he reminded her about their German church.

"Do you have any plans for Easter supper?" If she was already missing home today, she might appreciate the company—even if it was with a German family. "You're welcome to join us."

The wagon lumbered closer. Greta sat beside Elsa on the seat, a smile on her face. Elsa, on the other hand, didn't look pleased. Had Friedrick incited more gossip by walking Livy home?

"No, thank you. I actually have plans," Livy answered. "There's a family in town who've invited me over. The woman's mother used to be our neighbor back home."

Disappointment lashed through him, but Friedrick hid it behind a smile. "Glad to hear you have somewhere to go."

"Hi again, Miss Campbell," Greta called out as the wagon stopped beside the cabin.

Livy waved. "Hello, Greta."

Friedrick motioned to Elsa. "This is Elsa Wagner. Mother, this is Livy Campbell, the new schoolteacher."

Elsa nodded in response but didn't speak.

"Nice to meet you." Livy glanced at him. "Thanks again for the walk...Friedrick."

He met her gaze and wasn't surprised to see conflict clouding her green eyes. He wanted to reassure her, make her laugh again, but how could he when he knew he was the cause of her confusion?

"Happy Easter, Livy."

"Happy Easter." With one more pained look in his direction, she unlocked her door and disappeared inside.

Friedrick watched the door click shut. Something about the finality of the sound stirred him to irritation. At Livy, at himself, at Elsa for her coldness. He called for Harlan to come and marched to the wagon. Once the boy was situated in the back, Friedrick guided the horses toward home.

"What were you doing, Friedrick?" Elsa asked him in German, her voice a half whisper.

Friedrick didn't need to ask what she meant. "I was walking the new teacher home."

"But she is not German."

His hands gripped the reins harder. "I hadn't noticed."

Elsa frowned at his sarcasm. "This is not a joke, Friedrick. Do you think those men who came to our farm would like hearing you are befriending the American schoolteacher?"

The thought hadn't crossed his mind. Of course he'd been concerned about offending Livy and getting himself fired, but he hadn't considered the implications of simply being friendly to her.

"They might believe you are trying to influence her," Elsa continued, "to be sympathetic to our people."

Friedrick lowered his chin and stared at the horses' backs. His annoyance faded into concern. He couldn't put his family in danger again.

Elsa placed her hand on his arm until he looked at her. The empathy flowing from her surprised him. She wasn't angry; she was concerned—for him. Did Elsa sense the magnetic pull between him and Livy? "Promise me you will be careful."

He adjusted the reins to cover her hand with his. "I will, Mother." Avoiding Livy would be next to impossible with his new job at the school, but he would fight his attraction for her to keep his family safe.

* * *

Livy sat back in her chair with a contented sigh. "That ham was delicious, Mrs. Norton." The older woman smiled at her from across the table.

"Mother always did make a wonderful ham," her daughter, Mrs. Smithson, said as she began stacking the dinner dishes. Her husband and children had gone outside to take advantage of the sunshine.

"How are you holding up your first week here?" Mrs. Norton asked Livy.

Thoughts of Friedrick filled Livy's mind, but she shoved them aside. "I can't complain." She smiled at the woman. "My students are bright and my little cabin is quite comfortable."

Mrs. Smithson returned from taking the dishes into the kitchen. "Which township school is yours?" she asked as she joined them at the table.

"Number 1. It's northwest of town."

Mrs. Norton's mouth formed a perfect "O." "There are quite a few German immigrants living out that way, aren't there?"

Livy sensed the woman meant it as more of a statement than a question, but she nodded just the same.

Mrs. Smithson played with her hand-stitched napkin. "I don't think I could teach a room full of German children. They're a close-knit bunch—a bit suspicious of outsiders."

"Probably because they're conspiring with our enemies," Mrs. Norton added in a loud whisper as though someone might be eavesdropping on their conversation.

Shame flooded Livy to hear some of her former thoughts spoken out loud. "I don't think—"

"Is that the school where the teacher was fired for being a spy?" Mrs. Norton pressed. "Good thing for all of us they sent her away."

Livy stared askance at the woman. Didn't she know Miss Lehmann had been sent to prison? Whatever the woman's crimes, Livy still felt badly for her. She opened her mouth to tell them so, but Mrs. Norton spoke again. "You can't be too careful these days, especially with all the Germans in Hilden. I told Edith, here, we can't shop at Mr. Rosenthal's store anymore. Wouldn't do to be seen in a German-owned shop."

Livy recalled the yellow-painted building she'd seen in town. Was that Mr. Rosenthal's? Did he have any customers left, or had everyone in town stopped frequenting his shop?

Mrs. Smithson sighed. "Such a shame, too. His were the most reasonable prices." She folded her napkin into a neat square. "Now tell us, Livy. Where'd you go to church today? We didn't see you in our congregation."

Panic drained the color from Livy's face. She couldn't very well admit to attending the German congregation, not after what they'd just said. She licked her suddenly dry lips, wishing she still had her glass of water. "I...um..."

"Ma," one of the children hollered from the back door. Livy wanted to jump up and hug the youngster for his perfectly timed interruption. "When are we going to eat the pie?"

Mrs. Smithson shook her head, though she smiled. "We barely finished dinner, Timmy. I'll call you in when it's time." The screen door slammed in response.

"So tell us, Livy—do you still have eyes for the Drake boy?" Mrs. Norton grinned slyly at her. The ham in Livy's stomach was beginning to feel less delicious as the inquiries continued. The older woman laughed at her silence. "You keep your secrets then."

"I know a real nice fellow," Mrs. Smithson chimed in. "You know Walden's brother, right, Mother?" She turned to Livy again. "My brother-in-law only lives an hour away, so he comes to town quite often."

Mrs. Norton murmured in agreement. "Such a nice boy. Came home wounded two months ago, but he's coping well enough."

Perhaps with the use of a bottle? Livy wanted to say. Instead she settled for, "I'll keep that in mind, although my focus is on my job at the moment."

The two women exchanged a knowing look. "Of course," Mrs. Norton said as she tried to hide her smile. "But you never know when love might show up on your doorstep."

To Livy's chagrin, an image of Friedrick rose in front of her eyes and the way he'd studied her lips when he caught up to her after church. Had he been thinking about kissing her? She had to admit she'd thought about it, too. Especially during their nice walk together. But she'd thankfully been snapped back to reality—hard—when

he'd mentioned returning to the German church. And
when she'd caught sight of Elsa's disapproving look. Despite Mrs. Norton's predictions, Livy didn't expect love
to show up on her doorstep. Certainly it wouldn't be in
the form of Friedrick, no matter how handsome or kind
she thought him.

"I suppose we'll see," she said with a forced laugh.

Mrs. Smithson served pie soon afterward, but Livy
managed to swallow only a few bites. Her thoughts were
a cyclone of confusion after her conversation with the two
women. Finally she announced she had to go, using the
excuse of the long walk home. Mrs. Smithson offered to
have her husband drive Livy in their wagon, but Livy de-
clined.

"Don't be a stranger," Mrs. Norton said as she and her
daughter followed Livy onto the porch. "If you need anything at all, you come by."

"Thank you."

"I'm going to write your mother tonight and tell her all
about our lovely visit."

Livy managed a weak smile. "I'm sure she'd like that."

"I bet they're right proud of you. Teaching all those
German children how to be good citizens."

Livy stared at the porch boards in embarrassment. Is
that what people believed her purpose for being here
was—to make these German students more American?
Is that what Mr. Foster, the superintendent, wanted
from her? What her students' parents feared from her?
Her only desire was to provide the children with a good
education, regardless of whether or not they were German.

Did their ethnicity really matter? *It does to you*, her

head argued. *Why else would you be reluctant to get to know Friedrick more?* The realization stung.

She murmured a hasty good night to the two women and headed down the sidewalk, her mind as troubled as it had been during the awkward conversation after dinner. Why couldn't things be simple, straightforward? She'd wanted a teaching job, had obtained one, and now she wanted only to do her best at it. Why did the war have to complicate things, not just at home but here, too?

One thing Livy knew for certain now. Though her school might be away from town, she and her students were being watched nonetheless—by Germans and non-Germans alike.

Chapter Five

Livy tried to keep her eyes on the book before her, but her gaze rose again to the tall figure outside the school windows. The younger children were each taking turns reading out loud to her, while the older groups read silently at their desks. None of *them* seemed distracted by Friedrick sealing cracks in the schoolhouse brick.

Two weeks had passed since her troubling conversation with Mrs. Norton and her daughter. Livy had returned home that evening determined to be courteous and kind to Friedrick, but she wouldn't further their acquaintance beyond that.

Her resolve had held strong for a few days, until she realized Friedrick was also acting differently. Despite their lovely walk on Easter Sunday, he'd begun responding to her with equal aloofness. On occasion she'd catch a deeper emotion in his blue eyes when he watched her, seemingly unaware she was watching back. What she couldn't figure out was why he felt the need to avoid *her*.

She was supposed to be the one keeping him at a distance, not the other way around.

Once she'd realized he was equally resolved at maintaining a respectful friendship, Livy had found herself wishing for the exact opposite—in spite of the things Mrs. Norton had said or her own convoluted thoughts.

As much as she hated to admit it, she looked forward to the moment when he slipped into the school for his tools. The firm tread of his boots on the floorboards and the polite smile he gave her before starting his work outdoors brightened Livy's afternoons. Seeing him infused new energy into her, no matter how exhausting the teaching had been that day. And yet it bothered her to think he didn't feel the same.

Through the window nearest her desk, she studied his square face and cobalt eyes, narrowed in concentration. His large hands expertly wielded the trowel and mortar— those same hands that had held hers, more than once, in a strong but gentle grip. No wonder the matrons at church had been so protective of him.

"Miss Campbell? What's the next word?"

Startled, Livy swiveled around to look at her pupils. "Let's see, Helen." She looked down at the text, hoping to hide the deep blush on her face. "Which word were you on?"

"The bri . . ."

Livy saw which one the girl meant. "The word is *bright*."

"Bright," Helen repeated before continuing her reading in a halting cadence.

With effort, Livy focused on listening to the rest of the group read, then she stood and called the class to attention.

"Before we dismiss for the day, I want to remind you to tell those who haven't come to school yet, we are back in session." She indicated the three empty desks, which hadn't been claimed in the past three weeks. "Perhaps when you see the other children at church this weekend, you can tell them we'd love to have them join us. Thank you for your hard work. You're excused."

While the children raced about, preparing to leave, Livy asked Henry, the oldest boy in the class, to stay behind. He approached her desk slowly, wariness written on his face.

"You're not in trouble," Livy said with a laugh as she sat back against the edge of her desk. She waited until the rest of the students had filed out before she spoke again. "I'd like to know if you plan to attend the high school in town this fall."

Henry shrugged. "I thought about it. I'd have to walk every day."

An obstacle Livy and her older brothers had also overcome. "I think it would be worthwhile for you. Have you considered the possibility of going to college after you graduate?"

"College?" Henry repeated, his tone incredulous. Livy bit back a smile. "I hadn't thought about that."

"I've noticed you like to draw buildings when we do art, and you seemed especially interested in our discussion the other day on architecture."

"I like that kind of stuff."

"Then why not consider going to college to be an architect?" She bent slightly forward in excitement. "Someone who designs buildings and bridges."

Henry's eyes lit up at her words, bringing Livy a measure of pride. How rewarding it would be to see a student of hers continue on to high school and college. "Boy, would I like that."

"You'll have to go to the high school first," Livy explained, "and you'll need to save up money for college." His expression fell a little, but she gave him a reassuring smile. "Perhaps you could start by doing some odd jobs this summer. Talk to your parents about it, and be sure to keep studying and reading, even when the school year ends. Once you decide if you want to continue at the high school, I can talk to the superintendent and get some college information for you."

"Gee, thanks, Miss Campbell." He grinned and rushed toward the door.

"You're welcome, Henry." Livy rose to her feet and began gathering up the papers on her desk.

"Uh... Miss Campbell?"

She turned to see Henry standing by the coatroom. "Yes?"

"I think you should know the Keller kids ain't comin'."

"Aren't coming," she corrected. An uneasy feeling crept into her stomach at his announcement. "What is their reason for not attending?"

The boy's face flushed and his next words were directed at the floor. "My friend John Keller said his pa won't let him come. 'Cause Mr. Keller's wife's cousin was... I mean she still is... Miss Lehmann."

"I see." Livy stood tall, head up, though inside shock and anger battled for dominance. "Thank you for letting me know, Henry."

When the door shut behind him, Livy walked around her desk and sank into her chair. She lowered her head into her hands and massaged her now throbbing temples. Someone refused to let their children come to school because of *her*? She wasn't the enemy; she hadn't been responsible for Miss Lehmann's termination or her being sent to prison. Yet the Kellers laid some of the blame on Livy's shoulders anyway.

The unfairness of it festered in her mind until she could no longer sit still. *Maybe they'll change their minds once we've met.*

She gathered up her remaining things and headed to the door. After locking up, she stepped into the thin sunshine. Harlan and Greta were playing a game of tag behind the school, while Friedrick fixed the mortar along the south wall. He glanced up as she approached him.

"Afternoon."

The detached civility with which he greeted her only infuriated her more. "I need to know where the Kellers live," she said in a voice bordering on rude.

Friedrick pointed his trowel west. "Their farm is the one just down the road."

"Thank you." She kept her words clipped. Let him think what he wanted.

She left her sketchbook and lunch pail beside the school and walked in the direction of the Kellers' home.

A black dog jumped up from the shade of their porch and growled at Livy.

"It's okay, boy," she soothed as she came to a stop in the yard.

The dog ignored her attempts to placate him and began barking instead. A boy about Henry's age came out of the nearby barn. "Wilheim, be quiet," he hollered at the dog.

"You must be John Keller." Livy managed to relax her

clenched jaw into a friendly smile. "I'm Miss Campbell, the new teacher at the township school up the road. Is your mother here?"

John eyed her with suspicion, but he nodded. "I'll go get her." He jogged up the steps and into the house.

Wilheim threw out another menacing growl, but Livy knew it was a bluff. The old dog reminded her of those they'd owned on the farm at different times. As she'd suspected, he left her unharmed and trotted back to his spot by the porch.

Livy waited for Mrs. Keller, her heart pounding faster with each long second, her hands clasped in front of her. Finally the screen door creaked open and a woman stepped out. Mrs. Keller wiped her hands on the corner of her apron, her gaze distrustful.

"Mrs. Keller, I'm Livy Campbell." She took a step toward the porch. "I teach at the township school, up the road."

Mrs. Keller shook her head and called over her shoulder into the house. John strolled onto the porch, followed by two young girls. They stared in curiosity at Livy. Mrs. Keller pointed at Livy, then at her son.

"She doesn't understand very much English," John said.

"Could you please tell her, I'm here to talk to her about you and your sisters coming back to school?" Livy asked.

The boy translated Livy's request. Mrs. Keller frowned and shook her head again. She said something in German to her son.

"She says we can't come. Not until Marta is released or another German teacher takes her place."

Fresh anger leapt inside Livy. She gripped her hands

tighter to keep the emotion in check. "Even if the superintendent did find another German teacher, he or she would not be allowed to speak anything but English. We have to adhere to the new language law."

John conveyed Livy's message to his mother, but the steeliness in Mrs. Keller's face didn't abate one bit. She fired more German words at Livy before gesturing for her son to translate.

The boy glanced at Livy, then away. She braced herself for the words she knew would not be pleasant. "She says your kind of people should leave us alone. Then we wouldn't have to worry about things like language laws or non-German teachers for our children."

With a decisive nod, Mrs. Keller ushered the girls into the house and slammed the door. John descended the steps. He gave Livy an apologetic look and returned to the barn.

Livy whirled around and marched away from the house, the woman's accusation still smarting in her ears. *My kind of people?* she thought with a indignant sniff. She wasn't the one being biased. There was nothing she could do to change the law or bring Miss Lehmann back. She wanted to be a good teacher—to all her would-be pupils. Was that so wrong?

She returned to the school to collect her things and started toward her cabin. Her headache had worsened. Lying down would probably help.

"That was a quick visit," Friedrick said.

The remark, however innocuous, grated against Livy's fraying control. She spun around to glare at him. "Tell me, Friedrick. Do all the parents hate me?"

His brow furrowed in confusion, though she wasn't

sure if it was at her question or her anger. "Why would you say that?"

She stomped over to him, anxious not to have Harlan or Greta overhear. "I was informed this afternoon the Keller children won't be attending school this year, at least not while I'm the teacher. Apparently Mrs. Keller is related to Miss Lehmann."

Friedrick lowered the trowel and tipped his cap upward. "Now that you mention it, I recall there was a connection between the Kellers and Marta Lehmann."

· "I thought if they met me, they might change their mind." She pressed her things to her chest and frowned. "Did it?"

"No. Mrs. Keller was emphatic her children wouldn't be returning to the school. I couldn't convince her otherwise." Her gaze wandered to where his siblings were now climbing one of the trees behind her cabin. Her fury was fast fading into hurt. "Do the other parents despise me for taking Miss Lehmann's place, too? Or do they prize education too much to keep their children at home?"

Friedrick rubbed his chin, which was covered in tiny blond hairs. Livy had a sudden urge to touch the stubble. Would it be scratchy or soft?

"They don't hate you, Livy."

She blinked, trying to remember what they'd been discussing before her thoughts had been waylaid. This was the longest conversation she'd had with Friedrick in two weeks. "What about your parents? How did they feel about a non-German teacher coming here?"

She saw the hesitation in the line of his shoulders and neck before he gave her a level look. "I won't lie. They were a little disappointed." Livy opened her mouth to defend herself, but he wasn't finished. "That being said, Elsa convinced my father it would be good for Harlan and Greta to have a native English-speaking teacher. I think most of the parents around here feel the same."

Livy kicked at a clump of new grass. The thought of anyone—German or American—disliking her cut worse than she'd thought. How could she ease the concerns of her students' parents, assure them she was qualified to teach, even if she didn't share the same pedigree?

She lifted her gaze to find Friedrick at work again. "Looks like you're almost finished with this wall."

He grunted in agreement.

She searched for something else to say, suddenly reluctant to face her silent cabin. "What will you do after all the cracks are fixed?"

"I'd like to straighten the outhouse."

A glance at the leaning privy made Livy chuckle. "I wonder if it had a little help."

Friedrick looked over his shoulder at her. "How do you mean?"

"Before we got our indoor plumbing, my oldest brother, Joel, played a trick on our brother Tom. I think Joel was eleven at the time, so Tom would have been nine. He told Tom not to use the outhouse on Halloween night or some ghoul might snatch him."

The happy memory eased her hurt pride. She shifted the things in her arms and leaned against the dry bricks of the school. "Apparently, Tom waited in bed until he couldn't stand it any longer, then he sneaked out to the outhouse. Unbeknownst to him, Joel and a friend had been waiting in the dark for more than an hour. When

Tom went inside, the two boys shook the outhouse as hard as they could. Tom ran out screaming—woke the whole family. That outhouse never sat right again."

She caught Friedrick watching her, but this time he didn't turn away. Instead his eyes held hers. Livy's pulse drummed faster. His look said he admired her, even found her attractive, and yet he hadn't bothered to talk to her like this in weeks. Could they ever be more than polite acquaintances? Would that be so wrong? Surely no one would fault her for making a friend in a place where she so often felt lonely.

If only she could talk to Joel or Tom about her situation with the Kellers, with her students, with Friedrick. What would they say? She missed Joel's sage advice and Tom's ability to make her laugh—really laugh. Hilden might be far from home, but she'd brought the memories of her brothers right along with her.

"I miss them," she said without thinking. "I sometimes wish they hadn't gone to fight."

"Your brothers?"

"Yes." Livy shut her eyes and breathed through the sharp worry she felt for their safety.

"Some folks around here might take a statement like that for sedition," Friedrick warned, "German or not."

Livy opened her eyes and pushed away from the wall. "I didn't mean it like that." He wouldn't report her, would he? She hadn't shared a word of the few suspect things he'd said to her. "I'm glad we can help the French and the British. It's just…" She let her voice trail out, uncertain whether she should stop or continue.

Friedrick waited, the trowel unmoving in his hand. His expression remained open, interested. But could she trust

him? She watched Harlan and Greta, who were now examining something in the nearby field. Even after only
a few weeks here, Livy saw how much the two revered
their older brother. Friedrick might be hesitant to further
his friendship with her, but she felt certain he wouldn't
betray her.

"This war has taken so much from me." The words
spilled from her, bringing both pain and relief as she un-
burdened them from the silent tomb of her mind. "I had to
leave college to help out when my brothers enlisted, and
I fear every day something will happen to one or both of
them. Someone else very dear to me came back a different person after being over there. He can't stay away from
liquor."

She bit her cheek as fresh resentment and humiliation
washed over her. Why did everything in this world have
to be so topsy-turvy? Why hadn't Robert leaned on her
and her compassion instead of seeking solace in a bottle?
She missed being with him, at least when he'd been sober.
Or did she simply miss having someone around to talk to,
someone to do things with?

"I'm sorry to hear that," Friedrick said, his tone sincere, "about your friend."

A flash of recognition in his blue eyes made Livy
think he knew she'd been talking about Robert. Would he
surmise then that Robert hadn't shown up on her birthday because he'd been too drunk? To Livy's surprise, the
thought didn't embarrass her. She hadn't yet gathered the
courage to tell her parents about Robert's drinking, but
the weight of the secret felt less heavy after sharing some
of it with Friedrick.

"Do you have family over there?" She'd wanted to ask

the question since learning he was German, but no time had seemed appropriate, until now. "In Germany?"

"Elsa's grandmother and aunt still live there." Friedrick studied his large hands as he spoke. "She was very close to them before she came here. My uncle, my father's oldest brother, didn't immigrate with the family either. He and his family are still in Germany."

"Are you glad you're not fighting against them?"

He bent to capture more mortar on his trowel and smeared it onto the bricks. Would he answer? When he did finally speak, his words came out heavy with regret. "Most days I'm grateful not to be fighting, but there are times I feel useless here." He braced one hand against the wall as he smoothed the mortar. "Still, I hate to think what will become of my family's country and culture should they lose this war."

His admission stirred Livy's compassion, but the way he kept his back to her said he didn't want her pity. There had to be something she could say, though, to bring happiness back into his somber face.

"Sounds a bit seditious, too, don't you think?"

Friedrick glanced over his shoulder at her, his brow furrowed. She smiled to show she was teasing. Slowly the cautiousness ebbed from his face.

"I promise not to have you thrown in the clink if you'll do the same for me." He stuck out his free hand, his blue eyes crinkling with amusement.

"Agreed." She shifted her things to one arm and stepped closer to shake his hand. She loved the way his grasp engulfed hers, making her feel safe.

She knew she ought to let go, but she didn't want to. The way Friedrick peered down at her, he didn't seem in a hurry to release her either. Her breath caught as his gaze lowered to her lips. A flash of triumph rose inside her. For all his indifference lately, he still liked her.

Friedrick cleared his throat, the intensity of his look increasing. "Livy?"

"Yes?" Would he ask to kiss her? Should she allow him to?

"You're . . . um . . . standing in the mortar."

Livy blinked in surprise. *The mortar?* She stared at her feet and gasped. Her high heels were sunk halfway into the tray of grayish-white goo. Letting go of Friedrick, she tried to hop out of the mortar, but her shoes slipped and she teetered backward. Friedrick grabbed her elbow before she could fall.

"Thanks."

"Can you move?"

A giggle escaped her mouth as she shook her head. "I don't think so."

In one swift movement, he swept her into his arms, flicking mortar against the school, and carried her away from the offending goop.

At the sight of her white-covered shoes, Livy giggled again. The whole situation, coupled with the horrible encounter with Mrs. Keller, struck her as humorous. Once the laughter came, she couldn't stop. Tears of merriment leaked out.

"Are you all right?" Friedrick's concern brought another fit of giggles.

Livy wiped her eyes with the back of her hand and nodded. "What a fitting end to this afternoon."

She chuckled once more, but her amusement slowly faded as she realized Friedrick hadn't put her down yet.

He still held her, close enough she could feel the steady thump of his heartbeat beneath his shirt. Close enough to smell the scent of soap and sun on him.

Her heart ricocheted at his nearness, at the feel of his solid chest against her side. She hazarded a peek at his face. His serious expression hadn't changed, though he didn't appear angry. Instead he radiated surprise, in a somber kind of way. *But surprise at what?* she wondered.

"I...um...can walk now." She didn't want him to release her yet, but she worried someone might see them in such a familiar-looking pose.

Friedrick looked from her to her shoes, and a sheepish smile lifted his mouth. "Might as well get you to your door."

He carried her the rest of the way to her cabin, then lowered her gently to the ground. Livy took a much-needed step backward and bumped into the doorway. Her heart rate hadn't fully slowed.

"You sure you'll be all right?"

She gave a vigorous nod. "I suppose there's nothing I can do about the Kellers, but I can keep teaching the rest of my students."

"You're doing well."

The compliment made her blush. "Thank you. It's hard not to wonder, though. At least once a day," she added with a self-deprecating laugh.

"Do you need help with your shoes? You probably ought to get that stuff off quickly."

Livy studied the hardening goop. "No, I can do it."

"See you tomorrow then, Livy." He smiled and turned away.

"See you tomorrow."

He strode a few feet past the cabin, then suddenly he circled back. "Do you want to come to the dance hall with me tonight?" He ran his hand over his stubbled jaw. "It might do you some good, give you something else to think about other than the Kellers and teaching."

An irrational happiness filled her at his invitation. At the same time, though, a bell of warning sounded in her mind. If she agreed, she was acquiescing to far more than just a ride to the dance hall. "What about Maria?" she hedged, giving herself more time to decide. "Don't you usually take her?"

"She's helping her mother get ready for the spring social next weekend."

"Which dance hall were you planning to go to?" There was no way she would agree to go to the one near her home, where they'd met on her birthday.

Unspoken understanding filled his blue eyes. "There's one an hour's drive north of here that Maria and I haven't tried yet."

The inside of her cheek found its way between her teeth as she vacillated in indecision. What would her parents say about her going? What would the people of Hilden say? Mrs. Norton's accusing words about the Germans repeated through her mind: *they're conspiring with our enemies.*

She'd spent enough time around Friedrick and her students to know such rumors weren't true, but if she went to the dance hall with him, would she be branded a German sympathizer? Would her parents hear of it and be angry, or worried? Would Joel or Tom be furious with her as well?

She lifted her eyes to Friedrick's and saw only kindness there, a desire to help. And maybe something more? The possibility sent a pleasant shiver up her arms. Why should she allow others to dictate whom she spent her time with outside of her classroom? She was tired of long evenings by herself with no one else to talk to. She was a grown woman, and she would decide what she did and with whom. Besides, she told herself firmly, it was one night of dancing—that was all.

"What time will you come for me?"

Friedrick's face lit up at her words. "Six thirty."

"I'll be ready," she said, raising her chin.

He grinned. "Looking forward to it," he said before heading back to the school.

"Me, too," Livy whispered to his back as a thrill of anticipation, and a little fear, raced through her.

* * *

"Are you going somewhere?" Elsa asked Friedrick. She and Greta were rinsing the supper dishes. Friedrick had already hitched up the horses and had come back inside for his cap.

"Just dancing." He collected his hat from the peg by the back door. "I'll be back in a few hours."

Elsa frowned. "I thought you usually took Maria to the dance hall."

"She can't come tonight."

"Because she is coming here with her mother and a few of the other women from church. We are making decorations for the spring social." She handed Greta a dripping plate to dry. "Are you driving there alone then?"

It was Friedrick's turn to frown. He wouldn't lie to

her, but she wasn't going to like the truth. "I invited Miss Campbell to come to the dance hall with me. She's had a rough time of it this week, and I thought she could use the distraction."

Elsa met his level gaze with one of her own. "Is that wise?"

No, Friedrick wanted to say. It wasn't wise. Not for him, not for his family, probably not for Livy either. But he'd been powerless not to ask her after carrying her out of the mortar. The way she'd fit perfectly against his chest, strands of her soft hair brushing his chin, had both surprised and pleased him. He hadn't wanted to let her go. If that wasn't enough to make him extend the invitation, then her lingering melancholy about the Keller family and her ability to be a good teacher had tugged at his compassion. Surely there was no harm in helping cheer her up.

He'd been so vigilant in maintaining distance from her since Easter, despite seeing her nearly every day and wishing he'd been the one to make her laugh or smile instead of one of her students. Driving out thoughts of her beautiful face or her gumption or her kissable lips had been difficult, at times impossible. But he'd done a fairly good job of it—until now.

Friedrick realized Elsa was still waiting for an answer, along with Greta, who held the dishtowel unmoving in her small hands. "It's not as if we're only going to dance with each other, Mother. We'll be fine."

He bade them good night and strode out of the house. Why did helping Livy seem to come at the cost of helping his family?

As he climbed onto the wagon seat, Maria and her

mother pulled their wagon alongside his. Friedrick stifled a groan. He hadn't left soon enough.

"Hello, Friedrick." Maria smiled.

Knowing it would be rude to leave, Friedrick waited for her to hop down and walk over. Maria's mother threw them a knowing smile and took off at a trot toward the back door, leaving the two of them alone in the yard.

"Going somewhere?" Maria placed her hand on the side of the wagon. "I was hoping you'd be around while we worked on the decorations for the social."

Friedrick studied the girl's pretty face. He hated to hurt her with the announcement he was going dancing with someone else, but he couldn't let her keep thinking there was more to their relationship than friendship. "I'm going to a dance hall, Maria."

"Oh?" Her smooth brow scrunched in confusion. "Alone?"

"No. I'm driving Miss Campbell."

Her surprise hardened into a dark frown. "I thought she might be sweet on you, especially since she showed up at our church the other week."

Friedrick shook his head. "It's not like that."

She lowered her hand to her side. "It's not? What about you and me?"

"We're friends, Maria. Always have been." He pulled his cap more tightly onto his head, wishing he could erase the pain radiating from her. "Always—"

"Will be," she finished in a tight whisper.

"I'm sorry."

She held her head high. "So am I. But don't forget, Friedrick." She tossed her hair, her violet eyes flashing. "I'll be here. Whenever you need me."

He responded with a nod and gathered the reins. "Have a nice time tonight."

"You, too." Her words were coated with sarcasm. Friedrick could only hope she'd come to understand—and find her own happiness—someday.

Less than fifteen minutes later, he pulled the horses to a stop in front of Livy's cabin. He climbed down as Livy stepped outside. She wore a green dress that matched the color of her eyes. Her hair was arranged in a nice twist, leaving her slender neck and throat exposed, save for a few blond strands.

"Let me lock up."

"You have a coat?" he asked when she'd finished locking her door. The night was unusually warm for mid-April, but the drive home would be colder.

She smiled and lifted her arm to show him the coat draped there. He followed her around the wagon to help her up. He offered her his hand, and as she climbed past him, Friedrick inhaled a whiff of vanilla. The scent fit her exactly—lovely but not ostentatious.

Once they were both settled on the seat, he turned the wagon around and headed back in the direction he'd come.

"The school is looking much better," Livy said as they drove past the brick building.

With the new shingles and the freshly mortared bricks on the south side, the school looked nearly as good as it had when Friedrick had attended it. "The place was only a few years old when I first started there."

Most of his friends from back then had gone to fight overseas, which hadn't helped Friedrick's guilt over not being able to go himself. A few of them had even been killed, leaving behind grieving German-American families and sweethearts.

Would things be different once the war with Germany ended? Would he be able to see any girl he liked, without worrying what it would mean to her or his family? Or would there forever be a stigma surrounding him because he was from German descent and hadn't been able to fight? The thought made him suddenly tired.

Livy glanced at him. "Something on your mind?"

Friedrick shrugged. "Long day." Working on the farm and at the school had begun to take its toll. He'd nearly fallen asleep at supper the night before.

"We don't have to go tonight. I know how early you have to rise in the morning."

"And you get to sleep in," he teased.

She shook her head and laughed. "Not really. I'm waking up before the sun, as if I'm back on the farm."

"Then we'll both be tired tomorrow."

Livy needed this evening. As weary as he might be, he wouldn't give up the chance to help her.

"Besides, you've got to keep up your dancing skills for that boyfriend of yours back home." The statement was meant as more of a reminder to himself. He'd do well not to forget the pretty teacher seated next to him wasn't—and wouldn't ever be—his girl.

Livy's answer was directed at the coat in her lap. "Robert doesn't like dancing. He was injured in France and has to use a cane now."

"He's the one who's taken up drinking." Friedrick didn't pose it as a question, though Livy nodded in response. He'd figured out right quick whom Livy had been talking about earlier when she mentioned a friend with a penchant for drinking.

"Was it his dislike of dancing or his trouble with alcohol that kept him from showing up on your birthday?" He'd meant the words to come out lighthearted, but some of his annoyance bled through. Why would any man leave a woman like Livy alone on her birthday?

"It was the latter." She twisted her coat sleeve between her fingers. "I found out later he received word another friend of his had been killed. He spent the entire night passed out in his barn."

Friedrick clenched his jaw at the picture she presented of her beau. While he respected the man for fighting in the war, his behavior now was inexcusable. Especially when it caused Livy pain.

"What about Maria?" she asked, changing the subject. "Is she going to be upset that you're taking me to the dance hall instead of her?"

"She'll be all right." Friedrick pointed to his left without slowing the horses. "That's our farm there."

Livy leaned forward to see around him. "It's a nice place." When she sat back, she remarked in a playful tone, "So Maria hopes to live there one day as Mrs. Friedrick Wagner?"

He released a derisive chuckle. "I hope not." Especially after he'd let Maria know tonight where he stood on the subject. "I can't see a girl like her being willing to move into the home of her in-laws, especially when one of them is dying."

"Is that why you haven't married?" Livy asked with characteristic directness.

"I suppose." He fixed his gaze on the road up ahead.

"I owe a lot to my father and Elsa. He raised me on his own for three years after my mother died. I know he missed her, but he tried hard to let me know I was still important to him. Then Elsa came along and helped us both out of our melancholy. I can't abandon them now by going to live somewhere else." He urged the horses into a trot. "We don't have extra money to build me a house anyway."

From the corner of his eye, he caught her biting at her cheek. He could practically see the wheels turning in her head. She had something to say, but wasn't sure if she ought to say it. He swallowed a chuckle. "What is it?"

"What's what?" She feigned a look of innocence.

"You're biting the inside of your cheek, which means you're either nervous or dying to say something."

The corners of her mouth lifted. "I was thinking that perhaps money isn't your problem."

He frowned. "How do you mean?"

"Well." Her cheeks pinked as she hesitated.

"Go on." He could certainly take whatever ribbing she could throw at him.

"Maybe you just haven't found the right girl yet." She sat up taller on the seat as she said it. "There must be someone out there who wouldn't mind making her home with your family."

"Maybe," he echoed in a calm tone, though his thoughts were anything but serene.

He knew Livy wasn't talking about herself—she couldn't be. But her confidence prompted a seed of hope to sprout inside him. Not for her necessarily, but for the belief he'd find a girl someday who was beautiful, spunky, and willing to love and care for his family as

much as he did. Too bad Livy shared all the same qualities with his dream girl—those and a whole lot more.

*   *   *

The fox-trot came to an end, and Livy's partner released
her hand. Grateful for a chance to catch her breath, she
joined the young man and the other couples in applauding
their appreciation for the band. Since she and Friedrick
had arrived, the dances had been one lively one-step, two-
step, or fox-trot after another, much to Livy's delight.
She'd danced to every song, something she hadn't done
in ages, but only twice with Friedrick.

Where was he? She went up on tiptoe and searched the
crowd for him. His tall frame wasn't difficult to spot. He
caught sight of her and waved. Livy waved back as he
started through the throng in her direction.

He reached her side and leaned close to ask, "You
ready to go?"

Livy shook her head. "One more dance. Please?"

His warm, deep laughter brushed the hairs on the back
of her neck, causing her skin to tingle there. He looked
so handsome when he stared at her in that amused way of
his. "With me?"

She nodded.

"All right. But I might come pounding on your door
tomorrow morning so you can help me milk the cow at
dawn."

At that moment the band struck up the next song,
but instead of a toe-tapping number, the music flowing
through the room had a languid tempo. It was a waltz.

Friedrick lifted his hands into dance position, but Livy

hesitated. The energetic tension in the dance hall had transformed to something elegant and romantic. The other two dances with Friedrick had been lively and fun, not intimate like the waltz.

"Change your mind?" The teasing challenge in his blue eyes was unmistakable, though he lowered his arms to his sides.

Livy took a quick breath and tilted her chin upward. "No. I like to waltz."

"Good." The word was hardly audible, but Livy heard it just the same and his confident tone produced a strange thrill in her stomach. She stepped into his arms, and they joined the other couples spinning about the room.

Waltzing with Friedrick was nothing like swaying to the music with Robert or even doing the fox-trot. He held her closer but in a way that made her feel completely safe and cherished. She felt a heightened awareness of him in every sense. His firm touch on her back, the masculine scent of his shaving soap, the pleasure of his laughter in her ears.

Livy's pulse danced its own chaotic rhythm, completely out of sync with the fluid dance steps. Not for the first time, she contemplated what it would be like if he kissed her, what it would be like if they were to dance like this all night.

Afraid he'd read the longing on her face, Livy kept her chin lowered, her eyes trained on his shoulder. She shouldn't be thinking such things about Friedrick. She'd only ended things with Robert right before coming to Hilden, and then there was the whole dilemma of Friedrick being German-American. They couldn't be more than friends, no matter how much she secretly wished for something different.

Try as she might, though, logic couldn't hold its power over her for long. Especially when Friedrick peered down at her and smiled slowly. She couldn't have asked for a better evening. The night had been the perfect antidote to her frustration about the Kellers.

All too soon the waltz ended. Friedrick kept hold of her hand as he led her through the crowd to the dance hall entrance. Outside he helped her into her coat. The night air felt much cooler. Livy shivered and pulled the thin material tighter around her.

They drove through the streets in silence, Livy still trembling with cold. If only she'd brought along her thick winter coat instead of her more stylish thin one.

"Are you cold?" Friedrick asked, breaking the quiet.

"Why would you say that?" Livy joked through chattering teeth.

"Because you're bouncing the seat." He chuckled as she tried to stop, but she couldn't.

"Sorry. It's colder out than I thought it would be."

He turned to look at the wagon bed. "I don't have a blanket."

"I'll be all right. Just give me a—"

He put his arm around her shoulders and drew her against him. Immediate warmth spread through her arm and thigh where it connected with his coat and pant leg. She told herself she'd only stay there long enough to end her shivering, then she would move. But even as her trembling stopped, she couldn't force herself to scoot away. The same feeling of refuge, of safety, she'd experienced while waltzing with him washed over her again, driving out all thoughts of the cold. Friedrick's embrace felt not only secure but completely natural.

She wished she could see his expression. Did he enjoy holding her this way? Or was he simply being kind? "Thank you for bringing me tonight."

She sensed more than saw his smile. "You're welcome. You dance very well."

"I was going to say the same for you."

He chuckled in her ear. The low, rumbling sound, especially seated close to him in the dark, stirred her stomach to flutters. "Any time you want to go again, let me know."

She didn't answer, afraid she'd disrupt the feeling of contentment wrapping itself around them if she voiced the truth. There likely wouldn't be another time. But until they reached her cabin, she could pretend such a thing was possible as an American girl and a German boy going to the dance hall every night.

The motion of the wagon and the comforting heat of Friedrick's arm lulled Livy's eyes shut. The next thing she knew, Friedrick was giving her shoulder a gentle shake.

"Livy, we're here. At your cabin."

She lifted her head and blinked at the shadowed world around them. "That didn't take long."

"You've been asleep for a while," he said, the smile in his voice evident.

Friedrick helped her climb down from the wagon and walk to her door. She still felt half awake. After finding her keys, she unlocked the door and turned to face him. The light from the moon shone across his face, accentuating the crook of his masculine mouth and the angles of his jaw and chin.

"Thank you again, Friedrick. I had a lovely time."

"I'm glad. I hope it helped."

"Very much so." She hesitated on the doorstep, searching for something more to say. He'd been so kind to come to her rescue today. He always seemed to be helping others, but who helped him?

Friedrick cleared his throat and took a step backward. "Good night, Livy."

"Wait."

"Yes?"

The air felt suddenly charged with energy, an almost tangible force drawing them together. Sleepiness fled Livy's mind as she stared into his eyes. "You were wrong about one thing today."

His chuckle rolled over her. "Just one?"

"You said you felt useless here. But you're not." The cloak of night gave her courage to finish her thought. She stepped closer until their shoes nearly touched at the toes. "You helped me tonight, and you help take care of your family every day. Those things prove you aren't useless, Friedrick. Maybe you can't fight, but even a battle is made up of many individuals doing deliberate things. Just as you're doing here."

Unable to resist the pull between them any longer, Livy rose on the balls of her feet and pressed a kiss to the corner of his lips. For once, her own boldness surprised her. She threw Friedrick a quick "good night" and escaped inside.

She rested her back against the closed door, her breath coming in shallow bursts as though she'd run all the way home. She listened to the sounds of Friedrick's boots striding away, then the creak of his wagon as it lumbered down the road.

Would he think her forward or recognize the kiss for what it had been? A token of gratitude. *Nothing more than that*, she told herself firmly as she readied for bed. But the smile on her face wouldn't leave, no matter how logical her thoughts.

Chapter Six

Batter up," Friedrick announced as Henry stepped up to the makeshift home plate—one of the children's coats. Friedrick had come to the school early, hoping to finish fixing the cracks in the south wall, but the spring sunshine and Harlan's pleas soon had him abandoning his task to play a quick game of baseball.

Henry swung the bat a few times, then prepared for the pitch. Friedrick arched his arm and let the ball fly from his fingers. Henry gave it a light tap with the bat, forcing Friedrick to charge forward. By the time he snatched up the ball, Henry had crossed first base.

Friedrick called for the next student. As Anna took her place at bat, Livy exited the schoolhouse. The sight of her brought the vivid memory of her kiss to Friedrick's mind. He'd thought of little else the past five days.

She'd looked so vulnerable and beautiful standing on her doorstep in the moonlight, her hair slightly matted from sleeping against his chest. If she hadn't fled inside, he would have surely given in to his desire to kiss her, too. Such a realization had kept him awake more than once this week and filled him with equal parts regret and relief.

He'd told Elsa, and himself, that taking Livy to the dance hall the other night had been an act of kindness, a way to cheer her up. But he couldn't have been more wrong. The intensified awareness between them when they waltzed, the way Livy fit perfectly beneath his shoulder, the pleasure he found at both her words of encouragement and her touch, all combined into something far more dangerous than simply going dancing.

He could suddenly relate to the foolish moth, drawn to the lantern's alluring flame, wanting so much to be close to it, despite the peril it would bring. Try as he might, Friedrick couldn't curtail the need to see Livy. To be near her, to make her smile.

Anna frowned with impatience at Friedrick. "I'm ready."

"Hold on." He pointed his thumb in Livy's direction. "Don't you think we ought to let your teacher have a turn?"

Livy smirked and motioned to her shoes. "In these heels, I don't think so."

"Come on." Friedrick tossed the ball into the air and caught it. "I know you can throw, but can you bat?"

"Yeah, come on, Miss Campbell," Harlan shouted from behind Friedrick.

"Be on our team, Miss Campbell," Anna said. "We're losing by one. You can take my place."

Livy threw Friedrick a hard glare, which only made him laugh. He'd seen the way she stood up to challenges—she wouldn't back down, heels or not. "Oh, all right," she huffed.

The students cheered, even those on the opposing team, as Livy slipped off her shoes and hefted the bat. Friedrick made a show of stretching his arm in preparation for the pitch.

"Sometime today, Friedrick," she called, swinging the bat in front of her. He grinned. She positioned the bat near her shoulder and stared him down. The purse of her lips and the furrow in her brow made her look all the more attractive. Friedrick narrowed his eyes and threw the ball. Livy swung but missed.

"Strike one," he announced.

Livy frowned and lifted the bat again. Friedrick pitched the ball. This time the bat and ball connected with a loud *thwack*. The ball sailed over Friedrick's head toward left field.

"Don't let her reach home," he hollered to his team as he turned to face those in the outfield.

Out of the corner of his eye, he saw Livy sprinting to first base. Harlan and another boy ran after the ball, but they were moving too slowly. Livy reached second. She threw Friedrick a smug smile as she raced to third.

"Here you go, Friedrick." Harlan tossed him the ball, which he easily caught between his hands. He spun around and found Livy rounding third base.

"Oh no you don't." He ran forward to beat her to home plate. If Livy noticed him coming, she didn't show it. She ran as fast as her long skirt would allow, but Friedrick moved a hair faster.

He met up with her just before she could touch home plate. To avoid a collision, he gripped the ball in one hand

and wrapped his free arm around Livy's small waist. She laughed as he twisted her close to keep them both from toppling to the ground.

As their momentum slowed, he glanced down. She stared up at him, her lips parted as she tried to catch her breath. The noise around them faded into a dull roar, as it had when they'd danced the other night. Nothing else mattered but him and Livy and this moment. The yearning to kiss her was overpowering. He lowered his chin, so his forehead nearly touched hers. Her eyes widened, but she didn't move away.

He lifted his hand to cradle her face and realized he still held the baseball. Livy's gaze dropped to it as well. Wriggling out of his hold, she planted her foot on the coat.

"Home run," she said in a breathless voice.

Disappointment cut through him, but it was quickly replaced with rationality. He'd nearly kissed her in front of her students. "Well done."

Livy gave him a victorious smile.

"Ah, Friedrick," Harlan hollered. "Now we're tied."

Friedrick returned to his pitching spot. The next student stepped up to bat, but Friedrick struggled to focus on the game. He kept darting looks at Livy as she pulled on her shoes, her hair falling loose, her cheeks pink from the exercise. Distracted, he walked the next two batters, much to the consternation of his young team.

"You have ten more minutes," Livy said to her students.

Friedrick readied himself for another pitch when he noticed the postman coming across the yard toward the group.

"Something for you, Miss Campbell." The postman's

hesitant tone had Friedrick on sudden alert. Livy clearly heard it, too. She walked slowly toward the man, her shoulders pulled back, but Friedrick noticed she was gnawing the inside of her cheek.

He ignored the call of the children, who were anxious to finish the game before they had to head indoors. Instead he intercepted Livy and the postman. The man held out a short slip of paper—a telegram. The alarm in Friedrick's gut intensified.

Livy visibly swallowed, her eyes meeting Friedrick's. The raw fear reflected there cut at him. "Do you want me to read it?" he asked her quietly.

Still biting her cheek, she dipped her head in a quick nod and folded her arms. Friedrick took the telegram from the postman. He put his hand on Livy's shoulder and cleared his throat.

" 'Tom killed,' " he read out loud.

Livy flinched beneath his grasp and covered her mouth with her hand. A cry of pain leaked through her fingers, tearing at Friedrick's heart.

He swallowed hard and forced himself to finish reading. " 'Memorial service Friday. Stop. Will come for you tomorrow. Stop.' "

Friedrick crumbled the offensive telegram in his fist and drew Livy to him. Her love for her brothers was so strong. Losing one of them, without the chance to say good-bye, had to feel like losing her childhood friend all over again.

If only he could erase from time the last two minutes or been in France and saved Tom's life. But Friedrick couldn't do either, so he held Livy tight, her agony now his.

Livy didn't shed a tear. She simply pressed her cheek against his shirt, her arms wrapped around him as if he were the only thing keeping her upright.

The postman threw them a regretful look and walked away. The calls of the children from behind had stopped. Friedrick imagined they were curious and concerned about what had happened, but he didn't turn around. Instead he kept his arms around Livy.

How he wished it could always be his job to watch over and comfort her, but it would never happen. Not now. Not when her brother had just been killed in a war against his own people.

* * *

Livy stared out the window of her cabin, her mug of untouched coffee on the table in front of her. She couldn't swallow even one sip. Her throat felt too tight with unshed tears.

This isn't real, she kept telling herself. *Tom can't be gone. Tomorrow I'll wake up from this awful nightmare and he'll still be alive and well.*

She thought of her brother's easy smile, his quick wit, the way he'd always been able to cajole her out of a foul mood. He'd held her hand through Blanche's funeral service and gave her his best marble afterward to help her stop crying.

Did I really have to lose another dear friend, God? She rested her head beside her cup and squeezed her dry eyes shut.

Sorrow and shock sliced through her, making it hard to breathe. She forced herself to take deep, even breaths.

How were her parents managing? She'd lost a brother, yes, but they'd lost a son. And what about Joel? Did he even know what had happened to their brother? Had Tom suffered or had he been taken quickly? The unanswered questions made her head pound and her heart ache.

For the first time since coming to Hilden nearly four weeks earlier, Livy wanted to go home. She hated the idea of staying here, alone in her cabin with her grief, until her father arrived tomorrow to take her home. A longing to see her other siblings—to be with her family right away—filled her, nearly as fierce as her mourning.

A knock at the door interrupted her bereavement. She lifted her head to call out in a flat voice, "Come in." She hoped it was Friedrick; she couldn't stand the thought of talking with anyone else right now.

Relief flooded through her as he entered her cabin. "I called the superintendent from the neighbor's house." He left the door partway open and came to stand beside the table. "Mr. Foster said to close the school as long as you need. Just inform him when you get back."

"Thank you." She hoped he felt the sincerity of the words, even if they sounded a bit lackluster. He'd been more than kind—dismissing the children for her, making her coffee, and volunteering to telephone Mr. Foster.

"I've got Harlan making a sign for the school door to let everyone know it will be closed. Is there anything else you need?"

Livy shook her head.

"You didn't drink your coffee."

"I couldn't..." She gnawed at her cheek as fresh emotion crawled up her throat.

Friedrick crouched in front of her, one hand resting on

her chair back, the other on the table. The way he studied her with evident concern reminded her of the night of her birthday. He'd come to her aid then, too.

"It's all right to grieve, Livy. A good cry might help you."

"I want to, but I can't." Did her inability to cry mean something was wrong with her? How could she cry for days at the loss of her childhood friend and not shed a tear for her brother?

"The tears will come," Friedrick said as though reading her thoughts, "when you're ready." He placed his hand over hers. His touch warmed and comforted her, as his embrace had earlier. "My father told me the same thing when my mother died, and he was right."

His words eased some of her guilt, if only momentarily. "I keep thinking about my parents and what they must be feeling." She leaned her forehead onto her free hand and drew a shuddered breath. "I'm their eldest daughter. I should be there helping prepare for the service, not waiting for my father to come all this way to fetch me."

"Then we'll get you there today."

Livy lifted her head to look at him, hardly daring to hope. "How?"

Friedrick stood and pulled her to her feet. "Get what you'll need together, while I take Harlan and Greta home."

"But I don't live close, Friedrick. If we leave now, we won't reach the farm until supper." She wanted him to understand the implications of his decision, while at the same time, she hoped he'd still want to take her. "Are you sure you want to do that?"

His blue eyes darkened with an emotion Livy felt too

grieved and befuddled to identify before he offered her a shadow of a smile. "I'll be back in thirty minutes."

*   *   *

After a quick stop at the telegraph office to let Livy's parents know she'd be home today, Friedrick drove her south through town. The afternoon sun shone bright and warm, a mocking contrast to the news Livy had received.

Friedrick shed his coat once they reached the open road outside of Hilden. He shot a glance at Livy as he tossed the garment into the wagon bed. She gazed straight ahead, her green eyes devoid of spark. He refocused his attention on the road ahead, wishing there was something more he could do for her. Something to bring the life back into her.

To his great relief, Elsa hadn't objected to his plan to make the six-hour round-trip drive to get Livy home. She had asked if he meant to return that evening or stay over and come home tomorrow. Friedrick didn't want to impose on the Campbell family, especially at a time like this, but he wanted to see how tired he felt when they arrived before making a decision. Maybe he could bunk in the barn, then leave at daylight.

"I can't believe he's really gone," Livy murmured, speaking for the first time since they'd driven away from her cabin. "I wonder if they told Nora yet."

"Nora?"

Livy stared down at her hands. "She and Tom were sweethearts. He hadn't given her a ring yet, but it was understood by them and our whole family that after the war, they would be...be married." Several tears ran down her face. She swiped them away at once, but Friedrick was relieved to see she wasn't holding all her grief inside.

He hurt for her and her family, and for this other girl who'd lost her beau today. Having his mother die had been difficult, but he couldn't imagine losing the person one planned to marry.

"I didn't even get to say good-bye to him, just like with Blanche." A shudder ran through her. "Tom probably hadn't even received my last letter, telling him about coming to teach in Hilden."

Friedrick shifted the reins to reach for her hand. He locked his fingers with hers and set their joined hands on the seat between them. "What would you have said to him?"

"About what?"

"Tell me what you would have said, if you'd been able to say good-bye."

She sat in silence so long he thought she might not answer. "Well," she finally said, visibly swallowing. "I would have told him how much I loved him, how grateful I am to be his sister."

Friedrick nodded. "Anything else?"

"I would have told him I forgive him for all the teasing he did. I would thank him for making me laugh." Her voice wobbled with emotion. "He always did have a sunny personality, which could make even the most despondent of people crack a smile. He loved Nora dearly. He would have done anything for her. I always admired that."

What about your *beau?* he wanted to ask. Was this Robert fellow willing to do anything for Livy? Friedrick hoped so—she ought to be treated with the utmost respect and affection.

"He and Joel have been my greatest friends." Livy
brushed an errant piece of hair away from her face. Even
her grief and pale cheeks couldn't diminish her beauty.
"They let me tag along with them and their friends, at
least most days." A ghost of a smile appeared at her
mouth. "Tom often complained about me wanting to do
everything he and Joel did, but he was typically the first
to stand up for me."

"He sounds like a good man. I would have liked to
meet him."

It was the wrong thing to say. Livy tensed beside him,
her sorrow swooping down to blanket her again. She
pulled her hand from his and returned to her wordless
staring.

Friedrick ground his teeth together at his folly. He'd
been presumptuous to talk with such familiarity about
meeting any member of Livy's family. She wasn't his
sweetheart. While he wouldn't deny the strong attraction
between them, something he felt certain Livy recognized,
too, he could never be more than a friend to her. For her
sake and his and those they loved.

The rest of the long drive passed in awkward silence.
Livy had drawn into herself, perching at the far end of the
wagon seat, her grief wrapped as tightly around her as her
coat. She spoke twice, to give Friedrick directions about
which way to go, but he couldn't coax her into further
conversation. He gave up trying after the second time,
hating the helpless feeling in his gut at not being able to
do more for her.

The quiet forced him to face questions he wasn't sure
he wanted the answers to. Questions like what her family
would think about a German-American driving her home

or how her brother's death would change their fledgling friendship.

At last the home Livy had described appeared in the distance—a two-story, white-clapboard house and a large red barn. A wide porch extended along the front of the house, and a porch swing moved lazily in the breeze.

"There's the farm," Livy said, her voice lifeless.

Friedrick guided the horses into the yard and stopped the wagon beside the house to let Livy down.

"You can unhitch the horses and put them in the barn." She chewed the inside of her cheek before adding, "You're welcome to stay the night."

Friedrick didn't relish the idea of staying over, especially given the uneasiness between them, but it would do him good to get some sleep before heading back in the morning. "Thanks. I think I will."

She turned as if to climb down, but she stopped to look back at him. "Thank you for the ride, Friedrick."

The formality in her tone stung, but he told himself she was still in shock over the news. "Happy to do it."

She hopped down and hurried into the house. Friedrick drove the wagon to the barn. No one else was about, which meant the family was likely gathered for supper. The realization increased the discomfort churning within him. He unhitched the horses and led them into two empty stalls. After giving them feed and water, he reluctantly crossed the empty yard to the house.

Should he knock on the front door or use the kitchen entrance? The back door seemed less conspicuous than the front. Friedrick tapped a knuckle against the door. Silence met his knock. Now what?

He pushed the door open to find the kitchen vacant.

The family was near, though, judging by the murmur of voices Friedrick heard coming from the next room.

Not wanting to interrupt them in their shared sorrow, Friedrick decided to wash at the sink and return to the barn. Perhaps Livy could bring him something to eat later. As he moved toward the sink, the family's conversation rose in volume, making it impossible to avoid overhearing.

"He's German?" The speaker's voice teetered on the edge of manhood, which meant it had to belong to Livy's fifteen-year-old brother, Allen.

"German-American," Livy corrected.

There was a self-righteous smirk, then a girl asked, "Is there a difference?"

"That's enough," someone cut in. Friedrick guessed it was Livy's father. "We are not a house given to prejudice. A person is a person, no matter his or her heritage."

"But, Pa," Allen interjected, "it's the Germans who shot Tom."

Friedrick gripped the edge of the sink with one hand, anger and guilt warring inside him. He wasn't at fault for Tom's death, and yet he felt responsible in a way because of his parentage. One thing he knew for certain— he'd made a mistake coming inside. If he could slip back to the barn unnoticed...

Before he could make his escape, a middle-aged woman with light brown hair and an attractive face entered the kitchen. She gasped when she saw him, one hand resting against her heart. "Mr. Wagner, you startled me. We didn't hear you come in."

Friedrick removed his cap. "My condolences about your son, ma'am."

"Thank you." She appeared to sniff back tears as she went to the icebox and removed a bottle of milk. "We appreciate you driving Livy down here. That's not a short trip. You must be starved. Why don't you join us in the dining room? We thought we'd eat a special dinner in there tonight."

"That's all right, Mrs. Campbell. If you don't mind, I'll just wash up here and eat in the barn."

Livy's mother shook her head. "No, please. I insist you join us."

Friedrick couldn't refuse her again, no matter how much he wanted to. Not after what Livy's family had been through today. "Thank you, ma'am."

While she collected an extra plate and fork, Friedrick washed and dried his hands. He followed Mrs. Campbell through the kitchen door and into the dining room, wishing once more that he'd stayed put in the barn.

"Look who I found," Livy's mother announced as she set down his plate and fork. "I'll go get you a glass, too."

The open stares and frowns from Livy's four siblings made Friedrick feel much like the peculiar beetle Harlan had once found and pinned to a board for examination. Livy shot him a weak smile, then focused her attention on the food in front of her. Clearly she felt as uncomfortable as he did.

Her father rose from his chair at the head of the table and reached out to shake Friedrick's hand. "Mr. Wagner, I'm Josiah Campbell, and I see you've already met my wife, Ada. You know Livy, of course, but let me introduce the rest of our family." He motioned to each child as he said his or her name. "This is Allen and Mary, and over here, we have George and Charlie." Josiah sat back down and waved for Friedrick to follow suit. "Thank you for driving Livy home today. It was a welcome surprise."

Friedrick nodded and slipped into the only empty chair, beside Mary. She gazed up at him with wary brown eyes as her mother returned with the bottle of milk and a glass she set down in front of Friedrick.

"Thank you," he murmured. Ada dished him up a piece of fried chicken and some potato salad. She set the plate before him. Friedrick picked up his fork.

"We've got biscuits, too," she said, motioning to the half-full basket in the center of the table. Friedrick added one to his plate.

"Do you only eat liberty cabbage?" George asked from his seat across the table.

Liberty cabbage, the Americanized word for sauerkraut. "We do eat it sometimes," Friedrick replied.

George studied him. "How come you're not fightin' like Joel or Tom?"

"No more questions, George," Livy warned from her seat beside him. "Just eat your supper."

Friedrick smiled at her in gratitude. She didn't return the smile, but she gave him a determined look. She didn't regard him with suspicion anymore. He concentrated on eating his meal. He still preferred Elsa's German cooking, but the food was delicious.

The conversation around the table started up again. The family filled Livy in on the details of the upcoming memorial service and shared their favorite memories of Tom. They seemed to have forgotten Friedrick, to his relief.

The more he observed their camaraderie and listened to their stories, the more Friedrick sensed he didn't belong here. They didn't know what it was like to be considered an enemy to one's country, to be forced to buy bonds they couldn't afford, to fear losing one's job over a careless remark. He would never fit into Livy's world, and as hard as she'd tried, she wasn't likely to fit into his either. Not when the Kellers and other German-Americans opposed her presence at the township school.

Anxious to be gone, he climbed to his feet. The discussion ground to a halt as all eyes turned to him. "Thank you for the wonderful supper, Mrs. Campbell. It was just what I needed." He stepped away from the table and pushed his chair in. "If you'll excuse me now, I'm going to head back home."

Livy frowned as she set down her napkin. "Are you sure? You're welcome to stay."

Ada nodded. "It's no imposition."

"I ought to get back." Friedrick didn't want to cause offense, but his mind was made up. He had no reason to stay.

"Then we'll say good night." Josiah leveled a meaningful look at each of his children, reminding Friedrick of his own father when he'd been healthier. Livy's four siblings murmured, "Good night," before Josiah continued. "Thank you again for bringing Livy down here."

"You're welcome, sir." Friedrick gathered his dishes and carried them into the kitchen. Light footsteps, he instinctively knew belonged to Livy, trailed him.

Sure enough, he turned and found her standing there. "Wouldn't you like to rest up? It's a long drive back, Friedrick. You won't get home until after dark." Her earnest expression tugged at his resolve, until he reminded himself he had no business being here. He'd helped her, and now he had to do the right thing and leave.

"I think it's best if I head home." He set his dishes in the sink.

She stepped closer and touched his sleeve. "I don't under—"

A knock at the back door interrupted her. Before she could answer it, a man entered with the aid of a cane. He looked about Friedrick's age, though he stood a few inches shorter. Friedrick guessed at once who he must be.

"Livy, you're here already," the man said with surprise.

Livy spun around. "Robert?"

Friedrick watched as Robert embraced Livy. She looked startled.

"I'm so sorry, sweetie," Robert murmured to her. "I can't believe he's gone."

Livy shut her eyes and rested her head against Robert's shoulder. Jealousy lashed through Friedrick, sharp and hot. It had been his shoulder Livy had dozed on the other night when they'd gone to the dance hall. His arms around her when she'd heard the news of Tom's death earlier today. But he wasn't her source of comfort anymore.

He slipped past them and had his hand on the door-knob when Robert spoke up.

"Who's this, Livy?"

She lifted her head and moved away from Robert, but he kept a possessive hand on her back. "He—he works on the repairs at the school where I teach and was kind enough to drive me down here today."

Friedrick met Robert's cold stare. He was grateful Livy hadn't given his name—Friedrick didn't need the wrath of a former soldier directed at him tonight.

"Thanks for bringing my girl home." Robert pulled Livy to his side again.

His words, devoid of any real gratitude but full of aggression, grated against Friedrick's already rising temper. The room felt suddenly too warm, too small. "Good-bye, Livy. I hope things go well on Friday." He hoped for a parting smile or look from her, but she only nodded, her eyes trained on the floor.

Friedrick went straight to the barn and hitched up the team in record time. It wasn't until he'd left the Campbells' farm far behind that he felt he could breathe normally again. He didn't regret driving Livy home or the chance to help her at a difficult time. But the long drive had come at a bigger price than time or effort. He'd been confronted with the reality of how different her life was from his own. A few weeks of knowing her didn't change that. It was time for him to stop thinking so much about Livy Campbell.

Chapter Seven

Livy slipped barefoot outside, closing the front door on the hum of conversation inside the house. The parlor and dining room were still full of neighbors and friends who'd attended Tom's memorial service at the church two hours earlier. Thankfully the porch stood devoid of any guests.

She walked to the swing and sat down, not caring if she got specks of dirt on her black dress. Tucking one leg beneath her, Livy used the toe of her other foot to push the swing into motion. A nearby tree offered some relief from the late afternoon sun.

Her gaze wandered to the stand of trees across the road, where she'd often gone exploring with Joel and Tom. The memories resurrected the ache in her throat and head. She still hadn't cried, except for the few tears on the drive home and a few more at the memorial service this afternoon. Friedrick had told her the rest would come—at the right time.

Friedrick. The name alone conjured up a myriad of

images and emotions. She still didn't understand why he'd left in a hurry, instead of staying over. While her siblings hadn't exactly been welcoming, her parents had been kind, openly expressing their sincere appreciation for him driving her home.

Did they approve of her being friends with a German-American, though? Her father had pointed out they weren't a house given to prejudice, which was evident in the way he and her mother willingly served and helped others of any nationality or creed. Still, Livy felt like a traitor for befriending someone whose relatives may very well have killed her own brother.

She gripped the front of the swing and stared at the dusty floorboards beneath her toes. Why did things have to be so mixed up in the world? Why couldn't her brothers and Robert have stayed home, like Friedrick? *Then Tom wouldn't have been killed and I could have finished college.*

The glimpse at what life might have been didn't bring her as much comfort as she'd hoped. Without the war, she might never have had the chance to teach. She would have likely graduated, married Robert right afterward, and never gone to Hilden. Despite the challenges there, Livy found great fulfillment in being a teacher, even if that dream would end in a few months. Then she'd be right back here—with no hope of seeing both her brothers at the war's end.

What am I to do, God? she asked in pleading silence. *Give up the job in Hilden to be here for Mom and Dad?* That was her role as eldest daughter, wasn't it? She'd told herself that when she made the decision to leave college.

Should she stay and reconsider marrying Robert, despite her reservations? He'd been quite solicitous the past two days, holding her hand and getting her a plate of food this afternoon. She hadn't detected a trace of alcohol on his breath, despite his obvious sadness at losing one of his best friends.

How she wished Joel were here to talk to—he'd always been good at helping her sort out the jumbled mess her thoughts could become. *Sort of like Friedrick.*

The screen door squeaked open and Nora Lewis stepped onto the porch. Livy's cheeks flushed with embarrassment, though her good friend couldn't know she'd been thinking about a German-American.

"May I join you?" Nora asked.

With a nod, Livy untucked her foot from beneath her and slid over to make room. Nora sat down beside her. They rocked back and forth for a minute without speaking. Livy hadn't had a chance to talk with Nora alone since coming back to the farm.

She shot her friend a sideways glance. This pretty girl, one year older than herself, with ginger-colored hair was supposed to have been her sister-in-law.

Livy twisted on the seat to face Nora. "How are you holding up?"

"I should be asking you that question." Her red-rimmed eyes focused on Livy.

"I keep thinking he's just gone out to the barn, even though he's been away from home since last year." Livy gnawed at her cheek against the swell of emotion rising in her throat.

Nora nodded. "I feel the same."

"What will you do?" While Livy had her other siblings

and parents for support, Nora only had her folks. All of their other friends were married and she had no sisters or brothers.

"I'll keep praying and living." Nora played with the wrinkled handkerchief she held. "What about you? Have you enjoyed teaching?"

Livy stared at the growing buds on the tree as if they might hold the answer. "It hasn't been as easy as I might have thought, but I thoroughly enjoy it. Except..."

"Except?" Nora prompted.

"I don't know, Nora." She brushed her toe against the smooth wood of the porch. "I want to keep teaching, and yet I wonder if my place is back here again. Mother and Father don't need another child gone from home right now."

"No." The firmness of Nora's tone surprised Livy. "From the few letters you've sent me, I can tell you're happy there, Livy. Don't quit the job because of Tom's death. He, of all people..." She pressed her trembling lips together until she'd regained her composure. "He, of all people, would want you to fulfill your dream."

"But what about you?" Livy countered. Sorrow for Nora cut through her, making her tone fiercer than she'd intended. "You and Tom had dreams, too—dreams for a life together."

Nora gazed out at the road without responding. Chagrin filled Livy at the thought of wounding her friend any more than Nora had already been. She couldn't imagine Nora's pain. What would it be like to lose the man you longed to marry?

Livy shut her eyes against the awful question. A face appeared before her, but it wasn't Robert's. The man in her mind had blond hair and a genuine smile. She quickly opened her eyes, erasing Friedrick's image. She couldn't think of him now.

"I'm sorry, Nora." Livy slid over and put her arm around her friend's bent shoulders. "It's hard not to dwell on the unfairness of the whole thing. But if you can be strong, then I can, too."

"I have my moments of despair," Nora said quietly. "But every time I think of a future without Tom, I force myself to my knees and I pray until I feel God's peace again. It always comes." She turned to look at Livy, her gaze as intense as her heartfelt words. "I don't know what's ahead for either of us, but I know God will take care of you and me, Livy. Just as he's caring for Tom."

Nora's conviction brought the first stirrings of hope and peace Livy had felt since learning of Tom's death. She would miss her brother terribly and she didn't have all the answers about what to do with her life right now, but if Nora could trust God, then Livy would try harder to do the same.

"I think I spotted some carrot cake in the dining room before I came outside," Livy said, standing. "You know how much Tom loved my mother's carrot cake."

Nora smiled, in spite of her tears. "Yes, he did." She rose from the swing.

"Then let's go eat two pieces each," Livy said, linking arms with her friend. "One for us and one for Tom."

*   *   *

Livy parked her family's wagon by the Drakes' front porch and climbed down. After looping the reins over the railing, she walked to the kitchen entrance and knocked. Robert's mother opened the door, a dish towel in her hands.

"Why, hello, Livy."

"Is Robert here?"

Mrs. Drake shook her head. "I don't believe so. He mentioned going into town after supper."

Strange, Livy thought. *I could have sworn I saw his car in the barn.* Perhaps Robert had taken his family's wagon instead.

"Evening, Livy," Robert's father called out to her in his thick British accent. He sat at the table, a newspaper between his hands.

Livy waved. " Good evening, Mr. Drake."

"I'll tell Robert you stopped by." Mrs. Drake smiled at her. "I know it wasn't the best of circumstances that brought you back down here, but Robert's missed you. It's good to see the two of you together again. Will you be headed back to your job soon?"

Livy hesitated, uncertain what to say as an answer. She'd been home a week already, and although she missed her students and her cabin, she hadn't come to any permanent conclusions about what to do. Being back at the farm hadn't been as terrible as she'd remembered, and she felt guilty leaving her family to deal with her brother's death without her. She and Robert had even gone to a performance at the opera house in town last Saturday and she'd had a nice time.

What would her students think if she didn't come back, though? They'd so recently lost their last teacher. Whichever choice she made, she was letting someone down.

"I think it would be best to finish out the school year," she finally said, "but I haven't decided what to do after that."

"You're always welcome here."

Livy smiled. "Night, Mrs. Drake."

Robert's mother waved good night and shut the door. Livy walked back to the wagon. In the waning light, she studied the two-story house with its gingerbread trim. Could she imagine living on the property as Robert's wife?

Is that what I'm to do? she prayed.

A low, plaintive noise reached her ears, interrupting her silent plea for answers. The sound seemed to be coming from the barn. Could it be a sick animal? Livy crossed the yard to investigate. Thick shadows filled the interior of the building as she walked inside. As she'd suspected, Robert's car was parked inside—in front of the wagon. Livy's stomach twisted at the sight of both vehicles. Robert wouldn't have walked to town.

The cry repeated itself, softer and closer this time. It no longer sounded animal-like but human. Livy bit down on her lip against the anger fisting in her stomach. She turned toward the door, prepared to leave, when Robert spoke.

"Who's there?" he slurred. "Whatdaya want?"

"It's Livy, Robert. I came to see if you wanted to go for a drive or something."

A shadow disengaged itself from the dark pile of hay in front of her. "I don't want to."

"Fine." Before going to Hilden, before she'd ended things between them, Livy would have tried to coax him into coming with her so he'd stop drinking. Tonight, however, she felt too weary. Memories of finding Robert in a similar state suffocated her mind. "I'll be by to see you tomorrow."

She turned to go, but his next remark stopped her retreat. "Glad to see you're over Tom's death so fast."

"What did you say?" She slowly spun around, her heart pumping faster.

"You heard me. Wanting to go for a drive and goin' to the opera house last week."

Livy ground her fingernails into the palms of her hands. "Tom loved those things. He wouldn't want us to be sad all the time." *Or drunk.*

Robert gave a bitter laugh. "You ever seen someone blown to bits, Livy?"

"I don't want to talk about this—"

"You ever seen men screaming in pain after a shell's torn 'em up?"

Livy pressed her hands over her ears, trying to block out the images his words inspired. She didn't want to imagine her brother suffering, especially in such a gruesome way.

"Stop it, Robert," she whimpered. She couldn't seem to command her feet to leave.

Suddenly he was standing beside her, one hand supporting his weight on the side of the wagon, the other holding his bottle. "You ever had bullets flying 'round you?" he said, loud enough she could hear through her fingers. "Had your friends mowed down while you managed to get out with just a bum leg?"

She unstopped her ears as understanding replaced her fear. "This isn't about Tom at all, is it? It's about *you*— and what you lost over there."

"You don't know nothin'." He lifted the bottle and took a long swig. "I lost me another buddy last week."

Something snapped inside Livy as she stared at his shadowed face. Red-hot anger seared her veins. How many times had she tried, in vain, to help him? Robert wasn't the only one grieving.

She jerked the bottle from his grasp, whirled around, and threw it as hard as she could at the tack wall. The glass hit the wall with a satisfying *crash* and splintered into pieces.

"I lost my brother, Robert," she cried, turning on him. "My brother! But you don't see me or any member of my family drowning our grief in a bottle." She took a deep breath to calm her rage. "I'm sorry for what you had to see and do over there, but I won't tolerate this behavior any longer. We're through. Please don't try to contact me again."

He snatched her wrist in his hand. "That's what you said last time."

Livy tipped her chin up. She wouldn't let him frighten her. "It's as true tonight as it was then."

"I've been nothin' but nice to you this week," he hissed.

"Yes, but it's not enough." Being in Hilden, befriending someone like Friedrick, had shown her that.

Robert tightened his hold on her hand until it began to ache. "You're makin' a big mistake, Livy. There are plenty of girls who'll like me as I am."

"Then I'm happy for you. Now please let me go before I yell for your father."

The mention of Mr. Drake did the trick, as she knew it would. Robert released her at once.

"Good-bye, Robert. Take care of yourself." She didn't wait for his reply. Instead she strode quickly from the barn to her wagon. Once she'd left the Drake farm behind, she forced a cleansing breath of the chilly, night air.

Thank you, God, for letting me find him that way—again.

Robert's reaction to Tom's death had made her decision for her. She would return to Hilden—first thing tomorrow, if her father agreed.

Her mind now made up, Livy felt the rightness of her decision but also a sense of urgency. Whether the feeling of anxiety had to do with her job or something else, she didn't know. Either way, it was high time she went back.

*   *   *

Friedrick blinked as he stepped from the church into the bright sunshine outdoors. He shook hands with Pastor Schwarz—Pastor Black, as he was calling himself now. He wished he had something to say regarding the man's sermon, but to his chagrin, Friedrick hadn't paid much attention. He'd been thinking about a certain blond schoolteacher instead.

He'd done a poor job of keeping his resolve to rid Livy from his thoughts. All week, memories or concerns about her had entered his mind and lingered there. How was she faring? Would she return to her job soon? Would they still be friends?

"Friedrick?" Elsa said, jerking him back to the present.

"Yes?"

"You are frowning again," she said in German. She

motioned to the sun-filled sky. "What makes you so un-happy on this beautiful day?"

"I'm fine."

"Is it Maria?"

Friedrick shook his head. He hadn't told Elsa yet about squashing Maria's hopes for a future as his bride. Despite making his feelings plain, Maria had been as flirtatious as ever at the church social the week before.

"Does this have something to do with that teacher?"

"English, Mother," he said in a firm voice. "We're still in public."

"Ach." She rolled her eyes. "I will visit with my friends then. Anka Rosenthal said she had something to tell us."

He wished she would follow the law better, but he welcomed the chance to avoid talking about Livy. "Where are Harlan and Greta?"

Elsa pointed to some children playing tag, Harlan and Greta among them, before she crossed the lawn to join the group of women gathered around Anka. Friedrick debated taking a nap under one of the trees, while he waited for his family, until he spotted some of the men talking with Rolf Rosenthal. They were shaking the man's hand as if bidding him good-bye. Curious, Friedrick walked over.

"Where will you go?" a farmer by the name of Amsel asked Rolf.

Rolf pushed his glasses higher onto his thin nose. "To my wife's sister in Wisconsin. There are more Germans in her town. We will try to open a store there."

The men murmured in response. "You're leaving Hilden?" Friedrick stuck out his hand to shake Rolf's.

The older man nodded. "Can't afford to stay anymore.

We haven't had any customers in two weeks—German or not."

Shame seared Friedrick. Ever since discovering some-one had painted Rosenthal's grocery store yellow, signi-fying his ties to Germany, Friedrick had encouraged Elsa to go to the other grocer in town. He hated not supporting his fellow German-Americans or the inflated prices they paid somewhere else, but his desire to protect his family came first.

"You are not to blame, Friedrick," Rolf said, with per-ception, as he lowered his hand to his side. He turned to look down the street; the corner of his yellow-painted building was just visible. "We've lived here for twenty years. Brought Anka here as a young bride."

"You'll be missed."

"Thank you." Rolf faced him again. "Please tell your father good-bye for me. I have missed seeing him at church and in the store these last few years."

Friedrick offered the man his sincere wishes for a bet-ter go of it in Wisconsin, even as anger replaced the sting of regret. What kind of a world did they live in if good, honest folks like Rolf and Anka were forced to close their store and leave their home for good because they were German? Worse still, there wasn't anything Friedrick could do to change it.

After making certain his family was still occupied, he pulled his cap snugger onto his head and started down the sidewalk, away from the church. He needed to pound out his troubled thoughts against the pavement.

* * *

Livy lingered in front of the brick church, reluctant to walk home. She'd arrived back in town the day before. Though she'd chosen not to attend services at the German church again, she had hoped she might see some of her students—maybe even Friedrick—before she opened the school again tomorrow.

"Lovely day, isn't it, Miss Campbell?"

She turned to find the school superintendent approaching, hat in hand. Earlier, she'd seen him and his wife among the congregation.

"Good morning, Mr. Foster." The glorious spring sunshine warming her back added to the contentment she felt at being back in Hilden. The realization brought a momentary pang of guilt. Tom had been gone less than two weeks. Was she not mourning him properly as Robert had accused her? Her own reply to him repeated in her mind and eased her worry. *Tom wouldn't want us to be sad all the time.*

"May I offer my condolences again about your brother. He must have been a brave soldier."

He was so much more than that, Livy wanted to say, but she knew what the man meant. "Thank you."

"Are you sure you're ready to start teaching again?"

"Yes, sir."

"Very good." He shifted his weight, his focus on the bowler hat he held. "I did want to ask you something, Miss Campbell. Have you talked much with the man I hired to look after the school?"

Alarm crept up Livy's throat, snuffing out all feeling of happiness. Did the superintendent know about her friendship with Friedrick? Or worse, had someone seen them talking or at the dance hall or riding to her home together?

Would she be fired on the spot, even though she'd just returned?

"I have spoken with him, yes." Her calm tone belied her mounting fear.

Mr. Foster leaned closer, his voice dropping in volume as he continued, "Has he said anything to you that might reek of German patriotism? He seems a smart, hard-working one, but you never know with these German-Americans."

Disgrace brought a flush to Livy's cheeks. Is this how her siblings had sounded to Friedrick, after he'd been so kind to drive her to the farm? No wonder he'd returned home the same day.

A part of her still feared that a friendship with Friedrick meant she was betraying her brothers, but the importance of loyalty had been ingrained within her by her parents. In this moment, Friedrick was the one who needed her loyalty, regardless of his German heritage. She had no desire to have him or herself fired. Friedrick needed his position, and so did she. Teaching would keep her busy and give her heart time to heal from Tom's death and Robert's duplicitous actions.

Please, God, help me, she prayed quickly. *Help me speak the truth, but without getting either of us fired. Please.*

She opened her mouth, still uncertain how to respond to the man's question, but the words that fell from her lips rang with truth and confidence. "Mr. Wagner has been respectful, both to me and the children. He fixed the roof on the school and the teacher's cabin, as well as most of the cracks in the bricks. The school looks almost new, thanks to his attention and work."

"Good, good." Mr. Foster placed his hat back on his bald head. "There is something I need you to do, Miss Campbell."

Wary of what he might ask, Livy nevertheless gave a brief nod. He held the key to her continuing on as a teacher here in Hilden.

"I want you to let me know if he does or says anything suspicious. With that last teacher accused of being a spy, I'm concerned about other traitors in the area." He threw a cautious glance around them as though he expected someone to jump out and seize them. "You can never be too careful in times like these."

"I'll be careful," Livy answered. *In more ways than one.*

She would need to be more guarded in what she said or did when it came to Friedrick. She didn't want to cost him his job—or have her own taken away—by a misunderstanding.

The superintendent smiled. "I'm glad I ran into you, Miss Campbell. I have a war bond poster for you. I've been distributing them to the schools in our district, but you've saved me a trip to yours." He chuckled and motioned for her to follow him. He led her to a shiny blue Cadillac parked up the sidewalk from the church.

Livy gnawed at the inside of her cheek as he reached into his car and withdrew the poster. He held it up in front of her. It wasn't like some she'd seen—with frightening pictures of Huns. This one featured an eagle and American flags. Yet the bold type wasn't subtle either: ARE YOU 100% AMERICAN? PROVE IT. BUY U.S. GOVERNMENT BONDS.

"Put it somewhere prominent for the children to see,"

Mr. Foster said. "Then maybe they'll persuade their parents to buy more bonds before this loan drive is over."

Worry filled her stomach, making her feel suddenly ill. If she hung the poster, would more of her students' parents refuse to let their children come to school, like the Kellers? Even worse, what would Friedrick think if he saw it? He'd already expressed his guilt over not fighting, about not being American enough.

She wouldn't be the one to compound his regret. She'd simply take the poster and not hang it.

Mr. Foster's next words destroyed her simple plan. "I'd like to visit your school sometime in the next few weeks." The superintendent passed the poster to her. "See how you're getting along, how the school repairs are coming."

Livy rolled up the poster and forced a smile. "We'll look forward to it. Good day, Mr. Foster." She started up the sidewalk, but he called after her.

"Did you need a ride home, Miss Campbell?"

She shook her head. "No, thank you. A walk will do me good." She felt his gaze on her back as she spun around and headed away from the church.

What should I do?

If she hung the poster, she feared permanently offending Friedrick, who'd been more than kind to her. But if she didn't hang the poster, Mr. Foster would want to know why and she didn't have a safe answer.

She lifted her gaze from the cracks in the sidewalk and noticed a tall figure turning the corner on the opposite side of the street. *Friedrick.*

Livy froze in place. She couldn't be seen by him, in the presence of the superintendent, but she had nowhere to hide.

A quick glance over her shoulder confirmed Mr. Foster still stood beside his car, talking with his wife and another couple now. If Livy walked back by the church, he would surely wonder what she was doing—heading in the opposite direction from home.

Livy threw a panicked look at Friedrick. He was getting closer. Any minute now he'd spot her. Even at a distance, the sight of his handsome face quickened her pulse. Had it really only been a week since she'd last seen him? It felt more like months.

She longed to speak with him, to thank him properly for driving her home. But fear stopped her from calling out to him, kept her feet from rushing toward him. Mr. Foster couldn't see them together and acting familiar. There was also the matter of the bond poster in her hand. Friedrick couldn't see it before she'd had a chance to explain.

There was only one thing to do. She had to avoid Friedrick and pray he wouldn't see her. Biting her cheek so hard it hurt, Livy clutched the poster to her chest, feigned interest in the buildings on her left, and charged up the sidewalk.

Chapter Eight

Friedrick turned the corner and continued his walk south. A movement on the opposite side of the street drew his attention. A young woman was walking briskly, her head turned to face the buildings she passed, her hands full. Friedrick started to look away, but the woman's build and dark blond hair resembled Livy's so much that he stopped. As the woman reached the cross street, she glanced over her shoulder. There was no mistaking that pretty face. It was Livy.

Joy at seeing her quickly faded in the wake of sharp disappointment. How long had she been back in Hilden without his knowing?

"Livy," he called out as he left the sidewalk to follow her. He told himself he was making certain she was fine, nothing more.

She didn't cease her frantic pace until she'd rounded the corner and strode another few yards. Only then did she whirl around to face him, hiding whatever she'd been carrying behind her back. Her face looked paler than the last time he'd seen her.

"Hello, Friedrick." She wouldn't quite meet his eye.

"I didn't know you were back." He came to a stop in front of her. The breeze carried her lovely scent of vanilla to him. Her anxious expression made him want to hold her in his arms as he had done before she'd left. But the recollection of what had transpired while he was at her home marched painfully through his memory. He remained where he stood, his hands at his sides.

"I came last night." He could tell she was biting that cheek of hers. What had her on edge?

"How did the memorial service go?"

"It went well. Thank you." She kept throwing looks at something behind him. Friedrick turned to see what it might be, but he saw nothing out of the ordinary.

Was she embarrassed to be seen with him now? He tried to overthrow the thought, but it settled in the back of his mind, adding to the already strained tension between them.

"Will you open the school tomorrow?" he asked as he faced her again.

"Yes." She finally lifted her eyes to his. "Would you let Harlan and Greta know?" Her gaze beseeched his, but he didn't think it had anything to do with her question. A strand of hair blew across her cheek. Friedrick resisted the urge to push it back. How could she look so beautiful and yet be so unapproachable at the same time?

"You can tell them yourself." His frustrated tone made Livy flinch. "That is, if you'd like to ride home with us," he amended. He allowed himself another step toward her and touched her elbow. "I'd still like to help, Livy."

"I—I know." Her words sounded strangled and the

pleading had returned to her eyes. "I've got to go." She stepped back, breaking his grip. "I'm sorry. Good day, Friedrick." She spun on her heel and marched away without a backward glance.

Friedrick let her go, though the act of doing so had his hands clenching into fists. This wasn't the Livy he'd come to know. He'd expected her brother's death to affect their relationship, but not destroy it completely. Did their time together mean nothing to her now? Had she become like every other self-righteous American he'd run into during the last year?

The idea of Livy holding his heritage against him sliced deeper than anything else he and his family had suffered. He gave her retreating figure one final look, then walked back toward the church.

If Elsa sensed his darkening mood on the ride home, she gratefully kept her observations to herself. Instead she filled the tense silence by keeping up a steady chatter with Greta and Harlan. At home Friedrick unhitched the horses and put them away, while the rest of the family trooped into the house. The sound of raspy breathing and harsh coughs met him as he came through the kitchen door.

He hurried to his father's room. Elsa sat on the edge of the bed. "He's feverish, and his medicine is gone," she told Friedrick, concern marring her face.

"We can call the doctor." It wasn't the first time he'd been grateful they'd paid to have the telephone lines run to their farm.

"Yes, the doctor." Elsa rose and moved past him into the kitchen. Friedrick noticed Harlan and Greta standing on the stairs. Their worried looks squeezed at his heart, nearly as much as his father's distress. "Go change out of your church clothes. It's too nice to stay indoors this afternoon. Let's go exploring."

His siblings both offered him tentative smiles and raced upstairs. Friedrick trudged behind them to his own room. He'd hoped his father wouldn't need more medicine for a while—that the warmer weather would help him improve. Friedrick had planned to get his paycheck from the superintendent's office this week, but he'd been so busy running the farm and working at the school, he hadn't gone. Now he wished he had. With five dollars in the house, he wasn't sure they'd be able to afford more pills today.

He exchanged his Sunday suit for his work clothes and returned downstairs. Elsa was talking rapidly into the phone—in German.

"Mother?" Friedrick said firmly. When she didn't acknowledge him, he repeated her name a little louder. He couldn't seem to impress upon her the importance of speaking English in public, which included the telephone. "English, only English."

She shook her head at him as she kept up a steady stream of German. Finally she set down the earpiece and released a sigh. "He's waiting for a baby to come—a woman in Hilden. He said he would track down the pharmacist and bring the medicine as soon as he could. He can only bring half, since that is all we can buy now." She bustled around the kitchen, grabbing a pot and filling it with water. "I will make Heinrich soup and see if some cold compresses help."

Friedrick laid a hand on her arm, stopping her frenzy. "I know you're worried, Mother, but you can't speak German on the telephone, even with the doctor." His earlier annoyance over his encounter with Livy leaked out as he continued, darkening his tone. "The operator could report you and we can't afford to get into any more trouble. I can't lose this job at the school. Not when Papa's medicine is so expensive..."

One hand lifted to her mouth as she began to weep. Friedrick swallowed the rest of his lecture. He wrapped his arms around her thin shoulders instead and let her cry, though the sound tore at him.

"He used to be so full of life and energy. Do you remember, Friedrick?"

"Yes," he whispered back.

For years his father had woken him up before dawn so they could attend the needs of the farm together. Heinrich had been the one to make up the game of who could finish their evening chores and make it into the parlor first. He had impressed upon Friedrick, and later Harlan and Greta, the importance of learning English and getting an education.

Friedrick hated seeing him lying in bed, day after day, too weak to do more than read or sleep. His father's frailness was a constant reminder of something else he could not change.

Elsa stepped from his embrace. "I keep hoping he'll recover, that some miracle will happen." She drew a trembling hand across her wet cheeks. "But he isn't going to, is he?"

"We can't stop hoping and believing. Isn't that what you've taught us?" The reminder enticed a small smile from her, just as he'd hoped.

"You are right." She put a hand to his cheek. "What would we do without you, Friedrick?"

He knew she meant well, but the statement only succeeded in bringing to mind all the things he couldn't do for them—like get back their savings or cure his father or make the world see German-Americans differently. He bent forward and pressed a kiss to her grayish-blond head. "I told the children we could go exploring since the weather's so nice. Would you rather we stay and help with supper?"

Elsa straightened her shoulders. "No, no. You go on. I'll have supper ready when you return."

Friedrick went outside, where he found Harlan and Greta waiting for him. Greta slipped her hand into his as they set off down the road. She chattered at length about her friends and school. To Friedrick's irritation, she sprinkled her talk with Miss Campbell's name more than once, especially after he told them the school would reopen tomorrow.

He managed to find some unusual rocks for Harlan and some yellow buttercups for Greta before they trooped back to the farm. As they drew near the house, an automobile pulled to a stop beside the fence.

"Who's that?" Harlan asked.

"I'm not sure." Perhaps the doctor had purchased a car. Greta tightened her grip on Friedrick's hand in apprehension. "You two wait here."

A tall, muscular man emerged from the car. He looked nothing like the thin, aging Dr. Mueller. Or Miller, as he was called these days. Like the pastor and his family, the doctor had Americanized his name. This man didn't carry a doctor's bag either. Instead he sported a shiny badge on his vest.

"Can I help you?" Friedrick moved quickly to block

the path to the front door. If he could spare his family from witnessing another round of discrimination, he would.

"Afternoon. I'm Walter Tate, Hilden's sheriff." The man tipped his hat cordially. "Are you Mr. Wagner?"

"I am," Friedrick said, masking his concern at the sheriff's appearance behind a level expression.

"You own the farm here?"

"My father is the owner, but he's ill at the moment."

The sheriff pursed his lips and frowned.

"Is there a problem, sir?" Friedrick managed to sound conversational, despite the alarm pulsing through him.

To his dismay, the front door opened and Elsa came out onto the porch, a dishcloth mashed in one fist. "What is going on, Friedrick?" she said in heavily accented English.

"Ma'am." Sheriff Tate removed his hat. His glance jumped to Harlan and Greta, then back to Elsa. "I'm sorry to disturb you..." He swallowed, his Adam's apple bobbing. "However, I've been informed someone here has been breaking the law."

Friedrick kept his face impassive, but anger boiled within him. Livy must have shared the careless things he'd said. No wonder she'd been aloof in town. She'd probably been on her way to the sheriff's office when he saw her. He set his jaw, bracing himself to hear his own remarks repeated back to him. "What is the offense?"

"A woman telephoned from here and spoke in German. That's against the law now." The sheriff ran his thumb along his hat brim. "Which means I've got to take you to jail, ma'am. Just for three nights, mind you."

Friedrick's relief over Livy not betraying him was

short-lived. His annoyance and regret shifted from her to Elsa. He'd warned her not to talk in German on the telephone, for this very reason. What would his father do without her help? Friedrick couldn't be everywhere—on the farm, at the school, and caring for his father.

"I'd like to go in her place." The words came out before he'd even finished thinking them.

"Friedrick—"

"No, Mother." He pinned her with a stern look. Having worked extra hard the last few weeks at the school, he could afford to miss a few days. Things wouldn't suffer for his brief absence. "You're needed here. I can go."

Her face drained of color, but she finally nodded.

"I don't know if I can do that, son." Sheriff Tate studied Friedrick.

"All you need is someone to make an example of." Friedrick had to persuade him; he wasn't going to let the man haul Elsa to jail. "Let that person be me. My father's dying. He needs my mother's help."

The sheriff frowned. "I suppose it wouldn't hurt nobody to take you in instead."

"Then it's settled."

"All right." The man clapped his hat back on his head. "You'll be released on Wednesday."

Greta rushed forward to press her face into Friedrick's side. He put a comforting arm around her. He was grateful she didn't have to witness their mother leaving instead.

The sheriff glanced at Greta and shook his head, as if momentarily pricked in the conscience. "I got my hands full with this new language law," he grumbled. "I'll wait for you in the car."

Friedrick led Greta to the porch. Harlan hurried over to join them. "It's going to be okay," he told them. "It's only three nights."

"It's my fault," Elsa whispered in German. She rubbed at her folded arms. "I should go, Friedrick. I can't ever remember to speak English when I should."

"You're needed here, Mother. We both know that."

His words bolstered her into action. She waved Harlan and Greta into the house with her cloth. "Go get your brother some bread, Harlan. Greta, get him a book. I'll find a blanket."

Friedrick waited in the empty yard as they disappeared into the house. What would the jail be like? Cold? Crowded? Would he be able to keep the news of his arrest from Mr. Foster? His job was as good as gone if the superintendent found out what had happened.

Elsa and his siblings returned with a full bag. Friedrick swung it over his shoulder and braced himself to say good-bye. He'd never been away from them for more than a night. Thankfully he would only be gone four days, and this one was more than halfway over. If he'd been able to fight, the separation from his family would have been a thousand times longer and more difficult. For the first time since America had entered the war, he offered a silent prayer of gratitude for being home.

He gave Greta a hug. "Are you coming back?" she asked in a tear-choked voice.

"Of course. You heard the sheriff. I'll be home in a few days." He turned to Harlan and placed his hand on the boy's shoulder. "You be the man around here while I'm gone, all right? Help Mother with the chores." Harlan gave a solemn nod, his chin trembling.

"Don't tell anyone what's happened," Friedrick added. "All right?"

Elsa pulled him into a tight embrace. "We will be praying for you."

"Save supper for me on Wednesday," he said, easing back. He tried to laugh, but it came out strained. "I can walk home. Don't worry about driving into town."

With a wave good-bye, he walked to the sheriff's car and climbed inside. Sheriff Tate turned the car around and headed down the road toward Hilden. Friedrick hunched his shoulders over the bag in his lap—he didn't need anyone recognizing him.

Too soon the sheriff parked the car in front of the jail. Friedrick climbed from the vehicle and pulled his cap down as he followed behind Sheriff Tate. With his eyes focused on the sidewalk, he didn't see the woman in front of him until he'd bumped into her. Copies of the *Ladies' Home Journal* fluttered to the ground.

"I apologize," Friedrick said, kneeling to help her gather her magazines. As he handed the woman her belongings, he glanced at her face. Fear turned his gut to ice as he recognized her—it was Mr. Foster's secretary. Friedrick had spoken to her once, when he'd seen the superintendent about the school job, but her eyes widened in recognition, too.

He thrust the last few magazines at her and hurried through the jail door the sheriff held open. The feeling of dread churning inside him worsened as Friedrick followed the man down the line of cells. Two of the four were occupied. Sheriff Tate locked him in the third and mumbled something about supper in another hour. Then the sheriff turned on his heel and marched away, his footsteps reverberating off the stone walls and metal bars.

Friedrick sank onto one of the two cots inside the cell and dropped his bag beside him. Surely the secretary would tell the superintendent she'd seen Friedrick climbing out of the sheriff's car and entering the jail. He groaned and rested his head in his hands. Where would they get the money for his father's medicine if Friedrick lost his job?

He lifted his chin and gazed at the bare stone wall across from him. The cell was chilly and smelled of unwashed bodies and mold. Thank goodness he'd come in Elsa's place. He hated to think of her here, cold and alone.

The whole unfortunate day caught up with him, seeping exhaustion into every muscle. Friedrick shoved his bag onto the stone floor and lay down on the cot.

Have you abandoned us, God? he questioned, his eyes on the stone ceiling above. He stewed in his anger and weariness for a few minutes until he remembered something Elsa often said—*Trouble comes before the dawn, but the sun will always follow.*

Humbled, he shut his eyes and offered another prayer. *Forgive my doubts. I need this job, but if Thy will for me and my family is for greater things, help me find peace.*

He reached into his bag and pulled out the book Greta had packed for him. A sardonic smile lifted one corner of his mouth. His sister had chosen *Alice's Adventures in Wonderland* from Elsa's collection of German-printed books, which meant he'd have to be careful reading it here.

Resting the book next to him on the cot to hide the cover, Friedrick opened to the first page. Perhaps the story would erase the memory of the secretary's startled gaze from his mind, at least for a time. If nothing else, he could suddenly relate to the plight of young Alice. Today, his own world felt every bit as mixed up and bewildering as Wonderland.

* * *

The instant she woke up Monday morning, Livy's gaze flew to the war bond poster she'd set on top of the bureau. As she dressed, she kept shooting glances at it. Every time she did, she saw Friedrick's face from the day before—the frustration and confusion at her coolness. Guilt coated her stomach, making it difficult to swallow her breakfast.

She might have saved them both from Mr. Foster's notice, but she wasn't sure Friedrick would agree with the way she'd handled things. Especially after all he'd done for her.

She eyed the poster once more, then moved to the door. She wouldn't hang it until she'd explained everything to Friedrick. Surely he would forgive her behavior once he knew her reasons for it.

The morning air wrapped itself around her as she hurried to the school. Shivering, she lit a fire in the stove and prepared her classroom. The students filed in on time, exclaiming over her return, except for Harlan and Greta. They hadn't been late since her first day here. Were they sick?

Livy set aside her concern to begin class. The palpable excitement of her students brought a lift to her own mood. Twenty minutes ticked by before Harlan and Greta entered the room and slipped into their desks. Neither child looked at her as they pulled out their readers.

"Harlan," Livy said in a soft voice as she knelt beside his desk, "you and Greta will need to clean erasers during recess for being tardy."

He nodded, his gaze riveted to his desk.

"Are you feeling sick?"

"No, Miss Campbell," he mumbled.

"Were you helping Friedrick with his chores again?"

He shook his head.

She wanted to question him further, but one of the other students asked for help. The rest of the morning passed uneventfully. At recess, Harlan and Greta ate their lunches, then took the erasers outside for cleaning. Any attempt at conversation with either one proved futile.

Anxiety spoiled Livy's appetite again. Had Friedrick told his siblings about the awkward conversation between them in town? If she could apologize to him, she felt certain all would be right.

The hands of the clock seemed to move slower and slower as the afternoon passed. Livy busied herself with helping the children with mathematics and analyzing the caterpillar one of the older boys had caught and put in a Mason jar. All the while, though, her ears were listening for the sound of Friedrick's wagon.

When the last hour of class finally rolled around and he still hadn't arrived, Livy told herself he must have been waylaid by some chore around the farm. He wouldn't place his anger at her over his job at the school.

By the time she dismissed the students, though, Friedrick had yet to appear. Livy's concern turned to alarm when Harlan and Greta prepared to leave with the rest of the class.

"Is your brother coming to work on the school?" Livy asked Harlan in a nonchalant voice as she tidied up the room.

From the corner of her eye, she saw him throw a glance at his sister. "Uh, no, ma'am. He isn't coming today."

Livy averted her face so they wouldn't see her worried frown. "Is Friedrick unwell?"

"He just can't come. That's all."

What would prevent Friedrick from doing his job? A sudden thought made Livy bite the inside of her cheek. Perhaps Friedrick planned to come to the school much later, after she'd gone to her cabin. How was she supposed to explain things then?

On impulse, Livy called after the two children as they moved toward the door. "May I walk you home?" If Friedrick wouldn't come to her, she would go to him.

Harlan's face scrunched in confusion, but Greta smiled shyly. "Why'd you wanna do that, Miss Campbell?" the boy asked.

Livy grabbed her coat from off the back of her chair. "Because it's a beautiful afternoon. And I want to spend it with two of my favorite pupils." She lowered her voice and glanced surreptitiously around the room. "But don't tell anyone else—about the favorite part."

Greta giggled and walked over to place her hand inside Livy's. The small fingers within her grasp reminded Livy of her brothers. Tom had held her tiny hand like this when she'd been younger. She coughed against the rise of emotion the memory provoked. "Is that all right, Harlan, if I join you two?"

He shrugged and raced toward the door, but not before Livy caught the smile he tried to hide. Whatever had made the boy uncomfortable earlier had been forgotten. Livy locked the school, and she and Greta headed up the road. Harlan was already a ways ahead of them.

"Is Friedrick going to come to the school tomorrow?" she asked, keeping her tone light. "Or is he busy with spring planting?"

Greta stared down at the dirt beneath their shoes. "He won't be here until Wednesday when he gets—" She gasped softly as if she'd said too much and clamped her lips together.

Livy furrowed her eyebrows. What had Greta been about to say? She decided to change the subject to ease the girl's discomfort. Things would make sense once she and Friedrick had talked.

"Your reading is really quite good for someone so young, Greta. Do you read a lot at home?"

Greta lifted her chin and beamed. "Friedrick reads the Bible to us every night and sometimes he lets me read some of the words. Then he reads another book like Mama's fairy tale book. That's my favorite. But I can't read that one 'cause it's in German and I can't read German."

It was the longest speech Livy had heard from her. She could easily picture Friedrick reading to his brother and sister. Her own parents had done the same with her and her siblings when Livy had been young, and yet she couldn't imagine Robert doing such a thing with his children someday. Thank goodness she'd had the courage to end things with him.

"What's your favorite fairy tale?" she asked Greta.

"Hmm. Probably the princess ones."

Livy listened to Greta chatter on, as entertained by her retelling of the favorite stories as she was with how much the girl could talk when prompted. Harlan stayed in front of them. Every so often, he'd stop and let them nearly catch up to him before he hurried ahead again. The day felt cooler than the one before. But Livy's coat and the exercise kept her warm enough.

When they reached the Wagner farm, Livy was surprised to find it larger than she remembered from driving past it on the way to the dance hall. Her parents' place might be bigger still, but at least her father had the help of her siblings—and maybe a neighbor boy, if she had anything to do with it. Friedrick, on the other hand, was running this place on his own.

The front yard with its white picket fence appeared tidy and the two-story frame house boasted a nice porch and gabled windows. Harlan let himself in the back door, while she and Greta ambled after him. Livy glanced in the direction of the barn and the outlying fields, hoping to catch sight of a familiar tall figure.

"Do you know where Friedrick is working today? I'd like to speak to him."

Greta's cheeks flushed and she pulled her hand from Livy's grasp. "Friedrick isn't—"

"Hello," a heavily accented voice interrupted.

Mrs. Wagner stood at the back stoop, an apron tied around her faded cotton dress.

"Afternoon, Mrs. Wagner. It's nice to see you again," Livy said in a cheerful voice. She hadn't forgotten the wary look the woman had given her when Friedrick had walked her home after church, all those weeks ago. Or the fact that the woman was friends with some of the gossip-mongers at the German church.

"Miss Campbell. How do you do?"

"I'm well. Thank you." Livy watched the woman shoot a silent question at Greta, a suspicious glint in her blue eyes. "I hope you don't mind that I walked the children home. I know Friedrick normally picks them up, but he wasn't there today and I wanted to...to...talk to him. If that's all right."

"No, no. Not today." Mrs. Wagner shook her head. "Friedrick cannot talk today. He is not...well."

So he was ill. Odd that his siblings hadn't said as much. "I'm sorry. Is he very sick?"

"I cannot say. Thank you for walking the children. Good day." She cast another guarded look at Livy, then waved Greta inside. As the girl walked over, her mother scolded her in German.

"But, Mama, I didn't say anything about the secret," Greta protested as she paused on the doorstep. "Honest."

Secret? Livy took a step backward. She hadn't meant to get Greta into trouble.

Mrs. Wagner said something else in German, but Greta shook her blond head vigorously. "I didn't tell her about the empty bottle either."

Speaking in low tones, Greta's mother placed a protective hand on her daughter's shoulder as if to shield her. Livy pressed her lips together in frustration. Why did she constantly feel like the enemy?

"She may not be German, Mama, but she's nice." Greta threw a sorrowful glance at Livy and waved. "Bye, Miss Campbell."

"Good-bye, Greta," Livy managed to get out before Elsa shut the door.

She gazed up at the second-story windows. Which bedroom was Friedrick's? Her cheeks warmed at the question, and she spun back around to face the road.

What kind of ailment did he have? She guessed it had to be bad if no one would volunteer more information. A tremor of worry ran through her. Would he be all right? She didn't like the thought of him being ill. If only she'd been allowed to talk to him or been able to help in some way.

As she walked back toward the school, Livy thought over the things Greta had said to Elsa. What had the girl meant about a secret and an empty bottle? Livy shook her head. It didn't make sense, unless…Panic crept over her skin and she shivered.

Could Friedrick be drinking—like Robert? She'd never smelled alcohol on him or noticed any unusual behavior, but she hadn't discovered Robert's drinking troubles until they'd spent a lot of time together.

Her thoughts tripped faster and faster toward the awful and inevitable conclusion. How well did she really know Friedrick anyway? They'd talked in the afternoons when he came to work at the school, but the only evenings she'd spent in his company were the time they'd gone to the dance hall and the drive home the other week. He could easily hide a problem with alcohol from her. Perhaps he'd even been clever enough to hide it from his siblings until now. After all, Robert's father still had no idea his son was imbibing.

The horrible truth knifed through her, the pain of it stealing her breath. Livy stumbled to the side of the road and sank onto a fallen log. How could she have let herself be deceived again?

Friedrick had seemed much different than Robert—kinder, safer. She'd responded to him differently, too. His searching looks, teasing smile, and gentle touch had stirred something inside her that Robert never had. Only, like Robert's charms, everything she'd felt and experienced was a lie.

Anger mingled with the hurt squeezing at her heart and lungs. She'd been so concerned with how she'd acted yesterday, all in an effort to save Friedrick's job. And yet he'd been putting on an act, too—a self-serving one—by drinking behind her back. Livy dug her fingernails into her palms and squeezed her hands into fists. She wanted to hit something hard, ease the pain choking her.

When would she learn not to trust these men she knew so little about? She didn't need another drunken beau. *But Friedrick isn't a beau*, she protested.

Then why do I feel more betrayed by him than I did with Robert?

The question cut too deeply to examine wholeheartedly. Instead she conjured up a quick and logical answer. She'd come to rely on Friedrick and his friendship—that was all. But she refused to put herself through the same rigmarole she'd gone through with Robert. She would continue to be polite to Friedrick, for the sake of their jobs, but she would no longer be his friend.

First I lose Blanche, then Robert, and Tom, and now Friedrick.

Hot tears stung her eyes, but she refused to shed them. Thoughts of Tom sacrificing his life on the field of battle reminded Livy that she also had a duty to perform. It was teaching—she wasn't here to make or keep friends. She was here to do a job.

She sprang up from her makeshift seat and marched toward home. The walk was much shorter this time. She collected the bond poster from her cabin and returned to the school.

Livy nailed the poster to the front wall and stepped back. Her fury paled as she read the bold words through again: ARE YOU 100% AMERICAN? PROVE IT. BUY U.S. GOVERNMENT BONDS. She would likely offend some of her students' families—and Friedrick—but she'd been asked to do something by the superintendent and she needed to do it.

Her chin high, she headed for the door. From now on, she'd concentrate solely on her teaching position—and avoid interacting with Friedrick as much as possible.

Chapter Nine

"Here's your breakfast," Sheriff Tate called out as he approached the cell where Friedrick and his cell mate, an old man, were both lying on their cots.

Friedrick stuffed his book beneath his pillow, grateful the sheriff still hadn't noticed it was printed in German. He sat up, the worn cot creaking in protest, and stretched his sore muscles. The bed was anything but comfortable, and sleep hadn't come easily the last three nights. He kept half expecting, half fearing, the superintendent to march into the jail and fire him. No one had come, though, except the old man the night before.

The sheriff unlocked the door and slid two trays across the floor. "You're free to go this afternoon, Wagner," he said, locking the door again.

Friedrick's stomach rumbled from the smell of the mush. The food was tasteless and uninteresting, but he forced himself to eat it anyway. The jail inmates were fed only twice a day. What he wouldn't give for some of Elsa's delicious cooking right now.

Balancing the tray on his knees, Friedrick wolfed down the bland oatmeal and overcooked toast. His cell mate continued to snore softly. He probably ought to wake the old man since the breakfast would be a thousand times worse once it cooled.

He didn't know much about his cell mate. The man had come in after dark, and after a friendly nod at Friedrick, he'd curled up onto the other cot and gone to sleep.

Friedrick finished eating and set his tray near the door. He hoisted the full one to give to the old man. Even as unappetizing as it was, the untouched food called at him to sneak a few bites to ward off the hunger still clawing at his belly. But he couldn't do it.

He cleared his throat loudly and approached the old man's cot. When the noise failed to rouse him, Friedrick gave the bony shoulder a gentle shake with his free hand.

The man's eyes flew open, a wild look in their gray depths. He tried to rise, but his stiff body wouldn't cooperate. He collapsed onto his side once more.

"Sorry to wake you," Friedrick said. "The sheriff brought breakfast, and I figured you might want to eat it while it's hot."

The old man allowed Friedrick to help him sit up. "*Danke schön.*"

"*Bitte schön,*" Friedrick responded automatically as he handed over the tray. He hadn't expected his cell mate to be German-American, too.

Friedrick returned to his cot and his book as the old man began slurping the mush.

"Does the sheriff know you're reading a book in *German*?"

Friedrick studied the stranger. So that's how he'd known Friedrick would understand German. He hadn't expected such keen eyesight in one so old. "No, he doesn't, and he won't if neither of us tell."

The man barked a loud laugh. "Hah. I like you, boy. Vhat is your name?"

"Friedrick. And you?"

"Peter Hoffmann. My farm is due east of town." He spooned up more mush. Between swallows, he asked, "Vhat landed you in jail? Resisting enlistment?"

Friedrick shook his head. The matter-of-fact question from one of his own didn't incite the usual guilt. "No, I have a farm deferment, since my father's sick." He ran his finger over the lettering on the book's spine, thinking of Elsa and how much she prized these books. "My mother was overheard talking German on the telephone to Dr. Miller. She was needed at home, so I came in her place. What about you?"

The old man's barking laughter preceded his answer again. "This is the second time I have been thrown in jail for refusing to buy bonds."

Friedrick set his book aside, his interest peaked. No one he knew had resisted the wave of hate toward the Germans. "You told them no?"

"Ve are Mennonites, the vife and me. Ve do not support violence. That is vhy I vill not buy their bonds."

"Didn't you fear for your life by refusing?"

"Perhaps once or twice." Peter shrugged, but a determined glint filled his gray eyes. "I think they fear having my death on their hands, so they do not threaten real harm. They have ransacked my barn and house and painted them yellow. But I vill not give in, even if it means long days in this place." He waved his spoon at the stone walls and metal bars.

Peter's story infused Friedrick with the hope of vindication. What if he and his family were to resist? What if they refused to buy liberty bonds next time, refused to let someone rob them of their savings because they were German-American?

Peter wiped his mouth with the back of his sleeve and bent forward, his gaze focused intently on Friedrick. "Listen here, though, Friedrick. That is not always God's course, to make a stand. Every man has his own course to follow. This is mine, but you..." He pointed at Friedrick. "You must find yours."

Friedrick offered him a noncommittal nod and lay back down on his cot. He feigned interest in his book again, but inside, his optimism had changed to despair. Peter's last words echoed Pastor Schwarz's.

When would it be Friederick's time to resist—like Peter—his time to act against the injustice sweeping through their town? The idea of somehow avenging his people was dangerously tantalizing.

What of your family, though?

The simple question cooled his desire for revenge faster than water in winter. Friedrick couldn't bear the thought of his siblings or parents coming to harm or persecution because of his actions.

No longer glorying in thoughts of retribution, his mind ran through the questions he'd been asking himself for weeks. Was there nothing he could do to stem the tide of anti-German sentiment? Would he have served his people better by fighting overseas?

The old frustrations threatened to engulf him until a thought, quiet but reassuring, slipped forward. *There are those who need you here.*

"You mind helping me, Friedrick?" Peter asked, his words a near perfect echo of those in Friedrick's head. "I vould like to lie down again. My head is hurting something fierce."

Friedrick hurried to his feet. He took Peter's breakfast tray and set it on the floor beside his own. The man's toast hadn't been touched and Friedrick almost wished he'd eaten it earlier. He helped the old man lie back down on his cot, but before Friedrick could return to his own bed, Peter gripped his arm with surprising strength.

"You did right by coming here for your mother," Peter murmured, his voice low enough it wouldn't carry to the other cells. "You keep looking after those you love and you vill know if that means resisting or not. God vill let you know and make you stronger for it either vay. Remember that, boy."

Peter released him and shut his eyes. Friedrick walked back to his cot, marveling at the old man's perceptiveness. The way ahead might not look clear to him, but it didn't mean it wasn't plain as day to the Lord.

His mind more at ease than it had been in days, Friedrick settled down to read. Sometime later, a low groan from Peter jerked his attention from the page. The wan light coming through the barred window made judging the time difficult, but Friedrick guessed a few hours had passed since the man had fallen asleep. The temperature inside the cell had dropped, too. There had to be a storm brewing outside.

Friedrick sat up and swung his legs over his cot. "Are you all right, Peter?"

Another groan emanated from Peter's side of the cell followed by a loud whisper, "Is it varm in here, Friedrick? I feel so varm." Peter pushed his blanket to the floor. A sheen of sweat shone on his lined forehead.

Friedrick moved to Peter's cot and placed his hand on the man's brow. He wasn't just damp with sweat; he was hot to the touch. "Hold on, Peter. I'll call for the sheriff."

Hopefully the man would release Peter and let him return home to rest under his family's care. Friedrick went to the cell door and hollered for Sheriff Tate. After a long minute, the sheriff lumbered over, a deep frown on his clean-shaven face. "What's all the fuss, Wagner?"

"It isn't me. Peter Hoffman here is sick." Friedrick curled his hands around the cold bars. "He's got a fever and was complaining earlier of a headache."

The sheriff muttered a curse and unlocked the door. He stood over Peter for a moment, then touched the man's forehead as Friedrick had done. "Jiminy. He's roasting." Peter coughed and rolled onto his side. "I'd better phone Doc Miller."

In his hurry, the sheriff forgot to lock the cell door behind him. Friedrick eyed the unlatched door. He might be tempted to slip out early, but he wouldn't. Not until he'd seen his new friend cared for.

As he waited for the doctor, Friedrick placed Peter's forgotten blanket onto the end of the man's cot. He walked to the window and peered through the bars and glass at the sky. Dark clouds crowded against one another like frightened animals. He considered telephoning his mother to bring the wagon, then changed his mind. Elsa and the children would be busy getting the farm ready for the storm.

Friedrick returned to his bed and attempted reading again, though he wished he could do something to help Peter instead. By the time he heard the sound of footfalls coming down the hall, the cell had grown dim from the storm, making it difficult to see the words on the page. He stuffed the book under his pillow and stood.

Dr. Miller entered the cell, the sheriff right behind him. The doctor showed no surprise at finding Friedrick there. Elsa must have explained the situation to him when he came to visit Friedrick's father Sunday night.

The doctor examined Peter, then returned his instruments to his black bag. "He may only have a cold," he said to Sheriff Tate before climbing to his feet. "But I think you would be wise to send him home, Walter." There was a note of urgency in the doctor's voice that belied the simple prognosis.

"A little cold, huh?" Sheriff Tate drew the doctor toward the cell door, though Friedrick could easily overhear him. "Is that all it is, Hans?"

Friedrick sat back down on his cot and feigned interest in his bag as he waited for the doctor's answer. The familiarity between the two men wasn't lost on him. Had they been friends for years or only since the doctor had changed his name? Would the sheriff be so quick to throw the doctor in here if he spoke German in public?

Dr. Miller blew out a heavy sigh, his face haggard. He leaned toward the sheriff and spoke in hushed tones. Friedrick caught a few words—something about influenza and different symptoms. It didn't mean much to him. Now that the doctor had encouraged Peter's release, he was anxious to be going himself.

"What do you mean, possible *casualties*?" the sheriff barked at the conclusion of the doctor's speech. The word seemed to echo in the small cell. Friedrick chanced a look at Dr. Miller, but the man's solemn gaze remained on Sheriff Tate.

"I do not know the whole story, Walter. But I would send the old man home—for good."

"But Hans—"

"I would send them all home. We do not want this thing spreading. Drive Mr. Hoffmann back to his farm. Do you have a mask here?"

"One of them gauze things?" The sheriff shook his head.

"Go buy one at the drugstore if you do not have one and then drive the man home." He stepped toward Friedrick. "Be careful around your father, Friedrick. If any of you catch a cough or fever, stay away from him until you are well."

Friedrick answered with a nod, though he didn't understand all the fuss over a possible cold. At the offhanded mention of a scratchy throat, Elsa would quickly make one of her herb poultices and quarantine the person to bed. Friedrick disliked wearing the potent concoction, but he'd long ago realized the benefits. He and his siblings were rarely sick for very long and never with anything serious.

"I guess you're free to go then, son," Sheriff Tate said to him.

Friedrick gathered his things, slung his bag over his

shoulder, and crossed to the other cot. "Take care, Peter." He gently squeezed the man's shoulder. "Get well, friend."

"Good-bye, Friedrick," Peter whispered.

Friedrick followed the doctor and the sheriff from the cell. Neither one paid him any attention as he let himself out the jail's main door. Rain splattered the sidewalk outside. Ducking under the eaves of the building, Friedrick removed his coat and cap from his bag and put them on. He hunched his shoulders against the damp and set off down the street.

The drops changed to sheets of rain before he'd even cleared the block. Soon the street emptied of its few occupants. Friedrick kept his head bent, though that meant the rain slipped down his coat collar.

He trudged along, doing his best to avoid the puddles, past the homes and farms at the town's edge. Before long, his legs and back began to ache. Friedrick stopped to stretch his sore muscles. Clearly the inactivity of three nights in jail and two unsatisfying meals a day had drained him of his normal stamina.

Soon sweat broke out on his neck and arms. Friedrick loosened his coat and took it off, welcoming the rush of cold, wet air that swirled around him. He'd put it back on in a moment. The plummeting rain made it difficult to see very far down the road, but he figured he was nearing the school when a feeling of complete exhaustion stole over him. He tripped on something and nearly fell.

Friedrick removed his cap and let the rain wash some of the sweat from his forehead. Perhaps he was coming down with a cold, too. He returned the soaked hat to his head and continued on despite the sweat and fatigue. When he caught sight of Livy's cabin, he halted again.

He didn't like the idea of asking Livy for assistance, not after her coldness toward him in town. But he instinctively knew he wouldn't make it home in one piece if he didn't rest for a few minutes, out of the rain.

Once he'd dried off a bit and had some water to drink, he would head out again. He could surely be home by supper. The thought of something warm and filling to eat spurred him the last hundred yards to Livy's doorstep.

* * *

Livy glanced up from her sketchbook at the rain spattering against the windowpane. Thankfully the weather hadn't turned stormy until after she'd dismissed the children for the day. She didn't like the idea of canceling school—again—due to the weather, though she imagined the children might welcome another respite after yesterday.

The entire class had come in as noisily as usual, but the happy sounds had quickly evaporated when they'd noticed the poster at the front of the room. Livy had done her best to appear unruffled by their reactions. In a calm tone, she'd explained Mr. Foster's request and the purpose of liberty bonds before she had them pull out their reading primers.

Still, she couldn't forget the poster. It hung like a vulture behind her. Both she and her students hadn't been able to leave fast enough at the end of school the past two days. Unlike the children, though, Livy had little to distract her from her own guilt and loneliness.

If only Friedrick hadn't been absent from his job the past three days, then she would have had someone to talk to. The thought of conversing with a drunk was preferable to being in the solitary cabin with her memories of home and Tom.

How was the rest of her family faring? she wondered for the hundredth time. She'd written them a letter the day before, but it would take a few days before she received a reply. Did her siblings or parents harbor any of the same misgivings she felt at moving on with life so soon after Tom's death? Had she made the right decision by returning to Hilden? The silence held no answers.

She cleared her throat to disrupt the awful quiet and flipped through her sketchbook. More drawings filled it now. There was a picture of her sister, Mary, dressed in one of their grandmother's old gowns from the attic. Another of her parents, standing beside the lilac bushes. One of her and her older brothers, as children, in the hayloft at home. She'd even sketched one of Robert, looking as handsome and charismatic as he had his first week home from the war, before she knew the truth about him. This was how she wanted to remember him—his smile charming, his eyes bright with promise.

A sudden knock at the door yanked her from her despondent thoughts. Who would be out in this weather? Perhaps one of the children who lived close by had forgotten something inside the school. Livy unlocked the door and opened it just enough to peer out. A tall man in drenched clothes stood on her doorstep, his head down. Her heart beat fast with fear until he lifted his chin.

"Friedrick?" She pulled the door open wider. "What are you doing here?" Her surprise soon gave way to sharp annoyance when she remembered his secret. "What is it you want? You can't fix anything in this rain."

"I've been in town," he rasped, "and I'm on my way home."

"Where's your wagon?" She glanced past him but couldn't see much through the pounding rain.

"It's at home. I walked."

Probably because Elsa refused to drive him into town to buy his illegal alcohol. *Well, good for her.* Livy would be firm with him, too, something she should have done with Robert from the beginning.

"May I come in?" He voiced the question pleasantly enough, but Livy didn't miss the firm set of his whiskered jaw. He looked as though he hadn't shaved in days.

How could he be mad at *her*? She might not have been amiable during their last encounter, but she wasn't the one drinking.

To her chagrin, the old sympathies she used to feel for Robert blossomed inside her, bringing indecision. She wanted to refuse to help him, but his handsome face looked unusually pale and his clothes were soaked.

Oh, bother. She couldn't very well leave him outside. One cup of coffee, she told herself, then she'd go ask one of the neighbors to drive him home.

With a sigh, she stepped back and held the door open for him.

"Thanks." He stumbled over the doorstep as he entered and didn't seem at all bothered when he tracked mud and water onto her floor.

Livy shut the door with an irritated growl and pointed to his feet. "Your boots."

"Sorry. I suppose I should..." He glanced at the door and swayed a moment. "I think I need to sit down." Without waiting for an invitation, he collapsed into one of the chairs at the table, dropping his things, and removed his cap. "My head is pounding."

I'm sure it is. "I'll make some coffee," she said curtly.

Livy made no attempt to hide her irritation as she banged about the kitchen, preparing water and getting the coffee bean canister.

"Sorry to impose. I would have kept going, if I hadn't felt so poorly..." He lowered his head onto his arms as if it were too heavy to hold up anymore.

Livy slammed the canister onto the counter and whirled around. "Don't play innocent with me, Friedrick Wagner. I know all about your drinking habit and the reason why Harlan and Greta have been sulking about school the past few days."

Friedrick lifted his head. "What?"

"I figured it out." The words hurt her to say. "The secret your family wouldn't tell me."

"What are you talking about?"

"Come on, Friedrick." She folded her arms against the rise of anger his denial created in her. "I'm not stupid. I know the signs of a hangover. I saw it over and over again with Robert, but this time—"

"I am not drunk, Livy." He twisted around to face her. His eyes blazed with barely controlled fury, though his tone remained calm. "I've never tasted a drop of alcohol, nor do I plan to."

Her rising ire deflated like a pricked balloon. "But...but...Elsa asked Greta if she told me about the secret, and Greta said something about a bottle." Livy sank back against the cupboard, her cheeks hot. She'd been so certain her conclusions had been right.

"When did you see Elsa?" He turned back to the table and fingered his cap.

"On Monday. When you didn't come after school, I walked Harlan and Greta home. I wanted to…" She let her voice trail off as fresh embarrassment washed over her.

Friedrick blew out his breath, his shoulders slumping. "Elsa meant the secret about me being taken to jail."

"To jail? Whatever for?"

"Because I'm German-American," he said, his voice hard.

Livy shook her head. None of this conversation was making sense. "I don't understand."

"Elsa was overheard speaking German on the telephone, a direct violation of the recent language law. My father needs her home more than me, so I went in her place. I've been in the Hilden jail since Sunday afternoon." Friedrick massaged his forehead. "I told my family to keep it a secret. I didn't want Mr. Foster finding out."

Shame clogged Livy's throat as she went back to making the coffee. Friedrick had gone in his stepmother's place? Such courage and love of family heaped more humiliation onto her already tormented conscience.

"How badly are you feeling?" she asked. There would be time enough when he felt better to explain the reason for her uncharacteristic indifference in town.

"Just tired and sore." He ran his hands through his hair, making it stand on end. "The old man sharing my cell had a cold. I must have caught it."

"Old man?" Livy poured the hot liquid into a mug.

"He resisted buying bonds because he's a Mennonite."

"So they threw him in jail?" Livy set the cup of coffee in front of Friedrick.

He wrapped his hands around the mug and stared at the dark liquid. "It doesn't matter who you are or what you believe if you're German-American. We can't speak our native language in church and the liberty bond people don't care if they're robbing families of their savings. That's the bottle Greta mentioned. It's the one with our extra cash and it's empty now. Which is why I had to get this job."

Livy dropped into the other chair. Her chest felt tight, like the wind had been knocked from her. Her thoughts were a snarled mess. Joel might be fighting Germans across the ocean, but most of the ones Livy had met here in Hilden were hardworking people who cared for their families.

After a few sips of coffee, Friedrick set down his mug and put on his cap. "I'd better go. My family will be wondering why I'm not back yet." He slowly stood, one hand gripping the table for support.

Livy leaped up in alarm. "You're in no condition to walk home, Friedrick. You need to rest and dry off some more."

He threw a glance around the tiny cabin. "I can't stay here. It wouldn't be proper."

"The school then," she suggested, though the image of the bond poster rose before her eyes. He was likely too ill to notice it. "I can stoke the fire and you can rest there until you feel well enough."

He rubbed a hand over his stubbled chin. "All right."

Friedrick struggled to put on his coat and heft his bag, but Livy sensed he didn't want her help. She pulled on her own coat and grabbed a blanket from the pile she'd brought from home.

They went outside and started through the rain toward the school. Friedrick's breathing became more labored after only a few feet. He stopped and lowered his bag to the wet ground. "Just . . . give me a moment."

Livy worried the inside of her cheek. He had to be suffering from more than a simple cold if he could hardly walk without being fatigued. "Can I help?"

He eyed her skeptically, but he finally relented. "Would you mind carrying my bag? It isn't very heavy, but . . ."

She accepted the pack from him and slowed her pace to match his as he slogged forward again. The short distance to the school took twice as long as normal. When they reached the building, Friedrick sagged against the door frame, while Livy unlocked the door. She glanced up to find those blue eyes intently watching her from beneath his cap. Sick as he may be, he looked quite handsome with his blond beard and damp hair.

"Thank you . . . for your help," he murmured.

Despite her concern for his condition and her lingering embarrassment over misjudging him, the low tremor of his voice and the way his arm rested against her shoulder made Livy's stomach twist with anticipation. Robert hadn't thanked her—not once—when she'd cared for him while he was drunk or afterward when he was sober again.

"Y-You're welcome." She wanted to stay there, especially when his gaze flicked to her lips, but a rush of moist air at her skirt hem snapped her back to the present.

Livy opened the door and Friedrick stumbled inside. Thankfully the room still retained some of the warmth from the fire she'd kept burning in the stove throughout the day. She helped Friedrick out of his wet coat and stowed his things in the closet.

"Sit down, near the stove," she directed. *Away from that poster.*

Friedrick sank down onto one of the desks as Livy pushed some of the others away from the stove to make more room for him. She spread her blanket on the empty floor and checked the fire. She added some kindling to the glowing embers, her back to Friedrick.

"I see you hung a war bond poster."

The wood in her hand clattered to the floor as Livy whirled around.

"Even you don't believe we're really, truly American, do you, Livy?"

The rawness of his words didn't wound her half as badly as the disappointment emanating from him. That hurt worst of all. Only moments ago he'd stared at her with sincere appreciation, as if he might kiss her.

"Friedrick, it's not what you—"

He shook his head. "I need to lie down." He stumbled onto the blanket, knocking his hat to the floor.

"I didn't want to hang the poster." She picked up the wood she'd dropped and returned to stoking the fire. The rest of her words came tumbling out, too fast to stop. "Mr. Foster gave it to me after church on Sunday and told me to hang it. He also asked me if you'd said anything against the war, and I started to think of all the things *I'd* said. Then I saw you on the street and Mr. Foster was still down the block. I wanted to save us both from losing our jobs." She pulled in a shaky breath. "That was why I acted the way I did."

No response came. Livy shut the stove door and turned around. Friedrick's eyes were closed, his chest rising and falling with even breaths. Had he heard any of her explanation?

"Friedrick?"

When he didn't answer, Livy lifted his cap off the floor. She turned the wet wool hat over in her hands. It looked exactly like those she'd seen on her brothers and countless other young men. Was Friedrick any different from them? Like Tom or Joel, he'd been born in America. He worked hard; he cared about his family. In many ways—when it came to loyalty and love—his family wasn't so different from her own.

Fresh guilt washed over her as she set the hat on a nearby desk. Her gaze jumped to the ugly poster. She couldn't leave it up now, even with the superintendent's impending visit. If she did, she was showing she agreed with what was happening to Friedrick's people. And she didn't.

Livy stepped softly to the front of the room. With a quick yank, she tore the poster free from its nail. What should she do with it now? She eyed the stove, and a feeling of warmth and confidence filled her. It was the same emotion she'd felt when she applied for the teaching job, the same one she'd had when she drove away from Robert's house last week.

The poster was too big to fit through the stove door, so Livy slipped into the coat closet to tear the thing into smaller pieces. How good it felt to rip the offending words to shreds. When there was nothing left of the poster but two fistfuls of jagged paper, she went to the stove and shoved the scraps inside.

She would have to come up with something else to prove the school's patriotism to Mr. Foster, but first, she needed to help Friedrick get well. While he still slept, Livy hurried back through the rain to her house. She collected water from the pump and set some of it boiling on the cabin stove for tea. The stew she'd prepared earlier that afternoon would be thoroughly cooked soon and would surely give Friedrick needed energy.

She envisioned what he would say when he saw the blank spot where the poster had been. Livy smiled at the thought as she carried the remaining water back to the school. Once he saw what she'd done and heard her apology for her silly behavior, they could surely go back to being good friends.

* * *

A dry throat nudged Friedrick to wakefulness, though he didn't open his eyes. He'd had the strangest dream—Livy had an American flag draped around her shoulders and kept asking, *How American are you, Friedrick?*

He attempted to swallow and ended up releasing a hoarse cough instead. "Water," he murmured to the person he sensed nearby.

"Friedrick! You're awake," a female voice exclaimed. A voice that sounded like Livy's. But he hadn't seen her since Sunday when she'd given him the cold shoulder in town.

He pried open his eyelids to find Livy's lovely face above him, her gaze filled with concern. The schoolhouse stove loomed behind her. The object brought back vague memories of walking from town through the rain.

"Water," he repeated.

Livy dragged a bucket closer. "Can you sit up?"

Friedrick rose to his elbows, but every muscle in his body felt tethered to the floor. "I think...I need..."

Despite the fog filling his head, he relished the pleasant scent of Livy's hair as she assisted him into a sitting position. Her eyes lifted to his as she lingered beside him, her hand on his arm. Friedrick heard her breath catch in her throat, in contrast to the worry pinching her forehead. He wanted to smooth away those lines, rub his thumb over those inviting red lips, hold her close. But his body had turned traitor.

"Thank you," he whispered.

She cleared her throat and scooted away from him to fill a ladle with water. Friedrick drained it of liquid.

"More?" Livy asked.

He shook his head. As she reached for the ladle, he managed to capture her fingers beneath his. He'd been angry at her, but he couldn't recall why now. "Livy," he murmured.

"Yes?" She leaned toward him, her expression expectant.

Friedrick tried to form what he wanted to say, how to tell her how much he cared about her. But a wave of dizziness washed over him. He coughed again and slumped to the blanket. "I'm sorry...I..."

Disappointment momentarily filled her green eyes before she placed a reassuring hand on his shoulder. "It's all right. Just rest. I'm going to get you some tea."

Too tired to nod, he watched her leave, then turned toward the clock. It was a quarter to six. He'd been asleep for more than two hours. Elsa would be worried. He needed to get home.

Friedrick attempted to sit up on his own, but the effort left him short of breath and brought another wave of dizziness. He collapsed onto the blanket and shut his eyes against the dread making his head throb. How could he provide for his family if he was too weak to even stand? Maybe Livy's tea would give him enough strength to get himself home.

As he lay there thinking about her—her beauty, her strength, her smile—an unpleasant memory chewed at his awareness. Livy had done something before he'd fallen asleep, something that had frustrated him. What was it?

The memory of the poster smashed into him like a fist to the stomach. No wonder he'd dreamt what he did. He'd believed Livy's attitude toward German-Americans, and him in particular, was different, but her choice to hang such a poster confirmed it wasn't.

Why then was she bothering to help him? He could only conclude it was because they weren't in public, where others might see. If she were ashamed to acknowledge him as her friend publicly, then that would explain why she'd been aloof in town and why she'd hung the poster in the school.

The clatter of the door made him jerk open his eyes. Livy entered with a kettle in one hand and a cup in the other. The tea no longer sounded appetizing.

"I'd better go," he announced. He ignored the pounding in his head and forced himself onto his elbows to illustrate his intent to leave. "My family needs me, and we wouldn't want to cause you embarrassment by my staying."

"Embarrassment?" Her brow furrowed. "You're sick, Friedrick. I'm not going to turn you out into the rain, just to stop a few people from gossiping."

"I wasn't talking about gossip." He crawled to a seated position and ran his hand over his face. The fatigue was quickly draining his anger. "Why did you hang the poster, Livy? Because you're embarrassed to know me, because your brother was killed by the Germans?"

She set the kettle and cup on the floor and knelt beside him. "I was afraid, not embarrassed."

"Afraid of what?" he demanded, not caring that it sounded harsh.

Her words were spoken quietly. "Mr. Foster insisted I hang the poster. He also asked me if you'd said anything pro-German. I realized right then how much people are watching and listening. I didn't want to get either of us in trouble."

"Mr. Foster asked about me?"

The unease Friedrick had felt after running into the man's secretary rekindled inside him. Had the woman reported him to the superintendent yet? Would Mr. Foster show up one of these days and fire Friedrick?

"He was right down the street while we were talking in town on Sunday. I was afraid he'd notice if we acted more than . . . slightly acquainted." Her cheeks went pink. "I hung the poster because I thought I had to do it, but I took it down." Livy gestured toward the front of the classroom.

Friedrick glanced over to see the poster was no longer hanging on the wall. "Maybe you ought to put it back up," he said, more to himself than to her. He didn't want to be the cause of Livy losing her job—her dream. He might have already put her reputation at stake by staying here so long.

"I can't put it back. I burned it," Livy said, her voice firm. She'd clearly crossed a line in her mind. "It's not fair to you or the children or..." She swallowed. "To their families. We'll have to come up with some other way to show Mr. Foster our patriotism when he comes to visit."

Our patriotism. Her words, combined with her charming expression of determination, stirred hope within him. Hope for deepening their friendship, in spite of everything that had happened. He wanted nothing more than to kiss her, but he began coughing.

"Do you want some tea?" Without waiting for his response, she brought the teacup to his lips. The hot liquid soothed his sore throat, but only for a moment. Another coughing spell tightened Friedrick's chest.

"I've got to go," he said when his coughs subsided. He'd wasted enough time lying around the last few days.

Livy crossed her arms. "You can't walk right now, and I don't have a wagon. Sleep a little more, and then I'll have one of the neighbors drive you home."

Friedrick wanted to argue, but it required too much effort. The steeliness in Livy's gaze told him he'd likely lose anyway. He slid back onto the blanket and shut his eyes once more. Livy leaned near, evident by the vanilla scent he smelled again, and placed something beneath his head to act as a pillow. Her presence was as good as any medicine. He told himself he'd rest for a bit longer, then he would head home and reassure his worried family all was right.

Chapter Ten

Livy stopped pacing and stole another glance at Friedrick from across the schoolroom. She'd never observed a man sleeping before, except for Robert when he'd passed out from drinking. But that didn't count. His drunken snoring hadn't made her pulse skip faster like the sight of Friedrick's relaxed face and her awareness of him slumbering a few feet away.

Watching this strong, kind man sleep stirred emotion deep within her and resurrected the thrill she'd felt when he looked as if he meant to kiss her earlier. Thankfully Friedrick's coughing had jarred them both back to reality— it wouldn't do to be kissing him in the schoolhouse, alone.

Her pacing resumed along the north wall of windows, her steps soft, her arms folded. She couldn't deny a strong attraction to Friedrick, which had quickly replaced her anger over their earlier misunderstanding. He was still sick, though. There'd be time enough for sorting out her feelings once he was better.

A hoarse cough escaped Friedrick's lips followed by a violent shiver, which shook his body. He muttered something indiscernible.

Livy went to his side and placed her hand on his forehead. It felt hot. Fear prickled up her back—Friedrick wouldn't be going anywhere tonight. She searched the room for something to help him and remembered the water bucket. She plunged a corner of his blanket into the water. After wringing it out, she pressed it gently to Friedrick's face and neck. Was there more she should be doing?

At her touch, he stirred and opened his eyes. "Livy?" His voice sounded as dry and thin as sunburnt grass. "What are you doing here?" He blinked slowly. "W-Where am I?"

She put a finger to his mouth to shush him. The feel of his lips beneath her skin sent a bolt of emotion up her arm, in sharp contrast to her growing worry.

"Shh. You don't need to talk; just rest. You're in the schoolhouse, remember? You were walking home from...town." No need to conjure up his experience at the jail, if he didn't remember right away. Livy wet the blanket again and wrung out the excess.

"You have a fever, but nothing a little water and tea can't fix." Her voice sounded too cheerful, even to herself. In his condition, though, Friedrick wouldn't notice.

"No." He shook his head. "I've got to get home. Elsa will be..." He drew a shaky breath and struggled to rise.

Livy grabbed his sleeve. "Friedrick, you need to lie still."

He lowered himself onto the makeshift bed and moaned. His lack of protest frightened her more than anything. "It hurts something awful."

"Your head?"

He dipped his chin and shut his eyes.

"I'm going to warm some more tea." She rose to her knees.

"Don't go," he whispered. "Not yet."

Livy sank back down onto the floor, concern lodging in her throat. She grasped his hand. His skin instantly heated hers. "I'll stay, Friedrick. I'll stay."

The pain on his face eased at her promise. He mumbled something and drifted back to sleep. Livy held his hand, her thumb stroking his knuckles, until she felt certain he was completely asleep. She dabbed the wet blanket around the edges of his forehead, hoping to cool his fever. The various shades of yellow-brown in his hair beckoned her fingers. She brushed through the soft strands and traced the prickly stubble of his jawline. His face felt foreign and yet familiar beneath her touch.

Another cough shook Friedrick, bringing Livy back to the present. She blushed and removed her hand from his face. Thank goodness he was asleep.

She hopped up to add more wood to the stove. She stoked the flames, then wandered over to the windows. The rain had lightened considerably, but it would be dark soon. She darted a look over her shoulder at Friedrick. Would her parents, or Mr. Foster, or the parents of her students approve of her being here by herself with him?

"It can't be helped," she firmly told herself. Hopefully she and the students wouldn't catch whatever Friedrick had. Just to be certain, she would cancel school tomorrow. That would give Friedrick more time to recover.

She returned to his makeshift bed. Finding him still

deep in sleep, she decided to heat more tea and check on the stew.

Livy hurried through the light rain to her cabin, shivering all the way. She'd lent her coat to Friedrick to use for a pillow. The smell of cooking meat and vegetables greeted her at the door and made her stomach grumble. She worked as quickly as she could to put the meal together, hoping Friedrick wouldn't wake in her absence.

Once she'd placed the kettle, the stew, two bowls, and an extra blanket in a crate, she walked slowly back to the school. The measured pace tore at her impatience, but she didn't want to slosh or drop anything.

The noise of Friedrick's coughing hit her full force as she stepped inside. Was it her imagination or did his coughs sound worse? Her stomach churned into knots.

"I'm here, Friedrick," she said, setting the box near the stove. "I went to heat the tea and get you some supper."

"I'm...not hungry," he croaked out, his eyes still shut.

Livy ladled the stew into one of the bowls and knelt next to him. "A little broth might help." She scooped up some stew and pressed the spoon to his mouth. "Come on," she coaxed. "Take a sip."

He frowned, but obeyed. She managed to get a few spoonfuls in him before another hacking cough vibrated through him.

"No more."

"All right." Livy heaved a sigh of resignation. She couldn't force him to eat.

She sat against one wall to eat her portion of the stew. What other ways could she help him? She'd tried everything she could think of, but none of her efforts seemed to be working. Concern soured her stomach and she set her nearly full bowl aside. It was time to telephone the doctor.

Livy bent down beside Friedrick and cupped his burning face. "Friedrick, which neighbors have a telephone?"

He didn't answer right away, prompting her to repeat the question. Finally he asked, "Why?"

"I need to phone the doctor."

"Don't need the doctor." He grunted and rolled onto his side, his back to her. "Just need a little more rest. It's only a—" A cough ended his sentence.

Livy didn't have the heart to argue with him. "I'm sure you're right, but I want to see if there's anything more I can do. Besides, someone should let Elsa know you're here."

The mention of his mother did the trick. "The Kellers...have a telephone."

The Kellers? Livy's heart dropped to her shoes. Of course the closest telephone would be in the home of the family who refused to let their children attend school while Livy was the teacher. There was no way around it, though. She'd face the Kellers' wrath for Friedrick.

"I'll be back soon." She removed her coat from beneath his head and replaced it with the extra blanket.

She quickly left the school before she lost her nerve. Raindrops pattered her head and coat, making Livy wish she'd grabbed her hat. She shoved her hands inside her pockets to keep them dry. If the Kellers didn't let her in, she'd have to trudge through the rain to someone else's house.

Another few minutes brought her to the Kellers' front yard. Their dog, Wilheim, growled at her approach.

"Remember me?" she soothed.

Wilheim's memory was clearly flawed. Instead of being pacified, the dog set to barking loudly. The front door flew open in response to his warning. A giant of a man—whom Livy assumed must be Mr. Keller—stepped onto the porch. He hollered at the dog in German before he noticed Livy.

"What you want?" he asked. He scowled as he looked her up and down.

Livy swallowed and lifted her chin. She was here for Friedrick. "I'm sorry to bother you so late, Mr. Keller."

"Who are you?"

The two Keller girls peered out from behind their father. Livy saw recognition on their faces.

"My name's Livy Campbell. I'm the new teacher at the schoolhouse and—"

"No." He shooed at her with a wave of one of his large hands. "No go to school. Not till Marta come back." He began to retreat into the house.

"Wait," Livy called out. She marched forward, ignoring Wilheim's low growl. She already knew the dog was harmless. "I'm not here about school this time. I'm here about Friedrick Wagner."

The man froze. "Friedrick? What?"

"He's sick, at the school. I need to telephone the doctor and Mrs. Wagner."

Mr. Keller eyed her warily. Livy held her breath. Would he refuse her request? Finally he blew out his breath and motioned her inside. "Come in."

Livy exhaled with relief. Now she wouldn't have to traipse through the rain to another farm. She moved up the steps and into the warm house.

"Come," Mr. Keller repeated, gesturing toward the back of the house.

She smiled at the two girls and followed their father down the hallway to the kitchen. Mrs. Keller stood at the sink, washing dishes, while their son, John, sat reading a book at the table. Both of them glanced up as Livy and Mr. Keller entered the room. Mrs. Keller's eyes widened. She spoke to her husband in German, her tone surprised and cross.

Mr. Keller shook his head and replied in their native tongue. Livy could only pick out Friedrick's name. Mrs. Keller studied Livy, then pointed to the telephone on the wall.

"Thank you." Livy lifted the earpiece and gave the hand crank a good turn.

"Number please," the operator said.

"I need the doctor in Hilden."

"One moment."

Livy tapped her foot on the wood floor, aware of the Kellers' curious stares against her back.

"This is Dr. Miller," a tired, accented voice said.

"Doctor, this is Livy Campbell. I'm the new teacher at Township School Number 1, northwest of Hilden. Friedrick Wagner is there now—resting at the school. He's sick. I'm wondering what can be done for him."

"Friedrick Wagner? I just saw him, this afternoon at the…"

Livy gripped the earpiece tighter, willing the doctor not to say "jail." If the operator overheard where Friedrick had been, the superintendent would know before long.

The doctor cleared his throat. "Tell me his symptoms, Miss Campbell."

She let out her breath in a whoosh. Friedrick's time in jail would remain a secret. "He has a fever and a cough, and he says his head hurts."

A heavy silence filled her ears. "Doctor?" Had they been disconnected? "Dr. Miller?"

"I will be there in thirty minutes."

"Should I have someone take him home in their wagon?"

"No!"

Livy jumped at the man's loud voice. "Wouldn't he do better resting at his own house?"

"I am sorry, Miss Campbell." He released a sigh. "It would be best if he stays where he is for now. Has anyone else been around him since his symptoms began?"

"No," Livy said, shaking her head.

"Good."

"I need to telephone Mrs. Wagner." She chose her next words carefully. "Friedrick went into town and hasn't been back home yet. What shall I tell her?"

"Tell her where he is and I am coming to attend to him. She is not to come see him. Will you make that clear?"

Livy frowned. His instructions sounded a bit rash, but she was no medical expert. "Yes, I'll tell her."

"With his father already sick," the doctor added.

"Oh, yes, right."

"I'm on my way, Miss Campbell."

"Thank you, Dr. Miller."

She hung up the earpiece and turned to the Kellers, who had taken seats beside their son at the kitchen table. "The doctor's coming."

They smiled, their relief evident, but Livy couldn't shake the unsettled feeling in the pit of her stomach. Did the doctor suspect Friedrick was ill with something serious? "May I call Mrs. Wagner now?"

Mr. Keller nodded.

Livy informed the operator she needed the Wagner residence this time. After a long moment, a frantic female voice answered. "Hello? Friedrick?"

"No, Mrs. Wagner. This is Livy Campbell."

Livy quickly explained the situation and repeated the doctor's admonition about the family staying home, at least for the present. With much reluctance in her voice, Elsa agreed to wait for word before coming to the school.

"He is being cared for?"

"Yes." Livy wanted to tell Elsa how much she prized Friedrick's friendship, but she couldn't—not over the telephone with others potentially listening.

She hung up, hoping she'd eased the woman's worry. Her own had only increased since leaving Friedrick at the school. She attempted a smile for the Kellers. "Thank you for letting me use your telephone."

Mrs. Keller went to the counter, where several loaves of bread sat cooling. "You take?" She handed Livy a loaf.

"That's very kind. Thank you." Maybe there was hope for having the Keller children return to school after all.

"I walk you back," Mr. Keller said. He led her out the kitchen door. Thankfully the rain had stopped.

Livy plodded along beside him, the warm bread tucked against her coat. Though Mr. Keller didn't say a word, his presence helped her feel safe.

At the door, he stopped. "You do good—caring for Friedrick. We bring food tomorrow."

"He's likely going home tomorrow," Livy protested kindly, "but I appreciate the bread."

As the man strode away, Livy slipped inside the half-darkened room. The only sound came from the wood crackling in the stove.

"Friedrick?"

There was no response, no rustle of movement from him. Livy rushed over and fell to her knees at his side. She placed a hand to his chest, hoping, praying, he was deep in sleep. His chest rose and fell beneath her palm.

She bit back a relieved cry. "Friedrick, can you hear me? The doctor's coming."

He shifted restlessly on the blanket. "Hurts…"

Livy felt his forehead and found it still burning with fever. She bathed his neck and face again with water, not caring when she soaked his shirt. It would keep him cool.

The hardness of the wood floor gnawed at her knees and reminded her that Friedrick had nothing to protect him from the planks but a blanket. Surely he'd rest easier with something more comfortable beneath him. Livy glanced at the clock. If she hurried, she could drag her mattress over before the doctor arrived.

She raced across the yard to her cabin and wrestled the mattress off her bed. It was heavier than she'd expected, but she managed to drag it outside.

Once she'd maneuvered the mattress into the school, she used her coat to wipe it free of dirt and damp. She positioned it between Friedrick's blanket and the stove and glanced at the clock. The doctor was already ten minutes later than he'd promised.

Livy did her best to squelch her worry and squatted next to Friedrick. "I'm going to help you onto a mattress, Friedrick."

His only answer was a throat-tearing cough.

"Here goes," she muttered, more to herself than to him.

She gripped him beneath the arms and pulled him toward the mattress. His full weight dragged at her hands. She clutched tighter to his shirt.

A low groan fell from Friedrick's lips. "Hurts."

"I know it hurts," Livy said between labored breaths. She hated to add to his pain, but he would be much more comfortable in a minute. "This will help."

She hauled his upper body onto the mattress, then his legs and feet. "That's better, isn't it?" She removed his boots and set them near the stove to dry.

Satisfied with the new arrangement, Livy lit the lamp she kept in the classroom for gloomy days. The smell of Mrs. Keller's homemade bread filled the room. Perhaps Friedrick would eat a little more, now that he was off the hard floor. She tore a piece of bread from the loaf and softened it with some of the water.

"I've got a little bread." She brought the morsel to Friedrick's mouth, but he didn't seem to be aware of her.

"No, no. Don't take it," he muttered, his head jerking from side to side. Beads of sweat had formed once more on his forehead. "No, you can't have it." He shuddered as he murmured something Livy couldn't understand.

Another peek at the clock wound Livy's stomach into tighter knots. Had the doctor decided against coming? What would she do then? She had no idea how else to help Friedrick. She lifted his hand and held it firmly between hers.

"It's going to be okay," she told him, though the words tasted like lies on her tongue. "You're going to be okay."

A soft knock had her jumping to her feet. Livy raced to the door and threw it open. "Dr. Miller?"

"Miss Campbell." The doctor removed his hat and entered the school. "I am sorry I am so late."

"He's over here." Livy motioned for the man to come farther inside, but Dr. Miller remained near the door.

"Do you know where Friedrick was earlier today?"

Livy studied his fatigued face and piercing hazel eyes and instinctively knew she could trust him. "He was at the jail. He went in Elsa's place."

"Yes. Friedrick shared a cell with an old man named Peter Hoffmann. Peter took sick today, so he and Friedrick were released early."

With an impatient nod, Livy took a step toward Friedrick. "No wonder Friedrick's ill then."

"You do not understand, Miss Campbell." The doctor reached out to stop her with a hand to her elbow. "I am late because I was at the Hoffmann home. Peter is dead."

"Dead?" Livy whirled to face him, her breath seizing in her throat. "From a cold?"

Dr. Miller lowered his hand and shook his head. "He did not have a cold, and I do not believe Friedrick does either."

"Then what is it?" A dull roar filled Livy's ears.

"It is a form of influenza. Something I have not seen before." He moved past her into the room and set his doctor bag on one of the children's desks. "I have reports from a colleague this illness is striking hard against those young and strong like Friedrick. In several cases, it has proven to be deadly."

The roar grew louder, almost drowning out the doctor's last words. The room grew darker at the edges of Livy's vision.

"Please, sit down, Miss Campbell."

Livy felt him guide her to a desk, where she sank into the tight space of the seat. *Friedrick could die? Like Blanche and Tom?* She bit her cheek hard enough to draw blood, though she barely noticed the coppery taste on her tongue. Friedrick couldn't leave her now, not when she was beginning to realize how much she needed him. Her day—her life—wasn't complete without his friendship. Or his smile, or his gentle teasing, or the strength of his touch.

Her mind shied away from the horrible possibility, lighting on something she could focus on. "What can I do?"

"Good girl." The doctor drew a stethoscope from his bag and knelt beside the mattress. "First you must close down the school. No one is to enter this building. Especially not his mother or siblings. They could carry the illness back to Friedrick's father and he would not survive it." He bent down and listened to Friedrick's chest.

Livy clasped her trembling hands together as she watched.

"His heart and lungs sound good, for now." Dr. Miller felt Friedrick's forehead and frowned. "He has the high fever." His gaze moved from her to the bucket of water nearby. "Continue to keep him cool and try to get him to drink. He may not want food, but do your best to keep water or broth in him."

The doctor returned his stethoscope to his bag and removed a small round jar. Livy recognized it as Vicks VapoRub. She'd seen it in the drugstore back home.

"Put this salve on his chest at least once a day." He stood and passed her the jar. "I am sorry you must be the one to be here, Miss Campbell. But we cannot afford to have someone else looking after him, someone who hasn't been exposed to the influenza yet. My hope is your strong constitution will keep you from catching it as well."

Livy forced herself to her feet. The concern inside her had grown to a dull pain in her chest. A headache threatened at her temples. "I understand. Is there anything else I can do for him?"

Dr. Miller stared down at Friedrick, then back at Livy. "You can pray, Miss Campbell."

* * *

With his eyes shut against the pain in his head, Friedrick sensed more than saw the spoon Livy presented to his mouth. He forced his lips open and accepted the broth. Livy murmured her approval. He wanted to make her happy, but the slashing coughs and fatigue had drained him of all energy. A few swallows of broth were all he could manage from time to time.

How long had he been here in the school? Hours? Days? His family must be sick with worry. He needed to get well, if only his traitorous body would cooperate.

"Can you try a little more?" Livy coaxed.

Friedrick called on every ounce of strength within him to slurp more of the hot liquid. A wracking cough emanated from his throat, causing him to choke and sputter. Livy immediately lifted his shoulders and held him through the coughing spell. He hated being the invalid— he wanted to be the one holding and comforting her, not the other way around.

"Here's some water." She helped him drink.

Slowly the coughing subsided, but Friedrick's lungs still burned from the ordeal. "Need to...lie down." Livy eased him back onto his mattress. He gulped in air, every nerve aching. The physical torment never completely ceased; even his fitful sleeping only temporarily numbed the pain. Would he survive this?

As if reading his thoughts, Livy peered down at him, her green eyes almost black in the dim light. "I know it hurts something awful, Friedrick," she said in a fierce whisper. "But you must keep fighting. You're going to get well. All right?" Her voice snagged with emotion. Several tears dripped down her face. Despite all she'd been through since coming to Hilden, he'd only ever seen her come close to crying once—over Tom's death.

Friedrick lifted his arm, though it trembled at the effort, and brushed a tear from her chin. She seized his hand and pressed her lips to his knuckles. Her cool touch momentarily relieved his pain and exhaustion. She wore the same blouse and skirt she had on when he'd stumbled to her cabin, a testament to her vigilant care.

"I'm not giving up," he replied in a hoarse voice.

She offered him a watery smile. "Good, because we need you."

We. The word sounded as joyous and heavenly as angel choirs. "More broth..." He wasn't the least bit hungry, but he wanted to see Livy smile again.

Sure enough, she rewarded his words with a warm smile and reached for the bowl, her blond hair falling across her face. It was no longer confined in a bun, the way she usually wore it, but reached below her shoulders. She'd never looked more beautiful to him.

Friedrick made himself eat until he could stand no

more, then he rolled onto his side and closed his eyes again. Livy remained next to him, her fingers stroking his jaw, his forehead. He fell asleep with a silent prayer on his lips—*Thank you, Lord. Thank you for Livy.*

*   *   *

Someone rapped on the school door. "Miss Campbell?" a female voice called out. "Livy? Are you there?"

Livy froze, the wet cloth in her hand halfway to Friedrick's forehead. The visitor didn't sound like Elsa or any of the neighbors who'd come to talk with her at the door during the past five days.

She set aside her rag and scrambled up. The person knocked again before she could ease the door open. Mrs. Norton stood in the alcove, a covered plate in her hand. Livy's face drained of color. Had the woman heard about Friedrick? Or worse, about Livy caring for him, alone?

"Mrs. Norton?" she said with false brightness. She hurried out the door and shut it firmly behind her.

"I tried your cabin, but there was no answer." The woman studied Livy and made a *tsking* noise in her throat. "Look how dedicated you are, to be here so late after school."

Livy chose not to correct the misguided notion. "What brings you all the way out here?" *Into German-American territory*, she thought wryly.

"Oh, I couldn't stop thinking about you and your dear brother Tom." The woman shook her head in remorse. "Such a tragedy to lose them so young."

Sorrow washed over Livy, not for Tom alone, but for the man fighting for his life inside the school at this very minute. Livy cleared her throat to say, "Thank you for you thoughtfulness." However ill-timed.

"I couldn't very well let you starve in your grief." Mrs. Norton hoisted the plate. "Shall I bring this inside?"

"No." Livy's harsh tone caused the woman to lift an eyebrow in surprise. She forced a smile as she took the plate. "What I mean is, I'll run it over to my cabin."

Mrs. Norton's expression softened. "I'd love to see inside your classroom. Then I can tell your mother all about it my next letter."

Panic coated Livy's mouth. She couldn't let Mrs. Norton in now. If anyone found out she was looking after Friedrick, they might both lose their jobs. Worse, the woman might contract Friedrick's illness. Livy had strictly adhered to the doctor's demands that no one enter the building until Friedrick was well.

"Our…um…classroom is rather messy right now." It was certainly the truth. "Perhaps another time would be better."

"Oh." Her disappointment was plain. "If you insist."

"I'm afraid I must. You know how children are."

"German ones especially, I'm sure."

Livy gritted her teeth. "Thank you for the meal."

"You're welcome, dear." The woman patted Livy's hand and walked to the wagon parked in front of the school. "If there's anything else you need, let us know."

Livy waved in response as she crossed the yard to her cabin. She didn't want to leave Friedrick, but she didn't want to raise Mrs. Norton's suspicions either by not taking the meal to her home as she'd said.

Slipping inside, Livy set the plate on the table and waited until she could no longer hear the woman's

wagon. She breathed a sigh of relief when she peeked out
the door a few minutes later and found the road out front
empty. With the plate in hand, she retraced her steps to
the school.

The food smelled delicious, but she didn't think she
could stomach it. Worry continued to steal her appetite.
She set the plate next to the others on her desk and returned to Friedrick's side. Despite his will to eat and drink
when she asked, his strength was ebbing away. Livy read
it in his restless sleep and the thinning lines of his face.

"What else can I do?" she whispered, though she knew
he couldn't hear. He'd grown less and less aware of her
the last two days. She'd done everything the doctor had
asked, everything she could think of to help Friedrick.

Except pray.

The thought brought a wave of fear crashing over her.
She hadn't asked God for anything of real importance in
years, except for Tom and Joel's safety.

Livy lifted her hand and touched the light colored
beard covering Friedrick's jaw. The pain she would experience if she lost him would be worse than anything she'd
yet felt. Which surely meant she ought to pray for him
with more fervor than she'd ever done before.

Ashamed, she covered her face with her hands. *I'm so
afraid, God*, she pleaded silently. *Afraid to ask for what
I so desperately want. I care for Friedrick and I want
him to live. Please let him live.* Tears threatened, but Livy
swallowed them back, determined to finish. *But if Thy
will is for something different . . . If Thou who sees and understands all must take him home, then . . . then . . . please
help me accept that.*

A strangled cry escaped her lips and she hurried to

muffle the sound with her hand. Tears leaked down her fingers as she sobbed. All the heartache of the last year came rushing out. In its place, though, Livy felt a profound sense of peace. Whatever happened, God would see her and Friedrick through.

She curled up on her blanket next to Friedrick's mattress and allowed herself to slip into the first real sleep she'd had in days.

Chapter Eleven

Friedrick opened his eyes to bright light. The absence of the intense aches and exhaustion made him wonder for a moment if he'd died. Then he turned his head and the light faded, replaced by an even better sight. Livy lay on the floor, her back to him. Her shoulders rose and fell with gentle breathing, her hair spread out behind her.

A lump of emotion filled his throat at the realization he had survived—thanks to the mercy of God and this woman lying near him. Her constant care had saved his life. He blinked to dispel the tears in his eyes. Lifting his weakened arms, he scrubbed his hands over the whiskers covering his jaw and chin.

Livy shifted in her sleep, turning toward him. Friedrick seized the chance to study her unawares. Her dark lashes rested against her smooth cheeks, her lips full and relaxed. What he wouldn't give to see her like this every morning, as her husband.

Was such a dream possible? The misunderstanding

and frustration between them had been resolved, leaving Friedrick hoping for more than friendship from her. So many people stood in their way, though—her beau back home, her family, some of his own people, including Elsa. And yet all the complications faded into unimportance when he stared at Livy's lovely face.

Telling himself he needed to be certain she was real, he reached out and ran his thumb down her cheek and across her lower lip. Her skin felt warm and soft. Livy exhaled a sigh of contentment at his touch, stirring fire in his veins.

With great effort, Friedrick lowered his hand from her face. He wouldn't take advantage of her boyfriend's absence or their isolation, for that matter. Instead he slowly pulled himself into a sitting position and set his feet on the floor. A dull ache permeated his muscles and his neck felt stiff, but at least he could move.

"Livy," he called softly, resting his elbows on his knees.

She stirred and rubbed at her eyes. "What is it? Are you hungry?"

He chuckled as she tried to wake herself. "Starving, actually."

"Starving?" she echoed sleepily. "That's good…" He knew the instant his words penetrated her foggy mind. She suddenly sat up and gaped at him. "You're—you're better?"

He smiled at the confusion and delight in her green eyes. "Thanks to you."

She crossed the short distance between them and threw her arms around his neck. Friedrick hugged her tight, relishing the chance to finally hold her close again—if only briefly.

"I wanted so badly to believe you'd get well," she said, her voice thick with tears. "But I finally had to resign myself to what God wanted." She eased back, allowing him to brush away the moisture from her face.

"Apparently He wanted me to live," Friedrick teased.

Her lashes dropped as a shudder ran through her. "It's no laughing matter, Friedrick. I couldn't bear the thought of you . . ." Her words trailed off.

He tipped her chin up, so she'd look at him again. "I'm sorry to make light of it, Livy." He pressed his forehead to hers. "I'm just so happy to be alive . . . to be back with you."

She sat still, her gaze intent on his. The yearning to kiss her nearly overpowered him, but he fought it back as he released her. "Is there something I can eat?"

Livy looked momentarily startled or disappointed. Did she want him to kiss her? If so, what did that mean about her feelings for her beau? "You name it, we probably have it," she said with a laugh as she stood.

"Apple pie?" he threw out for fun.

She lifted a pie pan off her desk at the front of the room, her eyes sparkling in a way he hadn't seen for some time. "How big of a slice do you want?"

Friedrick chuckled. "I'll take the whole tin, if that's all right."

"Only if you share." She brought the pie and two forks back to her blanket. "I haven't eaten much myself and now I'm famished."

They each took a bite. Friedrick closed his eyes at the tart goodness. He felt as though he hadn't eaten properly in a month. "I hope Peter Hoffman received as good care as I did."

Livy's shoulders stiffened, her fork poised over the pie tin.

"What's wrong?" he asked, wariness stealing some of the enjoyment of the pie. "Did something happen to Peter?"

The sorrow in Livy's gaze told him the awful truth before she spoke it out loud. "I'm so sorry, Friedrick. He...he died the night you took sick. The doctor told me. That's how he knew the influenza you had was very serious."

Friedrick stabbed a piece of apple and stared at it. He hadn't known Peter Hoffmann very well, but the man had inspired him with his courage. A profound sense of loss settled over him. Peter's death served as another reminder of how close he'd come to leaving this world himself.

He cleared his throat. "Who brought all the food?" He waved his fork at the desk littered with plates.

"Elsa and some of the neighbors." Livy took another bite of pie. "They were very kind, even the Kellers. I think my caring for you may have helped them see the light— maybe." She threw him a smile.

"What about your family? Or your boyfriend?" he felt compelled to ask. "Will they understand when you tell them you cared for a German-American, here, alone?"

Livy stopped eating, her eyes on her lap. "I don't need to tell Robert. He isn't my beau anymore."

Her announcement sent a ripple of shock through him, followed closely by sudden hope at the possibility of a future together, but Friedrick hid it behind a calm exterior. "Since when?" he asked in a casual tone.

"I ended things with him before I came to Hilden." She fiddled with the fork in her hand. "I think he still clung to the idea of us being together, though." Friedrick couldn't fault the man for that. "But when I found him drunk after Tom's memorial service, I told him not to contact me again." She reached for another morsel of pie, her mouth tightened with determination.

Friedrick dropped his fork into the tin and captured her wrist before she could snag another bite. The realization that Livy was unattached infused him with new energy. He felt as though he could sprint home and back again. "You mean that? You're done seeing him?"

"Yes," she said softly. "I'm through with letting him hurt me like that. I want..." She swallowed and blushed. The color only added to her appeal.

He bent toward her, his focus as much on her words as her lips. "What do you want, Livy?" Did she want him, despite all the obstacles in their way?

"I—"

A knock at the door interrupted them. Friedrick stifled an audible groan and sat back. Of all the moments, someone would choose to drop by the school. He released Livy's hand so she could answer the door.

"That's probably Mr. Keller." Livy rose slowly to her feet. Her apologetic expression eased some of Friedrick's annoyance at the disruption. The neighbors had been more than kind to him and Livy.

He listened to the murmur of conversation at the door, which was followed by a happy shout. Both Mr. and Mrs. Keller entered the room.

"Praise be to God," Mrs. Keller said in German. She hurried over and gripped Friedrick's face between her hands. "We will get you home right now. My husband will fetch the wagon."

"Yes, yes," Mr. Keller said, hurrying toward the door.

"Your mother has been beside herself with worry," Mrs. Keller added. "She will be so happy." She glanced at the untidy room and said to Livy in English, "I help clean?"

"Thank you, yes."

The two of them set about gathering up the food and straightening the room. Friedrick watched helplessly for a few moments before he located his socks and boots. He pulled them on, though the simple task still took longer than normal.

His chance to renew his conversation with Livy never materialized, not with Mrs. Keller around. Her husband soon returned and told Friedrick the wagon was waiting out front.

"My children come next day you open," Mr. Keller said to Livy. Mrs. Keller nodded agreement.

Livy glanced between them, her face incredulous. "For school?"

"Ha. Not cleaning lessons." Mr. Keller laughed. "Surprised, no? You care for our Friedrick and now you teach my children."

Livy grinned and grasped the man's hand, propelling it up and down. "Thank you both so much."

He pulled his hand back and waved at Friedrick. "We go now, boy. Come." The man helped him onto his feet. Friedrick swayed a bit but remained upright.

Mrs. Keller and Livy led the way out of the school, their arms full of food. With Mr. Keller's assistance, Friedrick shuffled after them.

Even at his height, Friedrick still had to keep his feet moving rapidly to keep up with Mr. Keller's brisk pace.

The man's excitement was contagious, though. Friedrick couldn't help smiling as Mr. Keller helped him into the wagon bed beside the food. He would be home soon.

Of course, that meant leaving Livy.

He managed to sit up as Mr. Keller and his wife climbed onto the seat above him. Livy stood beside the wagon, her hand resting on the worn wood.

"Thank you, Livy." Friedrick covered her fingers with his. Would she sense all that he wanted to say but couldn't in the Kellers' company?

"You're welcome, Friedrick." Her green eyes deepened with emotion. "I'll see you soon?" It came out a question. The wagon lurched forward, forcing Livy to jump back.

"The first moment I can," he called to her.

Though his muscles screamed at him to lie down, he remained sitting until he could no longer see her standing, arms folded, beside the schoolhouse.

* * *

"Good morning, class." Livy almost convinced herself with her cheerful tone. "It's good to see all of you again. I would also like to extend a special welcome to the Kellers." She motioned to John and his sisters. They smiled at her from their respective desks.

She mustered a smile in return as she rubbed at her tired eyes. Despite sleeping nearly a whole day after Friedrick had left for home, exhaustion still plagued her. Nursing him back to health, scrubbing the school from top to bottom in order to reopen it, and several restless nights had depleted her energy, leaving circles under her lashes.

She missed Friedrick terribly, especially after spending every waking moment with him. Surely a lifetime had passed, instead of a week, since she'd seen him last. Did she come as often to his mind as he did to hers?

"Miss Campbell?" Henry waved his arm from his seat at the back, returning Livy's attention to the class.

"Yes, Henry."

"Where did that poster go?"

Livy cocked her head in confusion. "I'm sorry, Henry. What are you talking about?"

"The liberty bond poster." He pointed at the blackboard. "Where'd it go?"

As she turned toward the front wall, remembering rushed in. The poster—the one she'd burned the afternoon Friedrick had first taken ill. She hadn't given much thought to the children noticing its absence or how to explain her change of heart.

Livy offered a quick prayer for courage and rotated to face her students. It was one thing to admit she'd made a mistake to Friedrick; it was quite another to do so to a group of children who'd placed their trust in her.

"As you can see, I removed the poster," she said, squaring her shoulders. "I decided its message was not one I wanted us to ponder over each school day. Which means..." She wet her lips with the tip of her tongue. "I was in error and I apologize."

Henry's face scrunched in puzzlement. "I thought that school fellow told you to put it up. Aren't you gonna get in trouble?"

"Going to get in trouble," Livy corrected. "Possibly. But I hope I will have the chance to explain to Mr. Foster that we do not need to hang a war bond poster in our classroom to remind us we are Americans." The words resounded with clarity and truth in her own ears and strengthened her confidence in her decision to do away with the poster. "We show we are Americans by how we live. By how we cherish and honor freedom. By how we treat our fellow men and women. By how we act with strength and faith, not fear."

Her speech sparked a sudden idea. Livy smiled, her earlier fatigue forgotten. "Which is why we will not be doing geography this morning. Instead we are going to draw our own posters."

The children exchanged surprised looks. Excited conversations broke out among them like wildfires.

Livy clapped her hands to regain their attention. "I will turn you loose in a moment," she said with a laugh. "Instructions first. I want you to draw something you feel best expresses your love for this country. Something that honors America and its founding virtues. Then we'll place your posters around the room."

She pulled out her drawing pencils and paper from her desk and had the children come up row by row. Once the students were engrossed in their assignment, Livy sat in her chair and placed a blank sheet of paper in front of herself. What should she draw?

She thought a minute, then began making strokes across the page. The images soon took shape beneath her hand, a simple black-and-white rendition of a scene Greta had described to her.

When she'd finished, Livy blew on the paper and studied her creation. It was a sketch of Friedrick reading from the Bible. Harlan and Greta were seated at his feet, their backs to the viewer, so their faces weren't visible.

Livy crossed to the north windows and propped the picture up on one of the ledges. She stepped back to scrutinize her work. A genuine smile lifted her mouth. The simple picture represented her love of home and family and the freedom to teach the younger generation.

As the children completed their posters, they brought them to Livy to place on the various windowsills. There were flags, Fourth of July picnics, a soldier, families, and an impressive sketch of a naval ship by Henry. The sight of so many cherished drawings caused a temporary lump in her throat, and she had to swallow hard to dislodge it.

"Thank you," she said as the students settled back into their seats. "I hope the superintendent will be as impressed with your efforts as I am."

The rest of the day raced by, but Livy felt little of her earlier weariness. The thrill of doing something unconventional, and out of the ordinary, carried her through her lessons. It wasn't until she bade the children good-bye that the exhaustion caught up with her again and she sat back on her desk with a sigh.

"Bye, Miss Campbell," Harlan said. He and Greta were the last to leave. "I like your drawing. That's me and Greta, huh? And Friedrick?"

"Yes, it is." Livy climbed to her feet. "Is Friedrick coming to pick you up today?"

She knew the answer before Harlan shook his head. If Friedrick had meant to come, he would have already arrived. Sharp disappointment mingled with her tiredness. Another day without seeing him. "Is he fully recovered yet?"

Harlan's nose wrinkled in thought. "I guess so. He won't let Mama make him stay in bed anymore."

"That's a good sign," Livy said with forced merriment. Knowing Friedrick felt better and hadn't come to see her caused a dull ache to form in her middle. "Has he had lots of visitors?"

Greta took up the narrative. "Not really, but Maria's come by a few times. Mama says that's 'cause she likes him."

Harlan made a face, which made Livy laugh, despite the jealousy she felt at the mention of Maria. "What's the matter, Harlan? Don't you like Maria?"

"I don't know. She's kind of bossy, always makin' us leave the room when she comes over." His boyish face brightened a moment later. "But Friedrick usually figures out a way to have us come back in."

Good. A twinge of guilt made Livy take the thought back. She wanted Friedrick to be happy.

"You two better run along now. Your mother will be expecting you."

The pair waved good-bye and raced outside. The click of the door sounded loud in the silent room. Livy called on the last shreds of her energy to sweep the floor, straighten the desks, and gather the written assignments the students had done before leaving. When she reached Harlan's desk, she discovered he'd left behind the book she'd loaned him from her own collection.

"Oh well, I'll see he gets it tomorrow," she murmured to herself. She'd been doing that more and more the last few days. Without Friedrick to talk to or care for, the loneliness pressed in on her again. Only the sound of a human voice, even her own, seemed to hold it at bay.

What would she do when Friedrick did return to his job at the school? They couldn't go back to simply being friends, not after the familiarity they'd shared during his illness.

It hadn't taken Livy long after Friedrick's recovery to realize that she yearned to be more than friends with him. Especially when he'd taken her wrist in his firm grip and asked her what she wanted. She'd been about to tell him the truth—that she wanted him for a beau—when the Kellers had interrupted.

Livy shook her head at her own foolishness. She'd have to be content with being Friedrick's friend and nothing more. How could they be anything else, with so many people watching and their jobs in jeopardy should they make one false move?

Had coming to Hilden really been the answer to her problems all those weeks ago? she wondered as she divided up the written compositions by grade level. Or had this job simply created new challenges in her life?

At the sound of boots against the floorboards, Livy lifted her head. She hadn't heard the door open. Perhaps Harlan had returned for his book.

"Did you come back for your—" The words stuck in her throat when she turned and found Friedrick standing at the back of the room. Her heart drummed faster at seeing him again. He looked so tall and healthy and handsome. "I...um...thought you were Harlan. I loaned him a book, but he forgot it."

She faced her desk again, her back to Friedrick. She had to hide from those intense blue eyes. If she didn't, she feared she'd run straight into his arms and ruin everything she'd worked so hard for. She plucked up the remaining stack of papers and continued her sorting.

"I like all the drawings."

"They did turn out well, didn't they?" She glanced at the one she'd drawn of him. Had he noticed? Would he approve or be embarrassed, especially if he still harbored feelings for Maria? "I thought they might take the place of Mr. Foster's poster. Show we're still patriotic here..."

Friedrick made no reply, and the ensuing quiet thundered as loudly in her ears as her pulse. "Harlan said you were feeling better." Her high-pitched voice betrayed her nervousness. "Did they know you were coming by? I would have had them stay."

"I passed them on the way." He sounded closer, though Livy hadn't heard his footsteps. "I had to see about a few things here first."

Livy read the name on the paper in her hand twice before she was able to set it in its proper pile. "I won't be in your way; I'm almost finished." She didn't want him to feel obligated to talk to her simply because she was there. "Once I'm done sorting these papers, I need to clean my cabin. I scrubbed this place spotless so we could reopen it today. But my own house still needs a good..."

Her senseless chatter faded into silence when she felt his hands on her shoulders. His breath brushed the back of her neck, causing gooseflesh to run along her arms. She shivered and clutched the stack of papers tightly to her chest, the edges biting into her fingers. Maybe that would stop her heart from racing.

"I've missed you, Livy," Friedrick murmured against her hair.

"I haven't gone anywhere." The accusation didn't sound as angry as she'd meant it, but she was having difficulty thinking. Especially with him standing so close she could feel his strong chest against her back. She needed to stop swooning over him. What if someone saw them? She didn't want to lose her job and never see him again, even if staying meant pretending to be nothing more than friends.

"Why didn't you come sooner?" she asked softly as she turned to face him. Friedrick lowered his hands to his sides, but his tender gaze still held her captive and made her gulp.

"I would have, but regaining my strength took longer than I'd thought. Then there was spring planting to be done." He lifted his thumb and stroked her cheek. The action sparked a memory. Livy had been half-asleep, but she'd felt his caress on her face and lower lip the day he'd recovered. His touch felt as wonderful today as it had then. "I'm here now and there's something I need to tell you."

"Me, too."

He chuckled. The low sound sent a quiver of anticipation through her middle. "You first."

Livy took a deep breath and squeezed her eyes shut. The words would come easier if she couldn't see his handsome face. "I hope you and Maria will be happy."

"Me and Maria?" Friedrick tilted her chin upward, forcing her to look at him. She had to remind herself not to get lost in the blueness of his eyes, which had deepened to the color of twilight. "What are you talking about?"

She blinked, trying to remember. "Harlan... he told me Maria's come to visit several times. I'm sure Elsa approves of her..." Livy couldn't make herself say "more than me."

"You think I like Maria?" He laughed softly again, the warmth of his breath feathering her cheeks.

"Yes," Livy whispered, though the admission sounded foolish given the way Friedrick was smiling at her. "Er... maybe?"

She swallowed hard as his expression changed from amusement to somberness. He cupped her face between his hands and eyed her mouth. Livy's heart hurtled against her ribs; she couldn't seem to get a proper breath. Her eyes fell shut as Friedrick brought his lips down on hers—gently at first, then firmly. His kiss created a wellspring of emotion within her—happiness, safety, fear, joy.

When Friedrick stepped back, Livy sat down hard on the edge of the desk, her fingers straying to her mouth. Her lips still tingled from his touch. "So you... don't like Maria?"

He tugged the stack of papers from her grip and set them on the desk, then he helped her to her feet. His hands went to her waist and he drew her closer. "I am not, nor have I ever been, in love with Maria Schmitt. She is a charming, pretty girl. But she's not you. I told her as much before you and I went dancing. Her visits this last week have meant nothing to me."

"Really?" Livy didn't care that the word came out breathless. Friedrick cared as much for her as she did for him? The joyful realization was short-lived. "But... I don't see how we can do this, Friedrick."

"Why not?"

She folded her arms against a sudden shiver and leaned against him. His solid frame erased some of her fears, though not her logic. He wrapped his arms around her. "What about Mr. Foster? Or your mother?" Or her own family?

Would her siblings accept Friedrick as her beau?

Would her parents? They'd been courteous to him when he'd driven her home for Tom's memorial service, but they'd also been in shock. Would they feel differently now?

"You can't lose your job, and I don't want to lose mine either." She couldn't go home yet, not after realizing how much Friedrick meant to her.

"Livy, look at me." He released her so she could see his face, though he kept her close, his hands clasping her shoulders. "I care about you—a lot." He brushed an errant hair off her forehead. The simple gesture renewed the flutters in her stomach. "Somehow we'll make this work."

As she peered into his eyes, the deep sincerity reflected there filled and bound up her bruised heart. Here was a man she could trust—a man who would cherish and protect her.

"All right," she agreed.

Friedrick pulled her toward him and kissed her again. The gentle press of his mouth blocked all other thoughts from her mind, save this moment. Livy wound her hands around his neck as he deepened the kiss.

"Yuck!"

Livy's eyes flew open at Harlan's disgusted tone. She jumped back from Friedrick and knocked her legs against her desk.

Friedrick steadied her, then turned toward his brother. "What do you need, Harlan? Is something wrong at home?"

The boy studied the two of them for a moment. "Mama said to come get this." He crossed to his desk and grabbed the book. "Can I ride back with you, Friedrick?"

"Yes. I'll be out in a minute. Go wait in the wagon."

Harlan shot them another puzzled look, then headed back outside.

Livy pressed her hands to her flushed cheeks. "That was embarrassing." Would Harlan tell Greta or Elsa about what he'd seen? Was her and Friedrick's relationship doomed before it had even begun?

Friedrick lifted one of her hands and ran his finger against the back of her palm. "I don't think Harlan will say anything."

"What if it had been someone else who saw us?"

"But it wasn't." He squeezed her hand. "I'll be here tomorrow afternoon to finish up the mortar and start on the outhouse."

She nodded, though she couldn't keep from biting her cheek in worry.

He pushed her chin up with his knuckle. "We'll work it out, Livy. Promise me you'll remember that."

Livy hesitated. Her heart wanted so desperately to agree with him, while her mind argued the futility of being anything more than friends. But she was tired of letting other people dictate what she ought to do or feel or be. She was the one in charge of her life.

"I will," she said with conviction.

"Good." Friedrick smiled and pressed a quick kiss to her forehead. "Tomorrow then."

"Tomorrow," she echoed.

She watched him leave, hating the idea of so many hours to go before she saw him again. Even then they wouldn't be alone.

But we'll figure things out. Livy held tightly to Friedrick's reassurance as the door shut behind him.

Chapter Twelve

Friedrick plunged his pitchfork into the hay and tossed it from the loft to the ground below. A popular tune ran through his mind—"If You Were the Only Girl In the World." He sang the words to himself, not caring too much if someone overheard. His voice wasn't as polished as some, but he'd always enjoyed singing in church.

If you were the only girl in the world
And I were the only boy
Nothing else would matter in the world today
We could go on loving in the same old way

A garden of Eden just made for two
With nothing to mar our joy
I would say such wonderful things to you
There would be such wonderful things to do
If you were the only girl in the world
And I were the only boy.

The song adequately described his feelings for Livy. A week without seeing her, while he'd fully recovered from the influenza, had felt like a lifetime. But today he'd not only seen her, he had kissed her. Twice.

Friedrick grinned at the vivid memory of those kisses and the way Livy's mouth had felt so soft and perfect against his. He felt like the luckiest man in the world to have earned her trust and her heart.

He finished with the hay and left the barn. Blues and golds stained the western sky, pulling Friedrick's thoughts heavenward. Every day he saw evidence of God in the sky and soil, but today, he felt it inside himself. God had blessed him with life, despite being gravely ill a week ago, and now He'd blessed him again, with Livy.

Friedrick scraped the mud from his boots on the back step and entered the kitchen. "Smells good, Mother. I'm starving."

She glanced at him from where she stood at the stove, her eyes troubled for a moment. "We will eat very soon. I am just waiting for the bread to finish. Keep reading, Harlan."

The boy sat at the table, the book from Livy lying open in front of him. Harlan began reading out loud as Friedrick crossed to the sink and washed up.

After a minute or two, Elsa pulled the bread from the oven. "Harlan, will you please get some chokecherry jam from the cellar, then tell your sister it's time for supper? I believe she's playing upstairs."

Harlan grumbled under his breath until Friedrick shot him a pointed look. The boy picked up his book and disappeared out the door, though his loud, stomping footsteps attested to his annoyance.

Friedrick chuckled and went to the cupboard to collect four plates. He set them on the table.

"Did you work at the school this afternoon?" Elsa asked as she arranged the bread loaves on a dish towel.

"I will tomorrow."

"You drove Harlan home, though, didn't you?"

He glanced at her, curious as to why she was fishing for information. "I needed to talk to Liv—Miss Campbell. I brought Harlan home after that."

"Harlan said you and his *teacher* were doing more than talking."

Friedrick frowned in irritation as he pulled eating utensils from a drawer. "Did Harlan volunteer that particular piece of information?"

Elsa's heavy sigh filled the room. "I will not lie to you. I had a feeling where you were going and why. So when Harlan mentioned leaving his book behind, I sent him to collect it and see if you were working at the school."

"You sent Harlan to spy on me?" He stared at her in surprise. What had gotten into Elsa? She hadn't interfered in his life or questioned his way of doing things for years.

Instead of answering right away, she reached past him to collect four cups. She slammed each one on the table, reminding Friedrick of Harlan just now.

"Don't you think I know what you are feeling?" She gripped the back of one of the chairs, her voice soft, pleading. "I was young once, too. Don't you think I know why you have not sought out Maria as she has you?"

Friedrick finished setting the table and put his hand over one of hers. "Then give me your blessing."

"I can't." It was little more than a whisper.

"Why not?" he pressed. "Is it because she isn't German?"

Elsa's face flushed pink, but she shook her head. "German, American. It makes no difference—except in time of war. She is not good for you."

His annoyance festered into full anger, but Friedrick fought to check it. "How can you say that? Livy nursed me while I was on the brink of dying. She chose to stay in that school and care for me, even at the risk of her own life."

"I know," Elsa shot back as she lowered her head. "That is what I feared might happen. Don't you think I have come to love your father even more as I have cared for him these past few years?" She drew in a shaky breath, the threat of tears evident in her voice as she continued. "I do not want to see you hurt, Friedrick. But you cannot be with Miss Campbell. It will not work."

"Why not? She is the most extraordinary person, and when I'm with her, Mother..." He hazarded a smile. "I feel extraordinary, too."

"She is a wonderful girl," Elsa admitted. "But think what would happen if someone found about the two of you—someone who isn't German?

"She could lose her job, Friedrick. And what would we do if you could no longer work at the school? This job is a gift from God. We cannot take that lightly. How else can we pay for your father's medicine?"

"Livy and I both know there are complications." Friedrick placed his hand on Elsa's shoulder and gave it a gentle squeeze. "But they aren't impossible to overcome. You always taught me to do what is right, no matter how difficult."

Elsa twisted her apron between her fingers. "What if the right thing, this time, is to walk away from her?"

Harlan and Greta raced into the kitchen, bringing the conversation to an abrupt halt and stopping Friedrick from having to answer the probing question. He didn't agree with Elsa. Surely things would work out all right—that's what he'd promised Livy.

Friedrick volunteered to be the one to take his father's tray into him. He no longer had a desire to eat or remain in the tense atmosphere of the kitchen. Some space would do him—and Elsa—some good.

He entered his father's room and set the tray on the bedside table. His father's eyes opened as Friedrick took a seat in the nearby chair.

"A pleasant surprise," Heinrich said, "to dine with my son."

"Shall I help you or would you like to do it yourself?"

Heinrich's hands rose, trembling and pale, but he reached for the plate and fork Friedrick held out to him. "It is a good day. I shall do it myself."

Friedrick set the plate on his father's blanketed lap and watched as Heinrich scooped a piece of stewed carrot onto his fork. His father lifted it shakily to his lips. Most of the morsel made it inside, but some of it slipped onto his short gray beard.

"I'll take care of cleanup," Friedrick offered. He lifted the napkin from the tray and wiped the spill, then he arranged the cloth across his father's chest.

"Thank you, son."

Friedrick watched his father for a few moments, wondering how much Heinrich knew of the world outside this room. Had Elsa told him what was happening to their people?

"Elsa is worried about you," Heinrich said, as though

he'd been privy to the conversation in the kitchen just now. "She fears you still wish to fight."

Friedrick shook his head. "Not overseas, Papa. I am needed here, and this is where I'll stay." Especially now that he knew how much Livy cared.

He'd been so full of hope talking with her earlier—he'd convinced her, and himself, everything would be all right for them. Why did the war have to constantly intervene in his life? Why did he feel as if his own freedoms were constantly being threatened, when supposedly the country was fighting to regain freedom for so many others?

"Something on your mind, Friedrick?" Heinrich eyed him with parental concern. He seemed more lucid today than he'd been in months.

Friedrick had a sudden desire to hear his father's advice—something he hadn't sought in a long time. "You always taught us to be proud of our heritage, Papa. To stand for what is right and good in this world."

Heinrich nodded and brought another forkful of food to his mouth.

"What if doing so hurts, rather than helps, those you love?" Friedrick leaned forward, his arms resting on the bed. "What is the right course of action then?"

"Standing for the truth will always come at a price, Friedrick, whether it is being bold and sure or silent and strong. Neither one is easy." He pinned Friedrick with an intent look. "Only God can tell you which to be."

Friedrick hung his head. His father's words echoed what Pastor Schwarz and Peter Hoffmann had already told him. Wasn't there anyone who would tell him not to yield?

"Perhaps your real question is not *how* to stand for goodness but *when*. Am I right?"

"I suppose," Friedrick said, lifting his chin.

To Friedrick's surprise, his father chuckled—the sound of it was like the distant rumbling of thunder. "Remember how impatient you were as a boy? You wanted everything to happen right away, no waiting." Heinrich smiled. "You would watch the sky for the first snowflakes or a mother cat with her unborn kittens and grow tired when the tiny miracles did not happen immediately. It is not so different now, Friedrick. You want your chance to fight…"

Friedrick sat back in his chair, annoyance lashing through him. He'd just explained his desire was to be here on the farm, instead of at the front lines.

"I do not mean with guns, my son." His father's perceptiveness startled Friedrick. Though his body might be weak, Heinrich's mind was far from it. "I mean fighting for justice and decency and family. It will not happen on your timetable, but it will on God's. You must wait upon the Lord. You must trust He will guide and mold you to the task. As Elsa always says, the night is longest right before the dawn. But dawn will come, Friedrick, and when it does where, or rather, who will you be standing beside?"

The impassioned speech was the longest Friedrick could recall hearing from his father in some time. Regret cooled his earlier irritation. How much more wisdom did his father have to impart, if Friedrick would seek and listen?

"Thank you, Papa." He placed his hand over his father's heavily lined one.

How he'd always looked up to and revered this man. Friedrick would do anything for him and his family, even if it meant he had to go back on what he'd said to Livy this afternoon.

The thought of not being with her—or worse, of hurting her—cut him deeply. Somehow, though, he had to find the courage to let her go and hope someday the world would allow them to be together.

* * *

Surely the clock must be broken, Livy thought with a frown. The minutes had ticked by with painful slowness the entire day, postponing the moment when she'd see Friedrick again.

Concentrating had been a difficult task through nearly every lesson she'd taught. Her mind kept wandering to the memory of Friedrick's lips against hers, the safety of his arms, the tenderness of his words. When doubts or fears crept in, Livy banished them with reminders of Friedrick's promise—things would be all right; they'd figure them out together.

At last the clock dictated the end of the school day. Livy announced it was time to leave, her enthusiasm matching her students'. Any minute now, Friedrick would be here. She couldn't wait to see his smile, hear his voice, perhaps steal a kiss or a quick embrace.

Her students rushed out the door, including Harlan and Greta, while Livy hurried to set the classroom to rights. She wanted as much time with Friedrick as possible. The sound of wagon wheels on the dirt road out front sent her pulse pounding at a frenzied pace.

She smoothed her hair and skirt and walked calmly to the door, in direct contrast to the anticipation fluttering inside her. Friedrick was finally here. A day away from him had never felt longer.

Livy stepped outside and stopped short, her smile

freezing in place. Mrs. Norton's daughter, Mrs. Smithson, and two of her children were disembarking from their wagon. It hadn't been Friedrick after all.

"Mrs. Smithson," Livy said, doing her best to sound friendly instead of annoyed or surprised. "What brings you out this way?"

The woman had a basket on her arm and a look of pity on her face. Her two children trailed her to the alcove where Livy stood. "Mother and I just can't seem to get you out of our minds, Livy. We hate thinking of you all alone out here, away from your family, at such a time as this." She brightened her tone to add, "So I baked you a few goodies to eat."

"Um…thank you." Livy threw a furtive glance up the road. Any moment Friedrick would be here, but there'd be no hope of talking to him with Mrs. Smithson hovering about. "That's very kind of you. Especially to drive all this way."

Mrs. Smithson waved away her words. "No bother at all—not for a dear old neighbor of Mother's."

"Mama," her son, Timmy, said. "Can I go explore that field?" He pointed to where Harlan and Greta were playing.

His mother immediately frowned. "No, Timmy. You can play right here, while I visit with Miss Campbell."

"Ah, Ma. There's no one to play with here."

"Play with Emmaline." She gently pushed his sister toward him. "Better her than with those German children," she added under her breath.

Livy schooled her face to be the picture of calm, despite the anger Mrs. Smithson's comment inspired. Why did the townspeople have to be so narrow-minded, so ruled by fear? If they would only get to know Friedrick and the other German-American families, she knew they'd come to respect them as she had.

The rumble of another wagon reached her ears. She sensed without looking it was Friedrick. "Would you like to see inside my classroom?" she volunteered. She didn't want Mrs. Smithson lingering outside, ready to cast insults at Friedrick.

"That would be—"

Emmaline's startled cry drew their attention. The girl had tripped. Livy bit back a groan as she and Mrs. Smithson moved to the girl's side.

Mrs. Smithson handed Livy the basket and scooped up her sniffling daughter. "There, there, Emmaline. You'll be fine."

"Would she like to come sit inside?" Livy offered. Out of the corner of her eye, she saw Friedrick stop his wagon and climb down.

"I'm sure she would," Mrs. Smithson said. She followed Livy to the school. Livy allowed herself a breath of relief, but it was premature. The woman paused outside the alcove. "Who is that man?"

Livy meant to spare Friedrick a mere glance, to avoid raising Mrs. Smithson's suspicions, but once she looked, she couldn't turn away. The familiar sight of him renewed the rapid thrumming of her heart. She wanted so much to cross the distance between them and rush straight into his arms.

With great effort, she cleared her throat and moved to open the school door. "He is the maintenance man," she answered in a nonchalant tone.

"Looks rather young and healthy to be sitting out the war. Do you suppose he's refused to enlist?"

Livy pressed her lips together in frustration and forced a deep breath to quell saying something she shouldn't. "I believe he has a farm deferment. Something about his father being very ill." *There*, she thought, *that ought to quiet her*.

At that moment, Friedrick noticed them standing in the alcove. His eyes went to Livy's. She silently pleaded that he'd play along with her impartiality, though her heart begged the opposite.

"Afternoon, ladies," he said as he carried his tools past them.

"Afternoon," Livy repeated, her gaze following him until he disappeared around the corner of the school.

"He's rather handsome, isn't he?" Mrs. Smithson said as Livy led her and her daughter inside.

Livy chose not to respond.

"I don't believe I've seen him in church." Mrs. Smithson helped Emmaline into one of the desks. "What lovely drawings. Did your students do those?" She waved to the patriotic pictures adorning the windowsills.

"They did," Livy said as she set the woman's basket on her desk and causally walked to the drawing of Friedrick. Mrs. Smithson didn't need to see this one. She picked it up, along with a few others, as though she were collecting them.

Friedrick appeared in the window in front of her. She glanced over her shoulder at Mrs. Smithson. The woman was occupied with examining her daughter's scraped knee.

"Hello," she mouthed to Friedrick. He repeated the word silently back. Livy leaned forward to place her hand against the glass. Friedrick did the same. Although the pane separated her hand from his, Livy still believed she could feel the warmth of his touch as if nothing divided them.

"Is that man German?"

Livy bit back a cry as she whirled around. Thankfully Mrs. Smithson wasn't looking at her. She pressed a hand to her throat to still her racing heartbeat. She had to be more careful around Friedrick. The thought renewed some of her earlier fears. Would it always be like this? Stealing moments together and hoping no one saw?

What had the woman asked her? "Uh, yes, he is German-American." Livy added emphasis to the last word, but it made little difference to Mrs. Smithson.

"Goodness, Livy." She stood, her eyes wide with shock. "I don't like to think of you here, alone, with someone like him."

Someone like him? Livy wanted to tell her she felt safer with Friedrick than any other man she'd ever met, including Robert. Emmaline whimpered right then, saving Livy from having to formulate an answer.

"I suppose we'd better get you home," Mrs. Smithson said to her daughter. "I was hoping to visit with you longer, Livy. Maybe another time."

"Yes. Another time."

Livy set down the pictures in her hand and followed them to the door. As they walked out, Harlan suddenly rounded the corner, nearly colliding with Mrs. Smithson and Emmaline.

"Watch yourself, young man," the woman snapped. She pulled Emmaline to her side as though she feared having her daughter even stand near a German-American child.

Harlan ignored her and raced up to Livy. "Miss Campbell?" He motioned for her to bend down so he could say something in her ear. Livy obeyed.

"Friedrick said he'll stop by your cabin tonight," he whispered, "after evening chores."

Livy hid her smile, especially since Mrs. Smithson was watching. "That sounds like a good idea," she told Harlan by way of an answer. The boy seemed to understand. With a nod, he rushed away.

"I think we ought to walk you to your home, Livy." Mrs. Smithson clutched her daughter's hand. "It would make me feel ever so much better. Does your mother know your situation here?"

By "situation," Livy gathered she meant being surrounded by German-Americans. She chose her response carefully. "My parents are supportive of my dream to be a teacher, regardless of the potential challenges." *More from people like you than anyone else.*

"Well, that eases my mind some, but I would like to see your place before we go."

Livy swallowed a sigh. If the woman insisted on coming to the cabin, an opportunity to talk with Friedrick this afternoon would be lost. Even if Mrs. Smithson didn't stay long, the woman's unexpected arrival had shaken Livy's confidence. At least she'd see Friedrick tonight, with hopefully no more interruptions. "Let me get my things."

She entered the school and collected her coat, lunch, and Mrs. Smithson's basket. Friedrick was still working on the north wall. After quickly placing the drawings she'd gathered up back onto the windowsills, Livy tapped the glass to get his attention. He lifted his eyes, a silent question there.

"Tonight?" he mouthed.

She gave a vigorous nod. "Tonight," she repeated.

Somehow she forced herself to walk away from the window, knowing she wasn't just leaving Friedrick. She was leaving her heart behind, too.

* * *

Livy rechecked her appearance in the bureau mirror and pinched her cheeks. She'd put on her blue silk dress, as if Friedrick were picking her up for a real outing in town. For a few moments, she imagined a lovely evening out with her would-be beau, free of worries about their jobs or what others might think. Instead they had to meet here in secret as though they'd done something wrong.

She crossed to the little kitchen and laid out forks and plates beside the spice cake she'd made that afternoon. Everything was ready. She glanced at the clock on the mantel. Friedrick hadn't been specific about the time, but with an hour or so to go until dark, she figured he'd be over soon.

To pass the time, she picked up her sketchbook. She opened it to a blank page and began filling the white space with scrawls and lines. She wasn't entirely conscious of what she was drawing until she recognized Tom's face in front of her. She'd drawn him in his army uniform, his face lit with a grin.

As she stared at the sketch, she waited for the intense sadness to settle over her at knowing Tom was gone. Tonight, though, it didn't come. Instead she felt only gratitude—gratitude for having Tom in her life as long as she had.

The rumble of a car engine out front brought her head up. The room had grown dim. Livy stood and lit the lamp, throwing another look at the clock. Almost eight. Friedrick must have been held up by something at the farm, but surely he would still come.

A sudden knock at the door made her jump. She hadn't heard Friedrick's wagon. She tucked a strand of hair behind her ear and hurried to let Friedrick in.

"Fried—" The rest of his name died in her throat.

"Hi-ya, Livy." Robert swept his hat off and flashed a smile. "Surprised to see me?"

Livy gripped the door for support. This had to be a nightmare. How had he found her? Was he drunk? "Wh-What are you doing here, Robert? I thought we agreed not to see each other anymore."

With the use of his cane, he strode past her into the cabin, "That's no way to treat an old beau, is it? So this is your place, huh? Not much to look at—inside or out."

Livy bit back a retort as she frantically searched the road out front for a sign of Friedrick. Panic shortened her breathing when she realized no one else was about. She was on her own—with Robert.

Heart heavy, she shut the door and faced him. "You didn't answer my question. What are you doing here?"

He stopped his investigation of the room long enough to throw her another smile. "I missed you, so I got it in my head to drive up here today and see how you were faring."

"Did my…um…parents tell you where to find me?" Surely her father and mother wouldn't have sent him. Livy had told them everything about Robert before she'd returned to Hilden—all about his drinking problems and how she'd ended things between them.

"Didn't ask them. I knew you'd taken a job in Hilden, so I stopped by the superintendent's house in town. Nice fellow. He told me which school was yours." Robert crossed to the table and glanced down at her open sketchbook. "Looks like you still got time for your little drawings."

Irritation surged inside Livy at his comment, but she tamped it down with thoughts of how quickly she could get Robert to leave. She picked up her sketch things and shoved them into one of the bureau drawers. "How are your mother and father? I didn't get to speak to them very much while I was home."

Robert sat uninvited in one of the chairs. He set his hat on the table and leaned his cane against his knee. "My folks are fine. They asked about you the other day."

"That was kind."

"'Course I didn't have much to report, seeing as you haven't written once."

Livy searched his face—was he angry or resigned—but his eyes were focused on the low flames in the fireplace.

"You like it here?"

"It's been a good experience," she answered warily. What was his real reason for coming all this way?

He turned to look at her again. "Must get awful lonely here by yourself."

She lifted her shoulders in a noncommittal shrug and went to add another log to the fire.

"Have you missed me at all, Livy?"

The melancholy note in his voice was meant to secure her compassion, as it had in the past. But she'd changed during her time in Hilden—she wouldn't be so easily taken in by his calculated tone or words.

"I don't know why you've even thought of me." She

gave a false laugh as she clutched the mantel tightly in her hand. "There are plenty of other girls at church for you to see."

Robert rubbed a finger over the tabletop. "Things have been a little different since you left the other week."

"Oh?" Alarms rang inside her head. Robert was finally getting to his true purpose for seeing her, and she knew she wasn't going to like it.

"Mama swore she wouldn't give me money to buy more alcohol." His laughter came out harsh and bitter. Livy shivered at the ugly sound, even as she silently cheered Mrs. Drake for putting her foot down at last. "I haven't touched the stuff in days. Honest. But things are no good without you around. No one else listens like you. Or understands like you."

Livy refused to be pulled in by his persuasions or promises, but she could offer her sincere relief. She crossed the room to stand beside his chair. "I'm proud of you for giving up that awful stuff, Robert."

"Come back, Livy," he pleaded. "We can be married. You still love me, don't you?"

She squeezed her eyes shut, knowing the pain her answer would cause him. Though her feelings for him had changed, she would remember with fondness the happier memories they'd made together—Robert had been her first beau, after all. But she'd learned a great deal from coming to know Friedrick. Love meant hope and respect and affection between two people. Not manipulation and constant heartache.

"I can't. I told you that when I was home." She opened her eyes to look at him properly. "My life is here now. I'm sorry, Robert."

He didn't respond right away, and the silence between them stretched on for almost a minute, tight and sharp.

"Perhaps you'd better—"

The scrape of his chair as he stood bit off her words. "I'm sorry, Livy. But I can't accept that." He shoved his hat on his head.

"I don't know what you mean." She kept her head held high, despite the cord of fear winding its way through her at his sudden change in demeanor.

"You really think I came all this way to get rebuffed a third time? I need you to come with me." Robert gripped her wrist with his free hand. His fingers cut into her skin.

Livy's heart leapt in terror. Did he mean to forcibly drag her back home? She wouldn't go willingly. "Let go, Robert," she said in an icy voice. "I'm staying here."

"That's where you're mistaken."

Despite having to use his cane, he easily hauled her toward the door. Livy tugged against his grip, but it was like struggling against steel. He set his cane against the wall, long enough to yank her coat off its peg and throw it at her. She caught it with one hand and held it to her chest as if the thin fabric could protect her.

She'd never seen him so angry, at least not when he'd been sober. The absence of alcohol had brought out all the ugliness she'd sensed ruminating inside him.

"Like I said, things aren't going quite so well back home." Robert glanced around the cabin, his gaze dark and wild. "Once you left this last time, word got out about . . . my coping skills. None of the other girls in town will talk to me. Which is why I need you, Livy. Everything will be fine once you come home."

"I can't just walk away from this job," she tried reasoning. "I have to teach. My parents could use the extra money." She gulped in a few deep breaths to try to calm her pounding heartbeat. "Why don't you sit back down and I'll make you some coffee?" That had helped him when he was drunk—maybe it would also help him when he was mean and sober.

"No. We've got a long drive ahead of us. Now open the door."

Afraid to defy him, Livy reached past him and opened the door. Cool night air rushed in, bringing her renewed courage. Robert tightened his grasp on her hand as he started outside, but this time, Livy planted her feet and held on to the door frame. "I am not going anywhere with you. We're through, Robert. I'm sorry if you can't accept that, but I will not be bullied into—"

His unexpected slap sent her head reeling backward and into the edge of the door. Prickles of light danced before Livy's gaze, and a wave of nausea rolled through her. She gingerly touched the side of her forehead. Her fingers came away wet with blood.

Robert released a soft curse. "Look, Livy, I'm sorry." His voice sounded farther away, though he still held her wrist in a vise. "I just need you to get into the car."

She shook her head, but the movement only increased the throbbing pain. "No…please…leave me alone. I just…need…to sit…" The room had begun to spin. She couldn't keep Robert's stern face in focus. Would he haul her to the car once she fainted? She would be no match for him then.

Before he could drag her away, though, a familiar deep voice penetrated the fog in Livy's head. "Let her go—now!"

Chapter Thirteen

Friedrick strode toward the cabin, his hands fisted at his sides. Anger crackled along his skin. The dark trickle on Livy's forehead brought bile to his throat. With effort, he kept his voice calm as he repeated his demand. "I said, let her go."

Robert sneered at him without releasing Livy's wrist. A neglected cane sat in the dirt near his boots. "You're the fellow who drove her home the other week."

"Yes. And now I'm here to inform you that your visit is over. I suggest you get inside that automobile of yours. Unless you need an escort."

"Please, Robert," Livy whispered from the doorway. "You need to leave."

Friedrick stepped closer, ignoring Robert in his concern for Livy. In addition to the cut on her forehead, a red mark marred her cheek. A new surge of fury rose inside him. Robert had struck her.

Unable to contain his disgust any longer, Friedrick

grabbed Robert by the collar and shoved him up against the door frame. "You think you're someone important because you fought in this war?" Friedrick stuck his face close to Robert's. "You're nothing but a coward. A real man never strikes a lady. I ought to return the favor..." He let the threat hang in the air between them. He wouldn't make good on it, as much as he wanted to, unless Robert threw the first punch.

"Friedrick, don't." Livy stumbled to a chair and sank into it, her face pale. "Just let him leave. I'll be fine."

Friedrick forced his fingers to let go of Robert's shirt, then he stepped back.

"Friedrick, huh?" Robert's eyes blazed in the lamplight spilling from the cabin. "This is why you won't come back with me? You've taken up with some Boche?"

Friedrick lifted his fist partway at the ugly name, but he lowered his hand just as quickly. He needed to keep his anger in check. Ignoring Robert, he entered the cabin and walked over to Livy. "Are you all right?" he asked in a low voice.

She lifted her chin and nodded, despite the unshed tears glistening in her eyes.

"We need to wash that cut." He searched the room for a towel.

"A German!" Robert still sputtered from his spot in the doorway. "You throw me off for a German? Never thought of you as a traitor, Olivia Campbell."

Friedrick rose to his feet and glared at the man. Robert didn't look or act drunk, which likely made him all the more dangerous tonight. "You've said your piece. Now get out before I have to throw you out."

Robert drew himself up to his full height—several

inches shorter than Friedrick. "Why don't you, Boche? You call me cowardly, but you're not fighting in this war. What's the matter? Too afraid?"

The anger Friedrick had managed to assuage for a few moments boiled up with new energy. His pulse throbbed hot and hard in his neck, and his jaw tightened.

"Or maybe you're collaborating with your little buddies overseas. Is that it?" The unmasked hate in Robert's eyes as he spoke matched the feeling searing Friedrick's throat.

He fought the voice in his head screaming for him to pummel Robert, and instead he walked calmly to the door. He wouldn't strike an injured man, no matter the poison seeping from Robert's mouth. "It's time for you to go—now."

Robert's punch hit Friedrick square in the jaw, radiating pain through his head. Friedrick stumbled back. He heard Livy gasp.

"You're wrong if you think I'm gonna leave now," Robert snarled. "For all I know, you might be waiting around to take advantage of Livy. Just like your soldier buddies over there in Germany. A good citizen like me has to protect our women from vicious brutes like—"

Friedrick rammed his shoulder into Robert's midsection, dropping them both to the ground outside the cabin. The impact stung his arm and leg, but Friedrick scrambled up quickly enough to avoid Robert's flying foot. He blocked the doorway to keep the man from entering a second time.

"Get going," Friedrick hissed through clenched teeth. He scooped up Robert's cane from off the ground and tossed it at the man's feet.

Robert used the cane to rise slowly. "You"—he pointed at Friedrick—"will regret this. You, too, Livy," he hollered. Friedrick sensed her standing behind him. Robert shot a final look of loathing at Friedrick before he limped to his automobile and cranked the engine.

Friedrick didn't wait for him to climb inside the vehicle. Instead he shut the door and led Livy back to her chair. She collapsed into it with a soft cry. One hand rose to cover her mouth as she leaned her elbow on the table.

The sight of Livy so despondent destroyed the last remnants of his fury, replacing it with guilt. Always guilt. If only he'd finished the evening chores sooner, he would have been here when Robert had first arrived. Then the man wouldn't have hurt Livy—again.

"He's gone now," Friedrick offered lamely. What could he say or do to make things better for her? "I'm sorry I wasn't able to come sooner." He put his hand on her shoulder and felt her shaking.

Livy stood and buried her head against his chest. He wrapped his arms around her and held her tight. Her quiet sobs flooded out onto his shirt as he stroked her soft hair and murmured reassurances in her ear.

Several minutes later she eased away from him. "I got your shirt wet." She touched the water mark near his shoulder.

Friedrick didn't even spare a glance at it. "It'll dry. How's your forehead?"

Livy fingered it. "A little sore."

"Let me clean it up before I go." Friedrick located a towel and dipped a corner of it in the water pot on the stove. "Sit down."

When she complied, Friedrick knelt in front of her and gently dabbed the rag to the cut. His careful ministrations washed the dried blood from her forehead. His gaze kept straying to Livy's large, green eyes and her kissable mouth pursed in concentration. He wanted to taste her lips again as he had yesterday, but he knew the impropriety of doing so with the two of them alone in her cabin. Still, he drew out the simple task of caring for her for the chance to stare into her pretty face a little longer.

Digging deep for resolve, he lowered the rag and sat back on his heels. "It doesn't look deep. I think it should be fine in a day or two. What will you tell the children tomorrow at school?"

"That I walked into a door?"

Friedrick gave a humorless laugh. "That might work."

"Do you think he'll make good on his threat?" she asked.

"I don't think there's much he can do."

"I didn't expect him. I opened the door, thinking it was you. If he'd just stayed away." She reached for Friedrick's hand and locked her fingers in his. "You look a little worse for the wear, too."

Friedrick rubbed his jaw. "That former beau of yours has a solid right jab." As he watched Livy, an idea formed in his mind, a way to salvage the evening and bring a smile to her face. "In fact, I think my jaw needs some doctoring." He feigned a pained expression.

A knowing glint entered her eyes. "I see. How about this?" She leaned forward and whispered a kiss against his jaw. He fought a grin—his plan had worked. "Any better?"

"Some, but it hurts here, too." He pointed to his chin.

She placed a kiss near his mouth, as she'd done the night they'd gone to the dance hall. "Better now?"

"Sort of. Except I think my lip hurts the worst."

"Your lip looks fine to me."

"I know, but the hurt's deeper." His words, meant to tease, changed the air in the room from playful to serious. How could he let Livy go, even for the sake of his family? He loved her, plain and simple. With her, he felt like a hero—a man of worth and courage.

Livy bent toward him and pressed her lips to his. Friedrick gently held her neck with one hand and kissed her back for several long, glorious moments. Moments in which everything and everyone outside the cabin faded into unimportance. He had to call on every ounce of willpower to release her and climb to his feet.

"I'd better go. It won't look good if I leave too late."

Livy stood as well. "Thank you, Friedrick. If you hadn't come..." She visibly swallowed.

He brushed a finger over her mouth. "Promise me you'll keep the door locked. Don't open it unless you know who it is first."

"I promise."

He placed a chaste kiss on her forehead and moved to the door.

"Friedrick?"

He turned around.

"What was the reason you wanted to meet tonight?"

Reality crashed into him as swiftly and hard as Robert's fist. How could he tell her he'd come to end things between them?

"I wanted to see you," he said with complete honesty.

"Out from under the scrutinizing eyes of people like that woman today."

She nodded, seeming to accept his answer. "I'm glad you did."

Friedrick opened the door. "I thought I'd drive into town and pick up my paycheck tomorrow." With everything that had happened the past few weeks, he still hadn't gone into town to collect it. "Have you picked up yours yet?"

"No."

"Then I'll get it, if I'm allowed."

"Thank you." She rewarded him with the genuine smile he'd been hoping to coax from her.

"See you tomorrow, Livy."

"Good night, Friedrick."

He took another long look at her, then pulled the door shut behind him. Once he heard the lock click into place, he walked to where he'd parked his wagon beside the school. Above him the stars shone in a clear sky. Surely God hadn't placed Livy in his life, only to pull her right back out of it. She was the only woman who saw him as more than German or American—the one person who made each day richer, happier, more hopeful.

The opposition raining down on their heads had likely just begun, if they chose to remain together. But Friedrick wouldn't give Livy up without a fight. Somehow he would find a way to save his family and be free to love Livy, too.

* * *

Friedrick parked his wagon outside the brick building that housed the superintendent's office. The midmorning sun felt almost hot against his back.

Whistling to himself, he opened the door and stepped inside. He'd walked into this same building nearly two months ago, and yet so much had happened in that time, most importantly meeting Livy again.

He ascended the stairs to the second floor. Down the short hall, Mr. Foster's secretary sat at her desk outside the man's office, reading a magazine. Seeing her again reminded Friedrick of their encounter in front of the Hilden jail. His good mood faded at the memory. She obviously hadn't said anything to the superintendent yet, but seeing Friedrick might spark remembrance and action.

Friedrick paused, throwing a glance at the stairs behind him. If he left, he'd return to his family empty-handed. If he stayed, he might lose his job. He risked something either way.

But at least I'd be compensated for my recent work.

He removed his cap and strode up to her desk. "Is Mr. Foster in?" he asked in a confident tone.

"Not right now," the secretary said without looking up. "Come back at four."

"I need to pick up my paycheck. I'm Friedrick Wagner. The maintenance man at Township School Number 1."

The magazine slowly fell away from her face, revealing wide eyes and an almost frightened expression. "Uh...yes. I can...um...get that for you."

Friedrick watched as she sifted through one of the desk drawers. Her peculiar reaction to his appearance left him unsettled. She seemed to remember him, and yet he couldn't reason why she would act afraid of him. The secretary removed a slip of paper and handed it to him.

"Thank you." He folded the check and placed it in his shirt pocket. "Is it possible I could collect Miss Campbell's, too? She's the teacher there, but she doesn't have a wagon or a car to get into town. She gave me permission to pick hers up as well."

The secretary shook her head. "I'm sorry. I can't give you hers. Mr. Foster will be delivering it himself. He would've taken yours, too, but he wasn't sure if you'd be working at the school today."

"Is he coming up for a visit then?"

She ducked her head, her next words directed at her lap. "You could say that," she muttered.

Friedrick frowned—the woman acted as if she was hiding something, but he couldn't figure out what. Still, he had his check and she didn't seem inclined to bring up seeing him at the jail. "Thanks again," he said and turned to leave.

"Just a moment."

He faced her again, both curious and wary about what else she might say.

"There's something I need to tell you." The woman stood and came around the side of the desk. She glanced past Friedrick, down the hallway, before lowering her voice. "A man came in here today. He spent a long time in Mr. Foster's office. I wouldn't have paid the two of them any mind, but I heard him relay to Mr. Foster how he'd been to talk to the sheriff. Seems he was upset about a certain German striking a former, wounded solider."

Friedrick managed a nonchalant expression, though he ground his teeth together. He could easily guess who the man in Mr. Foster's office had been. Robert had made good on his threat after all—and exaggerated his tale in doing so.

"Did he say anything else?" Friedrick pressed. He had to know the details if he wanted to protect Livy.

"They both piped down after that, so I didn't hear anymore. After the man left, though, Foster came out grumbling about having to find another maintenance man and likely a new teacher, too."

Friedrick's jaw went slack as he stared at her. He—and possibly Livy—were being fired? It had come to this already. "What reason did he give for letting me go?" He didn't bother to disguise his frustrated tone.

The secretary glanced down at her hands. "I didn't ask, and he didn't say. I'm sorry."

Friedrick could only surmise Robert had found out about his jail stay and had informed Mr. Foster. Or shared a colorful version of the truth regarding Friedrick's relationship with Livy. "Was this man tall with dark hair? Walks with a cane?"

"Yes, a Mr. Drake."

Jamming his cap on his head, Friedrick paced away from her. "What does Mr. Foster plan to do at his visit to the school? Inform me I've been fired and tell Miss Campbell she might be as well?"

"I suppose." He caught her apologetic look as he retraced his steps to her desk. "I think he wants to see where Miss Campbell's loyalties truly lie. If she proves to be American enough for him, she'll keep her job."

Her words stopped Fredrick's agitated steps. He had to warn Livy. A handful of patriotic sketches—especially one of him—might not be enough to tip the scales in her favor. Not since she'd decided against hanging the war bond poster and not if Mr. Foster had learned about his and Livy's deepening friendship.

"When does he plan to make the visit?"

"This afternoon." She returned to her seat.

He needed to leave, but one final question compelled him to stay a few moments more. "How come you never told Mr. Foster about seeing me in front of the jail? Or did you?" he added when she remained silent.

The secretary lifted her chin, a gesture that reminded Friedrick of Livy. "I never breathed a word about that, and it wasn't because I didn't recognize you. I knew at once you were being hauled in there, for Heaven knows why." She bit her lip as if she'd said too much.

"Why keep silent then?"

Her response was scarcely more than a whisper. "My grandmother came here from Germany as a little girl." She leveled him with a look, then picked up her magazine. "I have some things to do, Mr. Wagner. If you'd be good enough to be on your way."

"Good day..." He paused, hoping she'd supply him with her name. He wanted to know whom to thank.

"Nellie," she said, her face softening.

"Thank you, Nellie."

"You're welcome," she mouthed before she glued her gaze to her magazine once more.

Friedrick hurried down the stairs, his boots echoing loudly off the walls. What would his family say when he told them he'd lost his job? They might try selling family heirlooms to pay for his father's medicine, though people weren't likely to buy things from Germans.

And Livy? Would he get there in time to warn her

about Mr. Foster's impending visit and tell her how sorry he was for complicating her life?

Elsa had been right. He and Livy couldn't be together—not with the whole world fighting against them. The realization felt like a punch to his gut, bringing more pain than anger. Friedrick might be able to save her job, though, which would keep Livy close. With that determined thought, he sprinted out the door to his waiting wagon and team.

Chapter Fourteen

Five minutes to go before school ended for the day. And not a moment too soon, Livy thought wryly. The sunshine had been taunting the children since recess, making them chattier and more restless than usual.

The rumble of an automobile outside made her stomach twist with sudden nerves. A shadow of the fear she'd felt after Robert struck her last night wormed its way up her spine as well.

It can't be Robert's car, she told herself. *He's long gone by now.*

Hands clasped together, she reined in her emotions and walked between the rows of desks as the children bent over their readers. Friedrick would be by soon, with a smile to make her day more complete. The thought soothed her nervousness. Everything was right in the world when he was near.

The sound of the door creaking open brought her head up, along with nearly every student. A moment later Mr.

Foster entered the room, a grim expression on his face. Livy's heart lurched in surprise. She hadn't expected him to visit today, and in the late afternoon, no less. What would he think of the patriotic pictures lining the windowsills on either side of the room? The one she'd drawn of Friedrick felt as large as the war bond poster she'd destroyed. If only the superintendent wouldn't notice it...

"Good day, Mr. Foster," she said, coercing calm and pleasantness into her voice. "Children, let's say hello to our school superintendent, Mr. Foster."

A chorus of "Hello, Mr. Foster" filled the room. The man removed his hat and gave them a stiff nod.

"Is there something you wish to say to the class?" Livy asked.

Mr. Foster shook his head. "No, carry on." He went to stand near the stove at the back of the room, his gaze settling on her in an unnerving way.

Livy straightened her shoulders and did her best to ignore him. "You may return to your readers, children."

She resumed her slow pacing, though her mind raced wildly ahead. Why did the man already act displeased? Had he noticed his poster was missing? If he questioned her, what would she say?

After another glance at the clock, she cleared her throat. "School is dismissed. I'll see you all tomorrow."

Her students noisily gathered up their things and moved in pairs and groups toward the door, ignoring the silent observer in the back. Livy longed to go with them. Even Harlan and Greta abandoned the school for the call of the outdoors.

When the last of the children had filed out, Livy forced her mouth into a smile. "What can I do for you, Mr.

Foster? If you'd come earlier, you might have joined us for our geography lesson."

The man stepped forward. "I'm afraid my visit is not to observe your teaching skills, Miss Campbell."

"Oh?" She busied herself with picking up the readers from the desks. The task gave her something to do besides stand still, facing the brunt of his irritation. She hoped he didn't hear the blood pumping in her ears. "To what do I owe this visit then?"

"Miss Campbell." The name was a command.

Livy set the stack of books down and turned to face him directly.

"I believe you have some explaining to do."

"About?" she hedged, still uncertain which of her choices had him most upset.

"To begin with, where is the poster I asked you to hang?" He gestured with his hat toward the front wall. "And what is all this falderal in the windows?"

She couldn't tell him she'd ripped the poster into shreds and burned it—she'd be fired at once. "I wanted to help the children find their own ways of expressing their love of their country."

"Their country—you mean Germany?"

Despite her fear, his words brought the sting of anger. Livy bit her cheek until she could respond calmly. "No, sir. Their love of America. Each picture is an expression of patriotism. And because the children drew them, I believe, the sentiment behind the pictures makes a more lasting impression."

"Humph." He crossed to the nearest window to examine the artwork. Livy's drawing of Friedrick stood only a few feet away.

"If you'd care to look over here, Mr. Foster." She waved to the opposite side of the room. "Henry is quite the artist. He drew a naval ship—"

"Which student drew this one?" He pointed his hat at Livy's sketch. Her heart throbbed with new dread, but she reminded herself she'd done nothing wrong. It was only a drawing.

"I drew that, Mr. Foster." She lifted her chin a notch, despite the clammy feeling of worry that made her collar feel suddenly hot and choking. "I wanted to contribute to the art project and thought a simple scene of a family reading the Bible captured the American spirit of hearth and home."

"It's a very good likeness of our maintenance man, isn't it?"

Livy pressed her lips together.

Mr. Foster spun around. "I imagine you've gotten to know him quite well."

"I'm not sure what you mean."

"You need not play innocent with me, Miss Campbell. I know far more than you might suspect."

Livy maintained a level gaze on his round face, though her pulse thudded faster with fear. "Is there something you find lacking in my ability as a teacher, Mr. Foster?"

He gave a mirthless laugh. "No, and that's the real shame." He tucked his hands behind him and walked past the windows toward the back of the room. "Do you recall a few weeks back when I expressly asked for you to tell me if Mr. Wagner said or did anything that might make one believe his allegiance lies with his mother country?" He paused to look at her.

"Yes." Livy had no remorse or regret at protecting Friedrick. "I remember."

"Would you consider a jail stay of three nights, even in his mother's place, smacks a bit of German loyalty? Perhaps Mr. Wagner was using his mother to conduct business against this country."

He pierced Livy with a long glare when she remained silent. How had the man learned about Friedrick's time in jail? As if reading her mind, Mr. Foster continued, "A new acquaintance of mine did a little digging around town today and found out about Mr. Wagner's time in jail. However, I'm more curious to know if you knew about it."

"Only after the fact, sir."

"Yet you did not feel the need to inform me?"

"I couldn't..." She'd been nursing Friedrick through his illness. Not that she would have gone to tell Mr. Foster anything, even if she'd been given the chance. Would he be further enraged if he learned how much time she'd spent here with Friedrick, alone? Would others find out? Would she be branded a German sympathizer?

"You couldn't come? Is that what you were about to say, Miss Campbell? And why is that?"

Tell the truth. Her father's repeated council from her youth entered her mind and gave her courage. She'd done the humane thing in caring for Friedrick, which was nothing to be ashamed of.

"I was not able to come, Mr. Foster, because I was nursing Mr. Wagner back to health." She kept her head held high. "While in jail, he came down with influenza. He was too sick to make it home, and so I stayed here in the school with him and cared for him until he was well enough to return to his farm."

A flicker of surprise crossed the man's face.

"You may ask any of the neighbors. They can testify to the truth of my story. A man was in need of help and I was the one who could provide it."

"I wasn't aware you were here in the school alone with him."

Livy hated the blush that crept into her cheeks. "I promise you nothing untoward happened. He was nearly at death's door for most of the time."

"I believe you, Miss Campbell, but your promise holds little weight with me." He plunked on his hat and marched toward the door, where he stopped. "You have failed to put up the poster I gave you. You have also withheld information from me regarding Mr. Wagner's loyalty or lack thereof to this country. We may not have evidence of any true wrongdoing on his part, but such is not the case with you."

Too angry and stunned to keep silent, Livy opened her mouth to protest, but the superintendent wasn't finished.

"I came here to get a feel for your own loyalties, Miss Campbell."

"I assure you, Mr. Foster, my loyalties—"

"Apparently he was right about you and your German sympathies."

Livy blinked in confusion. "He?"

"You are hereby released of your position, just as Mr. Wagner has been released from his." He withdrew a piece of paper and extended it toward her. "This is your first and final paycheck."

Friedrick had lost his job, too? The revelation stung as hard and biting as Robert's slap last night. "What is Mr. Wagner being fired for?"

"I can't very well employ a maintenance man whose mother broke the law, can I?"

She wanted to argue for Friedrick's innocence, but she knew she couldn't change Mr. Foster's opinion of the situation, at least not at present. The man had made up his mind, probably before he'd even set foot inside the school.

Sadness washed over Livy, making her steps feel weighted as she walked forward. She hated to think how the children would feel when they learned they had lost another teacher. And what would Friedrick's family do without the extra money?

"I'm sorry," she said as she took her check from Mr. Foster.

"So am I." The man shifted his weight as if suddenly nervous. "There is one other thing that must be done." When he lifted his head, his face had hardened. "But this is your own doing, Miss Campbell. Please get your coat."

Livy drew back, a worm of panic uncurling inside her. "I don't understand."

Mr. Foster went to the door. "You may take over now," he said to someone outside as he exited the school.

A man wearing a sheriff's badge appeared in the doorway. "Miss Olivia Campbell?"

"Yes?"

"I'm Sheriff Tate." He sounded tired. "I'm here to inform you that you're under arrest for seditious behavior against this country."

Her eyes widened in shock. "You can't be serious."

"Quite serious, miss. You withheld information from the superintendent and refused to show allegiance to America by hanging a war bond poster." He reached out and took hold of her arm, gentle but firm. "If you'll get your coat, please."

Too numb to think, Livy put on her coat. She stuffed her check into one of the pockets and allowed Sheriff Tate to lead her from the school. An automobile sat waiting out front, with Mr. Foster in the front seat.

"No, wait." Livy hung back.

"Please, Miss Campbell." The sheriff gave her a soft push toward the car. "Don't make things worse by resisting arrest."

"But I..." This wasn't happening. She felt as though she were moving through a dream. The nightmarish quality only intensified when her gaze jumped to a familiar car parked in front of her cabin. Robert leaned against the fender, a smug expression on his face. He'd threatened her and Friedrick, and now he was making good on his threat.

Fury burned through her as she averted her face. At that moment she caught sight of Friedrick driving his horses hard up the road.

"Livy?" he hollered.

Her heart twisted with both relief and panic. Would they arrest him, too? His family couldn't afford to have him in jail again—for who knew how long this time.

"Miss, please get in the car." Sheriff Tate opened the door with his free hand.

"Wait," Friedrick shouted. He drove past the car and jerked his horses to a stop.

"Come on, Sheriff," Mr. Foster grumbled from the front seat. "I need to get back to my office."

Livy stepped toward Friedrick. There was no mistaking the anguish in his eyes, even from a distance.

She wanted so much to break free—to find solace in

his strong embrace, to kiss him until she forgot all about the fear—but she wasn't free. And neither was he, not in the way they'd pretended.

"I'm sorry," she whispered to Friedrick before the sheriff placed her inside the car.

* * *

Friedrick watched, powerless, as the sheriff's car sped down the road in the direction he'd come. Why had Livy been arrested? His biggest fear had been over her losing her job, not being hauled off to jail. He gathered the reins, ready to turn the horses around and go after her, when he noticed another automobile and its owner.

His initial surprise at Livy's arrest exploded into rage as he sprang from the wagon seat and marched toward Robert. How dare the man try to hurt Livy again and again and again.

"You!" Friedrick forced out between clenched teeth. His hands, balled into fists, shook with fury. "You were the one who had us both fired."

Robert lifted his shoulders in a bored shrug. "I told you I'd get even."

"And for what? To see the girl you supposedly love carted to jail by the town sheriff?"

"I wasn't the traitor."

Friedrick came to stop near the car, his jaw so tense it hurt. "What did you accuse her of?" he demanded in a loud voice. "Why is Livy going to jail?"

"I told you." Robert stepped away from his car. "She's a German sympathizer."

"Livy Campbell is no traitor."

"Whether she is or isn't is not your concern," Robert said, his voice low and deadly. "You leave her alone from now on or you'll find yourself in a worse situation than losing your job. Seems I heard in town you got yourself a real sick pa and some kid brother and sister. Wouldn't want any harm coming to them, would you?"

The ugly words hit their mark, as Friedrick suspected Robert wanted. If the man found Joe and his crowd, there could be real trouble for Friedrick's family. This thought alone gave him the strength to unclench his aching fingers and walk away.

"That's right. You run on home now," Robert scoffed.

Friedrick climbed onto the wagon and snapped the reins. He needed to formulate a plan—a way to help Livy out of jail before she could be tried and sentenced to prison like Miss Lehmann—but the anger still pounding in his head made thinking difficult. If only he could have sent Robert back to where he belonged, more than a little bruised. But he wouldn't fight violence with violence.

The lash of the wind on Friedrick's face as he drove the horses hard toward the farm cooled his neck and his fury. Deep anguish rushed in to take its place, though. If he'd kept himself from falling for Livy, she wouldn't be in such a mess.

Could he really have stopped himself from loving Livy? He shook his head. He'd been destined to love her from the moment he'd gone over to cheer her up at the dance hall on her birthday. She was everything and more to him. As sure as the sun, he knew he would never find another girl like her. Someone who loved him back, in spite of his heritage. Someone who made him smile, made him want to conquer the world.

The thought of Livy spending even a few minutes in the cold, wretched jail tortured him. He had to get her out of there, but doing so might exact a price from his family.

Friedrick groaned in frustration. Why did everything have to come back to choosing his family or choosing to fight, this time for the girl he loved? His family had suffered enough already, but Livy wasn't guilty of any crime.

He jerked the horses to a stop, his breathing as hard as theirs. *Think, Friedrick. Think.* Could he save Livy and his family, too? He felt for the check in his pocket. It could buy his father more medicine. Or possibly Livy's freedom. But which should he choose? He owed his family everything, but what would life be without Livy? Even if he never saw her again, Friedrick could force himself to be content as long as she was safe.

What about Livy's parents? he wondered. Surely they would be willing to pay bail to have Livy released, if he notified them.

Friedrick dismissed the thought. He was largely responsible for Livy's confinement in jail, and he would figure out how to get her out.

Something tall and black, beyond the road, drew his attention. A tree trunk with a jagged top. The cause of death was evident—lightning. It reminded Friedrick of the war stories he'd heard about No Man's Land in France, where the bodies of the dead lay among splintered pieces of torched trees. The horrific image filled him with piercing despair.

Where are You, God? He rested his hands on his knees and put his head in his open palms. *Have You forgotten us, Thy children?*

Overseas, men and boys, on both sides of the trenches,

were being killed. Here at home, his life was slowly being stolen as well—his family's savings, their language, their dignity, and now Livy.

What am I to do?

"Friedrick?"

He jerked his head up and found Maria standing beside the wagon. He hadn't realized he'd stopped directly across the road from her farm.

"Are you all right? I saw you stop. Do you need something?"

A miracle.

"No." He gathered the reins to drive on, but the sincere compassion on her face made him pause. The beginnings of a plan sprouted in his mind. Maybe there was something Maria could do. Friedrick nearly laughed at the irony. God certainly had a sense of humor if the solution to Friedrick's problem was none other than Maria Schmitt.

"There is something I need you to do, Maria." He climbed to the ground and removed the check from his pocket. "Can you borrow your family's wagon and cash this check at the bank for me?"

Her eyebrows rose in obvious surprise, but she took the slip of paper from him. "My father took the wagon for an errand up north."

"I'd let you borrow mine, but someone in town might recognize it."

"Are you in trouble, Friedrick?" She frowned in concern.

Not yet anyway. "I lost my job today and things may go badly for me and my family if I go to town."

She eyed him for a moment, then shrugged. "I can walk. Will the bank let me cash your check?"

"The bank owner might not, but the young clerk who works there—the one who was wounded in the war—he most certainly will. Especially if you show him that dazzling smile of yours."

"Why do I need to impress the bank clerk?" Maria asked, her lips twitching with such a smile. "Are you playing matchmaker?"

Friedrick shook his head, all traces of humor gone. There was more he needed to do before Livy might be freed. "Miss Campbell is in trouble. She was fired and taken to jail. I'm going to try to post bail for her tonight."

"How much do you have?" She glanced at the check in her hand. "Twenty-five dollars surely won't be enough."

"I know." Friedrick climbed back up onto the seat. "I'm going to try to raise more. I think some of the families around here, at least those with children at Livy's school, might be willing to help."

Maria stepped to the wagon, one hand curling over the side. "You're asking us to help someone who isn't one of our own?"

"I am." He met her level gaze, silently pleading for her to understand. He needed her help; Livy needed their help. "Where does the bigotry end, if not now, Maria? When do we stand up against the injustice? Whether it's for a German or an American. That's what I am asking you and the others to do."

She bit her lip, her eyes especially dark and vulnerable. The lack of pretense enhanced her natural beauty. Maria would make some lucky man happy, even if it wasn't him.

"I'll get the check cashed." She tossed her hair and released her hold on the wagon. "You can count on it."

Relief flooded him. Livy wasn't free yet, but she was

one step closer. "Thank you, Maria. Bring the money by this evening."

"Anything else?"

"Pray that I can raise enough."

* * *

To Livy's surprise, the jail cells stood empty. Sheriff Tate opened the door to one and gestured for Livy to go inside. She stalked past him, not sure whether she felt more angry or concerned. Two cots stood on opposite sides of the cell, a dull white bedpan beneath each. A small window, covered with bars, provided meager light. Humiliation engulfed her as she sank onto one of the cots.

"How long do I have to stay?" she asked, though she feared the answer. She pulled her coat tighter around herself.

The sheriff focused on the row of stones at her back when he answered. "That all depends, Miss Campbell. If someone can post bail for you or if Mr. Foster drops the charges, then you're free to go."

"How much is bail?"

"A hundred dollars."

She fingered the check in her pocket, though she knew she wouldn't be allowed to go to the bank and cash it.

"Do you want to contact your folks?"

"They don't have a telephone."

"How about a telegram then?"

Did she want to tell her family she'd been branded a German sympathizer and thrown in jail? Would there be repercussions against them because she'd chosen to stand up for Friedrick and the other German-Americans? She shivered at the thought.

Despite the tears threatening to spill over, she shook her head. "No, thank you."

"Well, maybe tomorrow. Supper'll be around in about two hours." Sheriff Tate gave her a look of pity and left the cell.

Livy lifted her knees to her chest and wrapped her arms around her long skirt. Her gaze wandered over the blank walls. Was this the cell Friedrick had stayed in for three nights? How had he managed the boredom and inactivity during the day?

What would Nora say if Livy wrote to tell her dear friend about serving time in jail? Would she be upset or would she understand Livy's loyalty to Friedrick? More questions crowded in on themselves inside her mind. How long would she actually have to stay here? Could she request an audience with Mr. Foster and plead with him to drop the charges?

Livy squeezed her eyes shut as several tears slid down her face. Her life had once again turned to shambles. She'd left home to avoid Robert, the war, and the constant memory of her brothers. But even here, the war had found her. Now she would have to say good-bye to the people and the place that had brought her more happiness than she'd experienced in years.

A hard ache rose into her throat at the thought of never seeing her students or Friedrick again. To be denied the sight of his handsome face and the security of his touch was the cruelest of punishments—far worse than a jail sentence.

Sniffing hard, Livy opened her eyes. She noticed a dead moth sitting on the edge of the windowsill. The rest of the room had been swept free of insects and dust, but someone had missed this tiny creature. Had the moth known where it was going? Did it realize the window would never open, no matter how hard it beat its wings against the glass?

The pain in Livy's throat deepened with empathy for this lifeless insect. Was she, too, beating against the glass of fate to think she could freely love a man of German descent? Had she truly done wrong in helping Friedrick? She didn't feel like a traitor to her country, but she didn't know what that was supposed to feel like. At the moment, all she felt inside was empty and cold.

Please help my fear and confusion, God.

Had she misunderstood the feeling of hope she'd felt about returning to her job after Tom's death? Had God intended for her to remain distant friends with Friedrick and nothing more?

"I wish you were here, Tom or Joel," she whispered to herself. "I could sure use your help."

Memories of the two of them filled her thoughts. Tom, the tease. Joel, the sage. Friedrick reminded her a bit of both. Would they care that he was German-American when he treated her so well and loved her so fully?

A snatch of conversation, the night before Tom and Joel had left for training, returned to her memory. She'd asked Tom what he'd do if he came back from the war disfigured or blind. Did he think Nora would still have him then?

"I do," he'd said, his face uncharacteristically serious. "Nora lives that scripture we learned as kids in Sunday school. The one that talks about how God looks on the heart and not on what we look like on the outside."

God looketh on the heart.

Livy didn't voice the words out loud, but they echoed through her as if someone had shouted them. Could this be the advice her father had tried to give her when she'd first come to Hilden? To look on people's hearts, regardless of where they came from?

God didn't see Friedrick as German or American. He saw Friedrick's heart, just as Livy had been privileged to do. A heart full of kindness, hard work, and loyalty. If those were the qualities she'd exemplified in keeping Friedrick's secret and nursing him back to health, then she would do it all over again.

Livy climbed to her feet and brushed the lingering tears from her cheeks. She would send a telegram to her parents tonight and request they telephone her. Surely they would agree to pay her bail, once she explained everything. Then she would find a way to pay them back every cent.

Before she could call for the sheriff, he appeared at her cell door. "You have a visitor."

Could it be Friedrick? Livy hoped it wasn't, though seeing him would buoy up her spirits all the more. He didn't need to court further trouble, not after losing his job. "Who is it?"

"A Mr. Drake."

Anger boiled inside Livy at the name. Thanks to Robert, she was in this mess. "I don't wish to see him."

"He told me as much but said he had some information about your folks you might want to hear."

"My parents?" Worry challenged her anger. Had word reached her hometown already about her being friendly to German-Americans? Were her parents and siblings in any type of danger? She had to know, even if it meant talking with someone as odious as Robert. "All right, I'll talk to him."

Sheriff Tate left to get Robert. A few moments later he strolled into view. He came to a stop in front of her cell. "Afternoon, Livy." He doffed his hat to her as if making a social call.

Livy took a deliberate step back from the bars. "Get to the point, Robert. What's wrong with my parents?"

"Oh, they're perfectly fine." He glanced causally at his hat. "Unfortunately, I can't inform them their daughter has been thrown in jail for being a traitor."

Livy cringed. She didn't want her parents hearing the story from Robert. "Why is that?"

"Because Allen is the only one home."

Her next question came out slow and tense. "Where are my mom and dad?" She wanted to reach through the bars and shake him.

A glint of triumph lit up Robert's black eyes as he lifted his gaze to hers. "Your mother told mine your aunt isn't well. So your folks and the rest of your siblings took the train to go collect her and bring her back to the farm. They won't be returning for a week."

The news of her beloved aunt being ill barely registered in Livy's mind before she realized the import of Robert's last words. Her parents wouldn't be home for a week, which meant no bail and no freedom until then. Reality buckled her knees and she stumbled back onto her cot.

"Don't look so glum, Livy." Robert edged closer to the cell door. "I have some good news, which ought to cheer you up."

Livy doubted it, but she lifted her chin anyway.

"Come over here and talk to me, and I'll tell you all about it, darling."

The endearment grated across Livy's skin like sandpaper. Why had she allowed herself to be so dreamy-eyed over Robert that she hadn't seen him in a true light?

"I'll sit, thank you."

He shrugged, though anger momentarily clouded his face. "I'm here to strike a deal with you."

"A deal?"

"You can be free of this place within the hour," he said, his voice low, "and even have your job back, *if*..." How could one tiny word sound so ominous?

Wariness twisted Livy's stomach. "If..." she repeated.

"For starters, come here so I can talk to you proper without these hideous bars blocking the view."

A sharp retort rested on her tongue—she wouldn't be in jail if it weren't for him. Instead she swallowed the verbal barb. If she acted nicely, she might discover a better way out of her predicament than the fishy scheme Robert had likely concocted.

She stood and went to the cell door. Robert reached through the bars to hold her hand. Livy winced at his touch. Her wrist was still sore from where he'd gripped it so hard the night before. Had it only been less than a day since he'd shown up in Hilden and wreaked havoc on her life again?

"I told you last night I still love you, Livy. All you've got to do is agree to be my girl again, and you can walk out of here." He smiled, but it no longer held the charm it once had. "I'll let you finish up this silly teaching job and we'll be married this summer."

"Just like that?" she managed to ask in a calm voice,

though his patronizing tone churned new anger inside her. Robert had certainly done well in carrying out his threat to her and Friedrick, concocting this entire jail scheme and making himself her potential rescuer. All because he couldn't get another girl to love him as Livy had tried. "All charges against me would be dropped?"

Robert chuckled. "Not exactly. You'd also need to denounce these Boche friends of yours to the sheriff and the superintendent. Tell 'em you were verbally threatened to keep that man's secret about going to jail as punishment for the last teacher being fired." He spat out the words, his face hardening with each one. Apparently he'd garnered plenty of information from Mr. Foster, and who knew who else, about her and Friedrick's situation. "Tell 'em you made a mistake in going along with their plans. Tell 'em you're not a traitor to everything your brother Tom fought and died for, what your brother Joel is still fighting for."

Despite her revelation earlier, his allegations still stung and brought a moment of doubt. Would Tom and Joel see her actions the same way? Livy shied away from the question and instead pictured her students, their families, and Friedrick. She remembered the pain on his face when he'd seen the bond poster.

No. The word resounded in her head and heart.

She would not give in to prejudice. She'd experienced a taste of it herself when she'd first come here, and no one deserved such ill treatment. Joel might not forgive her, but at least she'd be able to live with herself by refusing to give in to Robert's lies and hatred.

"Thank you for your proposal. You're much more sober than the last time you brought up marriage to me."

She withdrew her hand from his and rubbed at the bruised flesh on her wrist. "Which also means you're sober enough to remember what I have to say now."

With head high, she stared down those darkening eyes of his. "I will not denounce these people. They are as American as me and you, if not more so. I will not break their trust, as you have broken mine, over and over again. I will wait for my parents."

Robert stuck his face against the metal bars. "You think you're so high and mighty? You've been duped, Livy," he hissed. "These people don't care about you. Where's your German boyfriend now, huh? I don't see him in here trying to negotiate for your release. And do you know why? He's too scared."

Livy gritted her teeth, trying to block out the misgivings Robert's accusations created. She'd seen the look on Friedrick's face before she'd been stuffed inside the sheriff's car—he loved her. But she also knew there was little he could do now, not without hurting his family.

"I gave you another chance, one you'll wish you'd taken before I leave town." Robert jammed his hat on his head. "Your Boche is goin' to wish you'd accepted me, too." With that, he strode away.

"Robert?" Livy hollered as she rushed to the cell door. "Robert?" Panic squeezed her throat and lungs. What would he do that he hadn't already done? Could she send a warning to Friedrick to be on the lookout? "Sheriff?" she yelled next, followed by a kick to the bars for more noise. "Sheriff Tate!"

The man lumbered toward her cell a few seconds later, a deep frown on his face. "What's all the ruckus, Miss Campbell?"

"You have to let me out—now. That man, Mr. Drake, is going to harm Frie—I mean, Mr. Wagner."

"Now, now." Sheriff Tate removed his hat and wiped his brow as if the exertion of moving quickly had tuckered him out. "Did he say what he intended to do?"

"No, but he made a blatant threat."

"You know I can't let you out. Not without bail or without Mr. Foster dropping the charges."

Livy slapped an open palm against the metal bars. "Then at least go to the Wagner place and make sure they're all right."

"Can't leave the jail while there's an inmate here." The sheriff dropped his hat back into place. "Not unless the deputy is present, and his wife's having a baby. Been having the pains most of the day."

"Errr." Livy pushed away from the door and began pacing the small space. "This is urgent. Is there nothing you can do?"

He shook his head. "Afraid not. But you get yourself some rest. Supper'll be around soon."

"I don't care about your blasted supper," she muttered beneath her breath as the man walked away. There was only one thing to do now. She stopped her frenzied pacing and sat down.

With her hands curled tightly around the edge of the cot, she lowered her chin. She prayed for the Wagner family's protection, for a way out of jail, for a miracle, if possible. When she felt too exhausted to sit upright any longer, she lay down on the cot. Shutting her eyes, Livy continued her silent pleas toward Heaven until sleep claimed her.

Chapter Fifteen

The noise of an argument jerked Livy awake. The light in the cell had diminished. A tray of food, likely as cold as the jail by now, stood by the door. She hadn't heard the sheriff slide it inside.

She'd had the most horrible dream, something about Robert threatening to hurt Friedrick. As she sat up, her conversation with Robert flooded back into her memory. It hadn't been a dream after all.

Livy shot to her feet and went to the bars. "Sheriff?" she shouted. "Sheriff?"

The arguing stopped at once, then Livy heard light footsteps rushing toward her.

"Hey, miss, you can't go back there," Sheriff Tate hollered.

Maria Schmitt appeared in front of the cell. "Maria?" Livy gasped. "What are you doing here? Is Friedrick in trouble?"

Maria shook her head. "He was fine when I left him an hour ago."

Livy's relief was short-lived. Robert could still be planning something. She had to warn Friedrick. "I've got to get out of here."

"I am trying to help with that." Maria lifted a wad of cash and several handwritten notes.

"I told you," the sheriff said, grabbing Maria by the elbow. "You aren't allowed back here."

Livy threw Sheriff Tate a beseeching look. "Please. I need to speak with her."

The sheriff frowned at both of them, but the hard lines around his eyes softened after a moment. "Fine. But being that your friend here is...um...German..." His round face turned red. "I've got to stay close by."

Maria arched her dark eyebrows. "Afraid I'm going to sell secrets to the enemy?" Sheriff Tate's red face flushed deeper in color, but he didn't move away. "Don't worry, Sheriff. I've been trying to tell you for ten minutes why I'm here and it's nothing so vial." She looked to Livy as she continued. "Friedrick collected money from the families of your students. He also donated his paycheck. But he was only able to come up with seventy-five dollars."

Friedrick had done that for her? Even at the price of punishment, he'd still tried to help—and she loved him all the more for it. She really and truly loved him. The realization brought warmth to Livy's cold body. "And the letters?"

"All written by the parents of your students." Maria separated them from the cash and passed them through the bars to Livy.

She read the first one, signed by Henry's father, though

Livy recognized that the handwriting was his son's. *Miss Campbell has helped my boy work to go to the high school and on to college. She is not a traitor, but a gifted teacher.* Another one had Mrs. Keller's signature on it. *Miss Campbell has taught these children well. She also helped save the life of Friedrick Wagner. She is innocent of wrongdoing.*

Livy read them all, including one from Elsa, stating her gratitude for Livy's teaching and nursing her son back to health. Their expressions of devotion, at the risk of their own reputations, brought fresh tears to her eyes. Like Friedrick, they, too, hadn't abandoned her.

"Don't these prove my innocence?" She shoved the notes through the bars for the sheriff to see.

"I told you, Miss Campbell," the man answered, his jaw set, "I've got to have twenty-five more dollars for bail or Mr. Foster has to drop the charges. I'm sorry." He gestured at Maria. "You've had your visit, now it's time to go." He started to walk away.

"Thank you for trying anyway, Maria." Livy mustered a grateful smile, but it faded quickly in the wake of her growing despair.

"I'm not done yet," Maria whispered.

"Miss Schmitt!" Sheriff Tate growled from down the hallway.

"Coming, Sheriff," she replied sweetly before leaning toward the cell door again. "Friedrick said if the money and letters weren't enough, I ought to find Dr. Miller. Apparently he and the sheriff are good friends, so the doctor might convince him to let you go."

"Try the deputy's house first. The sheriff said the man's wife is about to have a baby."

"Do you want me to lock you up, too, Miss Schmitt?" the sheriff intoned.

"I'd better go. But I'll be back, Livy." Maria strode down the hall.

Livy watched her go, then turned to face the high window. There was still a chance she'd be released tonight. Then she would beg the sheriff to drive her to Friedrick's so she could warn him about Robert. He'd assaulted her and Friedrick once. What would prevent him from physically harming Friedrick again? Or taking out his fury on Elsa or the children?

If Maria could get the doctor, if the doctor could change the sheriff's mind. *If, if, if...*

She paced the cell again. The movement helped ease some of the concern lodged in the pit of her stomach. *Hurry, Maria, hurry. Find the doctor, find the doctor.*

The remaining light in Livy's cell receded little by little as she circled the small room over and over. Light spilled from Sheriff Tate's office down the hall, casting shadows on the floor. Would she be freed in time? Had Robert gone after Friedrick already? Was the man she loved hurt, or worse?

Livy gnawed at her cheek until she thought she might bite a hole through it. *Please, God, please don't let us be too late.* She rested her forehead against the rough, cool wall. Voices filtered down to her cell. She rushed to the door and pressed her face to the bars to see who was coming.

"I only want to talk to her, Walter," she heard the doctor say in a weary voice before he reached her cell.

Hope rose painfully into her throat at the doctor's appearance. "Dr. Miller." Her voice broke on a sob of relief. "Thank goodness you're here."

"What is going on, Miss Campbell?"

"I was arrested for demonstrating sympathy toward the Germans."

The doctor glanced over his shoulder as Sheriff Tate came forward. Maria followed close behind. "Who accused her?" Dr. Miller demanded of his friend.

"John Foster," the sheriff said without looking at either Livy or the doctor.

Dr. Miller frowned. "On what grounds?"

When the sheriff remained quiet, Livy answered for him. "Mr. Foster asked me to share with him any incriminating information I might have learned about Friedrick Wagner. But I chose not to say anything about Friedrick being jailed or how I cared for him alone in the school when he was sick. I also took down the bond poster he asked me to put up in the school."

"That is all?"

Livy nodded.

"What was the reasoning behind your actions, Miss Campbell?"

"My decisions weren't based on any sympathy toward Germany. I did what I did because..." She swallowed hard. "Because I care about these people. Not as Americans or Germans, but as decent people trying to live right and care for their families, like all of us."

Lines of fatigue etched the doctor's face, but he held himself tall, his expression unyielding as he turned to the sheriff. "Let her out, Walter."

Sheriff Tate sputtered. "But, Hans, you heard her. She didn't tell Foster the truth. She hid information from him."

"Like Foster hid information about Miss Lehmann?" The doctor shook his head in disgust. "How Foster was pressured into firing her because she was German? How some of the evidence used against her was likely manufactured to suit that scoundrel Joe Hilly and his thugs?"

Livy stared openmouthed at Dr. Miller, trying to process what he'd said. The superintendent had been pressured to fire Miss Lehmann, largely because she was German? Instead of jail, though, the woman had been sentenced to prison. For the first time all evening, Livy felt a measure of gratitude she'd only been given a temporary jail sentence.

"I don't make the rules." The sheriff eyed Livy, then turned away. "I can't release her unless I get bail of a hundred dollars or Foster drops the charges. We've got to be careful in times like these. We can't have people conspiring with the enemy."

The doctor slammed a fist against the bars, making Livy jump. "She is not conspiring with the enemy. Miss Campbell endured great risk to herself by caring for Friedrick Wagner. If he had gone home instead, he might have given the influenza to his father, which would have killed him. According to Miss Schmitt here, Miss Campbell has also endeared herself to her students and their families. There is nothing traitorous about that."

Sheriff Tate ran a hand over his face.

"If that is not enough to convince you…" Dr. Miller reached into his pocket and pulled out his wallet. After counting out twenty-five dollars, he slapped the bills into the sheriff's palm.

Maria placed the money Friedrick had collected into the man's other hand and closed his fingers over it. "I believe you have the required amount, Sheriff."

His face red once more, Sheriff Tate stared at the cash.

"I can't take it, Hans," he said quietly. "Florence would make me sleep on the couch if I did, and she'd have every right to do so." He handed back the doctor's money and faced Livy, no longer hesitant. He drew himself up to full height and puffed out his expansive chest. "I'm the law here—not Joe Hilly or Foster or anybody else. I'll cover the twenty-five dollars you need, Miss Campbell, which makes full bail. You're free to go."

Livy grabbed the bars with both hands. "Thank you, Sheriff."

He unlocked the cell door and held it open for her. Livy raced out and gave the man a hug. The sheriff coughed with embarrassment, but she caught a glimmer of startled happiness in his eyes when she released him. Latching on to Maria's arm, she propelled the young lady down the hallway. They still had to get to Friedrick.

"We need to borrow your car, Sheriff Tate," she said without slowing down.

"My car?" The two men followed after them.

"Friedrick may be in danger, but we can stop it."

"Hold on, Miss Campbell," the doctor said. "What is wrong with Friedrick?"

Livy spun around. "There's little time to explain. A former beau of mine came to town yesterday. He's the one who convinced Mr. Foster to press charges and have me arrested. He threatened to hurt Friedrick, too."

Dr. Miller looked at the sheriff. "Sounds like you need to check it out, Walter."

"But I can't leave the jail."

"Who is going to break out?" the doctor asked, amusement and irritation coloring his tone.

Sheriff Tate growled low in his throat and threw up his

arms. "This better be real cause for concern, Miss Campbell. If I find everything nice and cozy at the Wagner place, I may drag you back here for good measure."

"Then you'll drive us?" Livy held her breath. She'd never get there in time if she and Maria had to walk.

"Why don't we telephone first?" Maria suggested.

Livy wanted to rush to Friedrick's side now instead of waiting, but if she could warn him beforehand... "You're right. That's a good idea."

She followed the sheriff to the telephone. The operator seemed to take an eternity to connect Livy.

"Hello?"

Livy sagged against the wall at the sound of Friedrick's voice. He was still there, unharmed. "Friedrick? Friedrick, you have to..." The line went dead. "Hello, hello?"

A moment later the operator came back on. "I'm sorry, miss. Something has interrupted the line."

"Could you try again? It's important."

"Hold, please."

Livy bit the inside of her cheek, hoping, praying.

"Still nothing."

Replacing the earpiece on its hook, Livy gulped with sudden fear. Had someone cut the line? Someone like Robert?

"We need to leave—now. I think their phone line has been cut."

The three of them hurried out the door after Livy. She and Maria jumped into the back of the sheriff's car. Once the engine started, Sheriff Tate slid into the front seat beside Dr. Miller. He jerked the car around and sped down the street, heading out of town.

"We'll make it." Maria gave Livy's arm a gentle squeeze.

Livy peered into the dark beyond the car, her heart beating wildly with dread. "I hope so."

* * *

"Livy?"

Friedrick could have sworn it was her voice on the other end of the telephone.

"Operator?" He gave the crank a good turn. "Operator?"

There was no reply. A feeling of apprehension crept over him as he hung up the earpiece. Why had the line gone dead? Did it have anything to do with Robert and his threat to hurt Friedrick and his family if Friedrick attempted to help Livy?

If it had been her on the line, did that mean his plan had worked? Had Maria been able to convince the sheriff to let Livy go with seventy-five dollars for bail and the testimonies of her students' parents?

Friedrick walked from the kitchen into the hallway and glanced through the open door of his father's bedroom. How strange to see the bed empty for the first time in years.

Heinrich had refused, at first, to go to the barn with Elsa and the children, and Friedrick couldn't blame him. A few hours in the old building might worsen his father's condition, but Friedrick wasn't taking any chances tonight. Not when it came to his family or Robert's threats. If the man had no qualms striking a woman, he certainly wouldn't let Friedrick get away unscathed for helping Livy. This time, though, Friedrick wouldn't stand down.

To his surprise and gratitude, Elsa had agreed with his plans. She'd voiced her approval of using his paycheck to help with Livy's release and had even dictated a letter about Livy for the sheriff. Friedrick wasn't sure what had prompted Elsa's change of heart, but he welcomed it. Whatever awaited them tonight, he could stand confident, knowing his family supported him.

A loud pounding at the door interrupted his thoughts. He'd been walking around the empty house for what felt like hours, anticipating trouble from Robert, but the sound of the knock still filled him with momentary dread.

He thought of Livy, alone and cold in the jail, and all because she'd helped him, loved him. His jaw tightened in anger. He would pay whatever price he must for securing her freedom, but he wouldn't surrender without a fight. Tonight was his time to stand against injustice.

Friedrick sent a silent prayer heavenward and strode with measured steps to the door. The scene before him mirrored the one from eight weeks earlier so perfectly, he might have thought he'd gone back in time. The mob filled the yard, their torches cutting up the darkness. Joe watched him with a mocking grin. Everything appeared as it had before, except for Robert's presence beside the mob leader.

"Where's Livy?" Friedrick demanded of Robert, dispensing with any false pleasantries.

"Gone home." The man's voice carried with resolve, though his gaze flicked away as he spoke. "She told me she doesn't want anything more to do with you, Boche."

The insult cut less than the knowledge Livy might have

left Hilden without saying good-bye, if there was any truth to Robert's assertion. Some of Friedrick's determination slipped at the thought of never seeing Livy again, until he reminded himself there were others he loved who needed his protection.

"What are you here for?" he asked Joe, his voice hard. It was time to show these men he wouldn't be bullied, as Peter Hoffman had done.

"Mr. Drake says you're not supportin' your country enough, son. Striking injured soldiers, swaying that schoolteacher toward the Germans, not enlisting. As the leader of Hilden's vigilance committee, this concerns me."

"We bought a hundred-dollar liberty bond in this last drive, as you may well remember." Friedrick took a deliberate step forward, forcing Joe and Robert back.

"Be that as it may," Joe said, "we're gonna need another show of loyalty tonight. Ain't that right, fellas?"

The mob murmured agreement.

"I'd say it's time for you to enlist, Boche." Robert laughed smugly. "No more hiding behind this farm deferment."

"No."

The word tasted sweet on Friedrick's tongue, fueling him with greater courage. He wouldn't bow to their whims and leave his family to fend for themselves. Even if he had to hide his parents and siblings in the barn every week until the war ended or swing at the end of a rope tonight, he would hold fast to what was right and decent. This was his time to stand and speak—he felt it in every muscle and bone of his body. His moment had come.

"No," he repeated with more force. "My loyalties have

and always will be to this country, but I won't leave my dying father or my family." He marched another step forward. The adrenaline coursing through him almost made him dizzy. "I'll ask you to take your leave—now."

For one tense moment Friedrick knew victory as the mob stared up at him with stunned expressions. Joe recovered first and tipped his head at Robert. They started down the steps as if to leave, but they swung back and seized both of Friedrick's arms.

"Bring the bucket," Joe hollered.

Friedrick struggled to be free of Joe and Robert, but they dragged him off the porch and through the crowd. Someone kicked Friedrick's legs and he fell forward. His knees slammed into the hard ground, but he clenched his teeth against a cry of pain. A viselike hand pressed his head to the ground, while someone else tore his shirt from his back. The taste of dirt filled his mouth.

The pressure on the back of his head ceased as something warm and sticky oozed onto his hair and down his neck. The smell of roofing tar assaulted Friedrick's nose and he coughed. He shut his eyes tight to save them from the thick liquid.

"Cover him up, Joe," a man yelled.

Tar spilled over Friedrick's back and pant legs. He kept his head down to keep his face clear and lessen the suffocating feeling creeping over him. *Just breathe.*

"Bring the feathers," Joe called out to someone.

Tiny pieces of fluff landed against Friedrick's nose and eyes. They made him sneeze and resurrected his cough.

"Change your mind yet, Boche?" Robert sneered above him.

"No," Friedrick croaked out.

"Then maybe this will," Joe said. "Luke, light the barn."

Friedrick opened his eyes to mere slits, but it was enough to see a man disengage from the mob and head toward the barn with his torch.

"Stop!" Friedrick screamed.

He lumbered to his feet, but the men held him back. He watched in horror as one corner of the barn caught the lick of the torch flame. The whole building would be gone in minutes, with his family trapped inside.

Within seconds, the fire jumped upward another two feet. Friedrick stopped his resisting and waited for the men's attention to be focused on the fire. When he was certain they were no longer paying him heed, he sprang forward. The men scrambled to grab him, but Friedrick broke free from their grasp this time.

He ran pell-mell toward the barn, intent on saving his family, when a single shot rang out.

Chapter Sixteen

Friedrick tripped and went down hard, the breath leaving his lungs. Had they shot him? He felt no pain. He rushed to his knees as a voice from behind shouted, "Friedrick!"

Livy? He whirled around. She hadn't left after all. Seeing her sprint toward him made the horrors of the last few minutes more bearable. Behind her, Sheriff Tate stood with his gun aimed at the sky.

"Livy, stay back," Friedrick cried as he lumbered to his feet. He needed her as far away from the mob and the fire as possible. He wanted nothing more than to crush her to him and never let go, but his family was in danger.

To his relief, Livy obeyed, stopping a few feet from him. "What did they do to you?" Her eyes were wide with fear.

"It doesn't matter. Just promise me you'll stay here, no matter what."

She visibly swallowed. "All right, Friedrick."

"Good." He hollered to the sheriff, "There are people in the barn. We have to get them out."

Livy gasped. "You don't mean..." She covered her mouth with her hand, unable to finish.

"We'll save them, Livy." He wouldn't lose his family, not when he'd finally stood up for them. Let the mob exact whatever punishment they wanted from him, but he wouldn't allow them to harm his family.

As Sheriff Tate began barking orders, Friedrick ran to the burning barn. Dr. Miller appeared at his heels. Together they jerked opened the barn doors. Smoke poured outward, along with a wave of heat that hit Friedrick square in the chest. His eyes watered and he paused long enough to wipe them. Above him in the loft, Greta could be heard crying. Hoarse coughs mingled with her tearful cries.

"They're in the loft!" Friedrick yelled to the doctor.

He raced toward the hayloft, keeping low to avoid the smoke and the flames climbing the nearest wall. Reaching the ladder first, Friedrick climbed upward and pulled his body over the lip of the loft. Greta screamed in fright.

"It's me, Greta." Friedrick held his hands up. "It's only me."

Elsa looked on the verge of fainting. "Is—is that blood, Friedrick?"

"It is tar and feathers," Dr. Miller hurried to explain as he topped the ladder. "We must get you out. Greta and Elsa first."

"Take them through the side door," Friedrick instructed. He helped his sister and Elsa to the ladder. "Harlan, you're next."

Harlan, his face white beneath a sheen of sweat, fol-

lowed his mother down the ladder. Friedrick turned to his
father, who leaned against the back wall, coughing. The
smoke had thickened in only a few minutes.

"Come on, Papa. Your turn."

"No, Friedrick," he said in German. "You saw how difficult it was for me to climb the ladder. It will take too
long for us both to escape. Leave me."

"Never." Friedrick lifted his father—saving his life
was more important than sparing Heinrich's clothes from
the tar—and set him at the edge of the loft. "Climb onto
my back." His father's frail arms wound around his neck,
his hold almost as light as the feathers spread over
Friedrick.

Friedrick twisted slowly and found his footing on the
ladder. He inched his way down, one rung at a time. His
eyes burned from the smoke until he shut them. He would
have to climb down blind.

The acrid smell of the burning barn filled his nose and
lungs. He coughèd in protest. Something hot singed his
arm and Friedrick flinched with the pain.

"I am slipping, Friedrick," his father whispered in his ear.

"Just a little farther." *Please, God.*

His neck and arms strained under the additional
weight, but Friedrick continued his descent. At last his
boots struck the floor. He opened his eyes to locate the
side door, but the smoke obscured his view. Alarm coated
his throat. Would his life and his father's end here? Had
his stand against injustice been his last? He hadn't even
told Livy he loved her.

"Follow me." Dr. Miller's voice sounded every bit as
heavenly and God-sent as an angel's.

Fresh strength coursed through him. Friedrick hoisted

his father higher unto his back and hurried after the doctor. Several heartbeats later, he burst into the cool darkness outside. Friedrick carefully lowered Heinrich to the ground and sank beside him. He gulped in great lungfuls of fresh air.

"Friedrick!" Greta ran to him, Harlan right behind her. The two of them threw their arms around him, nearly knocking Friedrick to the ground. He embraced them for a long moment, then gently eased them back. "We need to put out that fire."

Livy joined them. "The sheriff has Robert and the others doing that."

Friedrick stared unabashedly at her, her hair and face lit by the light from the fire. She couldn't be more beautiful, both inside and out. He'd never loved another person as he did her. He lifted his hand with a sudden need to touch her.

Livy locked her fingers in his and squeezed them tightly. "You're all right?" she asked. Her gaze roamed over him as if assuring herself he had no bleeding wound or broken limbs.

"I'm fine." Friedrick gave her hand a gentle squeeze in return. "Or I will be once I get this tar off." He longed to kiss her lips, hold her close, and promise never to leave her side again, but there were other things and people to tend to first, like his father.

Seeing Elsa help Heinrich to his feet, Friedrick released Livy's hand to stand as well. He might not be able to show her at this moment that he loved her, but he wouldn't waste the next opportunity.

He bent close to her ear and whispered, "Promise me you won't leave before we talk?" A shiver ran through her, which Friedrick suspected had nothing to do with the chill air. He smiled at the realization as Livy nodded agreement.

"I won't."

Friedrick managed to turn away from those luminous, deep eyes, to take Elsa's place beside his father. He helped Heinrich toward the house, while Harlan dashed ahead and opened the kitchen door. Friedrick carried his father inside and gently sat him on his bed. Elsa began pulling clean clothes from the bureau.

"You rest, Papa. I'll see to things outside."

Heinrich motioned for him to lean down. Friedrick obeyed. "You have made me proud, son." His voice came out hoarse but firm. "You fought for us tonight and that is worth more to me than seeing you in uniform."

Elsa murmured a quiet "Amen."

Tears blurred Friedrick's vision at his father's praise. It pierced his heart, bringing an overwhelming feeling of love and approval. He swallowed to keep the tears at bay as he slipped from the room to let his father change. Maria met him in the hallway.

"I ought to get back home."

"Thank you, Maria. For everything you did tonight."

She went up on tiptoe to kiss his cheek. "You're welcome. Good-bye, Friedrick."

He knew her farewell held more meaning than simply bidding him good night. Maria was ready to find happiness, with someone else.

After ensuring she had someone to walk her home, Friedrick went to the kitchen. Livy sat reading to Harlan and Greta at the table. The fear had ebbed from their faces, much to Friedrick's relief.

Livy glanced up long enough to exchange a smile with him before she continued reading. Harlan and Greta listened with rapt attention, their chairs pulled close to hers. Her presence in the kitchen felt natural and right. Perhaps he'd been wrong about her not fitting into his family. Friedrick squelched the desire to order his siblings to leave the room so he could snatch a few moments alone with her.

Elsa bustled into the room behind him. "Sit," she commanded in English. "We clean you off."

Friedrick took a seat at the table and submitted himself to Elsa's ministrations. The tar clung stubbornly to his skin and hair as Elsa attempted to pick off the dried bits. His forehead, neck, and back soon felt raw.

"Go change," Elsa directed. "We finish later."

Friedrick trudged up the stairs to his room. From his window he spotted several of their neighbors standing near the charred, smoking barn. Thankfully he'd stowed the horses in one of the fields and parked the wagon behind the house for safekeeping. He gingerly pulled on a clean shirt, changed his pants, and gathered his soiled clothes into a bundle.

The events of the night slid through his mind and filled his body with bone-weary exhaustion. He sank onto his bed, too tired to take another step. Bowing his head, he thanked God for his safety and that of his family. Pastor Schwarz, Peter Hoffmann, and his father had been right all along. God had not forgotten them. He had given Friedrick the strength to endure his darkest hour before the dawn.

"Friedrick, the sheriff wants to talk to us," Elsa called up the stairs. "We'll be in the parlor."

Friedrick brushed at the moisture that had resurfaced in his eyes and took a steadying breath. "I'm coming," he answered loudly. After dropping his tar-covered clothes inside the kitchen, he proceeded to the parlor.

The sheriff balanced on the edge of the armchair, looking uncomfortable. Elsa sat in her customary rocker with Greta at her feet, while Livy shared the sofa with Harlan. Friedrick took the empty spot next to her. He linked his hand with hers and rested it on his knee for all to see. It was time to let his family know this was the woman he intended to make his wife.

Sheriff Tate cleared his throat and glanced at Elsa. "I'm sorry, ma'am, for what happened here tonight. I assure you, Mr. Drake and Joe Hilly will not be bothering you again."

"How can you be sure?" Friedrick pressed.

"Because he and Joe will be cooling off in the jail tonight. I also told Mr. Drake if I catch him in town after tomorrow, he'll get the chance to experience a little tar and feathering himself." The sheriff sat up straighter. "Joe and his friends are welcome to similar consequences if they disturb the peace again or threaten violence against innocent women and children. I don't care if they are the vigilance committee in this town. I'm in charge of issuing the law around here.

"There is one other thing." He removed a wad of cash from his pocket. "I don't feel right accepting this. Not after what I've seen here tonight. Will you see this gets back to the people it belongs to?"

"I will." Friedrick accepted the money from the sheriff. He noticed Elsa wiping tears from her eyes. A similar feeling of gratitude washed over him. With the money from his paycheck, they'd be able to buy his father's medicine after all.

"Are we both still out of a job?" Livy asked Sheriff Tate.

The man stood, hat in hand. "If it's up to me, no. I'll work on Foster to drop the charges against you and give you back your jobs. In the meantime, I arranged to have one of the neighbors drive you back to your cabin, Miss Campbell. You have my permission to stay there until your position is worked out." He put on his hat and tipped the brim at Elsa. "Good night, folks."

Livy rose slowly. "Good night, everyone." Her gaze lingered on Friedrick. There'd been no time alone for them yet, but Friedrick was determined to snatch a few minutes.

"I'll walk you out." He trailed Livy and the sheriff outside. At the bottom of the steps, he took Livy's hand in his and led her around the side of the house.

Friedrick brushed a strand of hair behind her ear and cupped her beautiful face with his free hand. "Robert said you went home." He stroked her cheek with his thumb.

Livy shut her eyes and leaned into his touch. "He lied," she murmured.

"So I see. How did you know he was coming here?"

"He threatened to do something when I refused him— yet again—while I was in jail." She opened her eyes and gazed earnestly at him. "Thank you for helping me get released, Friedrick. I'm sorry I wasn't here sooner, to warn you about Robert. When I think what might have happened..." A shudder ran through her.

Friedrick drew her into his arms. She placed her head on his chest, while he rested his chin on her hair. How perfectly she fit against him. "Your timing was God-sent, Livy. I can't thank you enough for getting the sheriff and Dr. Miller here when you did." He pressed his lips to her hair. "Is that the only reason you stuck around after getting released?"

"No," she whispered. She lifted her head to look at him, her green eyes full of the same adoration and longing filling Friedrick's heart at that moment. "I stayed because..." She swallowed. "Well, because I love you, Friedrick. I know my family, or at least my siblings, weren't the kindest when you visited, but I believe they'll change their minds. That is, if you think you might... might love me back." She began chewing on the inside of her cheek in that unique, nervous way of hers.

"There's no 'might' about it." Friedrick reached up to hold her face between his hands and stop her worrying. "My love is fully and completely yours."

"Really?" Tears swam in her eyes.

He nodded, then bent forward to kiss each of her trembling eyelids.

Sunrise was still hours off, but Friedrick felt as though the sun were ablaze inside him. Not only had God paved the way for him to protect his family, but He had also brought Livy into Friedrick's life—a girl of spunk and compassion whose heart was his, to safeguard and cherish.

"Don't worry about your family. The only acceptance I need is yours, Livy. That is sufficient enough for me, for this lifetime and beyond." He eyed her lovely lips. "'Come kiss me, sweet and twenty,'" he quoted in a low voice.

"*Twelfth Night*," she said, her mouth lifting in a smile.

Friedrick chuckled. "You read it?"

"Out loud. While you were sick."

The remembrance of all she'd done for him, both tonight and while he lay at death's door, filled him with a surge of gratitude. Friedrick brought his mouth to hers and kissed her fervently.

How sweet indeed, he thought with a grin when he eased back.

"I guess I'd better go." She didn't make a move to leave, though. "What will we do if Mr. Foster won't give me my job back?"

Friedrick ran his thumb over the smooth planes of her lips—he couldn't wait for the day when they wouldn't have to part company. When they could hold each other and kiss to their hearts' content. "Your parents' farm is only a few hours' drive from here. One I'm willing to make, as often as needed."

Livy offered him a radiant smile. "Is that a promise?"

"It's a proposal." He lifted her hand and locked his fingers with hers. "Will you permit me to be your beau, Livy Campbell? To visit you and take you dancing? And one day soon to marry you, so I can show you every day how much this German-American loves you?"

She squeezed his hand tightly, her face aglow with love and joy. "Yes, Friedrick. I will."

Epilogue

July 1918

Livy peered into the mirror above her mother's vanity table. The blue and cream satin wedding dress highlighted the green of her eyes and the light brown tones of her hair, which Mary had expertly curled.

"You look beautiful," Greta announced from the bed where she, Mary, and Nora had gathered to watch Livy get ready. The open window behind them let in a nice morning breeze that ruffled the edges of Livy's cream-colored veil.

Her mother straightened the gauzy fabric, her eyes swimming with happy tears. "She does look breathtaking, doesn't she?"

"Wait until you see Friedrick in his suit." Mary grinned at Livy through the mirror. "If I were six years older…" she teased.

Livy pivoted on the seat and wagged a finger at her sister. "Then it's a good thing you aren't. Because Friedrick is mine." The words sent a happy thrill swirling through her.

Since her return home a month earlier, at the close of the school year, her siblings had finally welcomed Friedrick into their lives. He had won Allen and the younger boys over once he proved to them he was a worthy addition to their baseball games. Mary had taken longer to warm up to him, but Friedrick had been diligent in showing her the same sweet attention Livy had seen him give his own sister. Before long, Mary had nothing but glowing praise to say about her future brother-in-law.

Livy turned back to the vanity to apply a bit of powder. She met Elsa's gaze in the mirror and smiled. Ever since the night Livy had come to Friedrick's rescue, Elsa had been much friendlier to her. Still, the woman had remained on the edge of the group this morning, not quite joining in the happy chatter. As Livy watched, Elsa stepped forward, as if wanting to speak with her alone.

"Nora, why don't you come help me with the flowers?" Livy's mother suggested, throwing Livy a knowing look. "Girls, you can join us. It's almost time to leave for the church."

Livy smiled her gratitude. When the door closed behind them, she stood and smoothed the front of her wedding gown. "Do you think Friedrick will be pleased?"

Elsa nodded as she withdrew a box from behind her back. "You need something borrowed?"

"Yes." Livy's high-heeled shoes qualified as something old, her veil and dress were new, and the sapphire color of the gown fit the need for blue, but she didn't have something borrowed.

Opening the box, Elsa lifted out a string of bisque-colored pearls. "I wore these when Heinrich and I marry. They were my mother's. You wear them, if you like?"

"I would be honored." Livy sensed the gesture went beyond helping fulfill a wedding tradition. The pearls meant she'd met with Elsa's full approval at last. Livy accepted the necklace and fastened it around her neck. She fingered the smooth pearls. "I wish Heinrich could be here today."

Elsa gave Livy a watery smile. "I think he is. Before he die, he say he never see Friedrick so happy. It was comfort to him…and to me."

A knock sounded at the door. "Sugar?" Livy's father called. "It's time to head to the church."

"Ready?" Elsa asked.

Sudden nerves bundled up in her stomach, but Livy nodded. She followed Elsa into the hallway and down the stairs. She moved slowly past the family pictures lining the wall and stopped beside the ones of Tom and Joel in their army uniforms. How handsome and confident they both looked.

She had written Joel about Friedrick right after her jail incident, but she'd known his reply would be weeks in coming. As she'd waited, she couldn't keep from wondering if her oldest brother would be angry at her for marrying a German-American.

Joel's letter had finally arrived the day before. To Livy's great relief, he'd expressed sincere wishes for her happiness and a desire to meet Friedrick one day soon.

Livy smiled at the two faces behind the panes of glass. While she wished her brothers might have been here on this important day, she felt at peace with both their absences.

"Wish me luck, boys," she whispered.

The drive to the church felt as long as a drive across the

entire state. Livy bounced on the seat in her impatience to see Friedrick. At last, they arrived. Her mother and Nora each gave her a kiss on the cheek and told her how lovely she looked before taking their seats inside.

Livy linked her arm with her father's. The organist began to play as she and Josiah entered the chapel.

Livy's gaze went straight to Friedrick, standing in front of the pastor. Her breath caught in her throat as she drank in the sight of him, tall and handsome in his dark suit—just as Mary had described. His eyes lit up at seeing her, and a slow grin spread over his face, changing Livy's nervous flutters to ones of excitement.

Moving past the seated throng of their loved ones and friends, Livy walked to the front of the room and slipped her hand into Friedrick's. He squeezed her fingers, his look full of admiration and tenderness.

"I love you, Livy," he said, his voice for her ears alone, as the pastor began the ceremony.

"And I love you," she murmured back.

In that moment, she knew exactly where she belonged. At Friedrick's side, forever.

ABOUT THE AUTHOR

Stacy Henrie has always had an avid appetite for history, fiction, and chocolate. She earned her B.A. in public relations and worked in communications before turning her attentions to raising a family and writing inspirational historical romances. Wife of an entrepreneur husband and a stay-at-home mom to three, Stacy loves the chance to live out history through her fictional characters, while enjoying the modern conveniences of life in the twenty-first century. In addition to author, she is a reader, a road trip enthusiast, and a novice interior decorator. Her first novel, *Lady Outlaw*, was released by Harlequin Love Inspired Historical in 2012.

www.stacyhenrie.com

https://www.facebook.com/pages/Stacy-Henrie-Author/137610353020822

http://www.pinterest.com/stacyhenrie/

http://www.goodreads.com/author/show/5778153.Stacy_Henrie

https://twitter.com/StacyHenrie

From the Iowa heartland to battle-torn
France, take a journey back to the Great War
in Stacy Henrie's new sweeping romance!

Hope Rising.

Coming in December 2014

Turn this page for a preview.

Prologue

France, May 1918

Evelyn Gray breathed in the briny smell of the sea as she fingered the five shells in her gloved palm. One for each year without her father. From beneath her velour hat, she peered up at the gray sky overhead. The cool temperature and the possibility of rain made her grateful for the warmth of her dark blue jacket, shirtwaist and skirt that comprised her Army Nurse Corp outdoor uniform.

"Nurse Gray, come on." One of the girls down the beach waved for her to join the other three nurses in their walk along the shoreline toward the white cliffs in the distance.

Emitting a sigh, Evelyn turned in their direction, but she wasn't in any hurry to rejoin their conversation. The other girls on leave with her were full of talk about home and families and sweethearts, while she had only her aging grandparents waiting for her back in Michigan. As for a beau? Her lips turned up into a bitter smile. She'd been too busy, for some time, with nurse's training to worry about any of that. Besides, if she had gotten married, she wouldn't have been able to come overseas and prove her grandparents' financial backing of her career hadn't been in vain.

She lifted the first shell—a smooth, white one—and tossed it into the sea. "I still miss you, Father," she said as the seashell slipped beneath the surface of the water.

Five years today, since you left us. She could easily picture how he'd trudged up the porch steps that afternoon after tending to a patient—he'd never established a doctor's office in town, preferring instead to make house calls or take visits in their home. He hadn't looked well, but Evelyn's medical knowledge at seventeen wasn't what it was today at twenty-two. She still wasn't sure if he knew he was going to have a heart attack.

Tossing the second shell into the water, she swallowed hard against the flood of memories. She'd gone upstairs to make sure he was lying down and found him on the floor next to the bed, already gone.

She rid her hand of the third, fourth and fifth shells in quick succession, then brushed the granules of sand from her gloves. Blinking back tears, she straightened her shoulders. No one else needed to know what day it was or how much the loneliness tore at her heart.

"Afternoon, miss."

Evelyn whirled around to find an American soldier staring at her from a few feet away. He wasn't overly tall, less than six feet, but his handsome face, broad shoulders and dark eyes were an impressive combination.

"I didn't mean to disturb you." He smiled, looking anything but apologetic. "Beautiful view."

The way he said it she knew he wasn't talking about

the ocean. Evelyn didn't blush, though. She was used to lingering looks and flirtations from the wounded soldiers at the hospital where she worked.

Time to catch up with the others. She turned her face in the direction of the cliffs and started after the girls, who'd managed to cover quite a bit of distance in her absence. To her dismay, the soldier fell into step beside her.

"I'm Private First Class Ralph Kelley." He held out his hand for her to shake. "And you are?"

"Not supposed to talk to you," Evelyn said in her firmest nurse's tone. "You know the rules, soldier." Fraternizing was forbidden between nurses and enlisted soldiers. She tried to maintain a brisk pace across the beach, but the stones and sand underfoot made it difficult.

He chuckled as he lowered his hand to his side. "You on leave? With those other nurses?"

Evelyn responded with a nod—it wasn't talking after all.

"Do you collect pebbles?"

The question caught her off guard and she threw him a perplexed look.

"I saw you picking some up earlier."

How long had he been watching her? Heat rose into her cheeks at his intrusion upon her private mourning. "I need to go." She attempted to outdistance him again, but his feet kept tempo with hers. "The others will be wondering where I am."

"Have lunch with me."

The request, spoken in an almost pleading tone, halted Evelyn's retreat in a way his earlier charisma hadn't. She circled to face him, ready to reject his offer—gently.

Before she could voice her refusal though, he spoke

again. "I can't say I don't make it a habit of talking to nurses." He gave her a sheepish smile as he removed his hat and fingered the brown wool. "But you looked like you could use a friend back there. Like something was weighing heavily on your mind."

Evelyn managed to keep her mouth from falling open at his perceptive observation. Maybe there was more to him than his lady's man demeanor. Her earlier feeling of isolation welled up inside her, nearly choking her with its hold. Against her better judgment, she found herself admitting the truth to him. "It's the anniversary of my father's death—five years ago today. I've been thinking a lot about him lately."

"Do your friends know?" He nodded in the direction the other girls had gone.

Evelyn shook her head. "I didn't want to spoil their time away from the hospital."

"Will you tell me your name?"

She could feel her defenses crumbling beneath the sincerity in his black eyes. "It's . . . um . . . Evelyn. Evelyn Gray."

"Evelyn."

Hearing him speak her name brought butterflies to her stomach and the smile he offered afterward made her pulse run faster. When was the last time she'd felt this way? Probably not since she and Sam had kissed after high school graduation. Sam Harper had been her first beau, until he went away to college, and Evelyn had put all her time and energy into becoming a nurse.

"I discovered a place yesterday that serves excellent fish. If you like that."

Despite her best efforts to stop it, a smile lifted the corner of her lips. "Hospital food isn't much better than army fare, I'm afraid."

Private Kelley laughed; it was a pleasantly deep sound. "I owe it to you then, to at least provide you a decent meal while you're on leave." His expression sobered as he added, "Especially on a day as important as this."

Evelyn glanced over her shoulder at the three nurses far down the beach. She wanted to refuse—she'd never been one to break the rules. But he made her feel valued and important—something she hadn't felt in a long time. His notice eased her aching heart and soothed her loneliness.

She studied the sand below her feet, her lips pursed in thought. No harm should come from simply sharing a meal in a public place; that wasn't really fraternizing. At least she'd be spared listening to the other girls prattle on for the next few hours about their big families and parents who were still alive. She would only be trading one conversation for another.

"Let me tell them I'll meet up with them later," she said, before she changed her mind.

He grinned and replaced his hat on his head. "I'll wait right here for you."

Evelyn walked with new purpose toward the retreating group. She called to the girls from a distance. The three of them turned as one. "I'll meet up with you before supper, at the place we're staying."

They glanced at each other, then one of them shrugged and waved her hand in acknowledgement. Grateful they hadn't asked questions, Evelyn retraced her steps back to where Private Kelley stood waiting.

"All set?" He extended his hand to her.

Evelyn stared at it a long moment, then taking a deep breath, she placed her fingers in his palm. With a smile, he tucked her hand over his arm and led her away from the beach.

Chapter One

July 1918

You've become skin and bones since you came here, Evelyn. And no wonder; you eat like a bird." Alice Thornton waved her fork at the half-empty plate Evelyn had slid aside. "If my mother were here, she'd try to fatten you up. Unlike the hospital cook, apparently."

Evelyn smiled, despite the queasiness in her stomach. She could imagine Mrs. Thornton—a more rotund, matronly version of red-headed Alice—chasing her down with a ladle of stew in hand. Alice talked a lot about her family, particularly her three beanpole brothers who never put on pounds no matter how much they ate, much to their mother's chagrin.

That wasn't Evelyn's problem. The morning sickness that plagued her, even now in the middle of the day, prevented her from stomaching much of any meal. But she certainly didn't plan on telling Alice that.

Almost of its own volition, her hand rose to rest against the middle of her white nurse's apron. The tiny life inside her could only be ten weeks along by now, but her own life had been altered just the same. Would anyone else notice her lack of appetite, as Alice had, or her frequent trips to the bathroom?

Alice turned to talk with another nurse seated near them, giving Evelyn a moment to herself. She slipped her hand beneath her apron, into the pocket of her gray jersey dress and felt the letter tucked there. It brought instant calm as she withdrew the folded slip of paper. Though the letter had arrived less than a week ago, she had Ralph's words memorized. Still, she liked to see the bold strokes of his handwriting and read the reassurance in the words he'd penned.

I'm still in shock at your news of the baby. I find myself thinking at odd times of the day, even in the middle of a battle, that I'm going to be a father. I do want to do right by you and the baby, Evelyn. Not like my own father. So as soon as I get leave again, I'm coming to the hospital there and we'll get married. I know you'll be discharged after that, being married and all, but you won't have to worry what to tell your grandparents anymore. You can tell them you got hitched in France and came home to have our baby.

I miss you. I think of you every day and our time together in Dieppe.

Yours,
Ralph

"Did we get mail today?"

Alice's voice broke into Evelyn's reverie. Startled, she glanced up in confusion. "Mail?"

Her roommate pointed to Evelyn's letter.

"Oh, I don't know. This is from last week." Evelyn quickly folded Ralph's letter and shoved it into her pocket, away from Alice's curious gaze.

"Is it from your grandparents?"

Evelyn wanted to answer in the affirmative, but she wouldn't lie. She hadn't heard from either her grandmother or grandfather in several months. Their declining health made returning Evelyn's upbeat missives difficult. She hadn't yet broached the subject of the baby in her letters, out of shame and guilt. But she likely wouldn't have to. As Ralph had said, she'd be sent home once they married, but at least, she'd have a husband. She wouldn't have to return to the farm unwed and pregnant with an illegitimate child. What would that shock do to her grandparents?

"Better hurry up," Evelyn said, avoiding Alice's question altogether. She stood and picked up her plate. "I heard Sister Marcelle is doing a round of ward visits today or tomorrow."

Alice frowned and scrambled up from the table. "In that case, I'll skip the rest. Sister Henriette is likely to tell her that I yelled at Sergeant Dennis, good and long this morning. But honestly, the man refuses to believe he should rest. These doughboys think they can be shot up one day and return to the front the next, good as new."

The smile hovering at Evelyn's mouth curved down as she followed Alice to the kitchen. She'd noticed the way Sergeant Dennis watched Alice. The man was clearly captivated by the younger girl and would go to great lengths to garner a response from her—even if it was a good scolding. Evelyn could only hope her roommate remained blind to the man's attention. Thankfully Alice didn't seem the type to break the cardinal rule forbidding nurses and soldiers from fraternizing, but then again, Evelyn hadn't expected to disregard the rule herself. At least not until she'd met Ralph.

A torrent of French greeted them as they set their dishes beside the kitchen's enormous sink. Evelyn turned to see the cook at the back door, shaking her spoon at a dark-headed youngster.

"S'il vous plaît?" the boy entreated.

"Non," the cook responded. *"Pas de pain."* She muttered under her breath as she slammed the door in the boy's disheartened face. Throwing a pointed look at Evelyn and Alice, she returned to her table and began whacking dough with a stick.

"Come on, Evelyn." Alice retreated back toward the entrance to the large dining hall. None of the twenty nurses at St. Vincent's liked spending much time in the kitchen with the cantankerous cook.

"I'll be along in a minute. You go ahead."

Alice shrugged. The moment her roommate left, Evelyn slipped both their half-nibbled rolls from their plates and discreetly put them into her free pocket. She retraced her steps to the dining hall and let herself out the hospital's back entrance. A welcoming breeze loosened bits of her hair from underneath her nurse's cap. Evelyn tucked them back and eyed the sky. Gray clouds overhead promised rain.

Before her, the back lawn of the hospital extended long and wide, bordered by forests of beech and oak trees. The hospital itself had originally been a chateau, rebuilt in the 1860's and bequeathed to the Sisters of Charity. The living quarters for the hospital staff stood to her left in what had once been the orangery and beyond that sat an ancient stone church.

Out of the corner of her eye, Evelyn caught sight of black hair as the beggar boy rounded the hospital. "Wait! *Attendez!*" she called out as she jogged after him. "Please, wait."

He stopped so suddenly Evelyn nearly ran into him. Large black eyes peered up at her from a dirt-smudged face. They looked neither sad nor angry, but resigned and weary, though the boy couldn't be more than six years old. That wizened look constricted Evelyn's heart more than the other signs of poverty about him—the cuts on his shins and the disheveled state of his shirt and trousers.

"*Parlez-vous Anglais?*" she queried. She hoped he spoke English. Her French was still quite rudimentary, despite the months she'd spent in his country as a nurse.

He cocked his head and nodded.

"Wonderful. What's your name?"

"Loo-ee. Louis Rousseau."

Evelyn smiled. "*Bonjour*, Louis. I'm Nurse Gray."

"Got any coffin nails or chocolate?"

She shook her head and bit back a laugh at the familiar term for cigarettes. "You learned English from some soldiers, didn't you?"

Louis shook his head. "*Ma grand-mère* taught me the English. But *ma mère* takes our vegetables into the market and sometimes the Americans buy some. She didn't sell much today. I was trying to beg some *petit de pain* off that *tête de chou*. That cabbage headed cook. But she just say '*non, non.*'"

"Tell you what, Louis. I didn't finish all my bread today and I'd like you to have it." She removed the rolls, which were slightly squished now, and held them out to him.

His eyes widened as he stared at her, then at the bread.

"Go on. You can have it."

He took the rolls from her. One he bit into at once, but the other he held carefully in his free hand. "*Ma mère* can eat this one. *Merci*."

"You're welcome."

A flood of emotion filled her as she watched him lean against the hospital wall to eat his meager meal. He was clearly hungry, but he ate the bread slowly. Perhaps her baby would be a boy—a little dark haired fellow like Louis with an impish glint in his black eyes like Ralph. She could imagine the three of them, and hopefully the other children that would follow, sitting on the porch of her grandparents' house—*her house*—laughing and sipping lemonade. She would be a part of a family soon, a real family.

"Do you have any brothers or sisters?" she asked Louis, reluctant to return indoors. The heat and smells inside the hospital made her nausea worse.

Louis shook his head. "It's only me and *ma mère*."

"Where's your father?"

He lowered his gaze to the grass. "He was a solider... but he got killed last year."

Five years had passed since Evelyn had lost her own father, and she still missed him. Squatting down in front of Louis, she rested her hand on his thin shoulder. "My father died, too."

"Was he a brave soldier like *ma père*?"

"No. He was a doctor."

Louis lifted his chin to look her in the eye. "How'd he die?"

"His heart stopped working one day."

"Et votre mère?"

And your mother? Seventeen years without a mother still hadn't erased the tug on Evelyn's heart whenever people asked. "My mother died when I was five years old. She'd been sick for a long time." The word "cancer" settled on her tongue, but she swallowed it back. The boy didn't need to know and probably wouldn't understand the whole ugly truth about her mother's condition.

Louis' brow furrowed. "Who takes care of you?"

The inquiry was said with so much seriousness that Evelyn didn't dare laugh. "My grandparents are waiting for me back in America."

Her answer seemed to satisfy him.

"I'd better go," he said, wiping his sleeve over his mouth.

Evelyn stood. "So should I. Do you live close by?"

He pointed north and rattled off the French name of his village. It was the one closest to the hospital. *"Au revoir,* Nurse Gray."

"Au revoir, Louis. I hope to see you again soon."

He grinned, then spun around and darted into the trees. When he disappeared from view, Evelyn headed back to the rear entrance of the hospital. It wouldn't do to be late to her assigned ward, especially if Sister Marcelle chose today to make her inspection.

Evelyn passed through the empty dining hall. The sound of her footsteps echoed off the high walls and marbled floors as she hurried toward the opposite door. The room that now housed long tables and benches for meals had once been a ballroom. Evelyn liked to fancy herself in a silk dress, dancing here with Ralph who looked very dapper in his army uniform. Perhaps after the wedding, they could find a place to honeymoon for a few days. They could dance or explore. Just like they had two months before when they'd met on leave.

Smiling at the memory, Evelyn climbed the stairs to the wards on the second floor. The stone walls of the old chateau kept the place from being completely miserable now that it was the middle of summer, but still, she felt the air grow warmer as she ascended higher. At the top, she smoothed her apron. She tried to recall from her days assisting her father how early a woman's belly began expanding when she was pregnant. Four months? Five? Hopefully Ralph would be the first in his regiment to get leave again, so she wouldn't be showing too much by the time he came for her and they married.

"There you are, Nurse Gray." Sister Henriette met Evelyn outside the door of the ward. Her face glimmered with sweat beneath her wide, white headdress. It reminded Evelyn of the sailboats she'd seen as a child on Lake Michigan.

"I'm sorry I'm late, Sister. I had a quick errand to do first."

Sister Henriette waved away her apology. "Sister Marcelle wishes to speak with you."

"With me?" Something akin to panic wormed its way up Evelyn's spine, and with it, a new wave of sickness. She hadn't committed any infractions since transferring to St. Vincent's six weeks ago. Did that mean Sister Marcelle, the hospital administrator, had discovered her secret?

"You're not in trouble, child. She only wishes to ask you about a change in assignment."

Relief made her shoulders droop and relaxed her tight jaw. Evelyn dipped her head in acknowledgement. A new assignment she could handle, though it did seem odd Sister Marcelle wouldn't simply ask Sister Henriette to pass on the information.

"She is waiting in her office. Just report back to the ward when you are finished."

"Yes, ma'am."

She strode down the hallway with new confidence, passing the open doors of the other wards on both sides. The murmur of male voices and occasional laughter floated out to her. After climbing another set of stairs, Evelyn paused outside the worn wooden door of Sister Marcelle's tiny office. She knocked once and an alto voice called out, "You may enter."

Stepping inside, Evelyn stood before Sister Marcelle's large desk. Stacks of papers and ledgers stood in neat piles on one side. The only other furniture in the room was two wooden chairs, one occupied by Sister Marcelle. A large crucifix hung on the wall behind the sister. Just as Evelyn had on her first visit to this office, she avoided looking directly at the cross.

"Ah, Nurse Gray. Thank you for coming." The sister's blue-gray eyes, the same color as the dress she wore, shone bright with kindness. Unlike the other sisters, she spoke with nearly no trace of a French accent.

"Sister Henriette said you wished to see me."

"Yes." Sister Marcelle motioned to the chair opposite the desk. "Please have a seat."

Evelyn perched on the edge of the chair.

Sister Marcelle folded her hands and leaned forward. "I will get right to my request. As you know, Sister Pauline is getting up there in age. But we all are, are we not?" Her lips curved into a smile, increasing the laugh lines around her mouth. Evelyn smiled back. She'd heard from some of the other nurses that Sister Pauline, who was in charge of Sister Henriette's wards at night, mostly just slept. But she couldn't blame a sixty-year-old woman for dozing during the long, night hours. Lately Evelyn could hardly keep her eyelids from closing at the end of a day shift.

"Sister Monique will be taking over Sister Pauline's place, but her sister is ill and she has asked for time away from the hospital to tend to her. In the meantime, I would like to propose you supervise Sister Henriette's wards during the night shift. The other ward nurses will report to you and you will have access to the books and keys. It should only be a few weeks at most, until Sister Monique returns."

Evelyn's eyes widened with surprise. The sisters were in charge of all the wards in the hospital, while Evelyn and the other girls from the Army Nurse Corp served as ward nurses. The extra responsibility showed Sister Marcelle's trust and confidence in her, but Evelyn worried about not performing her best. Especially when her pregnancy sapped her stamina. She'd actually been grateful her turn for the night shift hadn't come up yet.

These were concerns she didn't dare voice, though.

"I'd be happy to help, Sister Marcelle." Her voice carried more assurance than she felt. Somehow she'd make it work, to keep her secret safe until she and Ralph were married.

Sister Marcelle's ready smile appeared again. "Thank you. Sister Henriette praises your meticulous work. You have undoubtedly proven to be a great role model for all our nurses."

Evelyn blushed, feeling less than worthy of the sister's last compliment, and glanced down at her hands.

"Do you enjoy nursing?"

The unexpected question brought Evelyn's head up. "It's the same line of work my father did, when he was alive. My grandparents were very proud of him. Naturally they hoped their only grandchild would follow in his footsteps. I-I do enjoy helping others, if that's what you mean."

Sister Marcelle nodded, her expression thoughtful, before she sat back. "We appreciate that help, I assure you. Especially now with our supplies being so low. That is something I will need you to be vigilant about. At night we need to use the pain medications spare—"

The rat-tat-tat of raindrops drummed the window behind her, but that didn't seem to be the sound that made Sister Marcelle stop and turn in her chair. Evelyn heard it too—the distant rumble of motor vehicles.

"It appears we have our next round of patients." The sister released a quiet sigh as she stood and crossed to the window. Evelyn joined her. Through the rain-splotched panes she could see the line of ambulances driving up the curved gravel driveway.

"More than usual," Evelyn said.

Sister Marcelle gazed at Evelyn, her expression grave. For the first time, Evelyn noticed the weary lines around the older woman's eyes.

"We do what we can." But Sister Marcelle seemed to

leave the sentence hanging at the end, almost like a question. The hesitation lasted only a moment, but Evelyn caught a tiny glimpse of the burden Sister Marcelle carried as director of the entire hospital.

Clearing her throat, the sister straightened to her full height, a few inches taller than Evelyn, and a tight smile pulled at her mouth. "You may return to your assigned ward for today, Nurse Gray. Can you start the night shift tomorrow evening?"

"Yes, ma'am." Unsure whether to curtsey or not, Evelyn settled for a quick nod before letting herself out the door. She hurried down the stairs to the wards. Many of the nurses had gathered at the open doorways along the hall.

"Did you see the ambulances?" Alice asked when Evelyn approached. "One of the sisters said there are at least four."

Evelyn cringed at the thought of all those suffering soldiers. As much as she couldn't wait to see Ralph again, she never wanted to see him carried out of an ambulance and placed on a stretcher. "I saw them—the ambulances. From Sister Marcelle's office."

Alice's green eyes widened. "What were you doing there?"

"I'll tell you at dinner." The first of the corpsmen had already reached the top of the stairs, an occupied stretcher between them.

Nodding, Alice disappeared into a nearby ward and Evelyn moved swiftly down the hall to her own. She passed a nurse smoothing a fresh sheet over one of the three empty beds. Evelyn lifted another sheet from the basket and went to the vacant bed in the far corner. A minute or two later the hallway outside boiled over with noise—nurses and sisters calling out directions to the corpsmen, wounded soldiers moaning with pain, the clatter of boots against the wood floors.

A rush of adrenaline throbbed inside Evelyn, driving out any lingering sense of nausea, as she heard Sister Henriette call loudly, "Bring those three in here." It was the same each time they had new patients. Her father used to say the adrenaline was the only thing that got him through those first agonizing minutes when he had to accurately and quickly assess an emergency situation and take action.

Evelyn finished tucking the sheet and pulled it back as two corpsmen approached the bed. The man on their stretcher had his eyes shut tight, his body shivering uncontrollably. His rain-dampened hair looked almost coffee-colored in some places, though the lighter scruff along his jaw and chin proved his hair wasn't that dark brown when dry. He had a nice-looking, unmarred face, but it was the dried blood on the lower half of his wool uniform that drew Evelyn's attention.

She backed up a step to allow the corpsmen to place the soldier on the bed, then she moved to his side as they rushed off to bring in the next injured man.

"Hey there, soldier," she said in a soft voice. "Let's get you warm first, all right?"

He didn't respond, but Evelyn placed a blanket over his shaking form. Once his shivers had receded some, she peeled back the edge of the blanket in order to assess his wounds. His right pant leg had been cut in order to place a bandage around his thigh and pelvis and his left arm had been placed in a hastily constructed splint.

Evelyn reached for the medical card pinned to his coat. She needed to know if surgery on his leg was required. She studied the scrawled notes, which indicated a blast wound with shrapnel in his right thigh, underdetermined damage in his pelvic area and a broken left arm. *He'll definitely need surgery to remove the shrapnel.*

"Water," a voice croaked.

She glanced at the man's face and found him awake. Hazel eyes gazed intently at her, though his body continued to shiver.

"I'll get you some water, but first, are you warm yet?"

He gave an almost imperceptible shake of his head.

Evelyn pulled up the sheet and blanket, nearly to his chin, then she procured a glass of water from a pitcher on a nearby table. "I'm going to hold it, all right? All you need to do is sip." She lifted his head gently off the pillow with one hand and brought the cup to his cracked lips with the other. He took a long swallow.

"Better," he murmured, but he gritted his teeth as she gently set his head back down.

"I know you're hurting, soldier. And we're going to get you into surgery soon. Most likely by tonight." At least she hoped. There would be others with much more immediate need for a surgeon, but she wanted him to know he wouldn't be forgotten. "In the meantime, I'm going to change that loose bandage for you."

Crossing to the supply cart in the middle of the ward, she removed a fresh bandage, a pair of scissors and a bottle of iodine. When she returned to the man's bed, she pushed the blankets aside, just enough, to reach his leg. Still she noticed the flush of embarrassment on his face as she bent to cut away the old bandage.

"Tell me where you're from, soldier," she said as she worked, hoping to ease his blushing and distract him from any physical discomfort re-bandaging his injury might cause.

"Iowa."

"Did you grow up on a farm?" So many of the dough-boys she'd served in France were sons of farmers.

"Yes."

Evelyn lifted her head to shoot him a smile. "Me too. I'm from Michigan." Once she had the soiled bandage off, she checked the leg for possible signs of infection—thankfully, there were none—and applied some of the iodine. She'd grown used to the acute smell, though it seemed much stronger now that she was pregnant. The man flinched as the chemical met his torn flesh.

"So your name is . . ." She glanced at his medical card she'd set on the bedside table. "Corporal Joel Campbell. Which regiment are you in, Corporal?"

He murmured the number. It was the same regiment as Ralph's. Worry flared inside her. Ralph must have been in the same battle as Corporal Campbell. Her worry grew stronger, more insistent. Was there a way to know if Ralph was safe or not? Perhaps the corporal knew him, though with so many men in a regiment, it seemed unlikely. *If they're in the same company, though . . .*

"What company are you in?" She did her best to keep the dread from her voice as she wrapped his leg with the fresh bandage.

"Company F," Corporal Campbell replied in a tight whisper.

His answer brought her head up and stilled her fingers. The corporal had to know Ralph. Was he safe or was he here, too? To think, Ralph might be in the next ward, his injuries being attended to. Evelyn's heart beat faster with equal hope and terror. If only she could see him this very moment, touch his handsome face, kiss those masculine lips. Assure herself that he was alive and well.

Evelyn ducked her chin, directing her next question toward the bed to appear as nonchalant as possible. "Do you by chance know Private First Class Ralph Kelley?"

Silence from the bed sounded louder in her ears than the racket in the room and hallway. She lifted her head and found Corporal Campbell staring hard at her.

"Are you all right, Corporal?"

Instead of answering, he countered with a question of his own. "Are you . . . Evelyn?"

She couldn't help the soft gasp that escaped her lips. "Yes, but how do you know my name?" Fresh panic pulsed through her veins.

"Because Ralph said it several times today." He turned his face toward the wall. "Right before he died."

A loud rushing sound filled Evelyn's ears as her mind shied away from his words. Had the rain picked up? One glance at the nearest window proved it wasn't raindrops causing the flood of noise in her head.

Ralph's dead?

"No . . . no!" Was that her strangled voice? Evelyn felt as if someone had torn the exclamation from her throat and hurdled it at the frowning corporal. She reached for the table to steady herself and knocked the scissors to the floor with a clatter.

"Evelyn?"

Who had spoken her name? Ralph? No, he wasn't

here. He was still at the front. He wasn't dead. He couldn't be.

"Evelyn," the corporal said with more insistence. "Look at me."

Slowly she dragged her gaze back to Corporal Campbell's. He reached for her hand and squeezed it. "Keep your eyes focused on my face, okay? Then you won't faint."

She wanted to; she tried. But she couldn't hear him anymore, though she could see his mouth moving. She looked at the rain-soaked windows and the walls of the ward, which were tilting at a funny angle. What was happening to the room?

Her knees felt too heavy, the sorrow in her gut too great. She attempted to look at the corporal's face again, hoping with all her heart to see the lie there instead of his earnest expression. But the edges of her vision had begun to fracture into tiny spots, which conjoined until all she knew was smothering blackness.

THE DISH

Where Authors Give You the Inside Scoop

♥ ♥ ♥ ♥ ♥ ♥ ♥ ♥ ♥ ♥ ♥ ♥ ♥ ♥ ♥ ♥

From the desk of Debbie Mason

Dear Reader,

While reading CHRISTMAS IN JULY one last time before sending it off to my editor, I had an "oops, I did it again" moment. In the first book in the series, *The Trouble with Christmas*, there's a scene where Madison, the heroine, senses her late mother's presence. In this book, our heroine, Grace, receives a message from her sister through her son. Grace has spent years blaming herself for her sister's death, and while there's an incident in the book that alleviates her guilt, I felt she needed the opportunity to tell her sister she loved her. Maybe if I didn't believe our departed loved ones could communicate with us in some way, I would have done this another way. But I do, and here's why.

My dad was movie-star handsome and had this amazing dimple in his chin. He was everything a little girl could wish for in a father. But he wasn't my biological father; he was the father of my heart. He came into my life when I was nine years old. That first year, I dreamed about him a lot. The dreams were very real, and all the same. I'd be outside and see a man from behind and call out to him. He'd turn around, and it would be my dad.

I always said the same thing: "You're here. I knew you weren't gone." Almost a year to the day of his passing, my dad appeared in my dream surrounded by shadowy figures who he introduced to me by name. He told me that he was okay, that he was happy. It was his way, I think, of helping me let him go.

I didn't dream of him again until sixteen months ago when we were awaiting the birth of our first grandchild. I "woke up" to see him sitting at the end of my bed. I told him how happy I was that he'd be there for the arrival of his great grandchild. He said of course he would be. He wouldn't be anywhere else.

A week later, my daughter gave birth to a beautiful baby girl. When I saw my granddaughter for the first time, I started to cry. She had my dad's dimple. No one on my son-in-law's side, or ours, has a dimple in their chin. He used to tell us the angels gave it to him, and we like to think he gave our granddaughter hers as proof that he's still with us.

So now you know why including that scene was important not only to Grace, but to me. Life really is full of small miracles and magic. And I hope you experience some of that magic as you follow Grace and Jack on their journey to happy-ever-after.

Debbie Mason

♥ ♥ ♥ ♥ ♥ ♥ ♥ ♥ ♥ ♥ ♥ ♥ ♥ ♥ ♥

From the desk of Kristen Ashley

Dear Reader,

Usually, inspiration for books comes to me in a variety of ways. It could be a man I see (anywhere), a movie, a song, the unusual workers in a bookstore.

With SWEET DREAMS, it was an idea.

And that idea was, I wanted to take a hero who is, on the whole, totally unlikable, and make him lovable.

Enter Tatum Jackson, and when I say that, I mean *enter Tatum Jackson*. He came to me completely with a *kapow!* I could conjure him in my head, hear him talk, see the way he moved and how his clothes hung on him, feel his frustration with his life. I also knew his messed-up history.

And I could not wait to get stuck into this man.

I mean, here's a guy who is gorgeous, but he's got a foul temper, says nasty things when he's angry, and he's not exactly father of the year.

He had something terrible happen to him to derail his life and he didn't handle that very well, making mistake after mistake in a vicious cycle he pretty much had no intention of ending. He had a woman in his life he knew was a liar, a cheat, and no good for anyone and he was so stuck in the muck of his life that he didn't get shot of her.

Enter Lauren Grahame, who also came to me like a shot. As with Tate, everything about Lauren slammed into my head, perhaps most especially her feelings, the disillusionment she has with life, how she feels lost and really has no intention of getting found.

In fact, I don't think with any of my books I've ever had two characters who I knew so thoroughly before I started to tell their story.

And thus, I got lost in it.

I tend to be obsessive about my storytelling but this was an extreme. Once Lauren and Tate came to me, everything about Carnal, Colorado, filled my head just like the hero and heroine did. I can see Main Street, Bubba's Bar, Tate's house. I know the secondary characters as absolutely as I know the main characters. The entirety of the town, the people, and the story became a strange kind of real in my head, even if I didn't know how the story was going to play out. Indeed, I had no idea if I could pull it off, making an unlikable man lovable.

But I fell in love with Tate very quickly. The attraction he has for Lauren growing into devotion. The actions that speak much louder than words. I so enjoyed watching Lauren pull Tate out of the muck of his life, even if nothing changes except the fact that he has a woman in it that he loves, who is good to him, who feeds the muscle, the bone, the soul. Just as I enjoyed watching Tate guide Lauren out of her disillusionment and offer her something special.

I hope it happens to me again someday that characters like this inhabit my head so completely, and I hope it happens time and again.

But Tate and Lauren being the first, they'll always hold a special place in my heart, and live on in my head.

Happily,

Kristen Ashley

♥ ♥ ♥ ♥ ♥ ♥ ♥ ♥ ♥ ♥ ♥ ♥ ♥ ♥ ♥

From the desk of Rebecca Zanetti

Dear Reader,

I'm the oldest of three girls, and my husband is the oldest of three boys, so we grew up watching out for our siblings. Now that we're all adults, they look out for us, too. While my sisters and I may have argued with one another as kids, we instantly banded together if anybody tried to mess with one of us. My youngest sister topped out at an even five feet tall, yet she's the fiercest of us all, and she loses her impressive temper quite quickly if someone isn't nice to me.

I think one of the reasons I enjoyed writing Matt's story in SWEET REVENGE is because he's the eldest of the Dean brothers, and as such, he feels responsible for them. Add in a dangerous military organization trying to harm them, and his duties go far beyond that of a normal sibling. It was fun to watch Matt try to order his brothers around and keep them safe, while all they want to do is provide backup for him and ensure his safety.

There's something about being the oldest kid that forces us to push ourselves when we shouldn't. When our siblings would step back and relax, we often push forward just out of sheer stubbornness. I don't know why, and it's sometimes a mistake. Trust me.

SWEET REVENGE was written in several locations, most notably in the hospital and on airplanes. Sometimes

I take on a bit too much, so when I discovered I needed a couple of surgeries (nothing major), I figured I'd just do them on the same day. Why not? So I had two surgeries in one day and had to spend a few days in the hospital recuperating.

With my laptop, of course.

There's not a lot to do in the hospital but drink milkshakes and write, so it was quite effective. Then, instead of going home and taking it easy, I flew across the country to a conference and big book signing. Of course, I was still in pain, but I ignored it.

Bad idea.

Two weeks after that, I once again flew across the country for a book signing and conference. Yes, I was still tired, but I kept on going.

Yet another bad idea.

Then I returned home and immediately headed back to work as a college professor at the beginning of the semester.

Not a great idea.

Are you seeing a trend here? I pushed myself too hard, and all of a sudden, my body said…*you're done.* Completely done. I became sick, and after a bunch of tests, it appeared I'd just taken on too much. So at the end of the semester, I resigned as a professor and took up writing full time. And yoga. And eating healthy and relaxing.

Life is great, and it's meant to be savored and not rushed through—even for us oldest siblings. I learned a very valuable life lesson while writing SWEET REVENGE, and I'll always have fond memories of this book.

I truly hope you enjoy Matt and Laney's story, and

don't forget to take a deep breath and enjoy the moment. It's definitely worth it!

Happy reading!

Rebecca Zanetti

RebeccaZanetti.com
Twitter @RebeccaZanetti
Facebook.com

♥ ♥ ♥ ♥ ♥ ♥ ♥ ♥ ♥ ♥ ♥ ♥ ♥ ♥ ♥

From the desk of Shannon Richard

Dear Reader,

When it comes to the little town of Mirabelle, Florida, Grace King was actually the first character who revealed herself to me, which I find odd as she's the heroine in the second book. I knew from the beginning she was going to be a tiny little thing with blond hair and blue eyes; I knew she'd lost her mother at a young age and that she was never going to have known her father; and I knew she was going to be feisty and strong.

Jaxson Anderson was a different story. He didn't reveal himself to me until he literally walked onto the page in *Undone*. I also didn't know about Jax and Grace's future relationship until they got into an argument at the beach. As soon as I figured out they were going to end up together, my mind took off and I started plotting everything out, which was a little inconvenient as I wasn't even a third of the way through writing the first book.

Jax is a complicated fella. He's had to deal with a lot in his life, and because of his past he doesn't think he's good enough for Grace. Jax has most definitely put her on a pedestal, which is made pretty evident by his nickname for her. He calls her Princess, but not in a derogatory way. He doesn't find her to be spoiled or bratty. Far from it. He thinks that she should be cherished and that she's worth *everything*, especially to him. I try to capture this in the prologue, which takes place a good eighteen years before UNDENIABLE starts. Grace is this little six-year-old who is being bullied on the playground, and Jax is her white knight in scuffed-up sneakers.

Jax has been in Grace's life from the day she was brought home from the hospital over twenty-four years ago. He's watched her grow up into the beautiful and brave woman that she is, and though he's always loved her (even if he's chosen not to accept it), it's hard for him think that he can be with her. Jax's struggles were heartbreaking for me to write, and it was especially heartbreaking to put Grace through it, but this was their story and I had to stay true to them. Readers shouldn't fear with UNDENIABLE, though, because I like my happily-ever-after endings and Grace and Jax definitely get theirs. I hope readers enjoy the journey.

Cheers,

♥ ♥ ♥ ♥ ♥ ♥ ♥ ♥ ♥ ♥ ♥ ♥ ♥ ♥ ♥ ♥

From the desk of Stacy Henrie

Dear Reader,

I remember the moment HOPE AT DAWN, Book 1 in my Of Love and War series (on sale now), was born into existence. I was sitting in a quiet, empty hallway at a writers' conference contemplating how to turn my single World War I story idea, about Livy Campbell's brother, into more than one book. Then, in typical fashion, Livy marched forward in my mind, eager to have her story told first.

As I pondered Livy and the backdrop of the story— America's involvement in WWI—I knew having her fall in love with a German-American would provide inherent conflict. What I didn't know then was the intense preju- dice and persecution she and Friedrick Wagner would face to be together, in a country ripe with suspicion toward anyone with German ties. The more I researched the German-American experience during WWI, the more I discovered their private war here on American soil—not against soldiers, but neighbors against neigh- bors, citizens against citizens.

A young woman with aspirations of being a teacher, Livy Campbell knows little of the persecution being heaped upon the German-Americans across the country, let alone in the county north of hers. More than any- thing, she feels the effects of the war overseas through the absence of her older brothers in France, the alcohol troubles of her wounded soldier boyfriend, and the disruption of her studies at college. When she applies for a teaching job in hopes of escaping the war, Livy doesn't realize she's simply traded one set of troubles for another, especially when she finds herself attracted to the school's handsome handyman, German-American Friedrick Wagner.

Born in America to German immigrant parents, Friedrick Wagner believes himself to be as American as anyone else in his small town of Hilden, Iowa. But the war with Germany changes all that. Suddenly viewed as a potential enemy, Friedrick seeks to protect his family from the rising tide of injustice aimed at his fellow German-Americans. Protecting the beautiful new teacher, Livy Campbell, comes as second nature to Friedrick. But when he finds himself falling in love with her, he fears the war, both at home and abroad, will never allow them to be together.

I thoroughly enjoyed writing Livy and Friedrick's love story and the odds they must overcome for each other. This is truly a tale of "love conquers all" and the power of hope and courage during a dark time in history. My hope is you will fall in love with the Campbell family through this series, as I have, as you experience their triumphs and struggles during the Great War.

Happy reading!

Stacy Henrie

♥ ♥ ♥ ♥ ♥ ♥ ♥ ♥ ♥ ♥ ♥ ♥ ♥ ♥ ♥

From the desk of Adrianne Lee

Dear Reader,

Conflict, conflict, conflict. Every good story needs it. It heightens sexual tension and keeps you guessing whether a couple will actually be able to work through those serious—and even not so serious—issues and obstacles to find that happily-ever-after ending.

I admit to a little vanity when one of my daughters once said, "Mom, in other romances I always know the couple will get together early in the book, but I'm never sure in yours until the very end." High praise and higher expectations for any writer to live up to. It is, at least, what I strive for with every love story I write.

Story plotting starts with conflict. I already knew that Jane Wilson, Big Sky Pie's new pastry chef, was going to fall in love with Nick Taziano, the sexy guy doing the promotion for the pie shop, but when I first conceived the idea that these two would be lovers in DELICIOUS, I didn't realize they were a reunion couple.

A reunion couple is a pair who was involved in the past and broke up due to unresolved conflicts. This is what I call a "built-in" conflict. It's one of my favorites to write. When the story opens, something has happened that involves this couple on a personal level, causing them to come face-to-face to deal with it. This is when they finally admit to themselves that they still have feelings for each other, feelings neither wants to feel or act on, no matter how compelling. The more they try to suppress the attraction, the stronger it becomes.

In DELICIOUS, Jane and Nick haven't seen each other since they were kids, since his father and her mother married. Jane blames Nick's dad for breaking up her parents' marriage. Nick resents Jane's mom for coming between his father and him. Jane called Nick the Tazmanian Devil. Nick called her Jane the Pain. They were thrilled when the marriage fell apart after a year.

Now many years later, their parents are reuniting, something Jane and Nick view as a bigger mistake than the first marriage. Their decision to try and stop the wedding, however, leads to one accidental, delicious kiss, and a sizzling attraction that is as irresistible as Jane's blueberry pies.

I hope you'll enjoy DELICIOUS, the second book in my Big Sky Pie series. All of the stories are set in northwest Montana near Glacier Park, an area where I vacationed every summer for over thirty years. Each of the books is about someone connected with the pie shop in one way or another and contains a different delicious pie recipe. So come join the folks of Kalispell at the little pie shop on Center Street, right across from the mall, for some of the best pie you'll ever taste, and a healthy helping of romance.

Adrianne Lee

♥   ♥

From the desk of Jessica Lemmon

Dear Reader,

A *quiz*: What do you get when you put a millionaire who avoids romantic relationships in the same house with a determined-to-stay-single woman who crushed on him sixteen years ago?

If you answered *unstoppable attraction*, you'd be right.

In THE MILLIONAIRE AFFAIR, I paired a hero who cages and controls his emotions with a heroine who feels way too much, way too soon. Kimber Reynolds is determined to have a fling—to love and leave Landon Downey, if for only two reasons: (1) She's wanted to kiss the eldest Downey brother since she was a teen, and (2) to prove to herself that she can have a shallow relationship that ends amicably instead of one that's long, drawn-out, and destined to end badly.

When Landon's six-year-old nephew, Lyon, and a huge account for his advertising agency come crashing into his life, Landon needs help. Lucky for him (and us!) his sister offers the perfect solution: her friend, Kimber, can be his live-in nanny for the week.

The most difficult part about writing Landon was letting him deal with his past on *his terms* and watching him falter. Here is a guy who makes rules, follows them, and remains stoic...to his own detriment. Despite those qualities, Landon, from a loving, close family, can't help caring for Kimber. Even when they're working down a list of "extracurricular activities" in the bedroom, Landon puts Kimber's needs before his own.

These two may have stumbled into an arrangement, but when Fate tosses them a wild card, they both step up—and step closer—to the one thing they were sure they didn't want...*forever*.

I *love* this book. Maybe because of how much I wrestled with Landon and Kimber's story before getting it right. The three of us had growing pains, but I finally found their truth, and I'm *so* excited to share their story with you. If Landon and Kimber win your heart like they won mine, be sure to let me know. You can email me at jessica@jessicalemmon.com, tweet me @lemmony, and "like" my Facebook page at www.facebook.com/authorjessicalemmon.

Happy reading!

Jessica Lemmon

www.jessicalemmon.com

OKANAGAN REGIONAL LIBRARY
3 3132 03618 6593